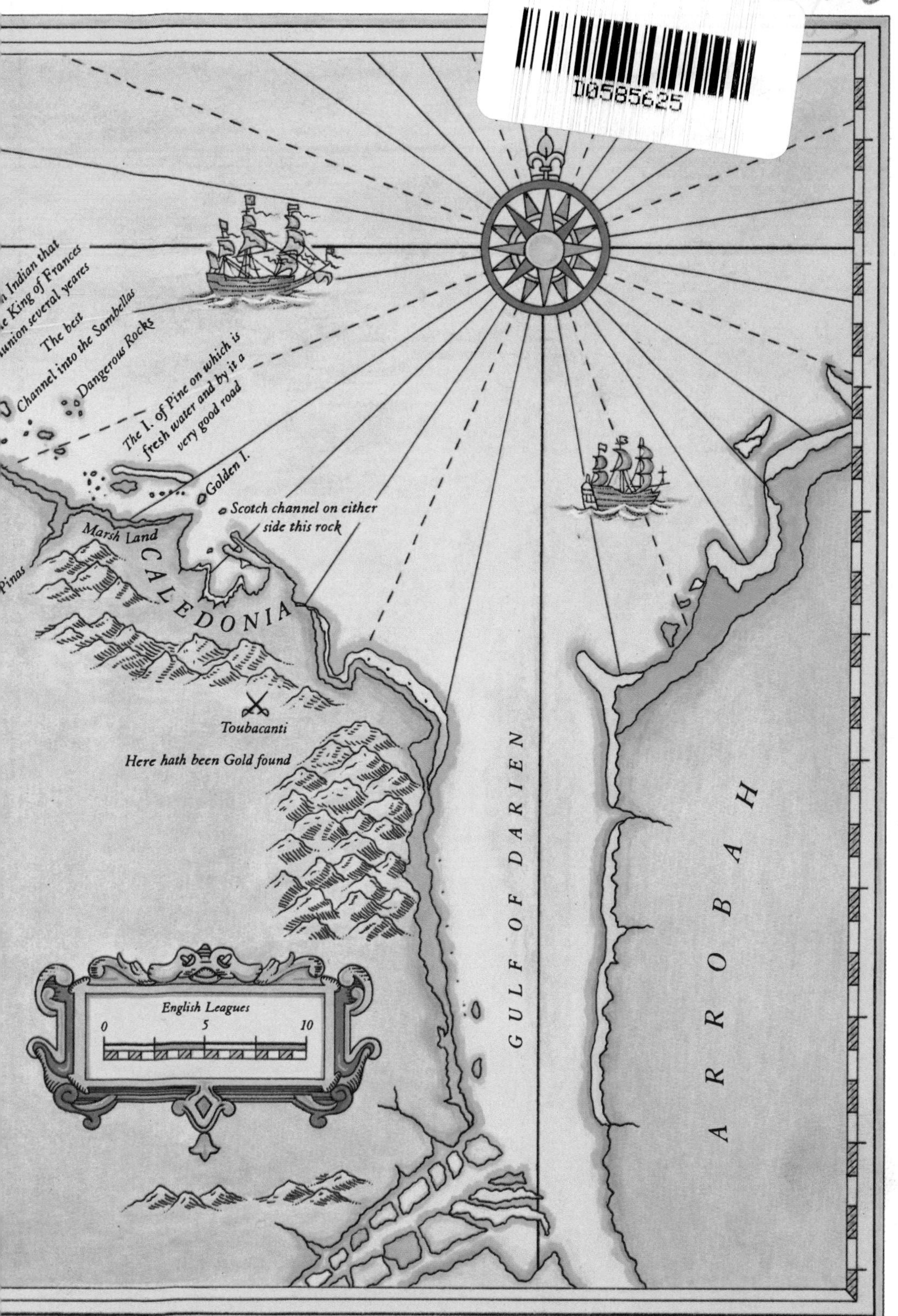

Indian that
King of Frances
several yeares
The best
Channel into the Sambellas
Dangerous Rocks
The I. of Pine on which is
fresh water and by it a
very good road
Golden I.
Scotch channel on either
side this rock
Marsh Land
Pinas
CALEDONIA
Toubacanti
Here hath been Gold found
GULF OF DARIEN
ARROBAH
English Leagues
0 5 10

The Rising Sun

Douglas Galbraith

The Rising Sun

PICADOR

First published 2000 by Picador
an imprint of Macmillan Publishers Ltd
25 Eccleston Place, London SW1W 9NF
Basingstoke and Oxford
Associated companies throughout the world
www.macmillan.co.uk

ISBN 0 330 37297 1

1 3 5 7 9 8 6 4 2

A CIP catalogue record for this book is available from the British Library.

Typeset by SetSystems Ltd, Saffron Walden, Essex
Printed and bound in Great Britain by
Mackays of Chatham plc, Chatham, Kent

DCH

Part One

THEY SAY THE MAD hear demons calling to them, as clear as a man in the street calling their names. I heard tell once that they would be mad and happy all their lives were it not for these voices. It is the voices that drive them to their destruction; moral, physical or both. So it may be with my numbers. I can no more forget twenty-three ells of bengal or the precise proportions of the blue crêpe to the incarnate and of the incarnate to the white than a man could shake the lunacy from his head by standing up and saying: 'I am whole.'

To be sure, the disease was common enough at the time. There was hardly one in the country who could not hear the sweet music of so many pounds, so many tons of this or that commodity, so many per cent. The demons whispered it in the taverns, it sighed out of the pillows in duchesses' bedrooms, the pages of merchants' ledgers and scholars' tomes fanned it into their ears, the bleating of the sheep on the high hills was strangely altered in the ears of their shepherds. If others further off could not or would not hear it, they were either ill-wishers or fools who deserved no part of the spoils.

I was the historian of these numbers. I became – may I say it? – the Herodotus of our comic tragedy. There was not a pound of ship's biscuit, a box of candles or a pint of lime juice but was counted out and set down in my chronicle. Kinghorn canvas: two thousand eight hundred and thirty two and a half ells to be sewn together as required by three hundred and thirty pounds of thread and five hundred needles. Enough to blow a nation's hopes half way across the world and over its insane edge.

The numbers keep me here, staring at my own form in the black glass of the window. That and the sound of my own blood too loud in my ears. Too much of claret and fine Virginia to thank for that.

One, two. Three? No, two of the clock. I'll not find sleep tonight, and to tell the truth am resolved not to seek it for fear of what might come to me. Even the clocks quarrel in this country. One, two again, further off. Now is the hour, it says. If they could heave up their stones and rush at each other I swear we would have a ten years' war of the clocktowers.

Two? Two of what? Two ounce of onion seed, butter two firkins, glass two hampers wherein granados four hundred, ninety and three. Or four perhaps? No. No, three definitely. There is so much to be forgotten now, but the numbers I swear will never leave me. I am a man haunted by numbers. They were my vocation. How gilded Fortune called me to them!

'I take it you can keep a ledger?'

'As well as any man, sir!'

'Well, then, we'll see what use we can make of you.'

Hence the numbers. I wrote in those ledgers but never read them. To have gone to the page would have dishonoured me: I was the Imam of the Grand Totals, they were my five-times prayers called out in account-room, warehouse, quay and hold.

'How much of soap, Mr Mackenzie?'

'White, four boxes, thirteen hundred pounds gross. Black, two firkins.'

Ah, yes. Thank God for the soap. We washed the seas clean with it.

Hammock hooks, twelve hundred; cordage (two inch), one coil; spunyarn thirty-six balls; pipes, nine casks being 129 gross; cheeses 77, being 940 pounds; guns 879; horn spoons, three dozen; deep lead one; hand lead one; shot, lead 223 pounds.

They pinch me in my sleep. I wake at four, bruised by memory. My skull echoes to the ghostly sound of 'Ship's biscuit! 10,000 pounds to *Dolphin*, 20,000 to *St Andrew*.' How fat the tropic fish must be today!

They will be my last thought, my very last I don't doubt it. Pale and enfeebled I shall lie on my fatal bed, my faithful daughter (should I ever have one) holds my fevered hand. Suddenly, I jerk upwards and with my last strength, shout, 'Shoes, eleven hodgets, being a thousand eight hundred and twelve pairs!' and fall back, a bloodied foam on my lips.

Tomorrow, at sunrise, I shall flee them, knowing as I go that they are no more to be evaded through time and space than the Furies themselves. I shall take them with me on my back, the original Scots pedlar, the chapman of my own and my people's past. Wherever and as fast as I go in the world, the numbers and the names shall come with me and this night I cannot see an end to it.

But three days ago I saw a nation fouled by its own failures. As did the unfortunate Captain Green from his fine vantage-point, kicking in the wind, his posthumous eyes looking at the wreckage of his own incorporated ambitions, ash to the waterline. They wouldn't even give him the drop.

Not all had lost their wits. I have the evidence here in my pocket, some privy-paper broadside thrust into my hand by one in the greedy crowd, or by the author himself perhaps, too proud of his own wit to ask for the 'Two Pence' demanded at the head. Here it is: *Every Man his Own Empire or, Worcester Sauce for a Scotch Lamb.* He should be thankful the bleating flock were not in the reading mood or he would have joined the enterprising captain. I would have spoken with him, but no sooner felt the paper in my hand than he was off into the crowd like a thief. Men of sense have become a secret fraternity, the members of which dare not open their mouths even to make themselves known to each other for fear of being set upon. As it is, I only took it from my pocket after returning to my lodgings. That was not a day to let men look over your shoulder.

He is right, of course: even in our revenges we are not one hundredth part of what we imagine ourselves to be, and the stretching of Captain Green's neck will not sweeten a single Scotsman's palate. I wonder if he is still there, staying on to fight, or was he that one that passed us on the road, galloping headlong for the border?

My head nods at my own image in the window as if my real and phantasmal selves would stop and talk awhile. But I will not have it. For days past my dreams have been nothing but drownings and hangings. What world is a man in when he must prefer the dead life of exhaustion to sleep?

A quarter of a day must be staggered through, or less. Half a night. My travelling companions and I have so stirred up the lees of our little tale that there is no help for it now. And so I have dug it out once again. Hidden like contraband, its cack-handed binding cracking as I open it. My old friend, my confessional, my hiding-place, my self, salted and dried, stitched in sailcloth, all but done with.

Hear the story of a Britishman.

I SHOULD NOT HAVE HURRIED. Delay after delay we suffered, and for all the confidence of the announcement no one believed that the next day would see our departure. The men who had refused to board were angrily protesting that they had been right and demanded to know why they had been shipped on a vessel that hadn't moved an inch since they had been drummed up in the town and put aboard. In the days before making sail Captain Galt paced his quarterdeck sending out black glances of fury in equal measure towards the city (the source of our unaccountable delay), and whatever colonists were airing themselves on the main deck at the time. It could not be denied that they are not all of the finest cut, but I was not without some sympathy for them. Besides, a characteristic that may prove troublesome in a period of enforced idleness might become a golden virtue in the circumstances to which we are committing ourselves. We must have the men to master whatever we find, and I do not doubt we have them here. In their further defence I might say that our good captain's attitude seems to come from the natural dislike of the salt for the fresh and, willy-nilly, I am of the latter tribe.

We itched with inactivity. The sound of brawling from the holds became common, and we suffered less intellectual irritations from the many millions of stowaways we carried in the form of fleas and lice. Dr Munro blamed it on our immobility. Little air passed through the holds and the weather continued unpleasantly warm. The currents about were slow and for hours each morning after the wastes were put out the water remained foul.

It was in the last hours of the day that I scratched and sweated in my cabin and made too much of my officers' allowance of brandy; another privilege of my inheritance of the ailing Mr Vetch's position. I drank his health, drank it again and then just drank. Towards midnight I went up on deck. Being but three days past midsummer there was still light in the north, even though I could hear the clocks striking midnight over the water. I stood awhile enjoying the sky and the quiet and for a few moments was relieved of that excess of human closeness which was weighing on us all.

Captain Galt appeared at my shoulder without a sound. I almost cried out in my surprise and was not a little chagrined to be found standing at the rail, bucket in hand.

'Sleepless, Mr Mackenzie?'

'A little, sir,' I admitted. 'I find it very warm down below.'

'It can be.'

We stood for some time gazing at the light over the hills and I began to learn of that costiveness which is our captain's chief characteristic. He caught me scratching at myself privily. 'That will ease when we are underway.'

With that he walked away as silently as he had arrived, and in a manner which made me feel that he had seen quite enough of me and that I had little more to expect from such a quarter. I reflected that I could have wished for a better introduction.

I went below to spend another uneasy night and with no expectation at all that the next day would be any different from the last ten. I had wished to ask Captain Galt his own opinion as to whether we would indeed sail, but failed at the necessary moment, partly for fear that the question would seem impertinent and partly because of my sudden awareness that my breath must have smelt strongly of brandy and that it would be better if I kept as much of it as possible to myself.

It was this shameful excess that accounted for my waking the next morning to find the ship already in full clamour. Feet drummed on the deck above my head and great shouts were made and answered in what seemed quite another language. I cursed myself and rushed up on deck in angry disbelief that I could have missed such a moment, only to find that we had not yet moved an inch. Feeling not entirely myself, I clutched the rail and felt a deeper swell push up through my feet. I noticed Captain Galt talking to Mr Cunningham by the helm and was trying to make my way into his line of sight and ask him if our great venture had indeed begun when a strange greenness seemed to overcome everything and I was suddenly aware of nothing but the smell of fresh timber and tar as my head struck the deck. I was told later that I was unconscious for no more than a minute and that in that time Dr Munro cast his eye over me and pronounced my case to be of no great interest and that the business of the ship should continue undisturbed. This it certainly did, for when I came to myself I found I had been propped against the rails and my first sight was of sailors stepping over my legs carrying between them a great coil of rope from one place to another. I put the matter down to the rudeness of my levee and the shock of thinking I might have missed the moment of our departure. Dr Munro thought little of my theory, however, and declared that I had been the victim of a 'spiritous syncope' and ordered no further brandy. I noticed Captain Galt's great back turned to me and hoped, vainly I suppose, that my humiliation had gone unnoticed.

By the time I had regained my full awareness, the activity was above me. Men, and sometimes boys who seem hardly more than half my age, were making their way about the masts and spars as if there was no possibility of error, as if they might step back and stand on the air a moment while untying some mysterious piece of harness before stepping back to cling to wood or hemp.

I struggled to my feet and felt the heightened and cooler air that we were setting ourselves to catch. About us I could see the same fervour on the *Endeavour* and the *St Andrew*. A little behind us the *Caledonia*, the command of Captain Drummond as he now is (and I hear he is most insistent on his new title), seemed to have got ahead of the rest of us in her preparations. A little sail was already set and she strained at her anchor.

Being at the time as completely ignorant of the science of the sea as it is possible to be, I imagined that the moment of our departure was still some way off. I was all the more certain of it when I noticed one of the small ferry-boats making its way out to us from the harbour. Only a moment later I was proved wrong when Mr Cunningham put his head back and bellowed up at the masts some word I was unable to understand. There came a strange sussuration from above, which rose to such a loudness that I ducked, causing some ungentlemanly laughter from the two or three nearest members of the crew. I looked up to see great sheets of whiteness streaming down from the spars; the sails that had so struck me when I first saw her approaching through the clearing sea-mists. For a while they fluttered ineffectually against the masts, but we were slowly turning windward and when the angle was sufficient they filled out, cracking like whips, straining after the wind. Our signal gun was fired and answered by all our companions. The commodore's pennant flew from our masthead as we moved as a group into the open sea.

For a moment it seemed as if even this departure might prove abortive. The boat that was making its way to us from the harbour (now with someone standing in the middle of it) did its best to reach us. As we started to move off I could see tiny puffs of smoke from it and hear the remote phuts of musket fire. All this I observed from the main deck and was sure that from their superior vantage-point on the quarterdeck Captain Galt and his officers would see the same, but they were talking closely together and were quite unaware of the situation. Torn between my relief to be under way and my duties as an officer of the Company I decided that I ought to draw Captain Galt's attention to what could be a matter of great importance. The quarterdeck being so busy with men greater than myself, my presence in that world being so new and unexpected, the unfavourableness of my first encounter with our captain the night before, my less than total recovery from my indisposition, in short for a multitude of good reasons, I did not succeed. I did cry out that someone was bringing a message, but was not heard, or at least not noted, and the boat soon shrank into the distance, the last I saw of it turning about to go back to the harbour.

For days we had bobbed in our own filth, land on three sides of us that a strong man could swim to. For the landsmen, we had taken but half a step from home and that was already strange enough. Then, within an hour of our departure, we were in a world transformed, all that we had known shrunk to the thickness of a ledger line. For the captains and the crews there was a return to their element at the very same moment we left ours. Looking back from the space of only a few weeks I can see that I suffered from no little pride in my sudden inclusion on the expedition. Yet that was a land pride, a coin of no currency at all at sea. I learned this quickly during the first days of the voyage when those born and bred in salt and tar lorded it over the rest of us, and I was made to feel at one with my charges, carried off with no more say on my fate than a box of wigs or a bolt of cloth.

On the subject of wigs and cloth, and of the ten thousand other things that men of business call goods, I may set down my new purpose on our great venture. More to the point, I may set down here my private irritation that for all my intrepidity and all my good fortune in Mr Vetch's difficulties my position has not been advanced by so much as the fourth part of a hair's breadth. Of course, I was never so beyond myself to suppose that I could fill Mr Vetch's shoes, and for the privilege of a place on the expedition I readily agreed that a new position be cut to my more modest dimensions. A day before being rowed out, I learned that I was to be Superintendent of Cargoes, which pleased me well enough. Since then the title had been likened to the uniform of an Irish field marshal: there is more to the wearing of it than the acting out. In effect I am doing what I was most particular to avoid doing, that is to say exactly what I was doing before, only now I do it afloat.

And the author of this gentle witticism? None other than him I call the fourth part of a hair's breadth. To wit: Mr Shipp (no less), my subordinate. I addressed him pleasantly enough on our first meeting.

'I am very pleased to make your acquaintance, Mr Shipp. Tell me, was it your name that led you into this trade?'

'It was my father's name, sir. And he had it afore me.'

Well, that was the way we started and there has been little improvement since. Mr Shipp's story, or what of it I can piece together from other members of the crew, is that he started as an ordinary seaman and served both in our and the English navies. This career came to an end when he suffered a rupture that made him unfit for strenuous work, whereupon, being able to read, write and calculate, he made a virtue of necessity and, as it were, moved up a deck. It appears that he has found himself suspended between one order of men and another, and his whole situation was rendered all the more uncomfortable by my arrival. He had started to move into my cabin and was therefore displaced by me and forced to go back and find a hook for his hammock with the other men. Whenever I think of him I pray for patience. To be fair, though, I cannot fault his work.

And so to settle at last to my theme. For surely not a grain of what we do now must be lost. The Scotiad (perhaps even the Roriad?) – Day the First: In which little honour was won, and the mystery of the boat explained.

The elation of being in motion at last was short-lived as we dropped anchor off the coast of Fife, barely more than half a day's good ride from where we had started. The weather remained fair and we could clearly see the towers of the old cathedral at St Andrews, about which I knew my brother might be walking. We did not enter the harbour, it being too meagre and silted for our vessels. I considered that if our halt was to be for some time I might take a boat and visit my brother, but the opportunity did not arise. At least, it did not arise legitimately: the next day when our journey had been re-started it was discovered that two men from our own *Rising Sun* had gone ashore, either by swimming or on a boat that came out to them from the harbour as part of a criminal arrangement. They took their two months' advanced pay with them. All officers of the Company were sworn to say no more of the matter for fear of the influence it might have. The precaution was pointless, however, as Mr Shipp was able to tell me the story in all its details. Indeed, he knew rather more than I did. There are no secrets on ships, it seems.

But to the point, to the point: what was interesting was not what went into the harbour, but what came out of it. Another boat, no less, with another figure standing in the middle of it, with three others aside from the oarsmen. A signal gun was fired from a little mound above the harbour, allowing for no mistake on this occasion. The boat came alongside and was greeted by Captain Galt in full view of the crew and all the colonists on deck at the time. Captain Galt showed no surprise at all, but I was astonished to see that it was none other than Mr Paterson himself. He called up to us. 'Mr Paterson and three to come on board!'

Captain Galt and Mr Cunningham conferred with one another and then Mr Cunningham called down to the boat. 'Three, sir?'

'My wife, clerk and Reverend Mackay.'

There was further conference, longer this time. Being perhaps conscious that more of the planters had come on deck and were taking a keen interest in the proceedings, a brief paper was written out and sent down to the boat. The contents of this were debated at length. Eventually a reply was written on the back of it by Mr Paterson and it was sent back up to us. Captain Galt looked at it briefly, handed it to Mr Cunningham, went up to the quarterdeck and into his cabin and took no further part in the business. Mr Cunningham, a little embarrassed, I thought, added another two or three words and returned the paper. The Reverend Mackay clambered on board, and as his chest was being hauled up on a rope, the boat pushed off and made for the *Caledonia*, on to which Mr Paterson, wife and clerk embarked.

It was shortly after this that Mr Shipp was telling me what he should not have known about the two deserters. I thought it might please him if I asked him his opinion about this new shipment of ours.

'Can't understand it,' was all he would say, 'can't understand it at all, young master. To take the Reverend on here and give the others to the *Caledonia*. It's not what you'd expect. Just can't understand it at all.'

Dr Munro was more helpful. He says Reverend Mackay, whom he describes as a great glorifier of God, is a close friend of Mr Paterson and would not come on the expedition, as the kirk party wished him to, without him. Which explains well enough why they came as a pair but not why they came at all, it being supposed so recently that they would not come. After all, Mr Paterson is not young.

Even so, I was happy to have our originating genius on board. It would have been nothing less than an injustice if he were not to share every part of a venture that would never have started to our minds without him. I took the opportunity to express this sentiment to him on a recent occasion and he seemed exceedingly pleased.

When we resumed our voyage on the next dawn there was a feeling that we were at last fully laden.

*

THERE, I have caught up a day. Though I can see nothing from this windowless hutch I am sure that sunrise can be no more than an hour or two away. Although I have taken only a single step I cannot write another line for the moment. The matter breeds monstrously and tomorrow I will lose everything I have gained as I must spend the day on the *Caledonia* examining a discrepancy Mr Paterson believes he has discovered in the stores.

Less than two weeks at sea have opened more secrets to me than all my days up to that wondrous departure. If Mr Paterson cares as much about a missing barrel of ship's biscuit, as his note suggests, I'll throw a guinea in the sea.

For now, sleep.

After our departure from the Fife coast things went excellently for several days. We sailed as a wooden archipelago, a new Hebrides with constant traffic between the islands plied by the jolly-boats carrying captains and councillors to discussions and, on several occasions, myself as I went from one hold to the other accompanied by Mr Shipp struggling under our stack of ledgers.

To get to the cargoes we had to descend through the middle and lower decks, which house the colonists – an experience that cured me instantly of any dissatisfactions I may have had about my own accommodation. Given that they were then ventilated by some forward movement and that we were moving into cooler air, I could only suppose that there had been some improvement but their conditions remained those of utmost foulness. The colour of ordure being what it is and the scantness of the light, one could do little to arrive at one's destination without having trodden in what one would have most avoided. Months of this must be endured, and even now the sound of coughing rises more frequently from the holds. Dr Munro takes a physicianly attitude to this. 'There's mortality for you, Rory,' he remarked the other day adding, as if to assert that he can be a man of business as well, 'Losses have been accounted for.'

I fell into a sober silence at such talk, almost wondering aloud whether, with such a view, Dr Munro considers himself employed to tend the sick or merely to wait and count the dead. The effect of this on me was clearly visible and we parted with some awkwardness, which I regretted particularly as I have yet to find any good friend in this village and was beginning to think well of Dr Munro.

As for losses, it is true that we have experienced none as yet and the spirit remains very high. The men take the air on the main deck in turns, twenty or thirty at a time, fifty on our larger vessels. There is one fiddler at least on every ship and some with other instruments. At night, after the rations have been consumed, there is music on the main decks for those whose turn it is to be above. Some play with a remarkable skill, and each in their own manner according to where they learned the art. The sailors play their own airs and some of the men dance, sailors and landsmen teaching each other their steps. When it is over for a moment and it is calm enough, the faint sound of other tunes comes across the water from our sister ships. Other men sit about with their pipes and take their allowance of brandy and talk about what they will make of themselves. Sometimes the Highlanders sing in good strong voices and very sweet melodies too. Of what they sing, I know nothing.

Humanity below decks is quite another matter, and it could only have been a few days later when, clambering down behind Mr Shipp on our way to make another reconciliation, I found myself thinking that if 'losses' reduced the appalling assault on my senses then I might be grateful for them. I prayed also that when they did begin, some power might make Dr Munro responsible for the noting of them rather than burden Mr Shipp and myself with the opening of another ledger and the scribbling down of more accursed numbers.

That night, on my knees as I end all my days, I begged for forgiveness. It occurred to me, just before turning down the lamp and while enjoying a moderate measure of my brandy, that I had experienced the meaning of the phrase 'sea change'. I am sure I could not have approached such brutal sentiments only a few weeks ago, let alone have spoken them so clearly to myself and with so little trouble to my conscience as I did when climbing down those ladders. Half slumbering, I recalled our day of departure and the swagger it put into the sailors. It seems to me now that we have undergone some kind of inversion or exchange of positions as in a dance. As the sailors returned to their true selves, we have been taken away from ours and left floundering, reaching out to find new selves or passively waiting for the sea and destiny to impose them on us. From this I was able to draw the charitable conclusion that neither Dr Munro nor myself has been quite at our best in these early stages. Still, we have hardly lost sight of the coast for more than a few hours at a time and had then still to turn Cape Wrath. If this process is progressive, I ask myself, what lies ahead? Something of great interest to the unbiased student of human nature, no doubt. I consoled myself before sleep with recalling that our destination is land as solid as any other, and will right whatever is put wrong during our journey.

My eyelids drop, my head nods, it is all I can do to stay awake and I have written hardly a word of what I intended. Our work goes easily enough, I suppose, and tediously according to its nature. I would rather forget it, extinguish it utterly from the few hours of consciousness that are left to me each day, but it is not so easily put away. In any case, its entire omission would be a dishonesty, albeit a venial one. I have hardly begun what was intended to be nothing more than an amusement, a private pastime on a long and doubtless tedious voyage that will not want for chroniclers, than I have developed an irritating scrupulosity that keeps me at my 'desk' too long.

In truth, there is little else for us to do except to give the appearance of earning our passage by confirming and reconfirming our own confirmation of our own inventories. While at sea, opportunities are limited. Where else could the stores go other than into the bellies of the colonists where they belong? The possession of sea-chests is a special privilege and so there are few hiding places in which someone could put what does not belong to them.

One consequence of our position which may well turn out to our advantage, or to mine at least, is that Mr Shipp and I surely know the fleet better than any other persons. At every suitable moment we find ourselves being rowed across from one vessel to another, ledgers on our knees trussed up in their oiled leather bags. We are like the only travellers in a little world of stay-at-homes and are often pressed for news of the neighbouring villages. In the last days of boarding there was such a hurry and a disorganization (it not being one of my responsibilities) that brothers, of whom we have several pairs, and cousins, of whom we have many, found themselves on different vessels. Some would be reunited and complained to their respective captains but the order came from Captain Galt, quite rightly no doubt, that every man was to stay where he was, there having been too much of trouble and delay already. Thus we inhabit not only an archipelago of our own creation but one populated by a diaspora scattered here and there by strokes of the pen. Naturally enough, they would make their thoughts known to each other, particularly after our recent disaster, and Mr Shipp and myself have been turned into a pair of unlikely Mercurys carrying notes to and from the ships as we go about our reconciliations.

About Mr Shipp I must say a word here. Perhaps by writing it down I will be better able to restrain myself with him in person. He has improved not a jot and has an unfortunate talent for quickly learning what will most irritate a person and then dedicating himself to becoming a master in that art. The perfection with which he achieves his effects quite rules out the possibility of chance. It is a deliberate campaign! For one thing he is a monster of efficiency and industry. No sooner do I give him a task in one compartment of the hold and settle myself in another for an hour's recuperation than he returns, lists in hand, with some story about the water in cask number seven being two inches lower than it ought to be. At such moments, indeed at all moments now, he puts a First Footman expression on his face as if to say, 'I can't understand why you're up there and I'm down here, because it is very obvious that it should be the other way round.' Our work would be an agony of tedium to any rational being, but Mr Shipp goes about everything I set him with a most absolute earnestness. It could only have been in the middle of the second week when we had already begun to repeat ourselves that, rather than count the casks of biscuit in the hold of the *Endeavour* for the second time in a few days, I made do with the previous list.

'Oh no, young master,' said Mr Shipp, when I presented it to him for collation with the ledgers, 'this is Tuesday's list, you must have mislaid today's. Perhaps it's on the deck somewhere, between some casks. Shall I bring another lantern?'

This was nothing but insolence, and I had to be very firm with him. It has, however, had little effect and he continues to do everything he can to give the impression that he has been appointed to look after me as much as to look after the goods. Our positions are almost the reverse of what they should be, but I am in despair of knowing what to do to put the matter right. I can only suppose there is some trick to authority which I lack. I cannot believe the men who strut about the quarterdeck would have any such difficulties. And here is another irritation which I might as well confess – my office gives me the right to stand on that stage with the rest of them, but I have not as yet had any good reason nor, it must be admitted, any encouragement.

But why delay? Why put off like this when it is already too late for me to make good sense of my thoughts? Why, then, am I in so short a temper? For the sheer incomprehensibility of it, the downright rudeness of being invited into a game and flatly refused an answer when one requests a hint of the rules. Or perhaps I have mistaken even that, perhaps there is no such game save in my imagination. And yet, what sort of game would be best for a group of players who would prefer not to be found playing it, who might at any moment wish to turn round and say, 'But my dear sir, what do you mean?' One whose rules required a cultivated vagueness about its very existence would surely be ideal.

The required signals having been made, we were rowed across to the *Caledonia* early over a nauseating swell. Captain Drummond looked down on us from the quarterdeck as we boarded but made no acknowledgement of our presence. The third mate was equally unceremonious and thought no more than a couple of grunts sufficient to direct us to where we might find Mr Paterson. Conscious of the honour he was doing me in allowing a personal interview, I took some deep breaths and started to climb down below.

Perhaps I should not be the one to record it, but Mr Paterson, the author and impelling genius behind all our efforts, received me most generously. 'Such a pleasure to meet you at last, Mr Mackenzie, such a pleasure.'

A little dumbstruck, I think, at the realization of who I was talking to, words seemed to desert me. 'An honour,' was all I could mumble, bobbing down towards his shoes. 'An honour, sir.'

'Your reputation precedes you, Mr Mackenzie. A man of precision, a man of industry.'

I must include this, if only for fulness' sake.

'Your work has not gone unnoticed, I do assure you. Rowing this way and that with your great ledgers, how you must know us inside out!'

'I do my best, sir. I do my best.'

'Pardon,' said Mr Shipp, who had been standing behind me and chose to draw attention to himself at that moment by breaking wind with equine vigour.

'Shall we give your man something to do?' asked Mr Paterson, in a tone that warmed my heart.

'Indeed,' I replied, hoping for a demonstration of how to handle this animal.

Mr Paterson indicated the row upon row of barrels stacked just behind us. 'It's the biscuit that concerns me, Mr Mackenzie. Nothing like empty stomachs to unsettle a ship. One can't be too sure of these things. I understand from our good captain that we should have forty-seven thousand and eight hundred pounds of it, or a little less given what has been consumed since our departure. But one can't be sure.'

There was a pause during which Mr Paterson looked at me and then at Mr Shipp.

'Well see to it, Shipp,' I said sharply.

'See to what, young master?'

I was a little slow perhaps and looked back to Mr Paterson only to find him already leaving the hold.

'If your man would be so good as to let us know if our calculations are correct. This way, Mr Mackenzie.'

I threw the ledger I was holding on to a bale of something and started to climb after Mr Paterson. The words 'Instantly, young master' were just audible as I regained the main deck.

The wind was picking up as we made our way aft. I wasn't entirely sure of the words that blew back to me but I believe I heard: 'Captain Drummond has been good enough to find me a little space to myself.'

And this while Captain Drummond himself was on the quarter-deck, his back to us, hand on his hat, as he spoke with the third mate who had brought us aboard so unmannerly. A plain enough statement, I thought, until I followed Mr Paterson not up to the quarterdeck from which we might have entered more suitable accommodation but through a door leading directly off the waist. We had taken no more than two or three paces down a lightless passage when Mr Paterson pulled aside an ox-hide and gestured that I should enter the large cupboard behind it, dimly lit by an oil lamp hanging from a hook screwed into the timbers.

'I'll have to ask you to make do with a sea-chest. I hope it won't offend you too absolutely. It is somewhat hobnailed I regret to say; an oversight on the part of its maker who, no doubt, thought it would never, em, come to this, as it were.'

I sat on the chest, embarrassed both at the circumstances and at being apologized to by the architect of our nation's fortunes. 'No, no, please,' I said, 'you would be doing me too great an honour in any circumstances.'

'You're too kind, Mr Mackenzie, too kind.'

He seated himself on another chest opposite me. Between us was a warped and knotted plank, fixed at one end to the timbers of the hull with a couple of twisted nails and supported at the other end by two slender battens that looked as they might break if two men rested their elbows at the same time.

Mr Paterson bent down to a small wooden box by the side of his chest and came up with a glass decanter with swirls of colour in it that twisted up to the neck where they disappeared behind a band of silver. Beside it he placed two glasses with stems braided like girls' hair and gilding around the lips.

'I still have some pearls, Mr Mackenzie. Nothing like a little pearl here and there to maintain the, eh, the *esprit*. You'll join me?'

I agreed, of course, and watched him as he poured two glasses of Canary. He wears a sober topcoat for the much cooler weather we have had of late but he maintains, nevertheless, an appearance that admirably defies his surroundings. A sign, I think, of great strength of character. There is a little light blue silk at his throat, and as he poured the wine I noticed two rings on his fingers which I had never seen in all my earlier and more distant views of him: a heavy signet on one hand and on the other a lighter ring with a stone. Lace brushed the edges of the glasses as he filled them.

'There! Shall we restore our spirits?'

I lifted my glass, unsettled by the thought of how complete a disaster it would be if I were somehow to let it smash on the deck or clumsily snap its stem.

'Of course,' he went on, 'I have always despised excess. A little privation early in life can be an excellent lesson and one I learned well. Keep the material element in its place, I say. Besides,' the lace cuffs expanded to take in the surroundings, 'many have less, I understand.'

'The late arrangements must have made things difficult,' I said. 'There was great surprise at your arrival. Everyone was so pleased.'

'You're well accommodated on the *Rising Sun*?'

I thought of the considerable superiority of my quarters and admitted: 'Tolerably.'

'Of course, you and your man must be almost the only people who can compare. Tell me, Mr Mackenzie, what do you think of the *Caledonia*? Are we as shipshape as the *Rising Sun*? Better, worse?'

'Well,' I said, 'I suppose I'm loyal to my own ship. To my home town, as it were, for the moment at least.'

He seemed to appreciate this comment rather more than it warranted and moved on more directly to express his desires.

'I understand from some talk amongst our colonists that you have delivered letters between the ships?'

I had, of course, but I was unsure of his tone and conscious that the practice had grown up without authority. I thought that perhaps there had been an objection and started to say that I had only done what had been asked, that relatives, men from the same village, had found themselves on different ships.

'Of course, of course! It's very good of you to add these little trifles to your burdens. You are doing what you have been asked. It is, I suppose, a sort of custom now.'

'Of sorts.'

'But you are not our appointed postmaster. Why should you be? We have no need of such formalities. Tell me, Mr Mackenzie, you carry for the captains, for the councillors?'

'Oh, yes. That's how it started. One of our colonists saw me going down to the boat with a letter from Captain Galt and handed me one of his own. From that it has become, as you say, a custom.'

'You would carry one for me, to Reverend Mackay?'

I said I would do it willingly, that it was always an honour to serve him and the Company.

He smiled a little at this, and I was all the more sure that I had made the right response.

Mr Paterson was about to speak again when the greasy ox-hide that provided his only privacy blew in an inch as if a door had been opened. He paused a moment until an opposing pulse of air sucked the hide back against the opening.

'I assure you, Mr Mackenzie, you may serve me and the Company.'

He produced a small, sealed packet from under his coat and

handed it to me. 'Every great man has Rumour as his enemy, Roderick. You will discover that for yourself one day. I trust in the confidence of good men. There is no greater security.'

And with that, he gave me my *congé*.

I found Mr Shipp waiting for me on deck, talking with one of the crew and sharing a pipe in the lee of some structure for which I haven't yet learned the name. They stopped speaking immediately on my appearance and Mr Shipp gave me a good long look before deciding to get to his feet.

'Well, young master, you'll be pleased to hear there's not a crumb where there shouldn't be, give or take a hundred pound or so. Not even the rats have had more than their due.'

'Knows better than to eat it,' opined the toothless crewman, who gave the appearance of living on nothing but rum and tobacco.

An almost painful incomprehension was beginning to steal over me as a result of my conversation with Mr Paterson. The *Rising Sun* seemed more than ever to be my home town and I was anxious to get back to her when the surly third mate arrived to let me know that Captain Drummond would be glad to share a glass or two. Lacking a ready excuse, I followed him to the captain's cabin where he tapped twice on the door, opened it and walked off without a word, as if I might choose whether to go in or not.

I found myself in gracious surroundings: an apartment as broad as the ship herself and, with one wall entirely taken up by the stern-lights, almost as bright as the day.

I was received unsmilingly by Captain Drummond. He gave a little nod as he took my hand and said: 'Superintendent.'

As I consider it now I am not so sure, but there was something in his expression that I took for anxiety and the thought pleased me, as if I might not be so insubstantial a figure as I imagined. I noticed too that he was shorter than myself.

'A little port, Mr Mackenzie?'

The glasses and decanter were of a different stripe, but their contents fine enough. As he poured them I tried, without seeming to take too great a notice, to see what was on the vast chart table that dominated the cabin. The chart on it was grubby and frayed at the edges where books had been placed as weights. A pair of brass dividers lay in the middle. The sight of it amused me a little as it is well known that Drummond had changed his red coat for black not more than three months ago and has no more experience of the sea than I do. But I learned soon enough that there is no pretence to the man. As he handed me my glass he demanded, 'So, does it look captainly enough?'

He went on before I could muster a suitable reply.

'There's no need to tiptoe, Mr Mackenzie. Two landsmen such as ourselves. I have been having my lesson from my first mate, my junior and master.'

He gave me a strange sort of smile, which I took to mean that he knew I was in the same situation with respect to Mr Shipp. He picked up one of the books, letting the chart curl up, and held it out to me. I read *Elements of Navigation* on the spine.

'You see? I am trying to learn my trade, or to learn another I should say, gentlemanly employment on dry land having . . . well . . .'

'Dried up?'

'Not been so much to my taste of late. Please.'

He indicated the chair I should take and took his place behind the table. Toying with the dividers, he asked: 'Well, then, Mr Mackenzie, tell me the worst. Shall we starve, shall we parch?'

'The stores are in perfect order, Captain.'

'Are they? Mr Paterson was mistaken then. He miscalculated perhaps?'

'He thought it best to be sure.'

'And now he is?'

'Yes, I believe so.'

His expression hardened. 'Well, I'm glad you checked this for us, Superintendent Mackenzie. As you know, I'm sure, Mr Paterson's calculations are not always to be relied upon. You cannot be unaware that he comes to us under certain . . . how shall I put it?'

I watched him massage his face and draw his nails through his beard as he groped towards the word.

'Under certain embarrassments?'

From this point I began to see his intention, or enough of it anyway to know that I disliked it. Our meeting took on the difficulty I had expected, the awkwardness and almost feline caution that seemed already to have seeped out of his cabin and permeated the air of his command. My instinct was one of outrage that anyone would seek to cast doubt on the designer of our whole enterprise.

'Of course,' I said, 'in my position I think I must have heard it all, including the details, Captain. There were others involved, in whom any one of us might have trusted. If Mr Paterson has taken responsibility it's because he's an honest man of business and a gentleman.'

'Maybe so, but it's an unfortunate habit, Mr Mackenzie, putting one's trust in the wrong men. As for responsibility, that's all very well, but gold and silver's another matter. You may have wondered at our good fortune in picking up Mr Paterson and party so late. I understand he was unable to pay his debts, that he has nothing to offer but his labour.'

'I am surprised the Company feels he owes them anything.'

'Well, they do, Mr Mackenzie, having more respect for what they can lay their hands on than for what they can't. There's men of commerce for you, deplorable though it may be. Perhaps he didn't mention these difficulties during your conversation?'

He leaned forward to fill my glass with port I would leave undrunk.

'No? He didn't say anything of interest at all?'

'Nothing I feel obliged to repeat.'

'Forgive me. You're a gentleman too.'

He seemed to relax at this, to sink a little lower into his chair so that I somehow got, or was given, the impression that the game was over, that the pursuit had ended in an honourable draw. In any case, it seemed all too likely to me that he knew exactly what Paterson and I had discussed.

He stood up and went to the stern-lights to look down at the *Caledonia*'s wake. He turned quickly, taking me by surprise and demanded: 'So, Mr Mackenzie, you are a Patersonian?'

'A what?' I spluttered. 'I've never heard the word.' I made to leave, declaring as boldly as I could: 'If I have satisfied you as to the state of your stores, Captain, you'll permit me to carry on with my duties.'

Sadly, the sound of it wasn't quite what I hoped and when Captain Drummond smiled and tacked about and said that perhaps he had not expressed himself properly, that he had been in the company of the common soldier too long, that he spoke only out of his zeal for the interests of the Company, I found myself still sitting in my chair.

He sat down again behind his chart table and resumed the scratching of his beard.

'You must think me a very rough fellow, Mr Mackenzie. Well, maybe I am, but let me ask you this before you go: what sort of a place is it do you think we are going to?'

'Darien,' I said simply.

'It's a pretty word, but I think it must be a strange place. From my crew and my colonists I hear so much about it and always different. Sometimes you would think they are all going to different places. And then I think, No, you old dog, you've had too much of blood and fighting to be fit for the company of decent men and women such as these. We're all going to the same place, sure enough, it's just that we describe it differently. Nothing to worry about there. And what a fine place it is. One might almost say, if it weren't for fear of blasphemy, that it's a paradise. Well, now, Mr Mackenzie, don't you wonder why the world has left such a paradise for us? Could it be simply that they have not had the benefit of Mr Paterson's ingenuity, or might there be some other reason?'

I recovered a little of my boldness and told him straight: 'I can't understand why you are here, Captain Drummond.'

'Oh, no? Perhaps you have mistaken me. I don't say it's not true, that there's nothing there worth having. I do say that if it's worth having then we can't expect anyone to hand it to us for free.'

I repeated what I heard in the directors' meetings so many times: that the land was unclaimed, unoccupied by any European power and that our Act gave us every right to take it.

Drummond laughed in my face. 'Is that so? And you and your Mr Paterson have been all the way to his Imperial Catholic Majesty to ask him? Or perhaps you've sent him a copy of our Act?'

He took on a sudden intensity and leaned over the chart table, brushing the dividers aside with his hand.

'You listen to me, Mr Mackenzie. I was younger than you when a man told me Flanders was a pretty place to visit and I've never believed a recruiting sergeant since, silked and pomaded or not. I'm here because I just about believe in a tenth of what I've been told. But there's no Eden for us, Mr Mackenzie, and the taking of Darien and the keeping of it won't be done with lace and silk. Mr Paterson, the directors, they're all very well when it comes to spending money but we'll need more than that.'

His eyes didn't moved from mine during this speech and although I felt I had heard more than enough, he somehow extracted from me the question he was waiting for: 'And what more is that, Captain Drummond?'

He returned his gaze to mine with the expression of a man who had at last been asked to discuss his passion.

'Lives, Mr Mackenzie. Nothing great is done in this world without the spending of money and men. It's all very well your Mr Patersons dreaming up these schemes, but it takes a different breed of man to turn them into realities. You see, Mr Mackenzie, we're going to need men who know what it is to have blood on their hands.'

'Such as yourself, Captain?'

'Precisely my argument to the directors and, as you can see, they agreed.'

He clearly expected me to make some response to his whole oration, but if there was a question in it I failed to find it. I sat, dumbly transfixed, stunned at how many of my assumptions about our Company, which seemed so certain on land, had melted away under the influence of only a few days at sea.

Drummond stood up and walked to the door of his cabin. Despairing of my understanding he spelt it out, as if to an idiot. 'This is no venture for those who can't choose.'

The door was open, and myself standing in the threshold. 'Captain Drummond,' I said, trying to ignore the fact that I had begun to tremble, 'if what you say is true, I'm sure you'll be ready to do the necessary.'

I was on the quarterdeck, shaking half with a strange fear of the man and half with fury. I found myself looking straight into the leering features of the third mate who, I now felt sure, had been skulking in the passage during my conversation with Mr Paterson. I had slammed the door behind me and now held the attention of everyone on the deck.

'Get the boat ready.'

Still emboldened, I had said this to the third mate but panicked immediately as I realized that I had left myself nowhere to retreat. He grinned more broadly, showing his teeth in a feral threat, and moved not an inch. The prospect of climbing down from the deck in complete defeat was intolerable. I risked everything and shouted: 'I am an officer of the Company and I am telling you to get the boat ready!'

The man became expressionless and I couldn't guess if he was about to do as I had ordered or to murder me. The opportunity to test my authority was short-lived as Drummond's voice blasted out from behind the cabin door: 'Do as he tells you, you piece of filth!'

It solved a problem for both of us: he could do what his captain had told him, and I could have my order obeyed. I followed him down to the main deck and found Shipp lounging on a pile of sailcloth listening to some yarn from Toothless. In a minute or two we pushed off from the *Caledonia* and began to labour through the swell towards the *Rising Sun*.

Mr Shipp remained as unperturbed as ever, although I am sure he must have heard both my voice being raised and that of Captain Drummond. Furthermore, I could not believe that he was totally incurious about the amount of time we had spent on the *Caledonia* on account of such a trivial matter, which, very clearly, was nothing more than a pretext. All the same, I was determined not to say the first word, having come to understand that his taciturnity is reserved only for me as another of his reproaches for my undeserved superiority. Here, also, I won another small victory. For we had not yet covered half our distance when he volunteered his opinion: 'He's a beast, I say. There's no good'll come of his being here.'

Thinking this might apply equally to Captain Drummond or to his third mate I asked whom he meant.

'Drummond, you . . . Captain Drummond, young master, who else? It's the devil's own luck behind him, I say. Hardly three year back he couldn't set foot in his own country for fear of the rope and now this. There's your great men for you!'

I was in no mood to defend Drummond, but was also aware that as an officer of the Company I could hardly sit by and listen to one of our captains being described in the most slanderous terms. I was about to ask what he meant by it when a wave overtopped our gunwales and threatened the ledgers. I must record, to his credit, that it was with admirable presence of mind that Mr Shipp hoisted them above his head a split second before all four of us in the boat were soaked from the chest down. From beneath this canopy he glowered and shouted through the wind, 'If we've need of a man like that, you wonder what we're heading for, young master!'

Later, with the great timbers of the *Rising Sun* solidly beneath our feet, I asked him what he meant, but he would say no more. I went straight to my cabin, sought out some less salted clothes, put Mr Paterson's letter to Mackay on my writing table and poured myself a royal measure of brandy.

*

THERE! Another fragment of our history preserved for grateful descendants. But what a hopeless task it seems; what I have just recorded was already an age ago, a full ten days. In a moment of confusion I considered using Shipp as a copyist. It brought a visitation from the voice of Dr Lennox: 'Zeus has taken away his wits, gentlemen.' It was indeed the stupidest idea I have had for some time – even for what has already been said, it is too late to share the burden with another hand. Still more impossible for what remains to be said.

Thanks to God we have had plain sailing for three days. At this very moment we roll gently and there is nothing to be heard but that constant creaking of the timbers, which is now my conception of silence.

I still have said nothing of the great fog, but can hardly write another word for fatigue.

Cracking the lice is still something I cannot hold my stomach to. I have found that if I leave a little brandy in the bottom of the glass and place them there, it extinguishes them very well by morning.

Enough! Out, dear flame, out!

FOR THE SECOND TIME I found myself abed at the start of great events, and for the second time a victim of a rude awakening. I had exhausted myself the night before in establishing our stocks of salt beef and in my own writing. Understanding that letters can be left at Madeira, I have written to my mother, brother, Dr Lennox, Mr Colquhoun and Mr Vetch, and also a brief report to the directors assuring them of my industry on their behalf and of the excellent state of all matters under my control. I could only have finished two hours or less before dawn and took a little brandy to ease my brief rest. A moment later I seemed to be dreaming of some indefinable disaster when a shattering explosion was unleashed. I jerked up, smashing my head into the beam above my bunk, and tumbled out of my cabin, certain we were under attack. Could the Spanish have come this far north, determined to snuff out our venture at the start? More likely, I thought, it must be some English privateers under secret instructions from London to do their worst and deny all. I paused a moment and was perplexed by a strange silence, more complete than any I could remember since taking ship. A distant bell seemed to be tolling, so much on the edge of my senses that I couldn't swear whether I truly heard it or not. I pulled on my breeches and made my way quickly to the main deck where I ran into a thick cloud of whiteness. From where I stood, roughly in the middle of the ship, I could just see the spectral outlines of its bow and stern and I realized that those at either end would be quite invisible to each other. I looked up and saw the great trunk of the main mast disappear into obscurity two-thirds of the way up. A man appeared from nowhere, sliding down out of the clouds on a rope. His bare feet landed with a slap on the deck five feet from me.

'Good morning to you, sir,' he said, as if he climbed up and down from the clouds every day. He turned and bellowed: 'Nothing at all. Worse.'

'Very well. Carry on.'

It was Captain Galt's voice from the quarterdeck, where I could see three or four indistinct figures. On the bow I could see other men and I went that way first past the forms of several of our colonists. Two crewmen were as far forward as they could go and had put one of the boys out on the bowsprit. A rope trailed back from his waist and was secured to some point on the deck. We moved sluggishly through the fog with little wind and light sail and such was its extraordinary density that as we moved through the thicker folds of it we could see only the knees, calves and feet of the boy. Then, as the wind quickened or shifted for a moment we could see him whole. He called out: '*Caledonia!* Fifty yards!'

The dark block of a stern loomed ahead of us and, just visible, the dull glow of its two red stern-lanterns.

'*Caledonia!*' relayed one of the crewmen to the invisible figures on the quarterdeck. 'Dead ahead!'

As we watched, her shape became clearer and the man spoke again: 'We're too close.'

The *Caledonia* suddenly lost what little speed she had and we were almost upon her, the bowsprit, boy and all, nearly smashing through the stern-lights into Drummond's cabin. We were sighted and could hear the shouts of command and response from the *Caledonia*, none of which, I noted, were Drummond's.

'We're going to ram her!' the crewman next to me shouted, and ran off into instant invisibility to warn our Captain Galt.

Orders and commotion came from behind us now, and from above the sound of sail being taken in. Looking along the line of our bowsprit I could see our course change sharply so that instead of breaking Captain Drummond's windows in the very next second we began to come alongside his vessel.

'God preserve me! Don't they know I'm here?' came from the boy, and a hiss of pent-up breath from the remaining crewman.

From behind, above the general clamour, came: 'The damn fool!'

It was Galt's voice.

I turned to the man beside me and asked where we were.

'The Pentland Firth, sir. Couldn't have happened at a worse spot.'

I can recall it clearly enough, but don't believe I fully heard it at the time. Certainly, I did not understand its implications. I began to doubt whether I had been woken by that explosion or not, such was the extreme strangeness of our situation. I watched us gain on the *Caledonia* till we were level with its main mast. The crewmen looked up and I did the same to see the spars of the two ships pass feet apart. A figure appeared at the rail of the *Caledonia* and shouted across to us: 'Do you know our position, sir?'

Again the voice was not Drummond's but that of the first mate, a man, I believe, by the name of Strachan. There was further cursing and swearing from our quarterdeck and then Mr Cunningham's voice shouting: 'The Firth. Middle, we think. Your reckoning?'

'Aye.'

The crewman beside me had dragged the boy back and was untying the rope from his waist when he gave a low gallows laugh and said: 'Then it's all hands to the Bibles.'

There was more shouting from the *Caledonia*, of which I could only make out a few words; something of ropes, of tying up. The voices of Cunningham and Galt came through the mist again, but there was nothing I could understand. Our change of course to avoid colliding with her continued to carry us away. Her hull and masts faded and were gone.

As I returned to the main deck I could once again hear the faint tolling of a bell far behind us, which I understood must be either the *Dolphin*, *St Andrew* or the *Endeavour*. The sense of fear at this soft, silent threat started to seep down into the holds and the deck was becoming crowded with colonists talking quietly in twos or threes or peering anxiously over the rails in the hope that they might be able to see something. The fog seemed to have sucked up every last grain of the sun's warmth and a sinister cold began to penetrate us. The vapour settled on our skin and clothes so that before long we were drenched through. A coldness ran down my back like a louse and I looked up to see the sails, quite limp and useless now, collecting the moisture from the air like great leaves and dripping it on to us.

A woman, one of the very few we have with us, pressed my arm and demanded to know: 'It's not dangerous, sir, is it? We won't come to any harm by it?'

As I looked into her face, rigid with worry, glistening with the moisture of the fog, it seemed the most preposterous question that had ever been asked and one she had already answered for herself a hundred times over. How bizarre that such a concentration of plaintive fearfulness should find itself drifting fogbound between two rocky coastlines. The question came to me at once: Who could have persuaded her to embark on such a voyage? She seemed the sort of woman who would not cross a street in darkness and I could only imagine that she was plucking my arm and asking me this question as the distant result of some terrible deception.

'No, madam,' I said to her. 'It's quite safe.'

Eager for a more honest account of our situation I finally decided it was the right moment to take my first steps on the quarterdeck. The thought, rather ridiculous as it seems now, that my identity and possible embarrassment would be concealed by the fog was also in my mind. I was hailed at once from a huddle of figures in the middle of the deck.

'Good morning to you, Mr Mackenzie. You managed to find your way to us in this infernal haar?'

It was Captain Galt, standing between Mr Cunningham and his second mate with a gunner and a steersman.

'Yes, sir. Captain,' I said, thankful for the fog at that moment when it became clear that I did not even know what to call the man.

'Excellent. I was about to send Mr Cunningham to ask how we had offended you.'

'Offended? In no way at all, Captain. Sir. I, er, assure you. I . . .' Or some such nonsense. In short, with a word he had put me in utter confusion.

'Good,' he said feelingly, but concentrating entirely on the papers before him. 'I imagined we must have done something to have been deprived of your company for so long.'

I saw Mr Cunningham smile and felt the moments in which I might make a response slip hopelessly away. Fortunately, I was overtaken by events. Mr Cunningham was looking intently at a device on the table and nodded to Captain Galt.

'Gunner?'

'Ready.'

'Give the order, Mr Maxwell.'

The second mate walked forward to the rail and shouted: 'All quiet! All quiet!'

'Two seconds,' said Cunningham.

'Fire.'

There was a flare of light from the touch-hole and a shocking explosion like the one that had torn me out of sleep. A concentrated silence ensued so that it seemed that I had been the only one to hear the blast, and was certainly the only one to jump out of my boots. From out of the muffled distance an answering explosion came. Mr Cunningham started at once to make a calculation. After half a minute or so he straightened and declared: 'A thousand yards, maybe more.'

Captain Galt expressed no opinion, but did not seem pleased. 'Carry on, Mr Cunningham. And see that you don't collide with that soldier boy dancing about in front of us.'

'Sir.'

With that he retired to his cabin, making our second encounter almost as brief as our first.

Two problems filled my mind: whether we were indeed in any

danger, and the precise nature and scale of the offence I had given Captain Galt and how I might repair the breach. I was struggling to find some way of broaching the matter with Mr Cunningham when he placed in my hand the instrument he had been studying. 'The finest Paris can produce, Mr Mackenzie. Cost you half as much as some ships.'

I looked down at a very plain-faced and very large pocket-watch, or at least at an instrument with the same shape as a pocket-watch but with no chain or place to attach one. 'And with this you can say where the other ships are?'

'Roughly. It counts half-seconds and stops when you press it down here.' He demonstrated. 'We were signalling the *Dolphin.* As soon as they hear our gun, they fire theirs. With an accurate idea of the time and an estimate for the speed of sound it's a simple calculation. Very crude still, but better than nothing.' He held out his hand for the return of his 'chronometer' as he called it. 'Clever, no?'

'Very,' I said, as he locked it away in its box.

A distant bell rang.

'The *St Andrew.*'

'And the *Endeavour*?' I asked.

He shook his head. 'No sign for an hour.'

As it seemed that there was nothing more to be done for a while, I decided to make an immediate start on my problem. 'Mr Cunningham,' I said, 'I am no seaman as you know, and I think that in my ignorance I have offended our captain.'

Mr Cunningham took such a long time before replying that I thought he must be trying to find the best way of conveying a particularly unpleasant piece of information. It was with equal measures of incomprehension and relief that I heard him say: 'You are a man, Mr Mackenzie.'

He told me this in a tone that suggested I had been unmasked as such, as if Captain Galt had seen through my attempts to pass myself off as quite another creature.

'That offends him?' I asked, astonished.

'Very deeply,' said Mr Cunningham.

I peered at him through the mist and tried to find some trace that he was amusing himself at my expense, but found only an expression of complete openness and sincerity. Aside from being a very curious remark it seemed to me a very intimate one and I asked him: 'You have served with him before?'

'A few times, and with other men and commanded myself.'

'You've been master yourself?'

'Yes,' he said, 'but when I heard he'd been appointed I asked for the *Rising Sun*.' He emphasized this and looked at me straight.

The bell sounded again, neither fainter nor stronger than before, and a cry from the bow of 'Stern-lanterns ahead!' told us we had drifted in sight of the *Caledonia* again.

'We're keeping together,' I observed.

'Well enough.'

Neither of us mentioned the *Endeavour*. I cannot say what was in Mr Cunningham's mind but my own was transfixed by Captain Galt and the hopeless thought that he might be offended by my very humanity. I tried to imagine myself in a position of indifference to this fact but realized, not without some humiliation, that I had become intensely interested in what the man thought of me. I considered the development of my unlicensed postal service and the audiences with Paterson and Drummond. Could these be the sources of offence? It seemed unlikely and I sent my mind off in search of other sins.

These driftings were interrupted by the heavy footsteps of someone making their way up to the quarterdeck. The bulky, ghostly figure of Reverend Mackay loomed. I nodded in the direction of the great glorifier of God and recipient of Mr Paterson's letter, but he failed to see me in the haze and went to stand on his own by the rail. Another thought occurred to me. I leaned a little closer to Mr Cunningham and asked quietly: 'Have I offended our captain especially? I mean, more than any other part of humanity?'

A relenting smile appeared at last and for a moment I forgot the danger of our situation when I heard him tell me: 'Rather less than some parts, I would say, Mr Mackenzie.'

It was only then that I remembered the second question in my mind. 'Are we in danger?'

Mr Cunningham looked at me solemnly and was, I think, considering whether he could trust me with this information. I told him I had already dismissed the fears of one colonist.

'Good,' he said, 'no point in causing alarm. With no wind we cannot steer. To the north we have the Orkneys, to the south the headland, neither of them kind to blind, wandering ships. If we are going to be unfortunate, we could be totally unfortunate.'

From his voice I knew this was not to be repeated and was grateful for the confidence.

The time for our next signal to the *Dolphin* was approaching and Captain Galt came back on deck holding a paper which he handed to Mr Cunningham. 'My estimate of our current positions; if you could give me your opinion.'

Mr Cunningham glanced over the paper briefly. 'All in accordance with my own calculations, sir.'

'Excellent,' he scowled about him at the thick vapours drifting over the deck, 'in so far as calculations make a bugger's worth of difference in this. Ah.'

He had sighted the shade of Reverend Mackay and went over to him. Some inaudible words were exchanged and Mackay walked smartly off the deck.

'Very regrettable,' said Captain Galt, as he returned to us. 'It appears that the presbytery can be of no help. Mr Mackay informs me that there is no prayer, hymn or incantation known to him which is effective in the blowing away of fogs. Alas, gentlemen, we must proceed without him. Ready?'

The gunner gave the nod while Mr Cunningham unlocked the chronometer from its box. The pains of hunger that had been rising since I had been blasted out of my bunk could no longer be denied.

I excused myself and went below in search of food, reassured on all quarters.

I found Munro softening his bread in a tankard of beer and looking gloomy. Mr Mackay sat reading at the other end of the table and was not inclined to acknowledge me. I had the steward bring me some bread, beer, some cheese and two oranges and sat with these opposite Dr Munro. He moved his eyes in the direction of Mackay then raised an eyebrow at me. We gave each other a slight smile. The signal gun boomed out again, sending its vibrations through the ship. Being below decks I could hear no reply. The steward came in again, put a glass of water by Reverend Mackay and left.

'Have you spoken with the tasselled one?'

In reality Captain Galt dresses very plainly.

I said I had been on the quarterdeck and had spoken about the situation with Mr Cunningham. I noticed, as I spoke, that Mr Mackay was having difficulty in concentrating on his book.

'And do they know where we are?'

'Pentland Firth,' I repeated.

'Is that good?'

Dr Munro affects an airy ignorance of most things, medicine not excluded.

'Not with this fog,' I said. 'I talked with one of the crew. As he put it, it's all hands to the—'

'Good Christ, we're not leaking already, are we?'

'Dr Munro!' exclaimed Mackay. 'Please.'

'No, no,' I said, 'not at all. But the danger is real. There are rocks to be avoided and even then we might lose each other. There's been no sign of the *Endeavour* for hours.'

'There's a thought,' said Munro. 'If we had to lose one of them which one would be best, d'you think?'

Mackay looked horrified. 'Dr Munro, that is a very disloyal comment.'

Munro gave an expression of exasperation and mumbled a word of apology. Mr Stobo came in, the other minister on the *Rising Sun*.

He nodded in our direction then exchanged a few words with Mackay in Gaelic. Dr Munro said something to them in the same language. They sent sharp looks in our direction and left.

'You were on the quarterdeck?'

'Yes.'

He leaned forward eagerly. 'Well, what happened?'

I paused, my mind going back to my recent encounters with Paterson and Drummond. Having been accused of being a Patersonian (to which I would not object if it had not the whiff of faction about it), I had no desire to make myself a Munrovian or a Galtian or whatever else we might be divided into.

'Something happened,' said Munro, 'the way he came in here.'

'Captain Galt spoke to him. I didn't overhear.'

'Ah,' said Munro, 'aaah. Captains and ministers.' He called the steward for another tankard of beer and then said with sudden anger: 'Aren't they doing anything about it at all?'

'Such as?' I asked. 'They can't see one end of the ship from the other. The wind has dropped so much they couldn't sail out of it even if they could see where they're going.'

'Quite the mariner.'

This last remark was gratuitous and I carried on with my breakfast in silence. The steward appeared with the beer and left us again.

'The damn stuff's getting below decks. Twenty-four hours of this and we'll have losses. I've got some weak chests already. How they chose these people I don't know. There's a young one . . .' He shook his head at me. 'Shouldn't be here.'

'It's bad for the stores,' I said.

'Well, I hope they don't die of it.'

'No, I meant that if they spoil—'

My defence was interrupted by a knock on the door. A man I didn't recognize came in and demanded: 'One of you's the doctor?'

Munro went without a glance in my direction.

I returned to the main deck to find that our situation had not changed. Hunger satisfied, my other great need forced itself upon me and I went below to find my bunk and some of the sleep that had been stolen from me by the writing of letters and by trying to ensure that this account does not fall too far behind. I went up to the main deck again at about three o'clock and was pleased to find an evident improvement. The wind was still very feeble, but the fog had thinned so that the entirety of our ship from bow to stern and main deck to top mast was clearly visible and we could see some way out over calm water. The sun was still invisible, but a brighter glow indicated its position and I could see that if only the fog would clear we would enjoy clear skies.

That morning had broken the spell of the quarterdeck and I boldly climbed up to find Mr Cunningham and our captain poring over charts. I offered some optimistic pleasantry about the lifting of the fog but received only a grunt from Mr Cunningham. My curiosity was intense and, at the risk of presumption, I leaned a little over the table from the other side to see what sense I could make of it. I assumed a long unbroken line represented the headland and below it (from where I was looking) was the central block of Orkney surrounded by its many irregular satellites. Lines were drawn through the broad channel between the two, marked off in segments accompanied by tiny neat numbers. The last segment terminated in a small cross well west of the islands and two or three miles north of the headland. It seemed as if everything had worked out perfectly.

I saw the signal gun covered in a tarpaulin and recalled that my sleep had been uninterrupted. 'No signals?' I asked.

Mr Cunningham explained that we had got out of earshot several hours ago and I noticed then that the bell of the *St Andrew* could no longer be heard. By this point the light was brightening perceptibly and Captain Galt gave the order to take sightings. Men stood by with spyglasses on either side of the ship, while two others went aloft, becoming only a little hazy as they climbed the ropes. The sun appeared, pale and without warmth, and instead of the uniform obscurity we had been in before, heavier and lighter billows of mist passed over us. Suddenly the light was brilliant and the sun's full warmth was on us. Instinctively, we looked upwards, smarting at the brightness and wiping tears from our eyes. A happy cheer went up from the colonists on deck, and as this sound carried the message below, the rejoicing spread. In front of us and from either side, the wall of fog rolled away so that with every passing second we could see further. There was a cry from above and all heads turned in one direction as land loomed. A line of harsh cliffs appeared, startlingly close. The headland, I thought at first, but as the mists rolled further back the cliffs receded and sank into the sea revealing a small island. There were other cries and as we turned to look to the north another larger island appeared. Between these two a third block of jagged land, some miles off and directly in front of us, was unveiled as we watched. There was a narrow channel to the south of it and only a very slightly broader one to the north.

A voice came from above: 'We're in the Flow.'

Captain Galt took a glass and scanned about. There were mutterings between himself and Cunningham and I could just see where another mark was made on the chart, very distant from the first cross. Instead of passing cleanly between the Orkneys and the mainland we had drifted northward while blinded by the fog and now found ourselves in a tangle of islands, each one edged with cliffs as sharp as teeth. I looked at the chart again and saw how fortunate we had been in not already having run aground. We were fortunate, too, in having lost contact with the other ships – our lead, if they had followed it, could only have led them on to disaster.

There was an Orkney man in the crew and he was called up to be questioned by Captain Galt. The island ahead of us was Graemsay. To the south of it the channel was narrower and made treacherous by a skerry that barely broke the surface. We would go to the north, through the Bring Deeps. All of which would have been easy enough had not our moment of clear sight been so brief. There came another cry from one of the men aloft: 'We're in an island.'

At first I thought I had misheard, but then I saw the rocky edges of the islands fade and disappear as I looked at them. On three sides of us the land was already invisible. I watched in dismay as the fog rolled towards us denser than before, squeezing our island of clear air out of existence. It didn't come gradually, but with a curious precision I have never seen before so that when it had half swallowed us we seemed to be on half a ship. Ahead of us, Graemsay and the channel to the north of it faded and were gone.

Captain Galt looked back to the chart on the table, then into the whiteness of the fog as if trying to fix in his memory our only way forward. The quickened wind, which had brought back the fog, gave us a chance to make good headway. But to where?

Mr Cunningham and Captain Galt put their heads together. Snatches came to me. There was talk of anchoring before we drifted into the deeps and waiting till the fog cleared, which surely could not be long. But what of the other ships? They must be getting further and further away, assuming they had not been wrecked. Besides, why should the fog end soon? It could be another day or more. There was talk of risk, of caution and then the conversation ended with Mr Cunningham looking the graver of the two.

A stream of orders was given. Sail was put out, crewmen went forward with leads ready to plumb the depth from either side of the bow. Muskets were issued to two of the colonists with soldiering experience with orders to blank charge them and stand by on the main deck.

It was impossible to judge our speed. Indeed, it was only from the filling of the sails that any movement could be deduced at all. More canvas was put out as another anxious word from Mr Cunningham to our captain was dismissed. He would not turn his head from the direction of the channel that had just been hidden from us. Time passed in silent invisible movement. We peered ahead, unable to see beyond our own bowsprit. I assumed (though I now doubt it) that some private knowledge of Captain Galt's, or the practice of some trick of seamanship unobserved by the rest of us, was preserving our lives.

'Soundings!'

The leads were swung, whipping the thin cord down after them. Every time the cord was exhausted with a jerk we knew we were in ample water. Then there was a cry from the left, and a second later from the right. All human sound and motion stopped as we listened to the diminishing numbers and imagined the rocky bottom rising up to our hull.

Attention turned to the side from where the cliffs of Graemsay might threaten us at any moment. The muskets were fired and their sounds sent rolling through the fog in search of the cliffs as we listened for their reflections. The wind increased and gusted suddenly, causing us to keel over towards where we knew the island must be. There were cries of alarm from the main deck and Captain Galt ordered it to be cleared of colonists. By the bows one of the crew gave a cry of pain as the cord was ripped from his hands and disappeared over the side, the lead caught on the rocks just below the surface. The fog began to break up as the wind between the islands became more intense. We got glimpses of land to the north, reassuringly distant. But then, as the fog was pulled apart by the gusts we found great cliffs lowering over us on our southward side. Captain Galt stepped forward to take the helm.

'Take in sail, Captain, surely?'

Mr Cunningham shouted the question so that it almost sounded like an order, but Galt seemed not to hear it. He leaned all his weight against the wheel. The wind and the currents strengthened and pushed us ever closer to the cliffs. As they approached, they seemed to race past at an impossible speed. I saw the second officer's lips moving and started to add my own prayers. I was almost convinced that Galt was intent on our destruction when, at the very moment we seemed bound to touch, Graemsay curved away from us and we were in open water.

Having contempt for the ordinary running of the ship, he returned to his cabin almost immediately, apparently oblivious of the effect his manoeuvre had had on everyone on deck. I glanced at Cunningham. 'You would have done it differently?'

I received only a look of reproach for having dared to ask.

PLAIN SAILING NOW, and for several days past. We need it and I am sure it has helped us overcome the shock of our great loss.

It was an hour after dawn when we were still anchored in the lee of Hoy and considering what to do that the watch sighted a sail on the horizon. It was the *Dolphin*. Captain Jolly had guessed correctly and had zigzagged northwards in the hope of finding other members of the fleet. We waited several hours side by side before it was decided to sweep southwards on irregular courses covering as much of the sea as we could. We then made for Stornoway to ask if there had been any news and to our great delight found the *St Andrew* and the *Endeavour* at anchor there, asking the very same questions of the fishermen. For two days we waited, hoping for news or a sighting. At the end of the second day the remaining four captains and the other councillors met. At dawn we steered well out into the ocean and then south for Madeira. The *Caledonia*, and with her the author of our venture, is lost.

I cannot convey what a great disturbance this has caused in me. What is more, the effect of the disaster has been compounded by my observations of how differently the matter has been received on the *Rising Sun*. Saving those of our colonists who had relatives or good friends aboard, only Mr Mackay has been deeply affected. In spite of this, whenever in his presence I put on a more cheerful and unconcerned appearance for fear of attracting overtures. It is already clear that his party will not prosper, still less so after our losses.

Perhaps it is better that the hardest lessons be learned soonest. Certainly, if it had been some other ship lost and Captain Drummond were still with us, he would have delighted in the proof of his harsh philosophy. In my prayers I ask forgiveness for feeling some satisfaction that the bragging spender of lives has himself been spent. Adieu, Captain. How right you were!

In spite of this we prosper. With steady winds and warm, sunny weather, the relief from the benighted summers of home has raised our spirits. We have made good progress. If we could see far enough it would be Portugal to our east, and soon Africa. Dr Munro tells me that the health of his 'cargo' is much improved.

The ease of our current situation has given me more time to devote to this account and I find that I am so taken with the writing down of my own words, and with my liberation from the hateful numbers that I am no longer satisfied with my first modest design. Consider what could be said of all the bones about the wreck of the *Caledonia* by future generations. Nothing more than that they exist and once framed out some men and women. All else would be mystery. Another thing set me on this line – a thing I was sworn not to repeat. Dr Munro came to my cabin to ask what stocks of bandages and medicaments are left to us. The new issue of brandy having just been made, we decided to make an immediate start on it and it wasn't long before he told me that he had served as a surgeon in the English navy. He said he had been unjustly treated in a matter of honour while in Portsmouth and implied he would not be safe if he showed his face there again.

Well, well, I thought. What is one to make of that? I should have seen it before – every man here trails out a thread of life behind him, and without knowing them all, nothing is comprehensible. I have made a point of becoming more sociable, and the more I talk with my fellow travellers the more I am ambitious to expand this simple journal into one more worthy of our project. The thought that I might not know a man's motives now gives me an itch, and I find myself being led on from connection to connection until I insist that I must know everything or nothing. There is a Highlander who learned whaling with the Norwegians. He bought his own boat in partnership with some Aberdeen men and saw it smashed to pieces beneath his feet by a leviathan and was the only one to survive. He came to Edinburgh to restore his fortunes. One very plain-looking man has been a minister of the Episcopalian persuasion. Despairing of an end to the exclusion and with his wife and children all dead – of hunger he claims – he was ready to exchange broadcloth for canvas. Another is a cheated merchant and another the fourth inheritor of a patrimony fit only for three. There is a rumour that there are several of the MacDonalds of Glencoe with us, though no one has ever come across one themselves, and the name is absent from my lists. We have many tired of breaking their hearts on the land through wet winters and cold summers. We are eleven hundred life stories twisted together into the very fibre of this venture. Near a dozen of Decamerons! I shall not want for entertainment.

Let me start with my own thread. Here is my everything, my all in all –

*

I FELL UPON THE WORLD able to rule a ledger as well as any boy my age, to write in it in a fine hand, letters and numbers equally, to add and subtract these numbers to and from each other and with a particular facility for the calculation of percentages.

I felt at the time – and still think I was not wrong – that I knew much besides. One afternoon I had the temerity to point this out as I stood beside my dominie and watched him write out the letter that began my journey.

'Perhaps I should add,' he said, 'that he is an arrogant young man with a displeasing self-confidence and a determination to know more than his elders and betters. Well, Master Mackenzie?'

'No, sir,' I admitted, 'I do not think that would be helpful.'

'Well, don't give me any reason to say it. There's one thing you don't know, Roderick, and that's what the world cares for. Look at that wall until I tell you otherwise.'

'Sir?'

'Do as I say!'

I turned my back and heard Dr Lennox's pen scratching the paper for another two or three lines. It crackled as he waved it in the air and started to fold it.

'You've seen enough.'

I turned back to see him making the last fold in the letter and reaching for the wax.

'I speak to my pupils as men once only, Roderick, and never again,' he raised his eyes to the rafters, 'please God! You may think it all very fine to know what *amavissem* means or to be able to tell the generations from Adam to Noah, or what Mr Boyle thinks about gases, but the world won't pay you a grain of barley for it. It would be ill-mannered to bore a man like Mr Colquhoun with things he has no business with.'

The wax was drooping and smoking in the candle flame. Dr Lennox smeared it on the back of the letter and pressed his signet into it. 'Give that to Colquhoun. Into his own hand, mind. I knew him once and he'll do what he can for you, though it'll be precious little. He's a drunkard and a fool. You'll learn much from him.'

As Dr Lennox walked down between the benches I trailed him to the end of the schoolhouse. He wrenched open the door as if expecting an eavesdropper on the other side of it and we stood together on the threshold.

'Whatever Mr Colquhoun does, observe closely and resolve to do the opposite. Learn the business as best you can then leave him.'

'Yes, sir.'

He looked about the blackening hills and seemed for a moment to become unaware of my presence. Then he looked at me fiercely and I felt a sting of embarrassment as I noticed that he was holding out his hand. I took it and tried not to wince at his grip. He returned his eyes to the hills and uttered his oration. 'Well, Roderick Mackenzie, I've done what I can for you. Whatever you make of yourself it won't be my fault. Tell your mother she can be proud of your brother, and don't let me hear your name again for ten years.'

Dr Lennox stepped back into his domain and slammed the door so hard that I could feel the blast from it on my face. I ran into the street, clutching the letter to Colquhoun, avid for everything his extraordinary viaticum promised.

With promises to write frequently, return every three months, work hard and keep good company I left my mother a little too hastily perhaps, impatient to escape her tears. I hauled myself up on to Hippo's back and let him walk slowly along the main and only street of my native town, turning to wave just as the bend obscured us from each other. Named by myself in a moment of scholarly enthusiasm, Hippogriff, soon shortened to Hippo, was an unperturbable Galloway who constituted a good part of our movable property. Consequently, I had instructions to leave him at Maclean's where he would remain until he could carry back whatever traveller next made for our obscure direction. The plan seemed unrealistic to me. That anyone should want to go from Edinburgh to Dryhope was surely very improbable, and I fully expected him to remain there for the prescribed three months until I myself was his first return passenger. Hippo had won his battle of wills early with us and ever after never went anywhere faster than a funereal walk. I have read whole books on his back and passed many of the hours on this particular journey with my back to him, using his hindquarters as a card table for endless games of patience. A more unlegendary animal never lived.

I had been given the money to stop at an inn at the half-way point, but when I reached it the long-threatened rain had still not started and I decided that the first of my economies in my new life would be to let Hippo continue and drowse on his back as best I could. This worked better than I expected in that after several hours of darkness I not only drowsed but fell entirely asleep and so continued my journey as happy as a papoose until first light woke me. Hippo had stopped and I nearly slipped down his neck as he tore the grass from the verge. There was no telling for how long he had stopped, or how far we had travelled. Nor even if he had taken the right road. It was certain that he would always take the easiest and most obvious way forward and I felt sure that this principle would be enough to keep us on the Edinburgh road. One thing was obvious – that I was in strange country and in those days that was all I needed to be happy.

I soon passed another inn and learned that I was only a few miles short of my destination. Tantalizing smells of breakfast wafted from it, but again I decided to hold on to my money, reasoning that there would be something better to spend it on in the city. Soon I was not alone on the road. I had to make way for cartloads of vegetables, fatted lambs, coal and slates. There were several carriages, one with curtained windows and a coat of arms, which I tried to see into, and many riders, all of whom travelled faster than I did, despite several sharp kicks into Hippo's ribs.

That dull, damp, cool, near-midsummer day was the first time I saw our capital. On breasting the hill on the road from the south it appears all at once, a spine of tall buildings running down a rocky ridge from the castle at its head to the palace at its tail. Blocked on its northern side by a loch, the city has long since spilled down the southern side of the ridge. Beyond a certain distance from the ridge some of the houses are very great and one can look down over the walls of wide gardens with lawns, lines of little trees and hedges. My first sight of land planted for pleasure excited me and confirmed everything I had promised myself from the city. I told myself I would walk there one day, at first behind the great men of affairs and then by their side.

As I approached, the road was soon flanked with buildings, low at first and for the most part very mean. Only another few paces on I was thrilled to notice the proper gutters that had been dug at either side and lined with stones. There was the smell of coal and wood fires, interrupted by the scent of bread as I passed a bakery, glimpsing the fire of its ovens, and then the odour of beer and sour wine from a tavern. It was the beginning of the city and within minutes of starting my life in it I believe I must have seen more people than I had ever seen in a month of my earlier, and from that day, joyously discarded existence.

I saw Maclean's on the left, exactly where I had been told to look for it. I was anxious to set my feet on the city's streets, to run into the heart of it and inhale until my lungs burst. I thrust Hippo's reins into the hands of the first stable-boy I came across, gulped in shock at the number of shillings he demanded, paid them without a word, pocketed the receipt and ran back outside. I followed the flow of people up Horse Wynd and entered the Cowgate which, in my innocence, I mistook at first for the High Street, not thinking there could be anything larger. I passed the meat-market, where the air reeks with blood and the gutters run red. At the auspicious sea-stench of the fish-market where tails still thrashed, crabs pinched, elvers swirled and knotted in pails and heaps of flat stones were offered for two shillings a dozen – oysters, I was later to discover – I turned left where many people were compressing themselves into Fishmarket Close and still climbing upward. I looked up with wonder at the height of the buildings, which left only a crack of dull sky to be seen. I was jostled and growled at and commanded in curious accents to hurry on. We issued into the great thoroughfare of the city, everyone but myself striding on to left or right or making the hazardous crossing: a brief run to avoid a carriage or rider, a halt to let another pass, a dart to one side to avoid the ordure thrown up by the wheels of another carriage and then a dash to the safety of the other side, earning as one went the curses of a dung-cart driver or water-carrier for forcing them to slow a second rather than tread you underfoot as you deserved. As I came to know the city, I saw the High Street as a scene of eternal battle between dung-cart and water-carrier fought out in the gutter of the nation – the flushings of which enrich our fields for miles around.

A carriage stopped right in front of me, nearly cutting off my toes. A man climbed down from the back and was trotting round to open the door when it flew open in his face and out bustled the grandest gentleman I had ever seen. He stalked across the filthy cobbles into a fine house just behind me. The sounds of bitter argument had preceded his appearance and before his servant could close the door I saw a lady within, toying with a handkerchief. I saw myself climbing into the carriage, declaring my consoling love to her and giving imperious orders to the servants. The door slammed in my face, the horses were lashed and the carriage started away, spattering me with mud.

'Get out of the way, will you!'

I did, jumping to the left and upwards towards the Castle. I stopped to gawp at a black man, was passed by two men speaking a language I could not even guess at, watched as a merchant and a Jew shook hands and parted outside a coffee-house by Riddle's Close. In my imagination this was what I had been saving my money for. I ducked and entered out of the rain that had started to fall.

I pushed past a man who offered me twopence to carry a message for him and found myself a small table in a shadowy spot by one of the many brickwork piers that held up the ceiling. The place was filled with the clattering noise of the serving of food and drink. To make themselves heard above this everyone had to raise their voices almost to a shout, the entire effect being nothing less than riotous. I had elected to sit by the narrowest point connecting the two great rooms of the establishment so that trays of steaming bowls of coffee and chocolate, warm loaves, plates mounded with blood puddings fried with onions, dainty little dishes of marmalade, smoked herrings, every conceivable form of eggs, sugared plums and apricots and all manner of tortures, which I can smell as freshly now as on the day itself, were rushed past my head. I say tortures because I soon discovered that on entering such places it is no simple matter to actually lay one's hands on food and drink – indeed, one's very existence becomes a matter of opinion. I can't say in what particular I lacked, but it was clear that in the opinion of the serving men I was no more noticeable than the air I had displaced. I was about to run out in humiliated defeat when a man near to me started to batter his table with the edge of a coin and bellow, 'Service!' I learned the lesson and soon had my breakfast: bread straight from the oven, the butter sinking into it, and a bowl of coffee, the city gentleman's drink from far-off lands. It smelt better than it tasted, but I drank it down determinedly.

A boy came in and called out for Mr Strachan, shouting the name at the top of his voice until he found him and delivered his message. He was stopped on his way out and handed another piece of paper and a coin before he dashed back into the street.

The crowd shrank as the breakfast hour waned. The piers were arranged so that they obscured my view of most of the other tables, but they seemed to play a trick with the voices of those who remained. Snatches of the many invisible conversations going on about me were suddenly clear and I was eager to play the spy.

'They're troublemakers through and through. I wouldn't have bothered with an enquiry in the first . . .'

Uproarious disapproval at this.

'If the King doesn't care what his ministers do, we should get another.'

'Husssh! You mustn't say that.'

'At least it sent Stair off with his tail between his legs.'

'Didn't you hear?' said another. 'They all killed themselves.'

'Have more respect, man!'

Another voice from another direction: 'How's your trade?'

'I'll be in the poor-house next week. Because of Willy's war they think we're against them too. I have to spend all day with a Frenchman acting the Jacobite to get a groat's worth of business out of him.'

'Perhaps our French friends can cook our Dutch goose for us?'

The voice of authority boomed: 'Out in the street with talk like that! I'll not tell you again.'

His patrons were uncowed.

I heard an accent like my own: 'If this weather goes on it'll not do the price of your grain any harm.'

'But shall we have any to sell?'

From yet another quarter: 'Will they touch the Act, do you think?'

'They'll throw us that scrap. Why not?'

'Tell them to tear up their Navigation Acts, then they'll show their true colours.'

'Navigate your way round them. Reith came into Glasgow last week, holds full of Virginia. He has a very fine piece of paper from a Spanish gentleman saying he bought it in Mexico. Seen it myself. He always uses the same one!'

This was heard everywhere with roars of laughter and much filling of pipes. I decided to get one myself.

I understood little of what I heard that morning, but did not doubt that it was all of the most enormous importance. Kings, wars, Acts of Parliament, tobacco, grain, Mexico! It was a poem, an enchantment. 'Affairs,' I repeated to myself. 'Affairs, affairs! Thanks be to God, at last I am among men of affairs!'

At the door I asked the way to Colquhoun's premises from a likely-looking gentleman.

'Who?'

'The claret merchant.'

'Who?'

The question had been overheard. This man told me I would find them in Dr Sinclair's Close. 'By Nether Bow Port but one,' he said, 'on the left.'

I started to retrace my steps down the High Street, ignoring a beggar, stopping a boy for the *Caledonian Mercury*, which I folded carefully, showing its title to the world, smelling the fresh ink.

I found the place after investigating several other stinking wynds. On my first sight of it I experienced a plummeting discouragement. The sign above the door was almost illegible for grime, the mole-eyed windows so encrusted that the interior must be in permanent gloom, as indeed it was. But I told myself the building was solid and of a good size.

Two steps just inside the door descended precipitously to the floor. These being invisible to my daylight eyes, I almost fell into the place headlong. The sound thus made did not seem to reach the ears of the clerk, who worked at a large desk under a candelabrum of a dozen lights. The room was enormous, barn-like, as I imagined a warehouse to be rather than any sort of office. A cold hearth stood at one end and in the roof were three skylights. Outside there was a break in the clouds. Three beams of light made grey bars in the mixed candle and tobacco smoke. One of these fell precisely on the great ledger the clerk was writing in, as if to prepare him for the arrival of an important message.

He stood up to get the candle-snuffer and noticed me. 'You should have said.'

'Good morning.'

'Of course,' said Mr Watson, my senior colleague-to-be whose conversation always made me feel that I had said something slightly different from what I had intended.

'Roderick Mackenzie. The new . . .' I tailed off, not knowing what I was.

Twelve tails of smoke rose from the candle wicks.

'Shall I take your introduction?'

'My?'

'Mr Colquhoun is in.'

I nervously handed him the letter, conscious as I did so that I was disobeying Dr Lennox's instructions. Mr Watson stealthily opened the door behind his desk only to be repelled by a loud 'Not now, Watson!' He returned to his copying unperturbed, hand moving steadily from left to right as he transferred the contents of some loose sheets into the ledger. As the information from each sheet was transferred he let it drop to the floor. I paced the enormous room, peered pointlessly through the tiny windows. Six or seven sheets lay about his feet when the door opened and two men came out speaking French. They went to the door where one took his leave and the other returned to the table and picked up Dr Lennox's letter.

He gave me an amused look that made me blush and said: 'Archie

Lennox, eh? Well, come in, my boy. Come in and let's have a look at you.'

Some of my anxieties about my employer were allayed as I entered the inner room. This, too, was lit from above. The light fell on a desk from which one could have governed an empire. Its surface was covered with letters, bills, receipts, and these gave me a most favourable view of the enterprise. The walls were wainscotted with oak almost to the ceiling where a gap of a foot showed the rough stone behind. There was an oil painting of a young woman holding out a branch with ripe cherries to a green and blue parrot. The centre of the floor was softened by a deep red carpet, which Mr Colquhoun would soon tell me had come 'All the way from Persia. Ten men went blind weaving it. Not another like it in the city.' The impression was almost domestic, save for the desk and the object that attracted my eye and interest most. In the corner, held to the floor by thick straps of iron, was an enormous black strong-box, its top pierced with holes for two great keys. This delighted me.

'Please, please.'

A chair was indicated while Mr Colquhoun went to the far side of the desk and sat in something almost throne-like. Before he blocked it from my view I noticed the velvet was a little worn, the gilding on the arms quite rubbed off at the ends where it gripped its own uprights with gryphon's claws. My heart began to pound as he unfolded Dr Lennox's letter and started to read. He uttered small noises at various points, of no clear meaning. By the time he had folded it up and dropped it among the others, I had half convinced myself I had been betrayed.

'Old Lennox clearly thinks very well of you. Very well indeed. I think I must be a lucky man.'

'Dr Lennox is very kind.'

'Is that what he calls himself now?'

I gave a disconcerted smile.

'We knew each other rather well. Did he tell you that?'

'He, er, made that clear. Yes.'

'Couldn't say how many years it's been. Many.' Then with a curious vulpine look I would come to know well: 'Did Archie speak of me at all?'

'Very highly, sir,' I said.

Mr Colquhoun smiled and declared that Dr Lennox had at least taught me one useful thing.

'Do you know claret, Roderick?'

I admitted I had never tasted it.

Colquhoun went to a cabinet on the right-hand wall and took three dark bottles from it. He swept a space on the desk and placed them there in a row. He poured some water into a glass jug and added it to the row. He made a second row of four glasses, setting them down with great care, moving one a little so that it was perfectly in line. 'Allow me to initiate you.' He beckoned and I came up to the table as he filled the first three glasses. 'Tell me which of these is the best.'

I took an over-confident mouthful of the first and just managed to swallow before I coughed.

'It doesn't smell of anything, then?' he asked.

I sniffed the wine and tried to think of some adjective other than 'winy'. I took up the second glass, sniffed, swallowed without coughing, repeated the actions for the third. I gave my opinion and was declared a natural connoisseur, thoroughly well suited for the business.

Mr Colquhoun half filled the fourth glass, added a quarter of water and a quarter of some other fluid from a small black bottle. 'You should be able to recognize this for what it is, too.'

I tasted it with equanimity and made a suitable expression of distaste.

'Not all our customers are gentlemen, Roderick, but they know what they like and they're good customers all the same.'

He pointed to each of the glasses in turn. 'Now here's the important bit – eighteen shilling, twelve shilling, nine shilling and five. Will you remember that?'

'Yes, sir,' I said, starting to sway a little and wondering what he was talking about.

'Let me show you the business.'

I followed my employer, listening to how a room had been rented in Baillie Ritchie's house (apparently I already owed him some money), to what my duties would be, to how much I would be paid, to how it was his father's business before his, to how 'established' it was – a thing of particular importance it seemed – to how everyone knew him as Claret Colquhoun.

We went further up the wynd to a structure that tottered even closer to the brink of dilapidation. Inside, however, was a thrilling sight: three rows of great barrels stacked on top of each other. A man at a table nodded to Mr Colquhoun but did not rise. Colquhoun gestured to him and said: 'Mr Beattie, cellarer.' He made an oratorical sweep of the hand towards the barrels announcing: 'Stock, young Roderick. Stock in trade, the heart and soul of Colquhoun, Merchant in Claret and Strong Spirits.'

A boy at one end of the warehouse was drawing off wine into bottles. Colquhoun gave his name as we passed him and went down a stairway to a lower level as large as the first. Here more barrels, and smaller ones heaped in pyramids like cannon balls.

'Our second string, Roderick.'

More glasses appeared. A measure of pale liquid was passed to me.

'Straight back with that, Roderick. Thirty-five shilling.'

My eyes watered as I was passed another glass of darker rum, which I swallowed immediately, thinking I might only suffer once if I sent it down after the brandy without hesitation. I followed Colquhoun unsteadily as he indicated where the carts came into the warehouse directly from Leith. I prayed for an end to the tour as I tried to make something of his theology of trading in claret – our Lord was a claret merchant while excise men were unquestionably the ministers of Satan.

The air in the lower warehouse began to stifle me and I am sure I would have fainted had not Colquhoun thrown open the carriage doors. The outer edge of the building being part of the city wall itself, we looked straight on to the Leith road, busy with traffic coming to and from the ships.

'You should go and see them,' I was advised. 'They're a fine sight. Come to Mr Watson tomorrow at eight; he'll show you what to do. Show them that at Baillie Ritchie's house.'

I accepted the note as Colquhoun stepped back into the shadow of his warehouse and closed the door.

By the time I found my quarters what remained of the claret, brandy and rum in my belly had made its way to my head and thence to my tongue. To Mrs Arbuthnot, the housekeeper, I presented a sorry spectacle. She inspected my note closely. She waved it to dispel the sinful vapours and looked at me as if I must have murdered the real Roderick Mackenzie and put myself in his place to claim his bed. I was commanded to follow. I did, stumbling once or twice on the endless flights of stairs until I found myself looking into a small, plain but very satisfactory room. I fell on to the mattress in more of a dead faint than a natural sleep.

My memories of Baillie Ritchie's house are happy ones and I took to the place immediately on coming to my senses that evening. For all the pains in my head and squirming in my belly, my spirits soared as I looked out of my tiny window for the first time. I was lucky enough to be at the front of the building and so could look down on all the life of the High Street, and beyond that over the whole southern half of the city. I drank down, almost to the bottom, the jug of water that had been left for me and so introduced myself to one of the rituals that so regulates life in the tall houses and gives it its special savour: the constant labour of ascending and descending the stairs for water. A good two-thirds of the intercourse of such households is conducted on the stairs and always with jugs and pots in hand. It is said that unlike all the rest of the world a good life in the High Street starts at the top and works its way down. A young man has a mountain to climb every night to reach his bed. As he prospers and becomes a man of substance, and perhaps a little less strong in the leg, he moves down to a more comfortable life. To say that a man is on the ground is to say that his life has achieved the summit of convenience, and that his next move is below ground.

Ritchie himself was an untroubling landlord. He and his family occupied the first and second floors of the house. These were the finest quarters, the street level being given over to a draper. The man dyed his own cloth and would sluice his wastes out into the street so that the soles of everyone who passed were red, green or blue according to the work of the day. Baillie Ritchie himself was one of those permanent members of the town council who are supposed not to exist. Like the house, he had more or less inherited the position from his father. If asked about his affairs he would describe himself as a merchant. If pressed he would say 'In tradeable goods, what else?' and make it clear he was not pleased. Although Mr Colquhoun had arranged my accommodation under his roof, he had no liking for the man. When I mentioned his name by the way he would scoff and say bitterly that being a councillor was the only profession a man needed, these days, and a very profitable one at that. I soon learned that the Ritchie household bought its claret elsewhere and that I was expected to put an end to this insult. Whenever two or three of his tenants met on the stairs, the talk would soon turn to how rich our rents were making him.

Our only regular sight of him was at table in the evening. He and his wife would take the ends and often exchange not a single word. The products of the marriage, the three Misses Ritchie, sat in a row on their mother's right hand. From time to time Baillie Ritchie would cast suspicious glances at the young men who shared his table, but to the best of my knowledge their virtue was tried only by our thoughts. Mrs Arbuthnot would not share our meals on account of there sometimes being wine on the table, a thing which her conscience would not allow.

My fellow tenants were a little older than myself and at first inspired a painful envy. Both were students: James Minto of advocacy, Douglas Whyte of medicine. I remembered old resentments against my brother; cursed Fortune yet again for making me the younger son, put to commerce like a horse to the plough. But I was soon reconciled to my state as I learned that even my meagre salary left me less poor than them. Besides, the compensations of a position with a claret merchant were by no means negligible.

I reported as required to Mr Watson on the morning of my second day in Edinburgh. Another desk had been set up for my use. It denoted my rank by being exceedingly small and too much resembled a piece of schoolroom furniture for my liking. There I sat for six days a week, adding up the figures on the individual sheets of paper I had first seen in Mr Watson's hands. After I had completed a certain amount I would carry them across to Mr Watson, who would stare at them for long periods as if checking my every calculation before writing the sums into his ledger. The sheets were headed in a shorthand I did not understand, so that I remained innocent of the significance of the figures that swarmed before my eyes and even crept into my dreams. Weeks passed without relief and I began to feel deceived.

Small changes gave me hope. Mr Watson no longer stared at my calculations with such suspicion, but copied them straight into his ledger. More and more he would declare the need to 'see a man about something', and would go away into the town for hours. As the sullen, damp summer turned to autumn he would sometimes leave just after noon and not return at all. Indeed, once I had settled in my position Watson began to lead a very easy life. At times gentlemen would come to see Mr Colquhoun and I would be the one to take their names, announce them and usher them into my employer's presence. I noticed them and they noticed me. I had already developed a sufficient understanding of commerce to know what this was worth. One day I found that the sheets of numbers had lost their cryptic titles and were plainly described as various classes of disbursements, receipts, dues and so on. I was at first delighted to have been received into the confidence of the firm, but then groaned when I discovered that this was merely the prelude to more work. Instead of Mr Watson copying my figures into his ledger I would now do this myself. I saw still less of him and gradually assumed his desk. He caught me there late one afternoon, but made no objection as he passed me to speak briefly with Colquhoun before leaving. In my frustration I became so bold as to suggest that Watson might soon be leaving us, but Mr Colquhoun just laughed and spoke of other things.

For all this, life was good. Every day I breakfasted in the coffee-houses, placing myself by the most prosperous-looking men I could find, drinking in their conversation with my coffee and bread. The dullness of Colquhoun, Merchant in Claret and Strong Spirits, had not at all dissuaded me from commerce. On the contrary, it was the postponement of these joys that helped them grow ever larger in my mind. I swaggered with every issue of the *Caledonian Mercury*, and when that disappeared with the *Northern Intelligencer* and when that too failed, with the *Edinburgh Courier*. When I saw some London merchants in Maclurg's I noticed they neglected all these in favour of the London reprints. And so I finally settled with the *Post-boy* and had myself a pair of spectacles made so I would not be mistaken for one of those who ran through the streets selling it.

I watched Aikenhead being hanged for blasphemy and heard the people hold their tongues for a whole hour. I walked to Leith to see the ships, admired the biggest – only to find it was Dutch – and ignored the sunken hulks. I bought a pipe and smoked it in the street. I ordered a yellow waistcoat from a tailor. I smiled back at the orange-sellers in the High Street. Guiltily, I received another letter from my mother.

Wishing to accelerate my career, I became particularly ingratiating with the better dressed of the gentlemen who came to see Colquhoun. Cultivation is a slow business, however, and Dr Lennox's advice repeated itself more urgently every day in my head. I began to despair of receiving an offer and decided it would be as well to apply the same stratagems to Colquhoun himself. One Sunday, I furtively cleaned the windows which looked on to the close and daubed over the sign to restore its legibility.

'Will you look at that? The good fairy has visited us at last, Roderick.'

'I thought it might help, Mr Colquhoun.'

'You invoked her? Well, that is clever.'

For several days after he delighted in calling me 'our good fairy'. But at the end of that week I knew my efforts had not been entirely in vain. He gave me his cunning look and demanded: 'So that scoundrel Ritchie still buys his claret elsewhere?'

I immediately bought a pint of vinegar and filled my pockets with corks before going back that evening. At the blackest hour of the night I would creep from near the top of Baillie Ritchie's house to the bottom equipped with corkscrew, corks, vinegar and spoon concealed under my night-shirt and chamber-pot in hand in case of encounters. I would uncork several bottles, swallow a mouthful from each, replace that with two spoonfuls of vinegar and push in the fresh corks, concealing all trace of my wickedness.

I anticipated the evening meals with particular relish. I had contaminated only a few of the bottles so that it was impossible to predict whether the sour or the good would be brought to table. On the first three evenings I was disappointed, then it was Sunday. The next evening, I tasted the wine first and looked forward to the fulfilment of my plan. To my dismay Ritchie, his wife, my fellow tenants (the Misses Ritchie were not allowed to partake), all drank the concoction down without the slightest complaint. In the nights that followed I redoubled the dosage, drinking two large mouthfuls from each bottle before refilling them with vinegar. The next day I awoke mid-morning with a terrible pain in my head and had to make my apologies to Mr Watson, but I was now confident of success. That evening at table I was astonished to find that my worst efforts provoked nothing more than a wrinkling of the nose. At the end of the meal I was alarmed to hear my landlord mumble something about having a word with his supplier. The possibility of my deception being uncovered loomed before me in the most ghastly colours: I would be thrown out of the house, my credit in the town would be lost, and for damaging the good name of Colquhoun I would be dismissed from my post and be forced to return home in disgrace. Decisive action was required. I crept down again, uncorked several of the bottles in the cellar and poured a good quarter pint of vinegar in each. There being no handy place where I could dispose of the wine – the door to the yard creaked impossibly – I could only conceal the missing wine in my own self and stagger drunkenly back up to my bed. The next day I suffered terribly for this determination but, come the evening, I was somewhat restored and looking forward to the daily household gathering. Persistence was rewarded.

'Pfleuch!'

The other partakers cautiously sipped the wine and winced. The offence was felt by all.

'This is too much!'

'It tastes like vinegar,' I suggested.

'It is vinegar!' insisted Ritchie, satisfyingly. 'This must have soured months ago.'

'Disgraceful!' said James. 'Take an action against him.'

'Don't drink any more,' advised Douglas, 'it'll make you ill.'

'Really, Robert,' said Mrs Ritchie, with a gratifying glance in my direction, 'you must do something about this.'

I mentioned that, with the intention of going early to a customer the next morning, I had a supply in my room. I fetched a bottle and the business was done.

The next day I presented a letter from our new customer to Mr Colquhoun. He pronounced it miraculous, a new marriage at Cana. More to the point, he pronounced me a true merchant and raised my salary by eight shillings a month.

Having noticed the tolerance of the household to vinegar, I was able to supplement this small reward by charging Mrs Arbuthnot eight shillings for six-shilling wine, thus generating a little private commission while keeping my customers' simple tastes fully satisfied.

In spite of this, Baillie Ritchie was still paying less for his wine and it flowed more generously than before. This endeared me greatly to James and Douglas, and I began to enjoy more of their company. I saw another side of the city, spending my nights in taverns as frequently as I spent the early mornings in the coffee-houses. When I found myself by the ear of a tavern-keeper I would disparage the other wine merchants and sing the praises of 'our' establishment, as I remember calling it. It was the finest education anyone could have in being ignored and insulted. All the same, there were times when my eloquence triumphed against every opposition and I was able to tumble into Colquhoun's mid-morning and pacify Mr Watson with an order from yet another new customer. Gradually, I became better known. When I walked the High Street I would exchange small nods of acquaintance with some of the more substantial tradesmen.

With James I went to see the courts sitting. With Douglas I learned the uses of the plants in the Physic Garden and sat with the students in the Anatomy Theatre as the Professor demonstrated the proper appearance of the liver, the morbidity of a shrunken kidney, the admirable length of the intestine, which he pulled from the desiccated, stinking cadaver on his table.

At last, overwhelmed by my companions' wickedness, I went to buy an orange. I knew from one of Mr Watson's moments of exasperation that this was something Colquhoun occasionally did, or at least something he was accused of. I knew also that, whatever it involved, it was mitigated by the fact that his wife had died seven years ago. I knew there was something ribald about it, and that Julia – the eldest Miss Ritchie – was turned quite scarlet one evening by a passing mention of the fruit by James. I knew also that the orange-sellers in the High Street had favoured me with the sweetest smiles all summer and that their sudden disappearance was more to do with a command from the town council than with the onset of autumn. It seems impossible now, a hardly believable measure of how little my education had progressed, but it is true: I knew all that, and nothing more.

The evening started criminally. It was a Saturday and the taverns were closing early in preparation for the Sabbath. After the meal at Baillie Ritchie's James caught my sleeve and told me that he knew of a few places, if I would care to join him and Douglas. I accepted eagerly, still flattered by the fellowship of these older men, never calculating what it cost me. Besides, might there not be some potential customers I had not yet met? We went down into a part of Canongate I had never visited before. I was half anxious, half excited as we went through the more ramshackle and high-smelling wynds. I kept my hand firmly on my purse. When we stopped it was by the most solid and well-maintained house in the area, but we were not to be guests above stairs. With a glance behind us we followed James down into a dingy hole by the side of the road and waited as he gave a conspiratorial knock on the cellar door. It opened two inches and we were examined by a long nose and a dark eye. James slipped a coin through the crack in the door and we followed him into a dingy stone corridor. An inner door opened to emit a gust of smoke, spirits and talk.

The distance between the two doors could have been a thousand miles. Most exciting of all was the fact that we were served by maids rather than the men and boys permitted in the taverns above ground. The term 'maids' was universally received as humorous. In James's words: 'It refers to their occupation.'

Every spirit and wine was being drunk at the tables, many of which rattled with dice or had cards slapped down on them. At others, there were more sober conversations, which I tried to overhear, still believing that everyone else's affairs must be more rewarding than my own. There were occasional outbreaks of singing. Even then 'Wilful Willy' was a favourite, and we all joined in till the glasses and bottles and tables shook with it. The fourth rendition was cut off half done when the long-nosed man reappeared and signalled for silence. Unschooled in the ways of such places, my own voice sang out alone until James clapped his hand over my mouth. 'Shhh! you fool.'

There was a pause while the church clerks went by in the street outside. After a minute of respectful silence, we returned to our revels in full cry.

My enjoyment of the Wilful Willy – it had been adopted as the name of the place – was tempered by embarrassment. I had quickly been identified by the serving-maids as their youngest customer, and therefore the one to whom they had the highest educational duty. In this they were encouraged by James and Douglas, who made an excellent entertainment of me. Every time more drinks were brought to our table, or empty glasses and jugs taken away, the maids would bend low over it and smile coquettishly into my reddening face. Embarrassment became fear when James whispered in my ear: 'She'll keep you busy. What will I tell Mrs Arbuthnot when she asks why your bed hasn't been slept in?'

'As a medical man I must warn you of that one,' said Douglas. 'She's killed three men already. Exhaustion! Dropped stone dead like overridden horses. Showed them no mercy.'

'For God's sake!' I pleaded, noticing with trepidation that the girls had put their heads together and were giggling threateningly in my direction.

The next thing I knew one of them had lost her balance while serving the table next to ours and, I need hardly say, fell into my lap. She batted at me ineffectually and made a show of trying to escape my lecherous clutches while holding me firmly round the back of my neck. 'Ooo, not now, darling,' she hooted raucously, 'not with all these gentlemen here.'

Our little play was greatly appreciated. Amidst the bellows of laughter from every table – James and Douglas treacherously joining in – I turned crimson as she rearranged my hair, stroked my cheek and kissed my burning brow. The girl returned to her colleagues who congratulated her on her success.

Attention soon shifted to another song, but the Wilful Willy was no longer tolerable to me – on that evening at least. As I was already the only one left with any resources, Douglas and James were easily persuaded to move on. We took Douglas's suggestion this time and descended another two streets to the Juniper. There would be no need to recall this place, were it not for the occurrence of two events which, at the time, were of no significance. Its aspect was hardly different from that of the Wilful Willy: similarly subterranean, similarly rowdy, its air entirely squeezed out by the heavy vapours of brandy and tobacco on all of which, I am sure, not a farthing of duty had ever been paid. In place of claret we were served with Rhenish and sweet geneva. In our company, too, we had, as it were, moved east and north. There were some Germans speaking with merchants of the town, some of whom I recognized. Others were from the Low Countries.

What fixed the Juniper in my mind rather more happily than the Wilful Willy was my first uncomprehending sighting of my future. There was a noisy dispute at one of the tables to which I cocked an ear, while James and Douglas bragged about who would be the richer, doctor or lawyer. For half of this table the issue was already 'The Company', or even, when the matter warmed, 'Our Company', though at that time they could hardly have had any position with it. For the other half it was a humorous object, soon to be chased out of London, sending its agents to Holland and London where fools, it was confidently asserted, were more easily parted from their money. The East India men weren't worried. They laughed. 'They'll scratch that flea from their arse when they're ready.'

The accent was far from home and sent a ripple of quiet through the room. The comment angered me, although I had not the slightest notion of what it referred to. More than that, it made some sort of call on me so that when the argument was on the point of going beyond words, I almost wished that it would. An imaginary brawl staged itself in my mind in which I wrote myself a most excellent part, astonishing the company with my heroics. The end was swift, and the vindication of my party's honour absolute. But which party, whose honour? I could not have said. If I were not now, as I write, sitting in the very belly of our cause, the moment would have been nothing more than a passing drunken fancy, long since forgotten. And yet, every subsequent turn has proved, it was nothing less than the first showing of Destiny's guiding hand.

The table became calm, the talk subsiding into a discussion of the price of money. I lost interest, wandering outside to relieve myself. When I returned, full glasses were on our table and a new entertainment had started. Several of our fellow drinkers were clustering around another of the tables. Three men sat at it, but throughout I seemed to notice only one, a huge black-bearded man, plucking his sleeves up in preparation for the sport, curiously paddling the contents of a water-jug with his hand. He glared about, pouting with mock ferocity, discountenancing everyone who caught his eye, growling. He was not easy to look away from, but every glance at him was returned eye to eye and I began to feel that I was favoured with more of his attention than the others. For some reason I wanted very much for there to be a smile for me hidden in that prodigious black beard. There was something else: beside him the few Dutch or German merchants who were there that night might as well have been born and bred in Edinburgh. But here was something truly different, a masterpiece of strangeness, the world's foreigner, a man whose every detail and motion demanded to be stared at.

Several coins were already on the table and it was clear that some wager was under way. A penny flew through the air to be caught by the Jew and slapped down on the table.

'A penny on the shaved one!' cried the owner.

'Your opinions aren't worth much, sir.'

The coins were swept into a glass, which was passed round and was soon almost full. Joseph Cohen d'Azevedo bleated at his victims: 'Come on, my pretty lambs! Come and be shorn by Joseph! I'll give you odds. Three to one.'

The coins were now tipped into a bowl as the flow of money increased.

'Come on, fools, throw away your money! See how they know their names, how they come when I call them.'

With every provocation, the wager increased. D'Azevedo marvelled at it. 'Such generosity! Such charity, gentlemen!'

With this, some silver was added to the mound of coppers. Here was a man who knew how to do business.

The landlord arrived bearing a tray of small glasses and a black bottle. The glasses were set three in a row before each of the men. They were filled, a raisin dropped in and the spirit set alight with a taper. The third man at the table also had a beard, although it was nothing to the mythic growth that sprouted from d'Azevedo's chin. This one was the first to approach his three glasses with their trembling blue flames. The room fell silent as he mouthed at it in a preparatory way. He essayed a quick dart at the first raisin, only to recoil with a cry of pain.

The crowd hurrahed and laughed. The man rubbed his charred moustache, from which a smell of singeing drifted, making the place stink like a farrier's shop. He made another attempt, this time burning his nose and then extinguishing the flame. This made the glass 'dead' and it was taken from the table by the landlord. The second glass was approached with a new and bolder tactic. With a great slurp the raisin was scooped from the fire. A cry of triumph was begun, only to trail away when it was noticed that this flame, too, was dead. The glass was removed as the man scowled at his last chance. He lunged at it, upsetting it and letting a puddle of blue flame flow across the table and drip on to his lap.

'Couldn't drink piss!' declared d'Azevedo, dismissing him with a sweep of the arm that sent him to the floor where others joined in the sport of extinguishing his breeches with rather more force than was necessary.

The crowd turned its attention to their great hope. Alas for them, the performance of the shaven one was no better. They groaned with despondency as he made a snuffer of his nose, clumsily plunging it into his last glass, drunkenly presenting it to his disappointed investors, rimmed in red where the hot glass had burnt the skin.

An unhappy quiet descended on the crowd as they eyed their bowl of money and offered up silent prayers for the Jew's failure. All eyes were fixed on the three glasses before him, topped with their domes of blue flame. D'Azevedo thrust his hand back into the water-pitcher and splashed half its contents on to his beard. Like a lady with her petticoats, he tugged his beard to one side and lifted each of the glasses in turn. He tipped the glasses away from him, letting the raisins float to his side before giving a curious twitch of the wrist and sucking each dragon from its fiery layer without the loss of a single whisker.

The three glasses still burned as Azevedo grinned triumphantly, showing three raisins in his teeth.

'You cheated!'

'That's right, he cheated. Cheat! Cheat!'

As, only minutes before, it had been axiomatic that only a clean-shaven man could perform the trick, it now followed that a bearded man could only win by fraud. To this indefeasible argument, another voice added the gloss of authority: 'You can't do that, it's not in the rules!'

Everyone was relieved to hear that the game had rules and agreed that by winning, d'Azevedo had broken them.

'Jew!' shouted the man beside me.

But he was shushed by his companion who spoke quietly in his ear: 'He's a very wealthy man.'

'It's true, it's true, I cheated,' said d'Azevedo, 'I didn't tell you you might lose. What wickedness! What duplicity! How like a Jew.'

He reached inside his waistcoat and produced a gold piece. He tossed the coin on top of the others and handed the bowl to the landlord. 'Console your guests.'

The game was over in a cannonade of demands for rum, gin, wine and brandy.

I was altogether enchanted by my first encounter with this exotic but, alas, had to take my leave of him almost at once. The room reeled, its shadows taking on ghastly, unnatural colours. An instant longer and they would have had to carry me out. As I realized I was about to faint, I stumbled through the swilling crowd and made a rush for the door. If there was a corner of my mind still intact at that moment, it was the corner where vanity lives and my only thought was that if it was going to happen, it would be better for it to happen in front of as few people as possible. I reached the night air in my last extremity, gulping it down as if I had all but drowned, clinging to the rail by the steps till my legs steadied and I could see clearly again. James and Douglas joined me after taking time to drink another share of the winnings. They conversed contentedly, agreeing something I could not understand.

To my despair we were soon before a third door. I stood alone with James while Douglas parleyed within. His suggestion raised the indignation of the mistress of the house. Her voice was suddenly piercing through the door. I believe it was when she was told there were three gentlemen that she submitted.

I asked what was happening.

'He's gone to buy an orange. Or, more precisely, to cast a professional eye over the quality of the fruit on our behalf.'

'What?'

He gave me a puzzled, almost remorseful look. 'You're not pretending, are you?'

'What's happening?'

All my mind could do was marvel at how drunk I had suddenly become. How had it happened?

Douglas reappeared. 'Sweet as could be.'

He held up slippery fingers, rubbing the tips together.

'You glutton!' objected James. 'You've had them all for yourself. I don't want mine now.'

'I think you do.'

Unwilling to be left in the street at such an hour and in an unfamiliar part of the city, I was forced to follow them into the house. My memory is vague but something must have gone wrong. I lost sight of James and Douglas almost immediately. I was climbing so many stairs I began to think I must be back in Baillie Ritchie's house, clambering safely towards my own bed. I fumbled at a door like my own, entered a room.

The girl was standing with her back to me, her hands behind her head untying her hair. She was dressed only in a white linen shift and the sheets on the bed had been turned back. She looked tired as she turned to me, annoyance and resignation in her face. 'It's late,' she said.

I started to apologize and backed toward the stairhead in confusion.

'How do you like it?'

I stared stupidly at the single candle by the bed and watched as she turned her back on me, knelt down by her bed. As if to pray, I thought. She pulled up her shift over her naked back and leaned over the mattress. 'Shall we get on with it?'

While she was saying this I had gasped in horror at the rising hem of the shift and clapped a hand to my eyes. There was laughter, unexpectedly beautiful and only a little unkind. Then she was standing before me, her hand on my wrist, pulling it down from my face. All my strutting four months' life as a city gentleman came to nothing as she caught one of my tears on her thumb and told me I was just a boy.

No sooner had she taken me into her bed than I fell into a state of utter oblivion. Pain was my next sensation, hideously aggravated with every pulse of my blood. First light was just visible through the curtainless window as I drank all the water she brought me and asked for more. There was more sleep and then a second waking to full day and a glimpse of perfect blue such as had rarely cheered us through the long and dreary half-summer that was finally ending.

Susanna conscientiously explained that I would be charged for my stay whether I availed myself fully of her hospitality or not. With this argument she eventually coaxed me into what she referred to as my 'shilling's worth'.

As I dressed she lay on the bed, not bothering to cover herself. I had had no particular expectation of what I should have felt beneath me, but as I looked at her in the Sunday morning light, the angularity of my first experience of love was shockingly confirmed. She had the ribs of a starved horse and her hips were points beneath her skin. I told her I would come back and bring her something good to eat. She smiled and told me I would always be welcome.

In spite of being referred to by James as the High Maharina of the Empire of Pleasure, Widow Gilbert, in whose house this occurred, is a weighty, domestic woman with a refined understanding of the connections between profit and respectability. She was dusting the flour from her hands as she intercepted me on my way out. It was quickly clear that she knew my name. 'Good morning, Mr Roderick. I see you've spent all night with us.'

The verb 'to spend' has only one meaning in Widow Gilbert's house. We settled in the kitchen as she apologized for the shutters all being closed on account of a neighbour who objected to the smell of baking on the Sabbath. She explained that Mr James and Mr Douglas had assured her I would pay for them as well. I pinched the bottom of my purse and up-ended it over her palm. 'Oh, well,' she said, looking severely at the coins, 'I'm sure you'll come again.'

The morning had brought the first frost of the coming winter. Never before had the city smelt so clean as I ran through its clanging streets, straight from my whore's bed to my pew.

MY REVERIE WAS BROKEN three days ago, and by what else but the accursed numbers? Captain Pincarton of the *St Andrew* took a panic into his head about the rate at which his weevils are gorging his oatmeal. A meeting of captains and councillors was called on board the *Rising Sun*, each of whom was treated to the sight of Mr Shipp lolling on deck, already with the complexion of a Turk, smoking his pipe and sharing some fantastical tale about himself with several of the crew. Given such an impression of idleness, it was no surprise that they came to the view that the Superintendent of Cargoes and his assistant should be put to harness again.

A general audit was ordered and we set off on our rounds again. Shipp has two natures, each pure and simple: total inactivity and total activity. My fear that too great an indulgence of the first must have leaked into and corrupted the second proved unfounded. He set to with the usual frenzy, relieving me of all but the most arduous parts of the task. This is just as well, for the heat that bears down on us and strengthens with every second of latitude that is cut from our position has made our work so much more offensive to the nose. My legs ache from climbing up and down, into and out of every stinking hole in our fleet. We have counted out every last comb, drum, fishing-line, knife and lantern horn. We have tasted the water in all the casks, sniffed all the meal tuns for rot, weighed each box of nails. In the *Endeavour* we are short by one sugar cake, for which a fat woman is suspected, though her accuser seems as likely a culprit. From the *St Andrew* a pewter trencher has made its escape (motive unknown). With respect to our own vessel all was found to be well, excepting the disappearance of two reams of paper, sedulously reported by Mr Shipp. I undertook to re-count these stores myself and was able to reassure him that he had been mistaken. To which he replied: 'If you say so, young master.'

I presented our report this morning, confirming that Captain Pincarton's oatmeal has indeed been sorely diminished by the weevils and that two casks of water on the *Endeavour* have gone foul. Saving these mishaps and the spoiling of two boxes of campaign wigs, which were serving as the nests of several rats (now evicted), the general state of our stores is as it was before, less what has been eaten in the meantime. Which is to say that the general state of the stores is as it generally is. This reassured the council greatly. Captain Galt received the information with eyes closed and even began to hum to himself before I had finished. He gave me a direct and slightly humorous look as I left the meeting, letting me know that he understood how my time has been wasted in all this scurrying about. The exercise is all the more futile as we will soon reach Madeira, by all accounts a most fruitful island. The order has been given for lookouts to be posted and it is said that we might see the outlying islands this evening.

All this was concluded in the forenoon and now I am skulking down here in the lamplight to avoid the heat and brilliance of the decks. After three years of near unrelieved gloom at home we find ourselves plunged into the very opposite excess. The more travelled members of the crews have kept out of it – unless they are one of the naturally tawny ones like Shipp. Many of our colonists, however, have been like men at the end of a desert journey: they have drunk too much and are suffering for it. Mr Mackay, who retains little of his natural covering, gave a lengthy sermon last Sunday on the gifts of the Lord and a much appreciated exposition of Isaiah 60: 20: 'Thy sun shall no more go down; neither shall thy moon withdraw itself: for the Lord shall be thine everlasting light, and the days of thy mourning shall be ended.'

Alas for our pastor, he gave it wigless, receiving the full bounty of the Lord's everlasting light flat on his head. By the end of the day Dr

Munro was in attendance for a slight fever and green spots before the eyes. Since then my first and only sight of him was this morning when he spent a little time on the main deck beneath the sailcloth awning that has been strung there. We exchanged a few civil words, but my mind was more on his head than what he was saying. All the hairless part is covered with watery blisters, which are joining each other under the skin like drops on a glass and giving a most unfortunate appearance.

Munro has been busy with many such cases, several of them much worse than Mackay's. At breakfast yesterday he presented me with a scientific curiosity: something like the thinnest paper, oiled so that it is translucent and softened by much crumpling and straightening out. He arranged it on the table until I realized with a start that it was in the shape of a shrivelled hand. 'Tell me what you make of that, Roderick. Nature's own glove stripped off by stupidity.'

I agreed that it looked better on its proper owner than off. It brought me a strange thought this morning, when I was still only half awake. Can the whole skin be shed in a like manner and still keep its shape like the ghost of the soul who once lived in it? I have read that some serpents do exactly that when they renew themselves. In any case, at this rate we will soon be black as Ethiopians with skins as fit for the new world as our white ones were for the old.

Aside from these sunstrokes, ever since the fog was driven from our holds the health of the colonists has been strong. The failure of Dr Munro's fatal predictions has made him very unhappy. He compensates for his disappointments by issuing still more terrifying prophecies of what lies ahead. He is a pessimist, I think, and seems to believe in a law of physic such that whoever is not on the very edge of expiry now must suffer even greater torments in the future. Health for Munro is merely a procrastination of one's diseases. I have none of this and have let him know as much. He responds with a puritanical expression and the all-conquering claim that: 'I have been in the tropics before, Roderick. You have not.'

When I ask how he survived he merely tells me that it is always unwise to ask such a thing and gives me to understand that the answer would be too terrible. From Captain Drummond I might have believed this, but from Dr Munro? I think not. It is another of these strange sea changes – it needs only a few days out of port for a man's past to take on whatever new majesty he pleases. When one leaves the land, one leaves contradiction too.

*

SWEET SOLID ROCK! How fine it is, and a little strange, to stand or sit in perfect steadiness. For the first few hours I imagined the ground still moving under my feet, as if giddy from having spun round and round, but now all is straight. And what a joyous discovery on our arrival!

For once, I was out of my bunk at the right moment. I had slept badly because of the heat and had gone up on deck early to empty my pot. First light was rising over Africa. Of the few stars left, Mr Cunningham, standing by the binnacle on the quarterdeck, showed me which one was Mercury. As I watched it disappear into the day I heard the cry from aloft: 'Land! Land!' Through the glass I could just see a short line of darkness, nothing more than a discoloration of the horizon. A few of the crew-members looked in the same direction, but others ignored the announcement and the rest of the ship, exhausted by the days of continuous heat, slept on.

There was a half day yet to spend on the sea, the island being mountainous and easily seen from twenty miles out. It was a little after noon that we made our approach, passing the small Holy Island to the north of Madeira itself and sailing round the rocky Desertas, which guard it from the east. A mile or two off Funchal, which passes for the island's metropolis, we dropped anchor and fired our gun for the *Endeavour*, *Dolphin* and *St Andrew* to come up by us. The four of us made a fine sight with just enough wind to hold our pennants out very prettily. As we were soon to discover, somewhat to our satisfaction, we also made a very fearsome sight. The activity in the town was by no means the normal bustle of the place which, in the middle hours of the day, usually has not a soul out of doors. It was all a panic caused by the idea that we were a fleet of Barbary corsairs come to do their worst. The fear was made plausible by what they had been told by the English on the island. Namely, that whatever the rumours of the Scottish Company, one thing was sure: our country could not produce such ships and we must therefore be some other, more terrible force.

Less glorious to relate – but my duty none the less – is that we were almost as alarmed by them as they were by us. An enormous Genoese, nearly as large as the *Rising Sun*, blocked the harbour mouth. She ran out her guns at our appearance and neither she nor the harbour battery made any friendly signal. Our standard was clear, but being such a new enterprise it meant little to them.

Captain Galt emerged from his cabin with Mr Cunningham and it was announced that a party would row ashore in the pinnace. We waited while Captains Jolly and Pincarton were rowed across from their own vessels to make up a more impressive embassy. Captain John Malloch, who commands the *Endeavour*, remained in temporary charge of the fleet. Pincarton brought with him Mr Benjamin Spense to serve as translator. I made his acquaintance for the first time. Of course, I had no purpose in such an elevated party, but I loitered about the rail where the boat was being made ready with such an evident appetite that I was invited to accompany them at the last moment. By the time we passed the outer breakwater my presence had been legitimated by having Quartermaster-General added to my titles and the task of provisioning the fleet from the island conferred on me.

We passed under the curious scowls of the officers of the *San Gianbattista* and watched a growing assembly on the quay. The Governor, standing at the centre of this group, disappeared for a while and was next seen wearing a curious velvet hat with a white feather. Being too small by half, it put me in mind of a cardinal's cap and added nothing to the man's authority. We had hardly come round the bow of the *San Gianbattista* and achieved a full view of the harbour when one of our oarsmen shouted out and we were hailed from behind in an unmistakable accent. There, hidden until that moment by the bulk of the Genoese, lay the *Caledonia*, not wrecked as we had assumed, indeed with not a rope out of place.

Captain Galt's assessment of the Governor and his party must have been the same as my own, for he ordered a prompt about-turn leaving them waiting on the quay, and had us rowed across to the far side of the harbour to take a report from our prodigal returned. The officer on the quarterdeck was the one I had encountered before and whatever my feelings on seeing the *Caledonia* again, we recognized each other without pleasure.

Captain Galt called up to him: 'Give me your report, sir.'

'All's well, Captain. Arrived two days ago. Yourselves?'

'Is it indeed,' muttered Galt to himself, 'and Drummond, where is he?'

'In the town, sir, with Mr Paterson, seeing to the provisioning.'

My heart leaped at the sound of that name whose apparent loss had, I believe, been more painful to me than to most others.

We rowed back to the quayside to make our courtesies to the Governor. He first addressed us in his small English but was unable to understand our replies, whereupon we communicated through Mr Spense. We satisfied him with a copy of our founding Act and an account of our intention to trade with Africa and the Indies, which is still our public purpose and must be maintained here for the ears of the English merchants. The formalities were concluded with a salute of ten guns, which Captain Malloch returned from the *Endeavour* with two extra.

Throughout this interview I could detect Captain Galt's growing impatience. As soon as it became clear that our presence on the island would be acceptable – it was agreed with the Governor that we should have a licence for ten days – he abruptly lost interest in the discussions and demanded through Mr Spense to know the whereabouts of Captain Drummond. With this information, he left with one of the Governor's men as guide, allowing Mr Cunningham to conclude the pleasantries.

By the time we had accepted an offer of accommodation for our most senior officers – myself excluded – and an invitation to dine at the Governor's mansion, Captain Galt reappeared wearing his own sword and carrying another. A disarmed Drummond followed ten paces behind him, his face dark with fury. Galt stopped by our party while Drummond walked on and climbed down from the quay into the pinnace. Galt thrust the papers he was carrying in my direction, telling me: 'These gentlemen have seen fit to start your work for you, Mr Mackenzie. Perhaps you could continue.'

The comment was loud enough to be heard by Drummond, intentionally no doubt. As the two men were rowed out to the *Rising Sun* Drummond sat in the bow and seemed to meet my eyes every time I looked in their direction. Anxious as I am to enjoy the confidence of Captain Galt, I cannot but regret this incident and have already, not two days later, heard from Rumour herself that I am now of the Galt faction. This, to the best of my knowledge, has no more existence than the elusive Patersonians.

Having to provide for myself, I made my way to the only hostelry that Funchal supports – though it is a very satisfactory one, except for its prices. To my delight, I noticed that my approach was being watched from a first-floor window by Mr Paterson himself, who hailed me and asked me to come up. I found him installed like a prince in the grandest room the establishment has to offer, with a table, a bed and even parts of the floor covered with copies of all his papers and charts, which had first been spread out in the directors' room at Milne Square. I picked my way over these, expressing my great joy at seeing him again. I said we had all thought him lost, that the whole expedition had suffered a great anxiety since the fog. He seemed, however, to be very preoccupied and not properly aware of the importance of what I was saying.

'And it's a great pleasure to see you again, Roderick. All is well, I take it?'

'Well, yes,' I said, surprised at the ordinariness of his tone. It was hardly that of a man being congratulated on still being alive.

'But what of you, of the *Caledonia*? How did you come through?'

'Through?'

'We thought you were wrecked.'

'How could you think that? I suppose we just had a better . . .'

'Your disappearance.'

These cold evasions came as a bitter disappointment to me, all the more so as I had, in the half-hour since I had been aware of his survival, imagined a very different reunion.

'But here we are, Roderick,' he went on. 'No disappearance, surely.'

'But in the fog . . .'

'We all disappeared in the fog.'

'The *Caledonia* didn't have any problems?'

'Blown straight through.' He moved his flattened hand smoothly through the air and offered an awkward smile, which faded as I declined to return it. He shrugged. 'A stroke of luck, I suppose, or something. I'm no seaman.'

'We spent two days searching for you.'

'*Voilà*, Mr Mackenzie! A needless waste of time. We would all have arrived together if Captain Galt hadn't ordered such a search.'

'You could have been wrecked!'

I didn't care that I was raising my voice and refused to be distracted by the odd mewling noises coming from a side-room.

'But as you can see,' smiled Mr Paterson, 'we weren't.'

'*We* could have been wrecked.'

'But you weren't. Really, Roderick, I don't see why all this—'

'Now you know we weren't wrecked. For the last hour you've known it, but what of the last two weeks?'

'Well, what of it? Could it have made any difference?'

'Could it! The orders. You had . . . We all had orders to wait!'

This, at last, was too much.

'You've persisted quite enough, Mr Mackenzie. A month at sea and a few malicious rumours don't give you the right to ask me anything in that tone.'

The side door opened and a snivelling, lined, red-faced woman walked in, handkerchief to nose. Dressed in brown wool that would hardly have been too thin for an Edinburgh November, she seemed already to have half evaporated, her skin now loose from excess capacity.

'Oh, William, William, hasn't that horrible man gone yet? Why do you let him talk to you like that? I don't understand. Where has Captain . . . Oh, I beg your pardon, sir.'

She mopped her eyes to get a better view of me or, perhaps, to improve her appearance. In the latter case at least, the gesture was not effective. Although it pains me, I am determined not to waver from the promise I have made myself to set down nothing but the purest truth in this history and I must therefore record that my first view of Mrs Paterson made it all too plain why I had never seen her before. The evasion of every opportunity in Edinburgh, her invisibility on the *Caledonia* and the embarrassment felt by all at that moment of her exposure were all of a piece. She is ugly, it is true, but not excessively so; no more so than many women to whom a certain age has brought the compensations of experience and character. Compensations, sadly, which have passed Mrs Paterson by. One is aware from the very start of being in the presence of a soul conjured from soured milk and cabbage water. Moreover, her face twitches constantly with private anxieties so that one cannot stay long in her company without feeling guilty of having offered some insult.

'My wife,' said Mr Paterson.

'Mrs Paterson.'

She recoiled from my hand, wiping her palms on her dress.

'This is Mr Mackenzie who has come to talk about provisioning the ships.'

'Oh,' she sniffed, 'another gentleman. I didn't know you had another gentleman with you. Oh dear, isn't it hot?'

Still wiping her hands on her dress, she returned to the side-room to continue her liquefaction.

Mr Paterson sat at his desk, nudging a weight from one of the plans, which rolled up with a snap. He leaned on his elbow, shading his eyes with his hand as another muffled whimper came from his wife.

'Is Mrs Paterson unwell?'

'She doesn't travel well.'

My anger melted away, impossible to sustain against the realization that only the most saintly devotion could have moved a man to bring such a wife on such a journey. I sat down opposite him and laid the provisioning lists on the desk.

'All these complications,' he sighed, 'and so unnecessary. As you know,' he indicated the papers, 'we just had words with Captain Galt before your arrival. Very difficult, very hot words I must say. I'm afraid Mrs Paterson was very distressed. It's something I find hard to forgive.'

'Of course,' I murmured.

'I was rather disappointed in him, Roderick. If anyone had still been listening to me at that stage I don't think he would even have been . . . But enough of that. He's here now. Here's a better idea.'

He poured two glasses of Malmsey and held his up to me in a toast. 'Peace, Roderick?'

'Peace,' I happily agreed.

We exchanged accounts of our voyages from the Orkneys, which differed in nothing of significance. After a second's hesitation he asked me: 'You saw Captain Drummond?'

I said that I had. Mentioning the detail of his sword in Galt's hands I suggested lightly that he might be 'Captain' no longer, but the remark was not appreciated. 'That would have to be discussed by the whole council. Galt can't do it on his own.'

I listened with astonishment as he told me: 'I do hope he won't attempt anything unwise. Drummond is an excellent man, you know. No, I'll go further: he is quite indispensable to the success of this venture. Indispensable, I say. We have too few of his sort.'

In the space left for my approval, I offered only silence. While walking from the quayside to the inn I had looked through the provisioning lists that now lay between us on the table and saw that they had been written in two hands. I then noticed two of Drummond's navigation books on another corner of the table and his red coat on the bench seat under the window.

'You are reconciled, then?'

'Reconciled?' said Mr Paterson. 'After what? I never spoke ill of the man.'

Thus it seems that the Patersonians have been disbanded. Or is it reformed with a new constitution? I immediately regretted the question as a lapse from my rule of standing aside from such talk.

'You could speak a word to Captain Galt on his behalf, Roderick,' said Paterson archly. 'You seem to have gained his confidence.'

I denied any influence and our meeting ended with a curt: 'As you wish.'

*

I FOUND MYSELF a more modest room and waited for the statements of supply to come in from the other captains. Mr Shipp and I collated these into a single list of our requirements. With this, and dressed in the fashion of the island – white cotton breeches, a short jacket of the same stuff and a hat as broad as Hephaestus' shield bought from the market – I set out with Mr Spense to tour the island like a great gentleman and to see to the ordering of all our needs.

We chose a donkey-cart to do our rounds, Mr Spense sitting beside me and a boy clinging to the back, suggested to us as a guide by an official at the Governor's palace. This vehicle was selected in preference to one of the extraordinary sledges drawn by pairs of bullocks, which appear to be the mainstay of the island's transport. I suspected a traditional jest when they were first shown to me and then amused our hosts even more by looking underneath to find the wheels which I was sure must be concealed there. They give the impression of waiting for a mythical snow to return or of being primitive essays in the carriage before that unknown genius gave the wheel and axle to the world. I declined, explaining that we needed greater speed which, in the event, our donkey hardly provided.

It was a great relief to me to spend some time quite away from the expedition and I left hoping that whatever ailed it would have mended by our return.

We took our directions from our young guide and started towards one of the largest sugar-cane plantations on the south side of the island. All Madeira's fertility lies in a narrow skirt between the sea-cliffs and the bare black rock of the mountains at the centre. Here the industry of the people and the benevolence of the climate has brought forth the greatest wealth possible from the little land available to them. To this they have added by cutting terraces into the foothills right up to the point at which they become almost vertical. As we trotted between fields of cane and maize and past their famous vineyards, a sort of ecstasy settled on me as I realized that Darien must be very like this, or at least capable of being made like it. Everywhere the lesson was plain: that only a little labour will make us masters of a similar paradise.

We were well received by the factor of the estate who greeted us volubly as the 'great Scots pirates', laughing a little, I think, at our humble mode of transport. Benjamin left most of this speech untranslated, but part of its purpose was clearly to demonstrate the man's knowledge of us. As I grinned stupidly, I caught hold of the occasional 'João Knox', 'King Stuart', 'Sheekspeer' and 'No popery', the last being a great joke.

He wanted to know if the Scots were as fierce as he had heard, if it was true that in Scotland soldiers grew like corn. I smiled and bowed and said we disembowelled those who cheated us.

'Then I must give you a fair price, Mr Makinzee, as I do to all my English customers.'

We followed him into the drying house where, as our eyes opened, we saw long lines of brown sugar loaves and breathed in the thick molasses sweetness of the air. After a brief negotiation we settled at a price, and the agreement was sealed with glasses of rum, distilled from the same sugar-canes. We agreed to buy a hogshead of the same and went on our way.

We had the good fortune to arrive at our next supplier in time for dinner. The meal is neglected by the natives in favour of sleep, but this was one of the English estates that proliferated after the Portuguese marriage of the last Charles, some thirty years back. The proprietor, Mr Edward Wallace, successor to his father in the trade, is nearly as black-haired and moustachioed as his adoptive countrymen and speaks his English in a very curious accent. I was ready for difficulties in this meeting, but found it to be quite the most pleasant of our journey. We were handsomely entertained with a meal of tunny-fish and tomatoes and black olives and herbs, all with mounds of excellent yellow bread from the maize flour we still had to buy. There was cheese from the goats, which cover the island like sheep, and strawberries as big as new potatoes. We were served outside under a pergola of the vines from which all this wealth flows, the grapes hanging down over our heads, still small and hard.

From the appearance of our host I would guess that his father married a native woman and he has done the same. Mrs Wallace and the three tiny Wallace heirs shared the table with us. They are as dark as gypsies and stared at our foreign features in amazement until dismissed. They never spoke a word, English or Portuguese. It was easy to forget that he was English, or that we were Scots. He expressed some very gratifying opinions about the unfairness of the Navigation Acts and is clearly no friend of the East India Company, saying that all the local merchants benefited by their exclusion from the island. He wished us every success in our venture and asked which part of Africa we intended to colonize. I made a plausible reply.

Our business was concluded amicably enough with the ordering of four hogsheads of his ten-year-old wine and half a dozen barrels of raisins, all to be delivered to Funchal at his expense in three days. The heat being still at its height, we accepted an offer of a few hours' rest on a covered terrace at the back of the house. This was ingeniously draped in muslin, which servants occasionally sprinkled with water. I woke before Mr Spense, hearing the children playing in the garden below the terrace. I parted the muslin to watch them trying to make a paper bird fly, the eldest throwing it up as high as he could only for it to come down again like a stone. The middle child tried and this time a breath of wind caught it and moved it sideways. There was an infant cheer, which turned to a concerned silence as the bird dropped into the fountain. An argument started, apparently as to whose fault it was and who should fish it out. An ear was twisted and a long wail let out, which brought a girl I hadn't seen before, maybe seventeen. She gave them each a slap on the head, which hardly ruffled their hair, and led them off. As the girl turned out of my sight, comforting the smaller child in her arms, I remembered that in a few days we would return to the stinking confinement of the ships. I gazed at the garden, silent save for the noise of the fountain, at the row upon row of vineyards that stepped up the hills beyond and wondered at the fickleness of my heart.

In the late afternoon we continued our clockwise tour of the island. Before we left, I found our young guide in conversation with Mr Wallace, using the local dialect which not even Mr Spense can understand. They stopped as soon as I entered from the terrace and we tried to find out, once we were back on the road, if the boy understood English. Every question put to him produced an expression of rather theatrical incomprehension blended with indignation at having his thirteen-year-old honour impugned. For the rest of our trip we were careful what we said in his presence.

The main town in this part of the island is Santana, modest in size by comparison with Funchal, but with an equally prosperous appearance. Here I saw the tunny-fish entire for the first time, and a very magnificent creature it is. They are great silver-bellied things, the largest weighing more than I do, laid out on the quay as soon as the fishing-boats return. They are so large the only way of killing them is to carve a great gash into the head. These wounds and the blood from them swarm with flies, which are constantly brushed away with a device like a cow's tail wielded by a man in a long white apron who struts up and down auctioning each fish to the crowd. We left them, thinking we could get the same and perhaps cheaper in Funchal.

There being no inn, we stayed in a private house, and left orders early the next morning with several of the farmers in the area for maize flour and oil. News of our presence had spread overnight so that on rising we were confronted by a delegation of these gentlemen eager to sell us their produce. When it came to the prices, however, this apparent surplus was vigorously denied. I stood by and watched the dumb show, receiving Mr Spense's account of its significance every few seconds. The gist was that only thieves and pirates would offer such prices as we suggested, it was a time of scarcity in spite of all appearances – had we not noticed the thinness of the children? one feeble tape-wormed individual was presented as proof of this – they had come out of Christian charity hearing we were in need, but could not let their families go hungry, however much they wished to sacrifice themselves on our behalf.

When I apologized for threatening their livelihood and had one leg up on our donkey-cart their demands fell, but only a little. With the courtesy due from a guest and realizing that the expedition should not seem short of money, I finally agreed some prices and placed orders sufficient for all the fleet's needs to be delivered to Funchal.

It was still early when we returned to the road and we were able to complete our circumambulation of the island, stopping only once for water and re-entering Funchal from the east. We rattled down one of the narrow cobbled streets between high-walled courtyards without seeing another soul. At the first crossing our guide hopped off, demanded his fee, and ran away up the hill towards the Governor's mansion – no doubt to say what he had learned and to collect another coin or two.

The place had a strange Sunday quietness about it that began to unsettle both of us. We turned into the harbour front still without having seen more than a half-dozen people, and those reluctant to acknowledge us. My first sight was of barrels, some on the quay, some in a lighter waiting to be taken to the ships, but without any men attending to them. The only humanity in evidence was two dozen of the Governor's guard in their carnival uniforms and an old woman brushing potsherds off her step with a besom before slamming the door on us as we passed. The guards gave us sullen looks as we dismounted and refused to answer Benjamin's questions. Two or three of the small boats from the fleet had been tied up but with no clue of who had come ashore or where they were. I noticed the pinnace from the *Rising Sun* rowing in through the windless heat, the officer not yet identifiable. The great Genoese had gone, leaving the *Caledonia* on her own in the lee of the harbour wall. Drummond appeared at the quarterdeck rail and gave me a lazy, mocking salute.

I made for the inn and heard, as I approached it, the sounds of revelry. A moment before turning the last corner, the cacophony resolved itself into the bellowing refrain of an obscene song, an obscenity all too clear to my ears as it was pounded out in some of the unloveliest accents our nation has to offer. And there they were, like a herd of long-tortured pigs who had finally broken through to the cabbage patch. One straddled the gutter, pissing on his feet as he swayed from side to side, another lay in the same, unaware of what was coming to him, like a dead man bloated by the sun, save for his snoring. Angrier voices were added to the song, which gusted out of the windows on a mistral of wine and farts. A clot of three squabbling bodies suddenly tumbled through the door, debating where that fifth ace came from until, deprived of mutual support, they each fell their own way, the cobbles of the street cracking some sense into their skulls. I looked up to see Paterson's windows tight shut.

Inside was an unbuttoned mêlée of our cheapest human cargo. My appearance caused a momentary lull in the din, but as soon as it was clear I was no one to be feared, it returned to its full roar. The aproned owner of the establishment wandered about in the midst of this with a stunned, Bedlamite expression on his face, raising his hands in an occasional appeal, uttering inaudible words. As our eyes met, shame was added to my anger. I pushed through to the stairs as a wine jar flew, shattering on the flagstones. There was no response from behind Paterson's door and it seemed to be locked. When I pushed a little harder it gave an inch and I heard his quavering voice declare that he had a pistol and the will to use it.

'It's me, Roderick Mackenzie!'

There was a gratifying 'Thank God!' and a clattering and scraping sound. I pushed in past the weight of a commode, almost tripping over one of the chairs that had just been cast aside.

'What in God's name is happening?'

'Are you all right?'

I said I was and received his breathless account of the last twenty-four hours as he rebuilt his barricade.

It seemed that for no good reason the bulk of the colonists, and all of the lower sort, had assumed they were to enjoy a full ten days of shore leave. To avoid disappointing them and risking a dispute, Galt – 'in his wisdom', as Mr Paterson insists on saying after every mention of his name – made no announcement, either for or against the idea. With the *Caledonia* in harbour, their crew and colonists apparently enjoying the earthly delights, and the smell of land in their nostrils, the injustice seemed more intolerable by the hour. Some swam ashore the day Benjamin and I left for our tour and some of these returned that evening with a boat borrowed from the harbour to ferry their less seaworthy friends into the town. News of this soon transformed itself into 'permission for shore leave' and a good half of 'the herd' made free with the small boats and pastured themselves in the town.

Trembling and sheened with sweat, Paterson sagged into his chair, giving a little jump as something else shattered below to the noisy pleasure of the men. 'This is the worst but there are others about the town, five hundred at least. It's a terrible blow for Mrs Paterson's nerves.'

'Surely something's being done about it?'

'Well may you ask, Roderick. I've done my best, but what authority do I have? Galt, in his wisdom, is suddenly concerned with more pressing matters. More pressing! I ask you . . . The Governor has resorted to the conviction, hardly surprising, that we are indeed pirates and fancies we'll slit every throat in the island if he lifts a finger against us . . . them.'

'And Drummond?'

'Playing Achilles. And not one of that lot is from the *Caledonia.* He at least has kept order.'

'The rest is sorted out?'

'The rest?'

'He's on his ship again. The last time I saw him . . .'

'Yes, yes, of course. Only a misunderstanding.'

I asked again what was being done about it, what were the orders?

'Mr Cunningham has gone to squeeze some out of him.'

The last word was pronounced with a contemptuous capitalization. I said I had seen an officer returning to the harbour.

'Go and ask him, will you, Roderick? They won't do you any harm.'

I had almost squeezed past the commode when he spoke again. 'And the Reverend Mackay, he may do something rash.'

'What?'

'If you see him tell him . . . from his friend . . . tell him to remember the reward of the meek.'

I almost collided with Benjamin Spense at the door. He had finally persuaded one of the Governor's guards to speak and was told they had received no orders. The man had added with a grin that the young men would soon be returning from the fields.

'I think those guards on the quay are the only ones,' said Mr Spense. 'I asked him and he said there were two thousand, which I thought was rather overdoing it. I met Cunningham.'

'And?'

'Said he was going to the Governor's mansion. That's all I know.'

I left him there with the idea of returning to the quayside but took the wrong street in my confusion and soon found myself in unknown parts of the town. The closed shutters and the pools of urine flowing from stains on the whitewashed walls marked the passage of other groups of my countrymen. Here and there, in small taverns which had not put up their shutters in time, miniatures of the scene at the inn were repeated. They knew who I was well enough and gave me sullen, guarded looks as I passed. Fearing I could only make matters worse, I said nothing and hurried on looking for a downhill street that must lead to the quay. Porcine gruntings came from the bushes beside a tiny chapel as another of our number thrust himself into one of the local women, his friend standing by, letting me see the knife at his belt.

I entered the second square of the town, which fronts the cathedral. All was quiet, red and long-shadowed in the last of the sun and I thought of sitting there a while to regain my composure. Alas, more Scots voices approached from the opposite direction, murmuring, low, as if trying to conceal themselves.

There appeared a sweating, black-coated procession led by Mr Mackay and Mr Stobo with Mr Borland, the minister from the *St Andrew*, a step behind. They brought with them their own dreary congregation, which plodded, heads down, as if labouring through a personal downpour. For an instant I thought I understood and took off my hat, but the expected coffin did not appear. The group assembled in the middle of the square, Mackay's head suddenly appearing a foot and a half above the rest as he stood on a box. He had found his text, filled his lungs and was about to start when I interrupted.

'The word of the Lord will not be shouted down! The word of the Lord is—'

He noticed it was me and at the sound of Mr Paterson's name consented to step aside and hear the message. At the sound of a few words from his less preferred Testament he was greatly offended. 'Do I tell you your business, sir? Do I tell you how to count and write in a ledger? Am I and my colleagues to have the stench of Satan's civet in our nostrils and not speak a word of truth to these poor benighted people?'

Having done my duty, I left him to his. As I left the square, I caught sight of some dim features peering past a half-open shutter in complete amazement.

On the quayside even the dozen or so of the Governor's guards who had been there before were now gone. As the last of the evening light faded I listened to sounds of increasing drunkenness in the town and strained to hear the first sounds of the riotous disaster that must have come from any meeting between our colonists and the men returning from the fields. Feebly pushing through the offbeats of this din came syllables of Reverend Mackay's sermon, making me smile as, in their strangeness, they recalled to my mind what I have read of the muezzins in the east.

A darkly dressed figure moved in the edge of my sight making me draw into a doorway. There was the sound of a sword drawn half out of its scabbard.

'Roderick?'

'Mr Cunningham!'

He opened the covered lantern he was carrying so we could see each other more clearly. I told him what was happening at the inn and of Mr Mackay's holy band, but was too ashamed to add what I had seen by the chapel.

'The Governor tells me they are our people and our problem. I notice the guards have disappeared.'

'And Galt?' I asked. 'It was you I saw rowing in from the *Rising Sun*?'

He admitted he had spoken with him.

'Well?'

'Captain Galt is very disappointed.'

'What?'

'Perhaps I should say he is in a state of disappointment.'

This meant nothing to me, and still does. It was incredible that he had not given orders and I pressed Cunningham to tell me what they were.

'To do the necessary.'

'That's all?'

'Without taking any more men ashore. Captain Galt thinks it probable that would only make things worse.'

As I pondered this, I could just see the lights and the last shadows of the *Rising Sun*, the *St Andrew*, the *Dolphin* and the *Endeavour* riding at anchor a mile beyond the harbour mouth. A hundred yards from us, laid up at the outer harbour wall, the *Caledonia* seemed dead, the stern-lights of Drummond's cabin black.

'Perhaps if we talked to Mackay together? And then we could deal with the men.'

Cunningham agreed, but it was with little confidence in this pact of weakness that we turned back up the hill towards the cathedral, that most offensive and maddening of buildings.

When we entered the square we could see that a fair number of the townspeople had come out to gawp at this curiosity from across the sea. Mackay, who was clearly less alarming than our ordinary colonists, took these spectators for a congregation. His rhetoric put out full sail as it mounted from the false prophets to the deceptions of Antichrist himself. Mercifully, not a word of this was comprehensible to our hosts who looked with either amusement or concern as flecks of righteous sputum arced through the lantern-light. One man, with a regretful expression, tried to make himself understood. I remembered the two or three words he kept repeating and asked Benjamin about them later: had the gentleman been bitten by a mad dog?

It takes one of our own to stop the flow of a homegrown preacher and he soon made himself heard.

'Shut up! Shut up, you old hypocrite! We've had enough of your skirling! Shut up, in God's name, you're nothing but a bag of old shite!'

The shock of being treasonously abused in his own tongue left Mackay gaping towards a dozen men who had entered the square by another street. More came from the same direction, not one sober. There was soon twenty, then forty, then a mob.

I still believe only Mackay would have come to any harm at their hands, but it didn't seem like that to the Madeirans. At once, the few women who had ventured out disappeared and more men came from the houses about the square and from the street behind us, looking very like the men from the fields with whom we had been threatened. Mackay, Stobo and Borland, with their little huddle of acolytes, stood in the middle, now silent and nervous, glancing from one group to the other, realizing their position. The Madeirans and our men moved towards each other, Mackay and friends scrambling out of their way. A glass was thrown, invisible until it shattered on the stones. There was a sudden move forward by our men, jerked to a halt as soon as it started, like a mastiff straining at the last link of its chain. A brief, sharp drum-roll of a dozen muskets being fired rattled out from the blackest corner of the square. All eyes peered to see twelve dragoons on their knees, reloading, another twelve standing behind them ready to fire. The brutal, inevitable, indispensable voice barked out: 'The next volley in your bellies if there's a word from any of you!'

He strode out into the light of the upturned lanterns, resting with one boot on Mackay's abandoned pulpit – Drummond in glory!

*

WE ARE NEARING the end of our short lease on Funchal; from dawn tomorrow it will tolerate us no longer. We will become another anecdote about the wickedness of the outside world. The provisioning went well in spite of everything, the last of the fresh stores being taken aboard this morning. Some murmurings about the cost came to my ears, but nothing of any significance. Our human cargo is all packed up too. I am one of the last on shore, waiting along with four oarsmen for Captains Pincarton and Jolly to return from the Governor's mansion where they have gone formally to take our leave. They carry a message from Galt who has not left the *Rising Sun*.

The last three days have been like the eve of a thunderstorm that never comes. Those of us still on shore have had to endure universal frowns of disapproval from dawn to dusk. We are not told the time of day, or which street is which.

Perhaps it was not as grave as it appeared. By nine o'clock Drummond's men had cleared all the streets and penned the colonists into the quayside, whence they were ferried back to the ships. Thus divided up, they once again became harmless. Not a life was lost, nothing more than a few bleeding heads. Reverend Mackay has complained loudly of an assault, but it went unwitnessed in the darkness and has left no wound.

Yesterday and this morning I passed profitably, completing my letters. I have had to omit more than I would have wished. With Benjamin I went to the harbour-master whose responsibility it is to place them on suitable ships. Through his mediation we had the following curious exchange.

'A pity you hadn't come a day or so earlier, it would have saved you a month of waiting.'

I asked him: 'Did Captain Drummond or Mr Paterson send letters by that ship?'

'Oh, yes, sir,' he told us, 'a great packet. From the whole ship, I suppose; that's what put me in mind of it. A day sooner and they could all have gone together. These might have to wait another month.'

And so our directors will have a month to think over Paterson's and Drummond's words before reading ours. A pressing reason for getting here first, or do I go too far?

They have returned. One of the oarsmen is calling me. These are the last breaths of clean air, the last of a table that doesn't yaw beneath the pen. The last of civilization, save for what we take with us.

Flying fish! They skim over the waves like skipping stones and some even strand themselves on the decks. They come to our lights – if we pass through a shoal of them at night there can be a good harvest at dawn. Until these I saw nothing I had not seen the like of before, and only now do I feel we have started.

The colonists have been kept below since leaving Madeira and will remain there until Captain Galt relents. As a consequence the fleet has a sullen, unhappy air about it, which was not improved by our passing, two days ago, a squadron of English frigates. We gave a friendly signal but received none in reply. They were sailing north-east, almost certainly for replenishment at Madeira where they will, no doubt, take a great interest in recent events.

What we thought was heat before was not heat at all. Now, our ships are becoming wooden ovens, burning us up. Twice already I have been asked to recalculate the water rations. We had our first death from fever yesterday, one of the older men, a widower from Stranraer, cooper by trade. Mackay spent half an hour on his obsequies before the board was tipped up by two crewmen, sending him feet first into the sea.

'There's a fortune not made,' was Dr Munro's comment. His mood has been much improved by this belated fulfilment of his prophecies.

I am happy to spend what time I can down here, letting my thoughts fly. That first winter in Edinburgh was a bitter enemy, but now the thought of it is precious as ice.

*

I ARRIVED BREATHLESS, not entirely of the required appearance and having to borrow a prayer-book. Baillie Ritchie liked to keep a Christian household and it was understood that any tenant not seen at the kirk on a Sunday morning had a short future with him. The Ritchies had the front pew on the right, that on the left being occupied in a similarly authoritative fashion by another family of whom never a word was spoken.

Several rows in front of me James elbowed Douglas and they both looked round. These two had clearly spent some time in their own beds, but in their fresh clothes and washed faces they seemed to fume with sin even more sulphurously than I did. For me the sermon had never been shorter, or the sight of my fellow worshippers more entrancingly suggestive. I stood in my own mingled incense: rum, brandy and tobacco, my own body, and that of my sweet, skinny whore. Each was a clear track in my senses, as I became my own hound, sniffing out the thrilling trail of these secrets. In my hands, the leather on that borrowed prayer-book was Susanna's skin.

The sermon was in one of its optional passages when Mrs Ritchie took the opportunity to turn and give me a nod, approving my presence. I smiled back and gave thanks to God that we were all so gloriously undetectable. As I looked over the solemn and attentive congregation I wondered how many others were with us. I vowed never again to satisfy myself with one life when to have two seemed so easy.

That day marked the beginning of an acceleration in my affairs and, though it would not become clear for some months, their convergence also with this great public enterprise on which we are now engaged. It marked also an expansion of my awareness of the world as I learned to view it with that double vision which reveals the whole – the significances of things as well as their appearances and the invisible, inevitable potentialities which could surely be no less in other men than in myself. By achieving what I imagined to be a mastery in the deception of others, I fancied that I made myself proof against similar practices.

In my first half-year of city life I had been absorbed more in myself than in my surroundings. Few enough were the things that impinged on me until that sight of Susanna's bony form in the Sunday-morning light. There was shock in that, as well as a thrill, which brought the rest of reality flooding through. The beggars were suddenly more numerous, and as the harvest fell below the gloomiest expectations, the streets began to fill with people driven from the land. The grain merchants put on funereal looks and shook their heads. They haggled with the English agents, but they were hard-hearted. Two were set upon one night and almost killed; the rest withdrew to the south. In the London reprints we read of ourselves as the barbarous, envious north. In the market, the prices were chalked up two or three times a day, always higher, more out of reach of those who clustered there to gather cabbage leaves and spilt grains with their fingertips. By the end of that month, icicles hung from the eaves, and thefts of coal and firewood began to be reported.

It was also about then that I noticed – though I should have seen it long before – the scarcity of young men of my age. I began to read the papers I liked to swagger with, and learned about the war in France. I attracted the looks of recruiting sergeants and took to crossing the street at the sight of a uniform. Some of the young men I did see lacked a leg or two. Maimed in an English war, their hands and hats were emptier even than those of the common poor. Our parliament sent petitions to our king for relief from the Navigation Acts; let us trade for our own grain, let us trade with the colonies and make your northern kingdom as rich as your southern. These were swept impatiently off his campaign maps – he was King of England too, King of the East India Company, or at least that's how one of the ballad-sellers put it, for which twenty pounds and a month in the Tolbooth.

Like the ballad-sellers, or those who weren't caught, I could observe all this without suffering it myself. At the start of the crisis men drank more as they ate less. We started to do business with the Wilful Willy and for us it had never been busier. I spent half my day in other basements around the city, selling wine in places where people burrowed down beneath the frost. I made the best of my opportunities while patronizing Susanna so that we started to sell wine to Widow Gilbert's establishment as well. Through her acquaintance I was able to cultivate other charitable matrons about the town who offered food and shelter to young women in a similar fashion. These measures, and a stroke of luck from the same quarter, helped keep Colquhoun's head above the rising waters.

I kept my promises to Susanna – very willingly, I admit – and as she ate everything I brought for her she became beautiful as well as more comfortable. By that time it had become an established custom that I would take private commissions from all the new business I brought to Colquhoun and these sums soon outstripped my salary. I could easily afford to visit her twice or sometimes three times a week, as well as to continue enjoying the costly company of James and Douglas and to make myself companionable to the more important men of the city when I came across them in the course of my affairs.

Susanna, to whom I was always 'my fine young gentleman', put up various objections to becoming my exclusive domain. Firstly, it was on account of Widow Gilbert's rules: as a highly moral woman she would not tolerate her lodgers making their own arrangements under her roof. Then it was because I could not afford her. At her prompting I had bought her a book of plates of great paintings from which she learned to loll naked on her bed like a Titian Lucrezia as she gnawed the flesh from a pheasant bone and haggled good-humouredly over her price. 'You see what a masterpiece you've made of me, my fine young gentleman? You've put my price above rubies.'

I argued that was all the more reason for me to enjoy the fruits of my improvement. But my claim was treated with a lordly contempt – I was nothing more than a peasant labouring to improve his landlord's field. My pleasures ended with my tenancy.

For much of that winter her tiny attic room was my chief rest and asylum from the world. Kept warm with the constant supply of coal I also paid for, it was the vantage-point from which I looked down on the world outside as it shivered and thinned. Occasionally, I had to pass other gentlemen on that last flight of stairs, but in the end that, too, turned to our advantage.

The one I glimpsed most frequently in the discreet tallow-light of Widow Gilbert's house wore an expression of such miserable furtiveness that it was difficult to imagine what pleasure he could derive from his visits. He gave the impression of having slipped his prayer-book in one pocket and his bands in the other and would give a quarter-look to every face he passed in an attempt to see without being seen, as if in risking recognition, he risked all. Needless to say, these traits made him an object of particular interest, and not only on my part. By and large, Widow Gilbert's visitors lived in a state of happy and shameless confederacy with each other, all mutually secured by our brazenness and the knowledge that one could not fall without a very great risk that the rest would follow. Indeed, in this respect, the regular attendance of four town councillors and even a peer made the house one of the safest in the town.

This single man, and what is more, this stubborn patron of Susanna and therefore undeserving beneficiary of all my cold pheasants, my pints of milk, pails of raisins and figs, my confections and the very last sweet oranges in Edinburgh – and of my coal! – withheld his faith from the rest of us and would not show his face. Suspicions of a clerical connection grew, but were soon cast aside. Some of our fellowship were well informed on such matters and dismissed the theory out of hand. Rather, such a vocation should have emboldened him, put him among friends and above shame. It was argued, therefore, that he must be something lower and more despised, something more vulnerable, as indeed turned out to be the case. Our curiosity was further aroused when it was discovered that Widow Gilbert had been sworn to secrecy on the matter of his identity. No small undertaking, we surmised, as extra discretion, as with extra anything in that good lady's household, could not be had for nothing.

I passed him again on that last flight of stairs in a late-November afternoon, already black as midnight, a day at the end of ten days in each of which we had sworn it could not get colder, but in each of which it had. The dawn watch had found several dead in the streets, while in the coffee-houses the talk was of a horse and cart found a mile short of West Port, man and beast frozen alike, the reins still in his hands, hard as iron. The faithless shadow hurried past my greeting under the brim of his hat.

Inside Susanna was as convincingly happy to see me as ever. Of course, I had asked her before who this man was but her answer was always the same. 'Well, wouldn't you like to know, my fine young gentleman?' And I would say I would, to which she would ask, 'Particularly?' to which I would say, 'Yes,' to which she, adopting another pose from her book of plates, would say: 'I suppose you must do, because he knows you, he takes a particular interest in you.' And there, or thereabouts, the tiresome game would end.

That evening I was determined to get an answer. As I picked at the ice around the window lights and we went through the irritating preliminaries, I considered using other methods. I never forgot what Susanna was. None the less – and I thank God for it – I decided otherwise, and was never kinder or more liberal with her than that night. It was in the morning, when I was preparing to leave to receive my weekly nod of approval from Mrs Ritchie in church when she eventually decided that I had outbid her other obligations. Our game began once again, this time at her prompting, and I was led by ways complicated enough to fall just short of a breach of confidence to ask: 'Is there an X in this man?'

'Maybe there isn't,' answered Susanna, 'and maybe there is.'

I do believe she even blushed – a thing I had never seen before.

The guess had become easy enough, but as for his name Susanna remained immovable. She had, after all, promised.

I had no opportunity to see Colquhoun until that Wednesday and turned this magnificent piece of information over and over in my mind until then. I remembered Dr Lennox's advice and had, in any case, come to a similar conclusion about my employer from my own observations. Seeing little of Mr Watson, I had become almost entirely responsible for the keeping of the books – indeed it was Mr Watson's neglect of his duties that put me on course for my current good fortune. As a result there was nothing of any import I did not know about the Colquhoun concern. I had seen how it was within a ha'pence of ruin when I arrived, how it had prospered since that time and how it was threatened by the general calamity that approached. All the same, the time for disembarking from Colquhoun had not yet arrived: none of the seeds I had planted had cropped, nor was likely to in that winter, and there was none other to whom the identity of Susanna's second patron could be of such value.

'Your whore has doings with an excise man?'

'I'm certain.'

'A whoremongering excise man?'

I watched joy triumph in his face after the briefest possible skirmish with whatever remained of his scruples. His expression clouded as the one terrible possibility that might render this fact worthless occurred to him.

'He's a married man?'

I admitted I had no name, but this presented little difficulty.

Colquhoun waved it aside: 'That's nothing, I know them all. Every tail, every pair of horns, every cloven hoof! All I need is a sight of him, just a smell of him, and I'll know who it is.'

Our quarry's visits to Widow Gilbert's house became irregular, a fact which cost my employer several freezing evenings lying in wait. We suspected that he had caught our scent and was staying away, but then, on the fourth day, there he was coming down the stair as I went up. It had been agreed that I would pretend to have forgotten something and would turn about and follow him out of the house. The man Colquhoun saw coming out immediately before me would be the one he wanted. It always seemed to be dark in those days, and everyone was disguised against the cold, Colquhoun doubly so. I watched him walk up the wynd a little, almost abreast of the man whose identity could save his business. He stopped suddenly and felt in his pocket. Colquhoun collided with him and I heard a mumbled word of apology and saw his head turn to see what he could between hat and scarf. A moment later, both walked into the Haymarket and went in opposite directions while I returned to Susanna.

The next morning Colquhoun summoned me to his office and presented me on entry with a glass of his private port. It was clear that, in his elation, he had already had several himself. 'Couldn't be better, Roderick. It just couldn't be better, my boy.' He kept repeating the phrase, almost hopping about the carpet. 'You've done a good piece of business here, Roderick, I'll say you have. And is he married? By all the bishops in hell there was never a man more married, married within an inch of his life.'

'So who is he?'

'Aeneas Caldwell.'

'Aeneas?'

'Ridiculous, isn't it? His father presumably hoped for better things but all he could do with his miserable wretched life was to become an excise man, and not just any excise man, no, but the wickedest and most vicious in the whole sorry history of injustice that has limped down all the ages since the Fall, since the first excise man forced the last morsel of bread from the mouth of a starving innocent. Caldwell, I tell you, is the direct descendant of that man, he is the publican of publicans. I heard tell that – have another glass, Roderick – that he stopped a man in the street once to tax the tobacco in his pipe! God's own truth! And when he looks at you, he doesn't see a man like himself. No, you're nothing more to him than a barrel on two legs and all he's thinking is how much he could skin you for if he hanged you by your ankles and drained your belly into a bucket. He's an evil and savage hater of mankind.'

Colquhoun paused for breath and another celebratory glass, refilling my own at the same time. I remember my surprise at discovering how very different this was even from the best that we sold. It had taken me a full six months in the wine trade to get anything a true gentleman would have recognized past my lips.

Colquhoun sat on his second-hand throne with an ineradicable smile on his face. 'Of course he does,' he kept muttering to himself, 'of course he does. How could he not?'

'What?'

'Spend his afternoons at Widow Gilbert's. You won't have heard of Mrs Caldwell, Roderick?'

I admitted I had not.

'Legendary, my boy. It's the only word. Truly legendary. Personal acquaintance is a pleasure that awaits, but the word has always been, and for the last twenty years, mind you, that Caldwell will be glad of his place in Hell when it comes, if only to get away from her. I hear she's almost punishment enough in herself.'

He began to talk to himself again, forgetting my presence as he pored over how to turn this knowledge into gold.

'Well, then, let's see. What if I . . . But then if that was to . . . No, no, that's not the way. Keep it simple. But what if he then . . . No, he couldn't; that's where we have him. I think all we need to do is . . . Of course!'

I reappeared to him as the mists of these delightful speculations cleared, presenting perhaps, indeed I hope, a slightly uncertain countenance.

'Of course we musn't involve you in any of this, Roderick. This isn't an affair for a young man such as yourself. What would Dr Lennox think of me if I permitted it? Good heavens, what would your mother say?'

At this point I reddened a little. I had so neglected my dear mother that I had given no thought at all to what she would say. A brief image came to me of her dropping dead from an apoplexy of shame. I flushed more deeply, my colour being nicely misinterpreted by Colquhoun.

'I see I've shocked you, young Roderick, and I'm very glad that I have. Some of the inner secrets of commerce are fit only for those whose hands are already soiled. I shall deal with it all, I assure you.'

By the time we had reached the door of his office my noninvolvement had ceded to the possibility of a little 'innocent co-operation'. With further assurances that it was God's will that excise men suffered for their sins, he dismissed me and I returned to the ordinary affairs of the business.

Nothing was said on the subject for six weeks or more. In that time there was no relief in the country for any person, whatever their rank. The only improvement came towards the end as the world turned and our afternoon darkness began at last to lift. All the same, January was the bitterest month yet. We began to hear of deaths by hunger in the country. There were more petitions for relief, but they were no more successful than before. Again our case was pressed for freedom of trade with the colonies but every proposal, however modest, was portrayed by the East India Company as the start of their inevitable destruction and therefore to be resisted at all costs. It was said that all our king wanted from us was young men to fight in his wars, and they went readily enough for the promise of two good meals a day. There was more talk of the Company and I began to put together the scraps I had heard, to see the greatness of what they aimed at and to think how I might steer my course across theirs. There were other voices too – the fainthearts, the easy men who raised their old song about union. But they were small and despised, and they had misunderstood the effects on our people of cold and hunger. Whenever a few gathered together to share their burdens it was not to the sky they looked for the author of their misfortunes, but to the south.

Mr Aeneas Caldwell plodded through these dismal weeks unaware of the part planned for him by a prominent member of the wine trade. I would pass him on the stairs as before and smile at his elaborate efforts to keep his face from my eyes. I began to think that Colquhoun might not make any use of his knowledge, or that he had already done so without my help as he had half promised. Indeed, I hoped it was the case and worried increasingly about the propriety of what he might do. I had already thought – though very prematurely – that it should be nothing that would prevent me from joining the great Company whose name began to fill the air.

Mr Watson still made the occasional appearance, but only to peer briefly over my shoulder at the ledgers and leave at once, silently and with a worried look. By the turn of the year the last reserves of money that the poor had saved to spend on drink were exhausted and the effect on Colquhoun's business became acute. I went about the town in those days only to collect the regrets and the cancelled orders of taverners, brothel-keepers and coffee-house owners, returning to the premises to add another few lines to the ledgers until the figures in the left-hand column first met and then sank below the figures in the right-hand column. I knew it could not be long before Colquhoun played the card I had given him.

It was at the end of the second week in January that he stopped me as I was about to leave and asked with a rather excessive solicitude if I would accompany him on a social visit on the morrow. He ensured my full complicity by saying it would be better if I did not ask to whom this courtesy was to be paid. The event itself was painful, though its aftermath, so far as I ever heard, was entirely beneficial to all who knew of it.

We walked for a minute or two beyond Nether Bow and then to the right by a row of the city's newest and most eminently respectable houses. A maidservant answered Colquhoun's knocking. He spoke to her, and she went within to announce us. Colquhoun, forgetting in his nervousness all pretence of saving me from the full odiousness of our business, leaned towards my ear and whispered: 'I've had a little friend of mine watching his movements. With any luck the man himself will be out for another half-hour. He'll come back to find us making conversation with his beldame. Perfect!'

Voices came from behind a door, one raised, abrupt. Colquhoun gazed about the hallway, then whispered again: 'It's a damned disgrace. Look at it! And every penny's worth squeezed from the honest toil of people like you and me, Roderick. It should really all be ours by rights, you know. We make the money Caldwell and his like cream off and, by the looks of things, precious little of it gets as far as the Treasury. If this is an honest excise man's house, I'm a Jew. He's worse than we are, just remember that, Roderick.'

The young woman was standing before us, solemn and just a little pink.

'I'm sorry, gentlemen, but I'm to tell you there's been a mistake. Mrs Caldwell isn't receiving visitors today.'

Colquhoun, in his most florid manners, said indeed there had been a mistake, perhaps he had not expressed himself clearly but we were there to visit Mr Caldwell and were willing to wait for such a good friend.

I gained an insight into Mrs Caldwell's character when I saw that this information put the maidservant on the point of tears. She took a half-step back, but was unable to bring herself to convey such an impertinence to her mistress.

'I don't think so, sir,' she said. 'Mr Caldwell never receives visitors.'

The nearness of complete ruination made Colquhoun bold. With a booming 'Perhaps you would allow me to explain?' he strode into the room and paid his victim such extravagantly verbose compliments on her husband, her house, her maidservant, her embroidery – we disturbed her in the illumination of the third S of 'The Lord casteth us down for our Sins' – and, least credibly of all, on herself, that he gained the advantage for a full minute and a half. When Mrs Caldwell drew breath for the first time, he forestalled her with an unnecessarily detailed account of how the offending arrangement had been made. When she made her second attempt he introduced me with much irrelevant information on my life to date. I bowed low and expressed my pleasure at being in her presence.

She seemed on the point of ejecting us but stopped after 'How dare . . .'

She calmed herself and was, it seemed to me, struck by a thought. She replied to all she had heard with a simmering 'Is that so?'

After commanding us to sit on a hard bench at the furthest point from the fire, she sat down with her needle and lay in wait for her husband.

The clock ticked, her needle pierced and pulled at the coloured threads. All seven of Colquhoun's attempts to engage her in conversation dropped like stones. The fire in the grate, meagre when we had entered, was allowed to die and at our end of the room our breaths were soon as visible as they had been outside. From entering as impostors we had somehow, without a blow being struck, become prisoners. We gazed in awe at the Caldwell woman. As she stitched another curlicue of flame on to her S, piety rendered her insensible of the glistening drip that gathered at the sharp point of her nose. Pity for our victim rose in us for the first time.

The door to the street was opened by someone who carried his own key. Mrs Caldwell's head sprang up like a cockerel's. Colquhoun leaned close to my ear. 'Say nothing!' he hissed.

For all my scruples – and they were considerable – I could not but admire the way Colquhoun handled that piece of business. He was in the hallway and greeting Caldwell like a lost brother before anyone else knew what was happening. Caldwell knew only too well who he was, but his protestations were drowned out by Colquhoun's tirade of joy at seeing him again. It was when he entered the room where I stood with his wife that all became silent. He recognized me at once from Widow Gilbert's, understood at once the hopelessness of his situation. In his own way, he turned out to be quite as fine an actor as Colquhoun. In an instant he remembered the appointment after all, apologized profusely for forgetting, for his unpardonable bad manners. He explained all to his wife, and with a wealth of convincing detail, indeed with a veritable flood of irrelevancies thrown up by his wits made quick with fear. Neither man, I thought, was entirely new to these games.

Caldwell's recognition of me, his moment of blanched understanding, was our crisis. Once that had passed there was little to do but make frigid conversation and sip our way quickly through the thin, bitter coffee he offered us. We soon extracted ourselves, the shrill tones of Mrs Caldwell's interrogation rising as we fled her doorstep. The following Monday Caldwell paid Colquhoun a brief visit and the matter was settled. From that day on he never paid a penny in excise and the figures in the left-hand column once again moved above those in the right-hand column. Caldwell himself enjoyed considerable unforeseen benefits from our visit. No longer required to conceal his shameful profession, he entered into full fellowship in Widow Gilbert's house. He drank and smoked and joked in the downstairs parlour with the rest of the frequenters – each insisting that his wife, bless her soul, was worse than all the others together. Much to my chagrin, this meant that he spent more time with Susanna, not less. Colquhoun allowed that he was almost human. Mrs Caldwell had a happier husband and was never, to the best of my knowledge, troubled as to the reasons why. As for the public purse, we were the least of its problems. All in all, we did more good that day than we intended.

*

FOR ALL THAT, the triumph was temporary. Before long the figures began to sink again. Selling our wares was hard enough, but then buying them also became difficult. Around the middle of February the French merchant was in town again, the one I had seen on my very first day in the capital. He came to see Colquhoun two or three times, but a price could not be agreed. A dozen French ships had been taken by the English since the beginning of the year. For these risks we would now have to pay. Colquhoun protested with all his eloquence. There was no treason he was not prepared to utter against that 'Dutch mountebank, that fraud, that thief, that gin-pissing pirate'. He was an English king, foisted on an unwilling Scotland that was still, as it had ever been, a loyal and honest friend to France. Had not Scottish ships loaded in Bordeaux for five hundred years, and the

French at Leith for nearly as long? If a Dutch pirate-king preyed on French shipping was that any reason to punish the Scots?

It was not so long ago, but I was naïve then and thrilled to hear such rhetoric as I pressed my ear against the door. Of course, these were not Colquhoun's opinions, he had no opinions. In place of such things that served for ordinary men and inspired his contempt whenever he came across them, he had at best a sort of policy. With everyone he was a diplomat, an agent of his own administration; the government of the Republic of Colquhoun. A handshake, a smile, a prediction of tomorrow's weather, sympathy for one's troubles: these were all acts of policy which aimed at leading everyone around him to believe that their interests coincided with his. I began to think that was what Dr Lennox meant when he recommended me to learn what I could from him and then leave. Lennox, too, is a cynic, then? Certainly, I flatter myself to think that I understand him better now than when I was his pupil. In any case, the idea added impetus to my direction – the more I knew Colquhoun, the further I was from him. He was nothing but a silk-stocking chapman.

As for Monsieur Montorgueil, who sat listening to his shameless huckstering, he enjoyed the entertainment, I think, but had no more interest in the real meaning of the words than Colquhoun himself. He had come out of the same school and, like two snakes of the same stripe, they could not poison each other. If anything, it was in my ear that his words had an unlooked-for effect.

The interview was over. By the time the door was open I was back at my desk, turning a page of the ledger. Colquhoun walked with Montorgueil in silence to the outer door. 'Good day, Monsieur.' He held it open for him as he stepped out into the close.

As soon as the Frenchman had gone he set to striding up and down in front of my desk. I studied my ledger until he could stand it no longer.

'Damn him!' he exclaimed, throwing a letter on the floor. 'Damn them all, damn that damned Dutchman! Well?'

I shrugged and looked blank.

'I, Roderick, I, Magnus Colquhoun, in case you didn't know it, am at war with France whether I damned well like it or not. What do you make of that? Well? While I try to make my crust, that tulip-eating hired-man of a king some fool brought in goes gallivanting about the rest of Europe making enemies. Twice the price he wanted, twice! For risks to shipping!'

With a final damnation he slammed himself into his bureau. Muffled curses and the furious clinking of bottle against glass emanated for some time.

*

AT LAST THE WORLD began to melt. Icicles fell from the eaves, the cobbles in the morning were no longer white with frost, the filth in the gutters softened, the reek rising up from them for another season. But it was not a happy spring. Clouds smothered us week after week, shutting out the longed-for light, pouring ceaseless rain on what little had survived of the winter crops, rotting them in the fields. Our streets turned from glaciers to rivers. James became a hermit, preparing himself for his final oral defence, which would make him a lawyer fully fledged. Douglas remained cheerful and liked to shock the Misses Ritchie by celebrating at table the fact that, because of the troubles, the morbid anatomy classes were in a time of plenty. There were now only three student-physicians to a cadaver, whereas before there could be as many as seven.

'It is the Lord's bounty,' said Mrs Ritchie, 'even in adversity.'

'Indeed so,' said her husband.

Watson reappeared in the business and between the two of them he and Colquhoun worked like galley slaves for a fortnight to fend off the inevitable. Wine was bought from warehouses in Glasgow and brought over by road. A small consignment of port was taken over from the wreckage of a Dundee merchant who had already gone bankrupt. The tap-boy was let go and happily went off for the short career of a drummer in Flanders. Dismal as sales were, we had little more than a week's supply left when Mr Watson, mud-bespattered from head to toe after his sodden journey, but with a smile of relief on his face, entered the office. A new supplier had been found: every two months a ship from Santander would unload at Glasgow, the barrels to be hauled across in ox-carts. From then on Colquhoun's 'claret' was to be Spanish. These ships were preyed upon by French privateers and took the longest route to avoid them, sailing west of Ireland before curving round the top and coming south on the last leg. It was to be my job to sell this wine at an impossible price.

The coffee-houses were half empty, those who remained in them being only of the better sort with the means to hold themselves apart from the common lot. As my rounds about the city and the lists of sales to be entered into the ledger continued to shorten, I could spend more time idling in these places, looking out at the dreary, sunless spring. I could ill afford it, but what little surplus I had I devoted to this activity, not out of reckless leisure but because this was where the last few pockets in Edinburgh with any money in them were to be found. A man with money in those days either had an uncommon amount of it, or an uncommon ability to make it while everyone else lost it. As I was by then certain of the eventual fate of Colquhoun's business, I felt an urgent need to be close to these men, to overhear their conversations lest, in a loose moment, one of them should let slip the secret. Less ambitiously, I hoped to make myself known to them, to habituate them to me sufficiently to receive an answering nod in the mornings, to look intelligent when their glance happened to fall in my direction, to spend as they spent, as if I too was above the flood that was washing so many others away. Back in Baillie Ritchie's house I crouched over candle-ends making anxious calculations. In reality, I would have snapped at the first offer they made me.

I was spending my time in just such a way on a morning in early April when I noticed that I was attracting the attention of one of these famine-proof gentlemen. When I raised my head he looked back to his own newspaper and I had the chance to assess him as a likely employer. He was dressed with costly simplicity and wore his own greying hair, rather than any wig, arranged with such perfection that it had surely received the attention of a French-trained *valet de chambre* that very morning. I was drawn to his hands, and hid mine under the table where the crusts of ink and wine lees that gathered under the nails could not be seen. I approved highly and was ready for any proposal. Our eyes met and we pronounced to each other a terse 'Morning!'

There was only one other man there and I became convinced that we were both waiting for him to leave so we could speak confidentially. This man dithered interminably over a pot of chocolate, pouring tiny amounts from it into his cup while he stared at a large piece of paper like a letter or a bill. He must have read it fifty times. I began to squirm with impatience, ever more convinced – with, of course, the most absolute lack of evidence – that the first man, the one who had met my eyes, wished to tell me something to my advantage. The thought occurred to me that I might be the obstruction, that these two might be waiting for me to leave. I looked straight ahead and pretended to jot down the latest price of East India stock as I strained my eyes to left and right. The man with the letter frowned, grimaced, became vacant, then frowned again. I decided he couldn't possibly have anything to do with the tastefully tailored gentleman on my right, and at last I was proved right as his chocolate pot gave up its last drop and he went out and walked up towards the castle.

'Sir,' I called after him, 'your letter!' But he didn't hear me.

The fine gentleman smiled at me and tapped a column on his newspaper. 'Have you seen this? Shocking, isn't it?'

The voice took me unawares. I doubted it for a moment and paused stupidly. 'What's that?'

'Or don't you eat, sir? The price of grain. It's shameful, all the more so when you know what it is in the south.'

'Terrible,' I agreed, thinking he must know that only too well as it was the south he called home. I hoped I had been able to conceal my reaction to this well-dressed, and possibly final, Englishman in Edinburgh, but I soon found I had not. He smiled at me more broadly, made a gesture at once of surrender and dismissal.

'Come now, I didn't put the price up.'

'Of course,' I agreed, and tried to return his easy manner. I had not abandoned the idea that there might be an opening here and would have considered myself mad had I lost any chance. And yet, from his first word something pulled me back, confused me, although there was nothing I wanted more than to escape the failure that loomed over Colquhoun.

He turned the news-sheet over, folded it and tapped another column. 'These are the ones you have to worry about. There's maybe a dozen men who control the East India Company and have the ear of the King. If they say, 'No,' then 'no' it is and there's many an English merchant – or Dutch, Spanish or colonial for that matter – who has found himself on the wrong side of them. You're not alone up here, sir.'

He held out the paper and I read how the India men had warned the London merchants not to take stock in the Company of Scotland Trading to Africa and the Indies. That was the first time I read our grand title in full.

The inexplicable Englishman had folded his paper and was standing ready for the off. 'So there's nothing for it now,' he said, 'you'll get your chance directly. All of you.'

He was almost in the street when he turned to take his leave with these words (if it is not too immodest of me to record them): 'A venture like that could make good use of a young man such as yourself. A man of courage, sir, I dare say.'

I was left standing in the front room of the coffee-house strangely amazed by this – as it seemed to me – annunciation. Why should a stranger say such a thing and, still more curious, why should he say it to me? Could he simply have recognized me for what I am – a man of affairs certainly, and a man of courage too? This would not be something any gentleman would wish to say about himself, but all the same, if it was plain enough to a stranger in a coffee-house, must it not be so?

The serving-maids yawned and discussed me behind their hands. I was about to leave when I noticed the abandoned letter and went to pick it up. I read only the first few lines: 'Order for sale to the benefit of the creditors of Abel John Wylie, cabinetmaker of Menzies Close, of stock in trade and personal property, real and movable to the sum of . . .' Just another bankruptcy order. They could be picked out of the gutters and all about the city men awoke in fright having dreamed those very words. I went outside where I felt the rain starting to fall again, from clouds so thick it was as dark as December. From every direction Destiny was beginning to talk to me and at last I was beginning to hear.

I was not the only one. The people waited for the spring, but when that too failed their last reserves of resignation were used up. This, and the indifference with which their every appeal was received by London, instilled in them a rare passion for action. At first it was unsullied by details – it was enough that there should be action. In itself this was food, and for a while at least the people were less hungry. The ballad-sellers helped, and when the town council neglected to pursue one of the sharpest-tongued, the gesture was generously interpreted. Within days, boys stood at every second street-corner selling heroic execrations of the King, the East India Company, the Continental war, the Navigation Acts, the English grain merchants, the English weather.

'By God!' Colquhoun would swear, as he paced in front of my desk. 'Is it not enough that they should be hungry, but now they go mad as well? We should be ink merchants!'

It was almost true. The bankruptcy sale of a printer and stationer was cancelled – 'due to excess of business', it said on the door. On a particular morning at the end of March the people rose to find ladders leaning against the windows of the Commissioner's house and a good crowd of joiners, masons and ironmongers busy beneath them. By the end of the day stout shutters had been fixed by every window. The compliment spurred the people on.

All this was before my encounter with the English gentleman in the coffee-house. Until that time the will of the people remained an abstraction, but in the first days of that cheerless April it began, as if directed by an invisible hand, to take a definite form. Slowly, the Company emerged from its chrysalis of paper and dreams. It began to live and move of its own. The ballad-sellers gave way to Act-sellers handing out fourpenny copies of the Act that had created the Company as a distraction at the time of the Glencoe Report. Ignored then, it now awoke in changed circumstances, more real, and to some, more threatening than was ever thought possible by those who had diffidently allowed it to be mumbled into existence on the last day of the Estates.

The Company was celebrated with many a libation. The Wilful Willy was full again, and Colquhoun's business, and therefore my own finances, enjoyed another stay of execution. Colquhoun, however, was by no means respectful of the hand that fed him. He would rail against the Company and the sudden enthusiasm for it. All was folly and madness; he the only sane man in the city.

'It shan't trouble me,' he would say, 'it's in the blood, you know. The Colquhouns have never had any trouble with this sort of thing. That's why we're still here, Roderick, after seventeen generations and never a day's madness in all that time. And where will all this fanfarole be in a month's time? Back in the devil's arse, I tell you, where it came from. Hunger's turned their wits. I've seen it all before, you know. Oh, yes – Father knew a man who thought he would make his fortune out of tulips. When I was starting out I was pestered by a poor loon trying to sell me shares in an elephant farm in Lauderdale. Ten times as much meat per beast than cattle, sir, do the sums yourself, make your fortune, came to you first, sir, being a young man who knows a good thing when he sees one, don't spread it about now, will you? Sign here. And, of course, some did and where are they now? Skeletons to a man, chained to the wall of a debtors' prison. Promoters! You'd think if it was worth anything they might keep a little for themselves, but oh, no: they're such good people they want you to go first. I tell you, Roderick, next to an excise man nothing stinks so much in the nostrils of all God-fearing and decent folk as a promoter!'

This particular speech, or something like it, was delivered after another worried glance at the figures. More and more it was the contents of Colquhoun's own ledger that led him on to these jeremiads. But for Colquhoun, too, it was in the blood, and his words were nothing more than attempts to lash himself to the mast in case the call should prove too strong. If I remember this speech more than the others, it is because promoters were a new species to me and because I was, or should have been, grateful for the reminder of how much I still had to learn. The hand that moved the people had been invisible only to my unpractised eye. In the face of the enmity of the East India Company and the indifference of the King, the Company's London directors had anticipated failure. They had sent promoters, some Scottish, others English, all recruited in London, to Edinburgh well in advance to break the ground in the last city in which the great vision of the man who led them might take root. They were the ones who had the Act printed and sold at the street corners and, no doubt, who flattered and held newspapers under the noses of any number of men idling away their mornings in the coffee-houses. Colquhoun had seen it all and I had seen nothing, still the country boy in town. I hated that, but where Colquhoun took the mere presence of promoters as proof of chicanery, I was undaunted. Besides, what was Colquhoun's oratory but an attempt to promote himself? He knew that his demise would come all the quicker without my help. He was the one I distrusted.

It made me cautious for a while, but I had not been deceived (as such), and saw no reason why the Company should not use these methods. Others, no doubt, did the same and, the people being wild with grievance, it was not unreasonable that the Company, too, should be cautious and reveal their hands slowly. The promoters found the fertile ground they were hoping for. Each day the people knew more without knowing how they had come by such knowledge. A morsel whispered in an ear by the castle was repeated at Holyrood within the hour – that night there was talk of nothing else as one half of the city excitedly told the other what it already knew. One name was at the centre of this fervour: Paterson. With this new and more human subject the poetasters redoubled their efforts. He was Glorious Paterson, Paterson the Prophet returning to lead his people to the Promised Land, he was John the Baptist to the Messiah of Prosperity, he was Paterson the far-sighted, Paterson Chrysostom. He was the bringer of gifts not only to his own people, but also to the naked savage of the ripe jungles the Company would possess. Soothed and refined by the gentle guidance of 'Patersonian Government' such sorry ones would clothe themselves in black broadcloth and give thanks in fantastic churches, roofed with banana leaves. Finest of all, the inspirer of the Company of Scotland became known simply as The Man Paterson. I knew well enough this was too much for any man, especially one we had not set eyes on. But these were the people's hopes, not Paterson's promises. I was ready to look this horse in the mouth when it came and, besides, how many of these hopes have not already been fulfilled?

Destiny is mixed for us all. Though she has smiled on me exceedingly since those days she has been pitiless in insisting that I am never quite present at the start of great events. The launch of the Company, of Hope itself in the midst of that blasted, rotting, rain-sodden spring, was to be no exception. Still marching about the town with my London paper under my arm and, as there was ever less to do at Colquhoun's, spending more time with Susanna, I was most absurdly taken by surprise. While half a dozen of the best rooms in the city were being taken up, while six horses of unusual quality were being admired in the stable-yards and while notices were being put in all the Edinburgh papers I somehow remained oblivious. It is true that, once arrived, the directors made quick work. Between the advent of Sir Robert Blackwood, Samuel Vetch, James Smith, James

Balfour, Sir Robert Chiesly and others and the opening of the subscription books in Purdie's, barely a week was allowed to pass. True also that for the best part of that week, sunk into a state of melancholic despondency about my prospects, I perched above the city in Widow Gilbert's top room beside or on top of Susanna, whispering earnest denigrations of Caldwell's character in her ears.

It was a Thursday, a little before noon, when I finally tired of hearing that his coin was as good as mine. I tumbled out of the house in a poor sort with nothing in mind but to wander through the streets and contemplate my situation. Making myself the entire object of my attention, I drifted for near an hour or two before noticing a strange reversal in the normal flow of people for that part of the city in the early forenoon. I assumed there had been a rumour of some cheaper grain or a cartload of turnips scavenged from a watery field and thought no more of it. When I came to myself again I was alone, as if I had mistaken the day and set out to work on a holiday. There was a sudden angry shouting in one of the nearby houses. I heard, 'I will go, I will!' and a door burst open, a youth of about fifteen almost knocking me off my feet as he ran up the close steps in the direction of the High Street. A man appeared in the doorway, straightening his hair, flinching when he found himself observed, folding up a torn and inky exercise book. He shook his head and with an expression of pain invited me to add my disapproval. I declined, turning on my heels to run after the boy. What else could it be?

I slithered on to the mud of the High Street gasping for breath. The boy had already disappeared into a crowd that engulfed the Mercat Cross and buzzed and elbowed its way about the entrance to Mrs Purdie's coffee-house. I ran to the edge of it and hoisted myself on a pair of convenient shoulders. Before being shaken off with curses and sent sprawling on the ground, I glimpsed the doorway everyone was jostling towards. I was right. It had started! Tacked across the lintel was a band of paper with the words *Company of Scotland* painted in black and below in smaller letters, *Subscriptions Received Here from Noon each Day*. For nearly two hours I had wandered about a half-deserted city like a foreigner not knowing what day it was. I added my own curses to the excited, jostling rumble of the crowd. Not against the man who had thrown me off, but against myself. How was such idiocy possible? As I scrambled to my feet and brushed the ordure from my clothes as best I could, those two hours loomed in my mind like a fatal error. The Company must already have employed clerks; those who had left their whores in time had been there before me. My place had already been taken! Desperate at the thought of this loss, I ran round to another part of the crowd and tried to push my way through. A vicious thicket of elbows and heels bit back at me. There is no rule of charity that requires a man to step aside from his last chance.

A stratagem was required and I retired to the far side of the High Street to consider. I thought over what I had learned from my models; Colquhoun and Caldwell, consummate liars both, the estimable Widow Gilbert, respectably passionate for money. A mood of urgency invaded me and, if it be not too impious, what I can only describe as a spiritual anxiety, as if a failure at that point would demand an unending repayment for the rest of my days. Every minute more people arrived on foot or in carriages. From the hired carriages, groups of five or a half-dozen would hastily unpack themselves and join the fray. The finer vehicles circled cautiously, their curious, perhaps amused occupants content to spectate. I eyed the crowd with trepidation as it began to give off a perceptible steam into the dank air. It had a menacing harmony about it as though, with a single corporate snap, it might swallow up an unwelcome intruder. I swallowed hard and strode towards it shouting to left and right in a puff-chested Colquhounish manner: 'Make way there, make way! Plenty of time, sir, nothing to worry about. Come back tomorrow, madam. Let a gentleman through, will you? There's work to be done here. Who are you pushing!'

Though there was hardly a Mosaic parting of the waters, I was able to struggle through to the doorway. Here the game ended when I collided with a towering block of a man hired, by the look of him, straight from the docks and solely on the strength of his obstructive properties. He looked down at me with an expression which seemed to say, 'I've had a dozen of you already today and you'll have no more luck than the rest of them.' What he actually said was nothing at all. The crowd pressed in behind me, lusting for my comeuppance. Seized equally by fear and inspiration I started my plea: 'Colquhoun!' I blurted, not knowing what I was saying but guided by some low instinct to the first word that came to mind in matters of bluster and fraud.

'Mackenzie, sir, of Colquhoun and Mackenzie,' I thought it best to elevate myself to partner status, 'victuallers. Come by order of the directors.'

'And which directors would they be?'

'*The* Directors,' I said, in a tone of incredulousness at such an idiotic question.

The fellow was unwilling to be shamed. '*Which* directors?' he asked, in a simpering imitation. There was some laughter behind me, and a sound like the grinding of teeth.

The only name I knew was that of Paterson himself, and it seemed absurd that I should speak it, like knocking on the door of a palace and saying one had brought a pie and a jug of beer for the king.

There was no greater crime that day than stealing another man's place – it had become more precious and more real than a loaf or a coin. Sure enough, the crowd was not long in throwing the first stone.

'Queue-jumper!' came from one side. 'Cheat! Pull him back!' from others. Hands scrabbled for the collar of my coat. Deliverance appeared in the form of an urchin who squeezed from between the legs of the crowd and made a dash for the door. Colossus lunged to the right while I made for the left. The sudden movement and indignant cries were misinterpreted by the rest of the crowd, which surged forward, thinking a general entry had been signalled. My interrogator soon had too much to deal with to worry about me. I was in, mumbling a prayer of thanks and reflecting that other great fortunes had, no doubt, begun in similar ignominy.

Inside, Mrs Purdie's coffee-house was more ordered, if no less crowded. My explosive entry brought some looks in my direction, but I was soon invisible again. Here the better orders were pressed shoulder to shoulder. The watches were gold, the snuff-boxes silver, the cuffs the finest lace from Bruges, the stockings all silk. The scent of the damp and slightly overheated human animal was only weakly detectable here under the masks of orris and violet. By a hundred subtle signs, the quietness of the voices, the cut of the cloth, the turn of a hand in making a point, the restraint of a laugh, an enquiry as to the health of one's Dutch stocks, I learned that I had entered a new world. Colquhoun could hardly have clung to these men with his fingertips. I cleared him that day, like a false summit.

The subscribers were in two groups. Those who had already done their business spoke amongst themselves of the state of the world, the weather, the war and so on while others waited in three lines before a long trestle bearing three ledgers, each inscribed by its own clerk. I cast a malevolent eye over these cuckoos, wondering which one I might oust in turn. By the scratching of their pens I could tell they had poor hands, while the one on the right was too slow and would frequently ask gentlemen to repeat themselves. I told myself there was hope yet. A white-haired ancient looked over their shoulders and made occasional announcements.

'A thousand pounds! Well done, Mr Farquhar!'

The phrase would be repeated about the room – 'A thousand pounds. Another thousand there. Well done, sir! Off with a bang, eh?' A polite gesture of amusement followed this. I had not seen the man before but surmised he was Farquhar of Farquhar and George, Gunsmiths, a good business to have been in over the last few years and one that would be better still when the Company started to equip its ships. I looked over those prosperous, settled men, each one the head of some concern, a nurtured inheritance from a father or a grandfather. Slow and steady is their religion, all care for what is mine and my son's. Of those I recognized and can still remember today, I am certain there was not one who did not get all his money back and more in the form of orders from the Company. Their money circulated through the Company, it jumped ship and swam back to shore before that signal gun was fired and we hoisted sail to move out of the Forth. What remained, what has paid for Direcksone in Amsterdam to build this ship, what paid for this paper, this ink and the oil in this lamp is the money of the common people, those who milled outside, who, as night fell and the books were closed, were told to come back another day.

As I watched the proceedings I became aware that, whereas I had previously attracted no attention at all, I was now attracting too much. A circle had cleared around me and unfriendly looks were sent in my direction. The filth daubed on my clothes when I was thrown down on to the street, now warmed by the air in Mrs Purdie's coffee-house, had begun to make its presence felt. My own senses, dulled by the intensity of my reflections on the scene before me, were the very last to detect the offence. As a consequence, when the stench rising from my stockings and coat tails finally brought me to myself I was the centre of an unkindly and universal curiosity. Retreat through the crowd being impossible, I excused myself as best I could and, crimson-faced, made for the only corridor open to me. I blundered along it and found myself in the back close where I stood panting, shaking, biting my lip.

I ran back into the High Street by another way and dodged through the opposing flow of people until I came to Baillie Ritchie's house. I changed clothes, caught my breath and then made the return journey, pushing my way past the crowd, which now blocked the High Street entirely, and going on until I could turn into the silence of Dr Sinclair's Close. I peered through the window fearing that Mr Watson might have come in to shake his head at the books, but the outer office was empty. I performed a slow dance across the floor, avoiding the most treacherous of the floorboards, and held my ear against Colquhoun's door – nothing, not even a snore. I went back to the close and let myself into the upper warehouse, pausing again to listen for any signs of my employer. Downstairs, Mr Beattie, the sole inhabitant of that intoxicating dungeon since our boy left to rattle his way through the wars, dozed over a half-consumed glass of brandy.

'Mr Beattie!'

'Wha'! Damn you, young Mackenzie! What are you doing skulking about like a thief? I was just in the middle of checking the brandy. These barrels aren't what they ought to be, you know, it'll need spirit adding before long, I was saying to him to—'

'Never mind that. He's not here.'

'Oh,' said Beattie, crestfallen. 'Shall I pour you one, then?'

I drained what was left in his glass in a single gulp. 'No, you won't. We've got some work on.'

'Really?'

'We need a hogshead of our cheapest and a keg of that port from Dundee.'

'For when?' he asked, not stirring a muscle.

'Now. At Mrs Purdie's.'

'What's their hurry? And, anyway, did the master say so? Where is he?'

'Yes, he did say so.'

I said it unhesitatingly, but was already half in a panic about how I would explain it to him. If he asked where I had learned to lie without blushing, I would tell him. But I knew that for such a crime more would be needed, much more.

After further exhortations to Mr Beattie and a brief excursion to find a horse, we rattled out fully laden and in two minutes drew up by the edge of the crowd. I jumped down, fixed the spigot in the large cask, engaged two vagrant children for a shilling each to do whatever Mr Beattie told them to and blew the dust out of some shoddy tin cups, a heap of which had occupied a corner of Colquhoun's warehouse from time immemorial. I was ready to make my first essay in public oratory.

'Free wine!'

'Awa 'n' bile yer heid, sonny!' was the reply, along with a noise I care not to reproduce here.

It was a harsh, but sound lesson. I learned that day that audiences, like women, need to be carefully prepared before having the essential business put to them. The idea of free wine was, of course, entirely incredible, not least to Mr Beattie himself, who looked at me aghast and declared I must have made some mistake. I ignored him and tried again.

'People of Edinburgh, future stockholders in our great Company,' a slight cheer here, 'on behalf of the Company I would like to offer you some free refreshment while you wait to subscribe to our great venture.'

I held out the first cup to a bleary Methuselah, deep in the confusions of age, who seemed merely to have tottered over to find out why there was a crowd there at all. The appearance of a cup of free wine answered his question. He accepted and drank. The nearest onlookers hesitated to see if I would demand a coin from him after all, cheats and sharpers being all around. When I did not, there was a general surge in our direction. I left a flustered Mr Beattie in charge, too overwhelmed to utter any further protest.

With the stronger of my two new employees I manhandled the keg of port towards the door of Mrs Purdie's. Without a word needing to be said, Colossus stood aside and let us in. Once inside, I set our burden on the nearest convenient table, announced myself as Mackenzie of Colquhoun and Mackenzie and asked if the gentlemen would care to accept a modest gift from us as a token of our good wishes for the Company. With the help of one of Mrs Purdie's servers, a supply of respectable glasses was produced and our compliment graciously sipped by one and all. I carried a glass of it myself to the withered supervisor of clerks and did my obeisance to him in the hope that he might have the power of taking on and putting off. This Mr Nixon – may he be eternally rewarded for his part in my ascent – received my compliments on his administration as his due and my criticism of how the nearest clerk distinguished his O from his zero as the word of one who knew. All in all, this timely libation to the gods of commerce had in fullest measure the desired effect. The waters of

Lethe themselves could not have done the job better. The well-bred memories of those gentlemen, some of whom I would come to know well, retained not a single trace of my mortification an hour before, nor did I ever come across any mention of that incident, nor any evidence, however indirect, that such a thing took place except in this record itself where I am sworn to keep nothing from myself.

The value of my stock restored I went outside to lend a hand to the beleaguered Mr Beattie. I clambered back on to the cart and helped to hand out the wine until our hogshead was dry. As the evening settled and urchins licked the drips from the spigot, I noticed a figure by the corner of Mrs Purdie's. It was d'Azevedo the Jew. The one I had last seen eating fire for coppers in the Wilful Willy. His involvement in the Company was not yet known to me and I believed his presence was coincidental. He was too far away and the light too faded for me to catch his expression, but I fancied there was approval.

The next day the common people were admitted for the first time and I was there before dawn to ensure a good vantage-point from which to view the proceedings and, if the opportunity arose, to exchange a lubricating word or two with Mr Nixon. In the mind of the people, as well as in my own, that day was the true start of the Company. There had been no show for the major subscribers – they had been spoken to privately by the directors and had, in any case, little need of explanations in the matter of companies, capital, subscriptions and the like. For the people, it would be different. When I arrived, men were finishing a wooden platform and erecting above it a vast sign painted on canvas: 'The Company of Scotland', it said, in letters as large as man. They formed an alphabet archipelago around which miniature puff-chested argosies sailed on a painted sea, trailing bright white saltires.

I sat on the edge of the platform, chewing the bread I had brought for my breakfast, and let three hours pass as the crowd gathered again. As the clocks struck nine Mr William Paterson stepped up on to the platform. He allowed a long, long pause to stretch out, testing the strength of the silence he imposed on us. He spoke simply and manfully: 'People of Scotland, I am William Paterson.'

There was a great cheer as they realized they were gazing on the hero of the balladeers. Of his own words I remember little. His speech was like music rather than words, and put a thrill in the chest of everyone who heard it, whether or not they grasped its meaning. Our grievances were recounted, and in that list every man recognized his own sufferings and saw how they were the sufferings of his country too. The piteous state at which we had arrived was set out in terms that struck at every heart. The causes were counted out one by one until we saw that it was not merely fortune that had brought us to such a pass, but insult too. Our merchants, the canniest and most upstanding in the world, had been kept out of the English colonies for no better reasons than malice and greed. Our trade with our friends the French had also been cut off as they had been cruelly set upon by a cynical confederacy, amongst whom our own king was to be numbered. Proof beyond question – his voice dropped almost to a whisper, such was the odiousness of the secret he had to impart to the people, pressing forward to hear it, ears cocked like dogs – proof, yes, that he cared not whose bed he shared. The crowd was stately – they shook their heads, wished it were not so, but could not deny it. We were reminded of the cold, eloquently made to feel it again. As for hunger, the briefest mention only was necessary. For a third of the audience it was present as they listened, for the rest a looming fear.

Perhaps others did not know of these sufferings. Perhaps the King himself did not know. True, the crowd admitted it; it wanted to be fair. I waited. Would he now soften their hearts as easily as he had hardened them? No, rather he was preparing them for their second firing. If the King did not know, it was because he did not care to know, because he had not once set foot in his northern kingdom, nor was likely to. If the people were hungry it was because the King cared not for his people's pains. He need only lift his little finger – there was Paterson's finger playing the role of the King. So easy it would be, so effortless. He need only lift his little finger to put a loaf in the hands of every poor man in the country. Paterson's hands held that loaf while the most ragged of his listeners smelt it, felt its warmth on their palms, ate it with their eyes. Their hunger bit more sharply as he discoursed on how full southern bellies were, how warm their fires, how heavy their purses. It was true, then, as many had always suspected – the English were red-handed in their wealth.

The cure for all these ills, for the implacable malice of the world? It could not be more simple, more transparent in its logic, more compelling in its morality or more audacious in its conception. We should go begging no more to those from whom we had received so many slights, but should make the lives we wanted purely through our own efforts. Cut off from all that could betray or deceive, relying on the purity of our own native will and genius, failure was impossible.

'People of Scotland, I come to put the means to that triumph before you.'

I enjoyed it well enough, I must admit, and thought that if I ever had to give wine away to a crowd again I would know how to do it. All the same, I did not join in the roar of acclamation that greeted the end of his speech. Something – and I have noticed it since in other situations – came between me and the crowd at that moment of unconditional 'Yes'. I cannot say I regret it, but wish to make it as clear as I can that my commitment to the Company is in no way less than those who so much enjoyed their own noisy enthusiasm that day. On the contrary, I would say it is a superior commitment, refined in its reasons beyond the sway of mere emotions. I realized that I was, in my nature, one of the black-clothed gentlemen whose company I had shared the day before rather than one of the yelling, yea-saying crowd, necessary as they are for such ventures. Like the price of grain, my ambition rose again, leaving me hungrier than ever.

After the excitement of the speech the crowd formed itself more or less into an orderly queue. The subscriptions now were for ten pounds here, fifty there, occasionally a hundred, never more than two hundred. Even so, not a few of the hands that signed on that day, and on the thirty days thereafter for which the subscription books were open, trembled as they wrote their names beside such impossible numbers.

As news of the Company spread, people began to make their way from further afield. The hidden gold of the nation now appeared in a great flood. Those who had sworn every oath they knew that they had parted with their last penny for a quarter loaf now levered up their flags, prised out their loose bricks, sprang the catches on their secret drawers, scrabbled in the darkest corners of their eaves, dug up their buried boxes to throw their all into the coffers of the Company. Hunger had not squeezed this money from the people, but the Company brought it flowing forth willingly, down to the last true and honest ounce. By a triple alchemy the heart and soul of our people was turned into that gold, and that gold into wood and that wood into these ships, the greatest of which creaks and sighs around me as I write.

*

OF LATE I have been a creature of lamplight, taking to the deck at dusk, which comes early at these latitudes. For the last few days there has been more to avoid than just the heat. Between the captains and the rougher sort of colonist there has been a creeping toleration as the boldest put their heads above the hatches first and have been gradually followed by the others. No cessation of hostilities has been signed, however, and both sides are unsure whether they are in a state of peace or war. Three days out of Madeira a half-dozen of the worst offenders were given their due on the main deck, all male colonists in compulsory attendance. The exercise was repeated on the *Dolphin* and the *St Andrew*. Mr Shipp shook his head sadly as he stood by me, watching the punishment. As the last was taken off, still steady on his feet, he sighed loudly. In my foolish tenderness I imagined some fellow feeling behind this, but could not have been more wrong.

'No,' he said decisively, 'no, that wasn't the way at all. It needed twenty lashes, or thirty maybe. More for that last one.'

I remonstrated with him but he would have none of it.

'Say what you like, young master, but that's not the way. There's them that punishes a man because they have to, and them that punishes him because they've got a job to do and a will to do it, come what may. If you're going to beat a man you should put your heart into it, do it good and proper. You should beat a man like a dog, once and for always, so he'll never forget. You'll only have to do it again if you don't.'

He went off to share a smoke and a jaw with some of the crew, still shaking his head. Captain Galt too full of the milk of human kindness? The thought came as a complete novelty to me – one I spent little time in dismissing. I turned my thoughts instead to Shipp and recalled that even on the hottest days I had never seen him without his shirt. Could it be that some unforgettable stripes lie beneath it?

With these unpleasantnesses and the progress of disease through our people at a rate that leaves only Dr Munro unconcerned, my airless closet below decks has become a blissful asylum, and my thoughts of the past its ideal furniture. I do not doubt that all will mend on land when, at last, we have our great work in our hands. We think on that as the moment of our salvation. Until then, the uneasy quiet of endurance will remain over us.

I am aware that after all this labour my place here remains a mystery. I have not yet brought the paths of the Company and my own life to their point of union. It was a simple enough train of events and my own part in it quite blameless. Yet it is, when you see it, a matter which you will forgive me for having delayed so long in speaking of.

My immediate crisis was Colquhoun and this pushed all other thoughts from my mind. Without negotiating him first I should have no employment of any kind, and against him I had committed the unpardonable sin, the ultimate violation of the sacred laws of trade: I had given away something for nothing. The most difficult part, namely the confession, had been made unnecessary by Mr Beattie, who had recounted every horrible detail at the earliest opportunity. It was a rational act of self-preservation from one who, I would guess, had not felt the prick of ambition since before I was born, indeed, since that forgotten day on which he joined Colquhoun and established himself under the great man's roof until he should be called to a higher place.

Mr Watson was examining the books when I entered the outer office. He told me in an expressionless, last-requests tone that I was 'required' by Colquhoun. He had been told an hour or so before and I found him in the eye of the storm. A litter of papers about the floor attested to the strength of the first blasts, while an empty bottle by a leg of the table and another by his elbow already half drained promised worse to come. At the particular moment of my entry he was mastering himself, picking distractedly at a last fleck of gilding on the arm of his chair.

It started quietly with a sighing, head-in-hand appeal to tell him that it wasn't true, that Mr Beattie, somewhat subject to confusion for all his virtues, had got it wrong. When I was unable to satisfy him on that point he embarked on his speech and, it must be said, it was one of his best. An incontinent cross-breeding of martyred apologia and shamelessly hyperbolical prosecution, it was the sort that, had it been declaimed by some feed rascal in a Roman court would, to this very day, be dinned into schoolboys as an example of the highest art. Where would I have been without him, which, of all my goods, did I not owe to him and the employment he had so generously provided? And now what does he find? The viper at the breast, so much the more bitter for having thought of me as a son, perhaps even as the inheritor of the business. He became lachrymose as he elaborated on my betrayal. Hitherto unsuspected learning was paraded – resources reserved only for occasions of unique importance such as this. From Brutus and his hellish fate through the bloody parricides of myth and history to the pelican, greedy for the blood of those who had given it life, the injured cry of his monstrous aggrandizement broke over me. Was I deliberately trying to destroy him? No, I needn't answer that.

The truth was all too clear. Was I a habitual thief, who else had I treated this way, how many years of hardened corruption had been required for me to arrive at this pitch of malevolence? He decided that it was not theft: it was too trivial a term. Rather it was bloodshed, a vandal raid on the sacred red fluid. He concluded by anathematizing me as the Antichrist. I had arrived at Cana to turn the miraculous wine back into water, indeed into nothing at all in an act of satanic annihilation.

'Pouf!'

His hands, wrestling with each other to this point, sprang apart to illustrate the vacuity into which I had enchanted his stock.

Dr Lennox's words repeated themselves in my mind once again: 'Learn what you can and leave him.' The time had nearly arrived and I was tempted to end the matter there and then. I wanted to take my turn on the stage, to talk of my honour, of my heroic but unrecognized labours on his behalf, of the dozen gentlemen of the highest rank who were waiting at that very moment to hear of my availability. The difference was that Colquhoun could afford his delusions, for a while at least, but I could not. I had a vision of myself with one foot on the Company, and one on Colquhoun. They drifted apart like a boat from the quay with cold water threatening beneath. More time was needed to make a safe jump from one to the other. So I lied. I said Mr Beattie had indeed misunderstood the situation. The people were not charged for the wine because the Company would pay. It had all been carefully arranged. In reality he was in my debt for having seen such an opportunity and being able to take it.

Colquhoun was not an easy man to deceive. He leaned closer to me and demanded, without his buffoonery now, but with genuine menace: 'So where's the money, Mr Mackenzie?'

I said they were creditworthy. He said they were charlatans and demanded to see it by close of business the next day. I said there would be no problem and started to wonder how I might find another employer.

I put my lie down on paper to make it more convincing and made up a bill for the wine I had given away. With this shameless fraud in my hand I walked up the High Street, feeling sure that my ambitions were on the very edge of extinction. There was no queue outside Mrs Purdie's by then, but a steady traffic of subscribers and spectators and, fortunately for me, provisioners of all the necessities of business buzzing to and from the great national customer. I entered the scene of the recent excitements and went upstairs to where the upper rooms had been taken over by various newly employed functionaries of the Company. All the doors were open, as if ready for the great flood of traffic between them, which might be necessary at any moment. In spite of this readiness, clock-ticks and pen-scratches were the only noise as I stood in the corridor. I determined that if my great career was to be cut short by the exposure of such an outrageous deception – albeit one sprung from the very best of motives – there was nothing to be gained by delaying the fall of the axe. I walked into the first room and was challenged by one unmistakably of the tribe of Nixon. There was something strangely unsettling about this etiolated creature of commerce with a body as slight as a child's but a face, as he raised it to me, creased with decades of squinting at ledgers in candlelight. The sort of face, I thought with a shock of repulsion, that might be my own one day.

I had so despaired of success on this absurd commission that I had not rehearsed a word of what I might say. My mouth gaped silently as he demanded to know my business, the single thought in my mind that it could only be a relief to be thrown out on the street. Well-used, it seemed, to idiot messenger-boys, he snatched the paper from my hand, returning it to me almost at once. 'This is Incoming. You want Outgoing, second door on the left.'

I went where he told me, this time with the presence of mind to say I had been sent by Incoming as I presented my forgery, hoping in this way to give the impression that I had already passed muster. This second man, by his appearance another of the wizened tribe of Nixon, took the paper and held it before his face in complete immobility, like a pointer frozen at the sight of a dropped pheasant. The blatancy of the fraud was surely obvious, it had stunned him, he was casting about for words adequate to the situation but had been struck dumb by the effrontery of it all. Or at least that is what I assumed, and that is what seemed to be confirmed by the ineffectual quiverings of his lips.

'A moment.'

He left the room with what seemed to me admirable composure. I waited, eager for it to be over, my wits struggling to make sense of such a grotesque situation. I was now trying to defraud the Company in which I had invested all my hopes! I did not doubt that the clerk would return mob-handed and that within the hour I would be gazing miserably at the inside of the Tolbooth. I had decided to confess – an appeal for mercy was my only way. After a few seconds of this I discarded the idea and elected instead to blame all on Colquhoun. The clerk returned on his own and forestalled me with a slight smile. He counted out the coins on his desk and asked that I sign a receipt.

Aside from grinding my teeth on my way down the stairs to stop myself laughing, my memory of that escape recalls two thoughts, both of which seem to me now to be equally outrageous. The first was a sense of anger that the Company could so casually pay out the precious resources of its subscribers. The second was one of that class of secrets that make one guilty merely by knowing and understanding them – namely, that the world is only as honest as it is because men have not guessed how easily they may deceive.

A commotion in the street announced what must at once be the happiest, the unhappiest and the queerest turn of fate in my story. There was a strange, desperate screaming, the like of which I had only heard before when an old dog, too slow or blind to avoid a hay-cart, had been run over in the street. There had been some collision and through the screen of onlookers I could see the hoofs of a horse thrashing until its traces were cut and it galloped off down the street. The screaming continued, always the same note, hopeless, uncontrollable, the sort of screaming that only ends one way. I pushed my way through and found an upturned cart and barrels of nails split open on the cobbles. Under the heaviest of these was no dog, but the white hair and scrawny neck of Mr Nixon. Not a hand went forward to help, such was the repulsive force of that ghastly noise. The edge of the barrel settled on his neck with a crack and there was silence.

Within five hours I was Secretary to the Company of Scotland.

UNTIL YESTERDAY Mr Shipp was obliged to mount a watch on all our supplies of wines and liquors. This is not, I am glad to say, the result of any sudden passion for intoxification but of Captain Galt's announcement three days previously that on crossing the line he would consent to 'the usual ceremonies'. This delighted the crew but baffled me. All the more so as several of them refused my requests for an explanation, one of them very brusquely. I finally persuaded Mr Shipp to satisfy my curiosity, whereupon I learned that amongst the sea-going fraternity there is a special virginity, a seal of the land, as it were, which is only broken by crossing the tropic line. The crew anticipated the event secure in their immunity, all having crossed it many times before, or so they claimed, and took some pleasure in alarming the more timorous colonists as to what they might expect. The celebration involves a rough baptism, indeed a near drowning, of several unfortunates who have neither crossed the line before nor are able to ransom themselves with what is known as the tropic bottle. Hence the guard put on that section of our stores although, come the day itself, so many were able to pay that fee that I suspect Mr Shipp of having come away with a pretty sum for all his guarding.

The winds would hardly have made a candle flicker and the ships, with all their sails reefed in, drifted so close to each other that it seemed for a day that we were a sort of village not so different from the ones we had left behind.

As the hour approached we took on the mood of a country fair, or a holy day in a small town after a hard year, determined to forget its troubles. Although under such conditions we would not have moved above an inch in an hour, Captain Galt and Mr Cunningham appeared on the quarterdeck to take our position. This they did with a theatrical deliberation, as actors wishing to convey the meaning of their business to the remotest members of the audience. At last Mr Cunningham came forward to the rail and, addressing the ship rather than Captain Galt who stood behind him, shouted: 'Crossing the line, sir!'

A great cheer went up from the crew, and a somewhat weaker cry from the colonists who swiftly divided into those who had their brandy or Malmsey about them and those who began to fear a ducking. As for myself, I made for the quarterdeck and stood in the protective aura of Galt and Cunningham. All the same, I had concealed a small flask of geneva in my pocket as a guarantee.

The announcement was the signal for our little world to be turned upside-down for the duration of the ceremonies. The crew gathered together on the main deck to elect their 'Admiral', whom they raised on their shoulders with a martial roar. He was paraded about in this manner, glowering at likely victims. He pointed to one who was instantly seized and brought for trial before the topsy-turvy court. The Admiral presided, his authority now symbolized by a velvet cap and a scarlet sash. Had he crossed the line before, or was it true that he was a hopeless landlubber? The man confessed, the Admiral's minions growled their disapproval. The sentence? Fined one tropic bottle, payable instanter! True terror had never been in the man's eyes and it was with a predictable grin that he paid up, first the Admiral, then a half-dozen of his men swigging it dry before tossing the empty bottle over the side. On the *St Andrew* revolution had taken hold even quicker. We turned just in time to see the splash made by one of the boys as they threw him off the main spar and then dragged him in like a tunny-fish, hauling him up the side feet first. A miraculous reversal of that other, funereal ceremony, which is becoming so frequent.

Infuriated by being beaten to the first ducking, our own Admiral declared that he 'smelt one below decks'. Three of his minions went down and soon brought up a struggling youth who demanded that they unhand him, then declared that he couldn't swim and started to squeal like a piglet, greatly exciting his captors. In a moment they fixed a rope around his ankles, hauled him up and sat him on the edge of the spar.

'Wet or dry?' demanded the Admiral.

'Wet! Wet! Wet!' was the universal response.

He was pushed off, falling on the water with a slap, flat on his belly. He started to flounder and thrash and cry out for help causing much amusement. They dragged him in quickly enough to make sure he came to no harm, hanging him by the ankles to get the sea out of his lungs, then clapping him on the back, congratulating him on being a true salt and reviving him with a mouthful from another of their extorted tropic bottles.

In this way the entertainment went on till darkness. Then, with their great half-tun in the middle of the main deck filled with liquors of every description, the music and the dancing started. There was a fiddler, much finer than you would guess from the look of him, and sometimes a boy with a fife. Both drank passionately at every break and their music became wilder and stranger as the night went on. The dancers would drag in their erstwhile victims, showing them the steps to complete their initiations. All were now dry and hale and bragging of the courage with which they had faced their ordeals. The Admiral and his men made much of them and all was soon forgiven. Nor were the sick forgotten, a ruffianly band being deputed to go about below decks so that soon, excepting the officers and a few gentlemen, there was not a sober man on board.

At eight Captain Galt, who had left Mr Cunningham to supervise the celebrations, held a dinner in his cabin for a number of the gentlemen on board. I enjoyed the honour of an invitation. Reverend Mackay and his deputy Mr Stobo were there, also Dr Munro, Mr Cunningham, of course, and three gentlemen I did not know so well. They are, as I understand it, gentlemen volunteers and two of them also stockholders in a small way. It turned out to be a rather curious evening, much of which I feel I did not understand, rather as if the conversation had occasionally drifted into a foreign language – that is, in addition to the few comments Reverend Mackay passed to Mr Stobo in Gaelic. In keeping with the celebratory nature of the occasion the company avoided discussion of our more immediate problems and we – or rather they, as I remained a mute observer – contented themselves with salon banalities until Captain Galt embarked on a series of metaphysical speculations of a most refined abstraction. These interested him very much more than the rest of the company which, after a lengthy struggle with the topic, began to show its irritation. Satisfied to have arrived at such a point, he allowed the matter to be dropped and remained in silence for a good half-hour as the rest of the table talked over general matters of business and their expectations for the colony. Dr Munro told us how he hoped to find new medicinal herbs and the two gentlemen less known to me enthused about the profits to be had from the Nicaragua wood and the great quantities of it that must stand in the forests, awaiting only a civilized hand to harvest them.

At this point Captain Galt asked everyone in turn if they had read Mr Hobbes's book and what did they think of it? No one knew anything of this but he was in no way discouraged and insisted on relating what remained of the evening's conversation to points he recalled from this book.

Reverend Mackay, having expressed the opinion that the book in question was not one which a man of the cloth was obliged to have any knowledge of, excused himself momentarily, causing a sudden crescendo of music and shouting as he opened the door of the cabin. Within seconds his voice, quite unmistakable, was raised in protest and then in alarm. This persisted for a short while with rising urgency until Mr Stobo commented: 'Captain Galt, I think I hear something.'

'Oh, yes?' said Captain Galt.

It appeared he would take no action until Mr Cunningham leaned across the table and had a few private words with him. He pushed his chair back and made for the door. The rest of the company, eager both to see the cause of such alarms and to take the opportunity to draw the evening to a close, followed closely on his heels. We looked down from the quarterdeck to see the Admiral directing three of his men in the business of throwing Reverend Mackay over the side. The latter, quite unmanned at the prospect of this salty baptism, was making more noise than sense as he clung desperately to the rail.

'Who is that man?'

As it was perfectly plain, I can only say that the purpose of our captain's question was to delay rescue to the very last moment. I think I also noticed a certain gleam in Dr Munro's eyes.

Mackay was now a third of the way over the rail, and the bulkier third at that so he seemed likely to tip over at any moment.

'Seaman Gillespie! That will do.'

Their burden was reluctantly dropped on to the deck.

'You are unharmed, Mr Mackay?'

Noises came from between two coils of rope, but no words.

'My apologies, sir. My men . . . in the darkness. Had they known it was you . . .'

With a nod to the rest of us he bade us goodnight and withdrew.

At midnight the Admiral's power was over, and though the singing and drinking went on for some hours, the ships at last began to quieten. From about four, snoring and the calls of the watch were the only noises that eddied out over the glassy ocean. After barely an hour, work began again. With sore heads and a thousand stories to tell, the crews and the colonists slowly reappeared. Mr Mackay did not show himself till late in the day. Neither, out of sympathy perhaps, did Mr Stobo. I cannot say that relations between the secular and spiritual arms of our enterprise have been at all improved by these events, but for the coldness we carried away with us from Madeira it has been the perfect remedy.

As if it had paused for no other reason than for our convenience, the wind rose in the mid-morning just as it had dropped eighteen hours before. In the two days since, we have made good progress, the ever-decreasing degrees of latitude being read out each noon as an encouragement to the colonists. For some, such encouragement has become a necessity. Uncertain that they will ever see land again, their fear aggravates their conditions and nowhere is this figure more eagerly awaited than in the sick bays where there is great faith in the curative powers of landfall.

These bays, constructed on one of the deepest decks according to Dr Munro's directions, consist only of canvas screens which the loblolly boys keep moist with a mixture of vinegar and tar water so that the infections are contained within them. These neither fully mask the odours of putrefaction nor the groans of those who lie behind them so that that part of the ship, which I am occasionally obliged to pass in the course of my inspections, has taken on a hellish aspect.

Two days before we crossed the line a feeble voice came from behind the canvas as I passed. 'Is it land? Have you seen it? Land?'

I kept silent, but the voice was persistent, demanding an answer at great cost to its owner, struggling through a terrible breathlessness and a deep rattling wheeze from the very depths of the lungs.

Dr Munro appeared behind me, carrying a shaded lantern and his box of drugs. He nodded and pantomimed the word 'Yes'.

'Yes,' I said aloud, 'it's land. In half a day.'

'God bless you, sir.'

Munro smiled and shrugged and disappeared behind the canvas.

I had an opportunity to speak with him the next day at which he told me the man was already dead.

'It didn't worry your conscience, I hope, that lie?'

I shook my head.

'I only ask because I had the good Mr Stobo down with me a while ago for a pastoral visit. You see . . .'

He constructed another morsel of salt beef and dried apricots, bit off half and continued his story as he chewed through it.

'. . . they all think they'll get better as soon as they reach land. Depends what sort of land, I suppose, but anyway that's what they think, it's all they talk about, the colonists, I mean, not the crew. Any land is home for them now and they've got it into their heads it'll do them good. They may well be right, and in any case believing it won't do them any harm. So down there we've been half a day – you picked the right answer, Roderick – from land for the last fortnight. Except, that is, when Mr Stobo visited us. He declined to bear false witness and went about ramming the last hope of salvation back below the horizon. I swear two of them gave up the fight before he'd got back to the main deck, and the third not more than an hour after. I'd rather have the yellow fever than that man at my bedside.'

I asked him if it was the yellow fever they died of. He denied it jauntily, tearing at his bread, gulping down wine. 'Not in the least! You've got to get there before you get that. Wait till you see it, Roderick, it's a grand disease, the yellow fever. No, these men all drowned.'

'Drowned?'

'Oh, yes. Any fluid will do, it doesn't have to be seawater. That's one of the less pernicious, in fact. They drowned in their own pulmonary mucus and rotten blood. A pint in each lung is all it takes, when they're weak enough.'

He emptied the bottle, dividing its contents between our two glasses.

'Are you interested in physic, Roderick?'

I almost confessed my visit to the Anatomy Theatre, but thought better of it as I watched his appetite increase as he talked of such loathsomeness while my own withered away to nausea. I left my wine or, as it seemed to me then, my glass lung drowning in diseased blood. He gave me a roguish smile, knowing full well the effect of the thoughts he had put into my mind.

He sat back and loosened his belt. 'No, what this lot have got they probably brought with them. They were weak from the start. That's why it's so much worse in the *Rising Sun*.'

'It is?'

'Of course. Never put a weak chest in a new ship. It's the green timbers: they exhale. It always does for them in the end. Still, if this were the English navy they'd be happy with losses of a third. Barring a pandemic we'll come in well under that, thanks to your ever humble servant. Those who do make a splash wouldn't have been much use anyway. The only other problems are a few venereals; souvenirs of Madeira. That's always the way: what you find on board has been brought from onshore, and if you do have a clean ship, at your first call after a long voyage your men will catch the port's diseases and die like infants. There's the secret of health for you, Roderick: one must never have lived on land and must never leave the sea.'

He turned to his pipe as a gentleman volunteer at the other end of our table made to leave. As the door closed Munro looked about.

'I think I've solved my patients' spiritual problem. Met Stobo this morning, and congratulated him on his enormous courage, told him how much I thought his faith in divine protection did him credit. "What a fine example you set, Mr Stobo, I told him, coming down to the sick bay to do your duty in spite of the malignity of the infections that lurk there, doing what little you can to ease the hideous suffering of the dying in their last moments, knowing that were it not for the especial protection of our Lord you would surely go the same way yourself." Guinea to a groat I never see his sleekit hide down there again!'

It was a wager I found easy to decline and our conversation might have ended there had his remarks not prompted me to put a last question to which I received a very curious answer. Was he not himself at a very great risk from his work?

'Roderick, did no one ever tell you about old doctors? They're immune. Yes, totally! As invulnerable to the darts of disease as to those of love.'

Our duties recalled us. Munro, no doubt, goes about his quite happily while I have been made suspicious of the very air. Till now the fresh timbers of the *Rising Sun* seemed to my landsman's eye the finest thing about her. Am I now to believe that our own ship is poisoning us? Munro delights in such ideas and I do not think I am obliged to believe him in every detail. I have, nevertheless, resolved to spend more time on deck.

*

SINCE CROSSING THE LINE there has been little to report except for our good fortune in the weather, exceptional, says Mr Cunningham, which has blown us steadily but never roughly in the direction of our goal. Providence keeps faith with us, as we do with her.

As anticipated, while the commander and officers of the ships and the common run of the colonists and the crews have all mended their fences, Reverend Mackay has declined to step back within the pale. It must be said that he has received no encouragement to do so, Captain Galt having all but abandoned his attempts to conceal his enmity for men of the cloth. Mr Mackay himself has not helped the situation by insisting on his right to walk the quarterdeck. As soon as he had fully recovered from the unfortunate error over his identity, he resolved to make good use of this privilege in an attempt to restore his position, but it has not proved to be a wise decision. The more Reverend Mackay has stood his ground, the more Captain Galt has made clear his irritation at him being there. Yesterday, he had hardly set foot on deck when Galt, scanning the horizon with his glass, declared the presence of an English naval squadron and gave the order to clear the decks of all 'unnecessary persons', myself included. Said squadron returned below the horizon, unseen by anyone other than Galt.

This morning, very early, I chanced upon him on the main deck. Wishing to be a good friend to all honest men and thinking that I might be of some use as a diplomatist, I bade him a good morning and stood by him a while at the rail. As soon as he spoke, however, I found myself on the back foot. He insisted on addressing me in the Highland tongue, and in no wise briefly until I interrupted him to say that I never learned the language and spoke only English, whereupon he continued in the same manner as though I might suddenly understand if only he persisted a little.

'Alas, sir,' I said to him, 'I am entirely at a loss, I assure you. I have not a single word of that language.'

He looked at me sharply, trying, I thought, to put me off my ease as he declared: 'That can only be because you have forgotten it.'

I could not help but resent his Lennoxish manner and was tempted to bid him a second good morning and walk away. And yet, where to? There seemed little point when I could carry my protest no more than a few yards. I decided to call it a game, and that it would be a great triumph if I could make some progress where all else have failed.

I said I thought it unlikely that I should once have known the language and already forgotten it, not having lived long enough to forget so much.

He smiled at this, encouraged I think by the sweet taste of controversy.

'It was forgotten, young man, before you were ever thought of. It is as forgotten as godliness is forgotten. Save for a single remnant of the just, modern mankind is as far from the true tongue as from Eden itself, sir.'

I made little of this, but was happy to press ahead with my peace mission, thinking it might at least yield some amusement along the way. I feigned interest, therefore, and let my fly fall upon the still waters of Reverend Mackay's mind.

'Your remnant of the just is, I take it, a reference to the Jews?'

He snorted.

'It is not, sir, and I think you know it. I am referring to our own people, our very own, sir. What is more, I do not doubt that I can prove it. I have examined twenty of the world's most copious languages as well as our own Highland tongue and am confronted at every turn by the inescapable evidence of its being the closest descendant of the Original Tongue.'

'It is the case, then, that Adam spoke Gaelic?'

'Not exactly,' said Reverend Mackay who, seeing that I desired a detailed account of his researches, was good enough to provide me with one, the entirety of which I do not care to set down here. The core of his discoveries, or perhaps I should say of his convictions, would appear to be that when the peoples were scattered from the Tower of Babel and the curse of incommunicability set upon them, some remained closer to the Original Tongue than others and that the closest of all made their way to our fair homeland, or at least the more northerly parts of it where, to this very day, they still speak Gaelic, that being the purest relic of the Original Tongue which sleeps in us all and is the closest man has ever come to sharing the language of the angels.

What readers there may ever be of this manuscript will, I trust, give me credit for sparing them a full account of the supporting authorities, textual proofs, subsidiary *notanda*, diverging *consideranda*, and dismissals in advance of objections from the weak-minded or the downright malicious. That reader must imagine that in the space of my brief paragraph a good forty minutes passed during which the sands of time dropped slow as thistledown and by the midpoint of which my last ember of goodwill towards Mackay smothered and died. It will not seem rude or intolerant, therefore, when I admit that when the good pastor fell silent for a moment my first thoughts were of escape. And yet, as it is said, he who hesitates is lost, and so it proved. My hopes that he had been exhausted by his exposition were in vain. He had, alas, merely paused for breath and continued in equally lamentable detail, on the utility of a universal language which, he demonstrated to his entire satisfaction, must be Gaelic. This opinion, I was informed, was one from which no one but a fool or a knave would dissent when the results of his researches were made public. I offered him my congratulations on this achievement but asked if his acceptance of a position from the Company was not an intolerable distraction from such important work.

'Sir,' he told me, 'I will do my duty by the Company in the fullest measure and so I need not hold back in telling you that I have a second motive in joining this expedition. It is to confirm my theories that I am here. In a matter of weeks, doubt will be impossible.'

'There is some scholar perhaps, you wish to consult?'

He exhaled dismissively.

'There would be little good in that, Mr Mackenzie. Your scholars are three to a farthing, sir. Leave them be where they can do no harm. It is the mouths of babes I go to hear. They will tell me the truth.'

He produced from his coat pocket a small tattered octavo and showed me the title page where I read in manuscript 'Wafer's Journal'. I was surprised to see a source of information which I am confident has not been printed, and of which the Company has always imagined itself to be the sole possessor. I said nothing of this, but admitted that, as one-time secretary, I did know the work. Mackay became visibly more animated. 'And you have read of the white Indians of Darien?'

'I have heard of them. Freaks, I believe. Wretched outcasts.'

'No, sir. Oh, no! You could not be more wrong there. I am going to speak with the white Indians of Darien and I—'

'And do you think they will understand you, Mr Mackay?'

'You have me, Mr Mackenzie. You have me!'

I thought perhaps that I might be going too far when I suggested that this would surely be because they spoke Gaelic, but was incredulous to hear Reverend Mackay half shout: 'Exactly! Exactly, sir. You run ahead of me. For what else are the white Indians of Darien but the descendants of the first Scots settlers who crossed the ocean centuries ago, centuries before that mountebank, that thief Columbus? And it may be stranger than that, Mr Mackenzie. It may be that we are not going abroad at all. No, indeed. It may be, sir, that we are going home. It may be that—'

'You're wanted below, Mackay.'

We both jumped and looked up to find Captain Galt overlooking us from the quarterdeck rail. He was in his shirt-sleeves, barber's basin in hand.

'A woman's poorly. Seems to think you could help.'

Mackay left with a brief confidential nod to me, as to one now within the fold of his secret religion.

As soon as he had clambered below decks I couldn't help myself from exclaiming: 'The man's deranged!'

From above, in the slow, growling tones of the now invisible Captain Galt, came the words: 'You're a slow judge of men, Mr Mackenzie.'

It may well be so.

One consequence of these encounters is that I have become reluctant to catch the eye of either Captain Galt or Reverend Mackay. But there is another and more sinister reason why it is timely for me to return to the gloom and stench of below-decks and spend my time with this book. There is, of course, not a word of truth in the affair but I should not fail to record it here for the sake of fullness. After a recent inspection of stores I had to report my concern at the depletion of our reserves of water, a problem made all the worse by two butts made of poorly seasoned wood going foul. Prudence required a reduction in the ration of one quarter and, on the advice of Dr Munro, a reduction of two-thirds of the spirit allowance was also ordered. Neither of these measures is at all popular and it was soon being put about that they are to be laid at my door. But Rumour's appetite was not so easily satisfied and this simple calumny was soon discarded for finer fare. It now appears that I spent my time in Madeira lolling in bordellos rather than attending to the Company's business and this explains the 'mal-provisioning' of the ships. It is no matter that our sister vessels have encountered no such problems, or that some amongst our colonists and crew have such a prodigious thirst for water only because they cannot count the difference between one glass of brandy and a dozen. Nor is it of any consequence that Mr Shipp and myself prevented a more serious problem by issuing our warning in good time.

There is an ambitious group among the colonists – a dozen or so who have found each other out and talk only amongst themselves and of what positions they will have in the colony. They would use me as a footstool, I think, to climb up to these positions and have addressed an indignant bill to Captain Galt on these 'grave matters'. I am assured by Mr Cunningham that he has, in his words, 'not yet found the time to read it'.

They do not concern me, I am sure of my ground. Be that as it may, their unfriendly looks and misfiring plots have been very tiresome and it is for these reasons that, in spite of my best intentions to spend more time breathing the wholesome air of the upper decks, I have returned to this gloomy hole to press ahead with our Company's history and my modest part in it. Whatever libels are laid against me, they are feeble creatures, and will not survive a few days' absence of what they feed on.

As for the most malignant effects of the below-decks vapours, I trust that by adding a little camphorated oil to my lamp and by burning a few grains of sulphur every day I can, God willing, keep them at bay.

NIXON'S DEMISE was my ascent. The speed was dizzying, indecent perhaps, the man hardly cold before I stepped into his shoes. I was not entirely unmoved by the circumstances. Equally, I did not reproach myself unnecessarily. Opportunities are to be used – what one man squeamishly drops another will pick up and prosper by.

I was the first to deliver news of the vacancy, returning at once to the rooms above Mrs Purdie's coffee-house. I encountered the clerk from whom I had taken the money a moment ago and asked with such solemnity to see someone in authority that he immediately did my bidding. He returned at once and led me through a door at the end of the corridor into another more finely appointed part of the building I had never seen before. I was left there, listening to voices coming through one door and a deep snoring through another that lay ajar. I approached the voices, positioning myself in front of a convenient print of ships in harbour in case the door should open suddenly. I could make no sense of what was being said but could hear an amiable tone, a genteel laugh at some piece of wit. The news had not yet reached them.

Left pacing for some time, practising my speeches of condolence and persuasion, I caught sight in the other room of a pair of booted feet, crossed and propped on a table. I moved closer, emboldened by the steady bass rumbling snores of their giant owner. I peered through the hand's-breadth opening to see the whole nether half of this person and the best part of the table whereon lay a great number of gold coins, some scattered about, others arranged in short stacks with these stacks in turn drawn up in rows and columns like an army. All in all there was a great fortune around those resting feet – enough to buy a ship, I should think, and with some left over to fill her holds. At that time, it was more gold than I had ever seen.

The sight of it had a strange, calming effect that made me forget for a moment about Nixon and his broken neck. I took it for a sign and was reassured that I was doing the right thing, that this chance was intended for me alone, that I had somehow a duty to take it. I wondered what sort of man could fall asleep with such extraordinary wealth on his table and snore away so contentedly behind a half-open door. I could never have closed my eyes on it. I pushed the door open another few inches, wincing at every tiny creak, listening with my other ear to the conversation in the second room. Closer to the edge of the table there were letters crusted with the remains of their red and green seals and one closed, ready for sending. There was a gold case that suggested a large pocket-watch but slightly oval. It lay on its back, its two sides opened till it was almost flat, like an empty cockleshell. On one side there was a radiating pattern of turquoise enamel and on the other a miniature half-portrait of a young woman with what appeared, from my position by the door, to be a squirrel. One last detail comes back to me: under the heel of his left boot he had carefully placed a folded pad of cloth. Here was a brigand who, overtaken by exhaustion in the midst of a triumphant accounting, had just time enough to take care of the polish on his table-top. From under the napkin covering his face a prodigious and unique beard extended down his chest. It was d'Azevedo, the Jew. I knew then it was no coincidence that I had seen him outside Mrs Purdie's a few days before. He was with the Company, a director perhaps? Success was doubly assured.

Suddenly, behind me, the voices were louder and a handle was turning. I stepped back smartly and adopted a respectful, waiting position. The two men took their leave of each other pleasantly and I wondered how they had managed to ignore the commotion in the street, which must surely have penetrated the room. I found myself facing the more impressive of the two. Dressed in the London fashion, his hair white as a wig and every bit as neat. His coat not quite of the usual black but of a cloth that seemed to have a thousandth part of white silk in it so that it had the black of a black pearl, or at least what I imagine to be a black pearl. A few minutes later, in the midst of that most vital conversation and while observing his strange, distracted, sideways manner I noticed that he had let himself go about the buttonholes, which were stitched with an imperial purple so dark it could hardly be seen. I had a vision of his tailor standing by his cutting table, drenched in a rainbow of silk yarns, waiting mutely for his best customer to decide how to meet the needs of both discretion and distinction. I should blush to describe him thus, for he is indeed a man of distinction and could wear it more brightly than he does without vanity. Moreover, like Mr Nixon, Samuel Vetch is another from whose misfortunes I have profited. I am in his debt for more than I can ever repay. Indeed, I owe him everything.

I was to learn that he was not an easy man to get to know. In my own case six months of hard labour would be required before the beginnings of a smile could be detected whenever our paths crossed. The process started unpromisingly with a wordless, half-enquiring look, which conveyed that he was not that interested in whatever I might have to tell him and that if I cared to turn on my heel and leave as silently as I had come, he would be all the more grateful.

I swallowed and declared myself to be the bearer of news of the utmost importance.

'And you are?'

I gave my name and was about to give my trade when he indicated his bureau, as he always put it, and went in, leaving the door open for me to follow. Inside, I noticed that a window on the left looked down on the scene from which I had just departed.

I announced directly that there had been a terrible accident and that Mr Nixon was dead. I offered my condolences. He seemed not to hear and continued staring over my shoulder. I was about to repeat myself when I realized my mistake.

'The secretary,' I said, 'or chief clerk, perhaps, I'm not sure, white-haired, very slender.'

'No!' he exclaimed, now looking over my other shoulder.

I turned to see if there was another in the room, only to find that in doing so I had made a fool of myself.

'A slight strabismus, Mr Mackenzie, I am attending, I assure you.'

I flushed, and to conceal this went straight to the window from where Nixon's body could still be seen, now covered in a length of canvas. Vetch joined me there, understanding at last.

'God have mercy on his soul.'

I added an earnest 'Amen' and wondered how I was going to get back from such pieties to asking for the man's job.

Whether deliberately or not, it was Vetch who made it easier. Once reinstalled behind his desk he asked if I was not the young gentleman who had been so generous with the wine. I said I was, feeling the weight of Colquhoun's money still in my pocket.

Once again, I became a partner rather than copy-clerk and tout. My views on the trade were solicited, on affairs with France, on the prospects for men of business. I let slip that there were methods for getting round such problems, regretted that discretion did not allow me to say what they were. In passing I mentioned my acquaintance with some of the more substantial of the tobacco traders and expressed my surprise when these imaginary merchant-princes were unknown to him. Did he not know Monsieur Montorgueil? No? Perhaps I could introduce him at some time. We concurred on the scarcity of capital – in my mind still a largely poetic concept – deplored our exclusion from English possessions and found ourselves to be in complete agreement on the need for an independent *démarche*. I expounded my views on how similar the wine trade must be to working in a maritime trading company.

The conversation arrived at a seemingly unbridgeable gap. I smiled desperately while Mr Vetch turned to bring his squint eye to bear on me.

'You are looking for employment, Mr Mackenzie?'

'I am willing to serve.'

Mr Vetch mused for a while.

'Perhaps if your current employer could have a word?'

I found Colquhoun haggling with a quayside tavern-keeper short of two fingers on the hand he was angrily waving in support of his point. As soon as the man was gone he put on his most mournful expression for me. 'You see what I am reduced to, Roderick? Half my customers look as if they are still with us only because the rope broke.' He sighed like a lover for his lost honour. 'Still, the resolute man of affairs knows that he must sometimes debase himself in the eyes of the vulgar to maintain his true integrity. That's the most important thing I can teach you, Roderick – to maintain your inner integrity. Did you get the money?'

I put the fruits of deception on his desk.

'Excellent! You have redeemed yourself.'

He swept the coins into a drawer.

'I may be able to retain you for another month or so.'

What pleasure it gave me to say that it would not be necessary! Greater still when I saw how coldly the news was received. I recounted the gruesome scene I had witnessed in the High Street and my conversation with Vetch. I admitted that I had allowed certain inaccuracies with respect to my position to creep into this, but the anticipated storm from Colquhoun when I said I had passed myself off as a partner was replaced by the merest lift of an eyebrow. His thoughts were already beginning to follow mine and I did not hesitate to spell them out.

'The Company has more money to spend than anyone else in the country . . .'

'That's because it's spending the whole country's money, Roderick.'

'. . . it has a number of very substantial gentlemen in its ranks with a taste for the finer things of life and, as we know from what you have just put into your drawer, is easily parted from its money. What more could you want than a man on the inside?'

I was, of course, retaining my inner integrity as I offered this outrageous argument. What lies I told – and these only by implication – I told to Colquhoun by way of tribute to a master.

'And my part in your elevation?'

'Vouch for me.'

The benefits of a 'man on the inside' were clear enough to Colquhoun and we both knew they would be greater by far than Mr Caldwell's relaxations at the Widow Gilbert's.

Together we immediately retraced the length of the High Street to Mrs Purdie's coffee-house. I waited outside while Colquhoun went in to have the all important 'word'. A half-hour passed with no result. I imagined that I had started to attract the looks of passers-by as I stood there idly and so started to walk up the street purposively before crossing to the other side and walking equally purposively back to where I had started. I stared at the cobbles, from which all trace of the accident had already been erased. Still no Colquhoun. The lamps were lit in Mr Vetch's office. I stood beneath the window hoping absurdly that amidst all the clatter of the street a few syllables of the conversation within might come to my ears. Perhaps not a word had yet been exchanged, perhaps Colquhoun paced fretfully in the corridor outside, his patience at the point of exhaustion as he prepared another tirade against the Company. Suddenly Colquhoun's voice boomed from just inside the doorway, magnified by drink and good spirits. He appeared with a holiday expression on his face, which he soured for my benefit as soon as he caught sight of me.

'Don't loiter there, young Roderick, like a common footpad, come and hear what I've done for you.'

He beamed as heads turned from all directions. The world wasted a genius when it allowed Magnus Colquhoun to follow in his father's footsteps rather than on to the stage.

'Well?'

He belched, picked his teeth with the fingernail kept long for the purpose.

'He knows a good claret. Apart from that, he's slippery. Didn't take to him at all. Still, as you're like a son to me, Roderick, and it's what you want, I've done my best.'

He nodded towards the doorway. 'He'll have a word with you now.'

I went up, almost trembling with trepidation, to find that not only had Colquhoun done his best, but that this had been good enough to entirely conclude the matter in Vetch's mind. All I had to do was to stammer my acceptance.

Outside, there was no need for Colquhoun to ask what had happened. I was elated, grinning like a lunatic.

'So he said yes, did he?'

The demand was abrupt, theatrically incredulous, for all his confidence in his own contribution. Colquhoun never approved of success in others, even in that train of young men who were like sons to him. He thought it apt to spoil them.

'Indeed he did!' I announced it with a flourish. 'You are looking, sir, at the Secretary to the Company of Scotland Trading to Africa and the Indies.'

'Pah! Couldn't find their own arses on a map! Much joy may you have of it, young Roderick. Just make sure you tell your mother I did my best to make an honest man of you. The madness is all yours.'

He heaved up his belt in a valedictory girding of the loins and made off through the evening for Maclurg's, where the wine merchants gathered to complain of their affairs. At twenty paces he stopped and turned and announced to the whole town: 'And another thing, Mr Secretary Mackenzie: I've told more lies for you in the last hour than in a month of Sundays, and not for nothing!'

Even this was not enough. After another ten paces he turned again, giving me once more the war-cry of the merchant Colquhouns for twenty generations: 'Not for nothing, my boy, not for nothing!'

I would have paid any price and thought it cheap.

That night I found Douglas and James – by this stage a junior to a Writer to the Signet – and lured them away from Baillie Ritchie's solemn table to share my triumph. We made a glorious procession through all the town's most iniquitous basements ending up as late-night visitors to the ever-welcoming Widow Gilbert, who was highly delighted by my good fortune.

'In amongst all those fine gentlemen, Mr Roderick, how proud you must be. They must have to work very hard, I'll say, in that company of theirs, all those fine gentlemen. Very wearying at times, I don't doubt.'

Susanna was asleep, but having achieved certain privileges in that area I was allowed to climb up to her room none the less. I slipped into her bed and into a sleep, chaste and drunken in equal measure. I awoke with a start in full morning, a dream of grand commerce fading from my senses, pepper dust and the tang of gold on my tongue. Susanna was unenthused by my presence, but I took her with the utmost vigour, my appetites having grown, it seemed, in accordance with my position. In a coffee-house I had the best of everything for breakfast, and then I had it again, which quite restored me from the effects of the many bottles I had downed the night before.

By a happy coincidence I was able to enjoy the benefits of my new position without delay as the apartment beneath mine in Baillie Ritchie's house became vacant. The greater cost of this, once prohibitive, was now negligible, and I agreed to take it at once, moving down towards the more gracious regions of the house and reducing my nightly travail by two flights. I returned to the tailor from whom I had ordered my yellow waistcoat and ordered another in red silk. To those of the destitute who took my fancy – and their numbers did not cease to swell – I now gave groats where before I had given farthings.

That Sunday I went to church twice to give thanks and to express my hopes for a just reward for the unfortunate Nixon. On the following morning I began my service with the Company of Scotland. Taking my predecessor as my model, I stood behind my three clerks and spent an undemanding day greeting subscribers and looking over the shoulders of my inferiors. I was assisted in my new role by the wearing of a pair of newly acquired pince-nez, which I secured about my neck with a black ribbon. This succeeded in making me look almost as old as the clerks I was supervising and would, as I hoped, ease their resentment at my sudden appearance above their heads.

I presided over the last ten days of the subscriptions during which few, if any, persons of note passed through our makeshift office. In the evenings I reviewed the ledgers, reading the great names on the first and second pages; those who had signed in the first hours of the subscription while I lay elsewhere, otherwise engaged. Sometimes I would stare for an hour at the first line – Anne, Duchess of Hamilton, for three thousand pounds sterling! You could have bought a shipload of Colquhouns for less. Then the Countess of Rothes, Lady Margaret Hope, the Earl of Argyll, Fletcher of Saltoun, Baillie of Jerviswood, Lord Belhaven, Lord Basil Hamilton, and none for less than a thousand. My mind thrilled to those names – and to those numbers – as dreamers thrill to Jerusalem or Samarkand. As I turned the pages I went down through the world: first the great merchants, then the lesser and then the unknown, some of whom, if one could judge from the amounts they promised, had spent miserly decades spurning every offer the world could make until that day when they had at last found something to which they could give their all. In the last days of this process I supervised the pledges of hat-doffing saddlers, threadbare tailors, unfashionable fencing-masters past their prime. The only significant sums came from the burghs. The good towns of St Andrew's, Glasgow, Paisley, Selkirk and Inverness sent solemn embassies to subscribe for their rich and their poor alike. When the book was closed on the last day of the month its pages described a truly universal corporation. Through these town collections everyone who had thrown a penny on the plate, or had meant to, was now as passionately connected with our grand project as those who had subscribed for hundreds or thousands. Indeed, more so. The poor never lacked for arguments and were soon sure that their contribution was the truest in spirit and by far the greater sacrifice. After all, if a neighbour signed for a hundred pounds, what was that when everyone knew he had ten thousand buried under his floor? He hadn't gone hungry for half a day.

Each of these unique penny-talismans became linked in the minds of the giver to an equally unique knot of rope or nail or dowel or candle or handful of shot. It was as like to be that pauper's penny that held the hull together in a storm, revealed the rocks to the watchman or shot out the brains of a buccaneer captain, as the rich man's sovereign.

Of these last subscriptions, the very last was different and, I am sure, has brought the undersigned nothing but grief and fear. It was a sly, shadowy act, committed at the very last possible moment, late on the final day of the subscription period when nothing more was expected. The clerks nodded or watched the clock and only occasionally took notice of what they later reported to me as a drunkard or a prowling pickpocket continually passing and repassing the door of Mrs Purdie's coffee-house, one time in five stepping in to look about without revealing his own face. He needn't have feared – I was looking over the figures in one of the upstairs rooms, Vetch's room in fact, the man himself having returned to London to supervise some business of his own. When the latest of the come-latelys had satisfied himself as to my absence he slipped in and did the deed in a trice. When the book was closed late that afternoon it seemed entirely suitable that Colquhoun's name should be the last before the heavy double line I ruled across it. At last it was complete: our book of numbers, our new pentateuch with all our saints and sinners alike.

I must confess that on the day the books closed my new position was already in danger of becoming a disappointment to me. One or two zeros had been added to the figures that swam before my eyes – and sometimes through my dreams – and I had inferiors (oh, happy word!) to write them down for me. And yet I was unpleasantly surprised at how ephemeral these pleasures proved to be. Four hundred thousand pounds sterling is a stirring figure to be sure, more than enough to while away a few hours in happy contemplation. Having done that, however, the problem with mere figures soon emerges. The imaginary appetites are intrepid and soon demand to press ahead and know what comes next so that between one nod of the dreaming head and the next the object of one's contemplation is multiplied a thousandfold. No sooner does a man delight in this new plaything than his joy palls at the thought that somewhere there must be a million times as much and that the current object of veneration is, as numbers go, a contemptible slip of a thing. That is the time to swear one is done with the romance of numbers.

Sadly, my position did not allow of such a moving on and in the immediate few weeks after the closing of the subscription books little of import happened. Mercifully, by early summer – indicated by a slight increase in the temperature of the rain – the first of two transformations arrived to refresh my jaded spirits. The first twenty-five per cent call on the subscribed capital was made, turning at least part of that great number into tangible coin. There was, needless to say, some anxiety that many of the names in those great tomes had been written down under the influence of momentary enthusiasms without a thought to the reality of the matter. In the event, we were made to feel ashamed of our doubts as hardly a penny that was called on failed to arrive in our vaults.

The calling in of our capital made vaults necessary, and a great deal more besides. The upper rooms of Mrs Purdie's no longer sufficed and a search was made for premises of a suitable scale and dignity. The new bank was also looking for a permanent home and the mood in the town revived as the agents of these two great corporations criss-crossed the streets, laboured up and down the tallest and widest staircases and received the obsequious attentions of the most substantial landlords. As the bank directors left Milne Square, we entered it, exchanging nods on the steps. It was the only building in Edinburgh they could not afford and within days I was supervising the transfer of a cartload of papers from Mrs Purdie's into the new accounts room, which occupied a corner of the topmost floor. I had a row of four desks installed for my clerks – the original three from Mrs Purdie's and a new man I had taken on from the provinces. In the space that remained I drew chalk lines on the bare boards to make a rectangle twice the size of Colquhoun's office and taking in the best three windows of the floor. I summoned joiners to build walls about this space with a stout oak door in the middle. I watched a signwriter paint 'Secretary' on the door and spent a pleasant afternoon leafing through a cabinet-maker's pattern book deciding on the details of my desk and chair. The resulting sheaf of bills caused me no little worry, but I sent them down to Markinch with a confident air and heard no more about them.

I was not the only one to make myself comfortable. The whole building vibrated with a continuous banging and sawing. There being no easy access from the rear, the main entrance was often enough blocked by competing queues of aproned tradesmen, half importantly insisting that they must go out and half that they must go in. The yard seemed to be preparing for a grand execution, it was so full of trestles and timbers and men everywhere cutting and measuring and joining, scuffing their way through an inch-thick snow of sawdust. When that was done it was the nose that was assaulted rather than the ears. A dizzying reek of paint and varnish billowed out of the doors and windows, every one open, and across the town. At the end there was the ring of the mason's chisel as, from the smooth slab of white sandstone above the portal, there emerged our arms, painstakingly copied out from our grant – Commerce's cornucopia spilled out her goods over the rounded world, from behind the arc of which rose an approving sun.

The draper at the foot of Baillie Ritchie's house flushed the gutters a deep blue-black as he prepared the cloth for the Company's new livery: tight tail-coats of a martial cut, piped in silver braid, knee breeches and caps of black velvet with the badge of the rising sun in silver thread. A few large outfits were stitched together in the tailors' shops for old boatswains recruited from the docks to serve as mastiffs on the steps to Milne Square, and a dozen or so small for the messenger-boys we took straight from the schools. These were kept scurrying about the town from morning to night. They carried orders, payments, specifications and contracts for the most part. On quieter days they bore sealed blanks with instructions on the back on when and where to hand them to another messenger who was to return them to Milne Square by a different route, and as ostentatiously as possible. Thus the ceaseless activity of the Company, which was true enough, was communicated to the people by an innocent ruse. If the doorkeepers were our mastiffs, the messenger-boys were our terriers and there were not a few street brawls with the bank-boys. Stern warnings were issued about behaviour unbecoming, but we were always pleased when they came off best, and the whole Company soon knew of it.

Markinch was in many ways my opposite. While I perched with the gods and the starlings, he hunkered in the dismal shadows of the lower basements. While I ran up bills (in the company of many others, let it be said), he paid them. Born and bred in Aberdeenshire, from which his speech retained an unmistakable imprint, he had made his way as factotum to an iron and coal merchant in England and had been enticed back to serve the Company. There was some liaison, which I never quite understood, with one of the directors.

At my first sight of him he cut a suitably vulcanic figure directing the blacksmiths as they made the vaults in the early days of the fitting out. I had gone down out of curiosity to see how it was done. A forge had been set up in the basement itself and was almost the only source of light. Sweat-drenched smiths flanked the anvil and swung hammers high above their heads to bring them down in perfect rhythm on thick ribbons of iron, red with heat. Other men held these with pincers and would move them forward to be struck again so that they undulated along their whole lengths and could be threaded through the uprights like osiers. Where the ribbons crossed, holes had been punched ready for the rivets. With a furious pumping at the bellows they were heated to a pale yellow and thrown across the room like shooting stars, to be caught in mid-air with another pair of pincers. Before its colour had hardly dimmed it was placed in the hole and struck from both sides at once with hammers I doubted I could lift. An error in timing of the slightest fraction would have sent the rivet flying one way or the other with the speed of a bullet, but while I watched, they never failed and the rivet was crushed flat at the first blow. Markinch was the one with the drawing in his hand and the measuring stick, requiring a piece to be thicker here, more immovably fixed there. He had, or so I liked to imagine, special knowledge of the lengths to which men would go to breach such defences.

I had a fascination for the vaults, which pulled me back to them on several occasions while they were being fitted out and then again when the first quarter of our capital was coming in. When all was done, they took the form of an enormous woven iron cage. A single narrow door secured with two enormous locks was the only access. The keys to these weighed a pound each and hung at the belt of an assistant, one at each side. Inside, steel rods had been fixed along the back wall and from these hung leather bags, puckered at the top where the four brass rings in each one had been gathered together so that the rod could be pushed through. No one seemed to understand Markinch's system or even, so far as I knew, asked about it. Complicated labels were attached to these bags, covered in his private shorthand. They were moved from left to right or from lower to higher rods like the beads on a giant's abacus specially constructed for the operations of what became known as Markinchmatic. As this worked to everyone's entire satisfaction its rules were left in happy obscurity. Markinch himself would sit just inside his cage at a modest desk, paying the bills that were sent down to him from the diurnal regions and issuing receipts to subscribers for their capital.

I was drawn to him in part out of social convenience – although he was the older and more experienced man he was, in the hierarchy of the Company, my equal and the only true equal I had, the others all being above or below me by unbridgeable degrees. He seemed almost to live in that iron cage and on those occasions when I and my clerks were working well into the night I would sometimes take a lamp down the backstairs and further down into the basements and find him there, looking over some papers by the light of a single candle. We would play a few hands and share a glass of port before returning to our respective labours. Perhaps a dozen, or maybe two dozen words would be exchanged. Of course, it wasn't just Markinch who drew me down there, it was what filled out his bags and bowed the steel rods they hung from as well. The numbers in my ledgers represented what weighed down those bags, but I was tired of the numbers, and envied Markinch his closeness to the reality. I was desperate to see inside them, to scoop up a great double handful of gold and let the pieces run through my fingers. He never seemed to notice them and I was always too ashamed of my desire to confess it. In all the time I spent with him I never saw a single coin.

The Company had its premises then, and a goodly part of its money. All that remained was for a head to be put on the beast to tell it where to go. This was the Court of Directors. Sober men all, broadclothed and bewigged. On formal meeting days they would process up the lawnmarket like a puritanical caterpillar before slow-stepping their way into Milne Square under the fresh-cut face of the rising sun.

Chiesly, Balfour, Blackwood, Haldane, Erskine, John Hamilton, Baron Belhaven, Mr Paterson of course, Mr Vetch and the infamous Smith. Even some of these are no more than names to me and there were others who attended more rarely whom I would struggle to recognize now if I passed them in the street. And yet, the most memorable of all was the rarest presence: Joseph Cohen d'Azevedo, the only butterfly amidst all those pious moths (Mr Paterson excepted, of course). He was there mostly in the form of his apologies: Mr d'Azevedo regrets that his affairs in Amsterdam . . . the office of Mr d'Azevedo in Antwerp regrets to inform the Company that . . . Mr d'Azevedo begs to intimate that delays to his affairs in Carthagena . . . They became ever more exotic and ever more exasperating to the dullards who were forced to listen to them. They could never offer more than an ague for their own excuses.

These meetings took place in the large room immediately below my office. To begin with I had no part in them, and as I laboured through an endless tedium of paper and ink with nothing but the idiotic conversation of my clerks for diversion I suffered an increasing fear that I would be condemned for ever to the periphery of the Company, out of reach of those events most suitable to my talents. Once behind my door I would throw off the dignity commensurate with my position, roll back the carpet and press my ear to the boards. Remote mumblings came to me, but never an identifiable word. I paced my office for hours at a time, racking my brains for the right course of action, certain that the most momentous decisions were being taken only a few feet below.

My mood lightened on receipt of a note from Mr Vetch. He would be grateful if I could attend the forthcoming meeting of the Court of Directors which, it was felt, might be particularly deserving of an accurate record. He hoped I would not find the task too tedious, but confidentiality was essential and I would understand why an ordinary clerk could not be used.

Around tables arranged to form three sides of a square, every chair except one was filled. A dreary, grey morning light fell across the scene from the three tall windows that illuminated the room, spotted with a tepid, early summer rain. An unseasonal fire burned in the grate but failed to dispel the dampness. I dipped my pen as Sir Robert Chiesly began the proceedings. He waved a note in his hand disdainfully. 'Mr Cohen d'Azevedo sends his fraternal greetings to his fellow directors.'

My pen remained still as I listened to groans and an ungentlemanly comment from Mr Smith.

'A misunderstanding in Cadiz requires his presence there.'

I believe I was rather pleased to find myself the only disappointed person in the room.

Sir Robert looked at Mr Paterson, who stood up and moved to the centre of the floor where two ironbound trunks stood, their lids forced open by thick sheaves of papers. Beside them lay two charts, rolled up and tied with green ribbon. Paterson contemplated these, his hands arched together, covering his mouth in a moment of silence that seemed almost sacramental.

'Gentlemen, I have here the records of an idea that has not been wholly out of my mind, waking or dreaming, since I learned the map of the world. Every year that passed I feared the chance would slip away, that others must see what I could see and would one day find the courage to make it real. Every London or Paris or Hamburg paper I read, every letter I received from my friends in Spain or from the West Indies merchants would, I was sure, tell me that it was too late and that I would have to stand by and watch other men and another country take the prize. With few exceptions I kept these thoughts to myself, fearing that the more I spoke of this treasure, the more would hear of it who would take it from us. To some I did speak – some in Amsterdam, some in Hamburg and Lübeck, but in each case I misjudged them. They saw the greatness of the idea but did not have the courage it demands. I thank God for their cowardice now. He has directed me more surely than I knew. He has directed me home, gentlemen, at the first moment in our history when we have the power to contemplate such a task. I come to you direct from London where my best and most discreet intelligence is that we still, if only just, have time.'

He bent to pick up the larger chart. I made to help but was motioned back to my place by Sir Robert, who took the other end and helped to unroll it. My part was to remain invisible, to listen and to write. And so I did: listen, write and watch all day. I watched the hands and the pointers move over the maps: the Spanish empire, the Portuguese (quickly discounted), the Indies where Mr Paterson had learned his trade and made his fortune, the English colonies to the north. My hand ached as I filled pages with talk of tonnages and distances. The principal ports were enumerated, their populations estimated, their trade examined. Mr Paterson talked of Puerto Colombia, Port au Prince, Kingston, Bluefields and of the great arc of Cuba and the riches of Havana, Trinidad, Santiago. Sugar and molasses, tobacco, rare timbers, dyes and a dozen other commodities were discussed and priced, and the means of harvesting and transporting them argued over.

I thought I understood, but what was in my mind was nothing more than what might have been in any commonplace mind. Mr Paterson was aiming higher, higher than any ordinary man would have dared, and it was only slowly that the rest of us could follow him. He knew this and took care not to alarm his audience by a premature unveiling. The talk widened and seemed aimless, though looking back I could see that Paterson never lost his way. There was talk of the Dutch and the great north German merchants, of France and the war. Then all Europe was the subject and the drowsing greatness of Russia behind her. Suddenly, like merchant Ariels, we flew to the East. We heard of India, of the spice islands, of Japan even and China. We heard of their teeming multitudes and of what they would sell from the products of their incalculable labours, and what they would buy to satisfy their still vaster appetites. From time to time the other directors would speak too, if only to show what they knew, but they shifted and looked at each other in puzzlement. They understood no more than I.

Another map was unrolled before us, for a moment unrecognizable. Europa had been evicted from her natural place and now hung strangely from one corner. On the other side were the barely familiar shapes of China, Japan, and the East Indies. Below, cherubim trumpeted the existence of the measureless unknown. In the middle, occupying a full third of the map, was the great hourglass of the Americas. Paterson's hand moved to its narrowest point. His finger pressed it to the board, obscured it.

'Gentlemen, my lord, we have touched on well nigh every part of our world that matters to the merchant or to the nation that would improve itself through trade. Observe that everything in one half of this world that would be bought or sold in the other half could more profitably and readily be transported if this fragile strand were broken. The name of this land is Darien.'

That was the first time I heard the word, but it has never left me, as ever-present as a lover's name, as familiar as a prayer. I would have jumped at it there and then. Indeed, I almost exclaimed, biting my tongue at the last moment. As I looked at each of the directors in turn I realized that I was the only one to receive the idea with such enthusiasm. I flushed and bowed my head back to the minutes, shamed by the knowledge that I was in the presence of men who had a dozen lifetimes' more experience than myself. Chairs creaked uncertainly, fingers tapped. Mr Vetch raised an eyebrow while Sir Robert might have died in the interim, such was the absolute impassiveness of his expression. Only Lord Belhaven seemed to show any interest. Mr Smith, scoundrel that he was, broke the silence first, his hand making the form of shears cutting an imaginary ribbon.

'Snip, snip, eh, William? Just like that? It might be a bit bigger than it seems on that map when you're standing on it. A bit tougher, too, than a strip of waxed linen.'

Mr Paterson was above such discourtesies. He smiled, as confident before this distinguished audience as he had been before the gaping crowd outside Mrs Purdie's.

'I see you are a man of vision, Mr Smith. Let me assure you, gentlemen, I am not. Mr Smith may dream of cutting continents in two – ' Paterson's hand imitated Smith's, bony fingers for blades, somehow sarcastic ' – but I cut my coat according to my cloth. A sea passage across Panama? A Moses of the rocks, parting the mountains to let the water through? One day, perhaps; man is great. But not yet, gentlemen. No, what I propose is simpler and cheaper and hardly less profitable. A trading station on the north coast at the narrowest point. A port, then a town, in time even a city. From that town a simple road leading a few tens of miles to the south or, as one could say, from one side of the world to the other. Transhipment in two days, gentlemen. Two days!'

All eyes were now on those same cloth-cutting fingers, not blades now but days. What might they be worth? Two days where now a sea passage of two months or more is required and on which one cargo in twelve ends on the floor. Silent calculations were made but soon given up. The answer lay in that vague, glowing, mythical region where titanic quantities drift beyond the reach of mere numbers.

Our attention snapped back to Mr Paterson as he let the lid of one of the trunks fall back with a bang.

'Gentlemen, my lord of Belhaven, there remains only a single question for practical men of affairs: is it possible?'

Most of the papers in the trunks were dusty and browned with age, but at the top were a dozen slender manuscripts, the paper a fresh white. Paterson gathered these up as he spoke. I was reminded of Dr Lennox about to distribute a stack of slates.

'I have spoken to the only white man with any reliable knowledge of Darien. These are his words. He has agreed, in return for a suitable inducement, that for a period of three months, your eyes alone shall see them. Should you agree to what I propose he will, for a further compensation, delay publication until the Company's ships are on the high seas.'

The copies handed out, Paterson leaned across the far table to exchange a confidential word with Sir Robert Chiesly. Sir Robert craned his neck round Paterson's body till he could catch my eye. 'I think we can let you have a rest now, Mr Mackenzie. An hour perhaps?'

Another half-dozen words were exchanged. Sir Robert's hand waved in a gesture of liberality. 'Two hours, please. We're very grateful.'

There were some murmurs of assent from heads that did not lift from the papers before them. I left unnoticed, closing the door on a scene of seminarian concentration. A single copy lay unregarded in front of Cohen d'Azevedo's empty chair.

Outside, the corners of the flagstones were drying under a sky that suggested only a short respite. A clock surprised me as it struck two. For five hours I had filled page after page, my hand moving with no more sense than an automaton as my mind followed Paterson from bafflement to wonder at the grandeur of what was being contemplated.

My legs bore me by force of habit to the nearest coffee-house. A half-hour passed before I looked down with surprise to find that I had consumed a plate of mussels in garlic and a flagon of claret with no more awareness than if I had been gulping down air. My mind was giddy with ambition and played endless delights before my eyes. I seated myself in a tropical customs house and entertained the son of a caliph while my factor calculated the toll for his ten ships of cotton bales. At my door he stepped aside with a bow to admit two merchants from Japan. After elaborate courtesies they at last make themselves understood: may they pay in black pearls?

A sudden burst of laughter from four men by the window shook the vision from my head. They started to make their way out and would have to squeeze past my table. As they approached I recognized some old customers and at the back, arms wide as he shepherded them to the door, Colquhoun himself. He started as he caught sight of me, hesitated between a sneer and a snub, and passed on making no other sign that he knew me. I watched them go with indifference. Paterson's words re-entered my head as soon as they were gone: 'Is it possible? . . . a single question . . . is it possible?' It was preposterous, then it was inevitable, then it was preposterous again. I thought of Paterson's steps, guided home after providential failures abroad. Perhaps he had been preserved especially for us. I wanted to laugh at the idea, the old cowardice pulling me back. It would have made me sound like Colquhoun.

Only an hour had passed. I dawdled by shop-fronts and refilled my pipe, but by the time the second quarter struck I had lost patience and returned to Milne Square. The reading of documents was most emphatically over. From behind the double doors to the directors' chamber voices rose to make themselves heard over each other. Discord? My mood sank for a moment but then turned to one of chagrin as I heard the accompanying scraping of plates and chinking of glasses. Through the keyhole there oozed the aroma of quail in redcurrants and of wines Colquhoun had never drunk, let alone sold. I was sorely tempted to apply my eye to that aperture to see what could possibly be going on, but feared being interrupted in such a disgraceful position. This proved to be the wiser choice as not another minute passed before five serving-men appeared at the head of the stairs. The first knocked perfunctorily at the door and went in at once, the last closed it in my face. They reappeared, balancing the debris expertly on hands and forearms, one even in a basket on his head.

'May we trouble you once more, Mr Mackenzie?'

The matter was briefly concluded, my part in it being the inscription of a single sentence in the minutes – That the matter spoken of by Mr Paterson having been heard and approved by a majority of the Court of Directors, it became the policy of the Company to bring that matter about as soon as may be.

'I needn't say, gentlemen, not a word. Not a word beyond this room.'

I am sorry to say he looked particularly at me while giving this admonition, an injustice compounded a few days later when I learned that my record of the meeting was not to be kept in my own offices but in Markinch's iron cage.

The directors filed out, each dropping his copy of Paterson's report in the grate as he went. Vetch went last, leaving me with a smile of encouragement. I was alone, watching that pile of paper smoking on the embers until it suddenly caught fire and blazed up brilliantly.

In front of one chair was a forgotten glass, never filled. Beside it lay d'Azevedo's copy of the document. I slipped it under my waistcoat and closed the doors behind me.

THE SECRET WAS WELL KEPT. That there was a secret was a universal certainty within days and there were few who could resist claiming they were privy to it. In one inn or coffee-house the fine details could be learned of how we had purchased Madagascar from the Emperor of the Ethiopians, while in another it was Zanzibar from the Arabs. In a third such nonsenses were dismissed with a worldly laugh – all men of sense knew that it was a mountain of lapis-lazuli in Tartary. Had they not heard that the price of ultramarine had fallen by a half?

As I lay exhausted under Widow Gilbert's eaves, Susanna pulled one of my ears and turned away. 'Don't tell me, then. Anyway, do you think I don't know?'

All predictions, from the most sober to the most wildly fabulous, gained support from the evident acceleration in the Company's affairs. For myself, although my days were fuller than before, time rushed on ever faster to the great goal that had suddenly become clear.

Daily, while the sun was still low, I made my way to Leith where two warehouses had been leased and cleared of the dross belonging to a score of minor merchants. On my first arrival I walked under the ladders of men whitewashing the walls with the single word 'Company' in monumental letters. The evening before, a note had instructed me to collect a giant key from Markinch who, punctilious as ever, insisted I sign a receipt for it. I turned this in the great north door of one of the warehouses, using both hands against the rust in the lock. Dust from the abrupt removal of our predecessors still hung thick in the air. Shafts of light ran through it from high windows to the floor like solid rods. One flickered as a pigeon broke it, flying from rafter to sill. I had the pigeons shot, the windows glazed and the walls scrubbed till the bricks looked as if they had been laid the day before.

Even before this task was finished the road from the city was blocked for six days of the week with a daily exodus of carts and wagons of all manner and size. What little space was left was trodden by men and boys struggling with smaller packages on their shoulders or slung on poles between them. I was now the master of another half-dozen clerks, each of whom inscribed a ledger that was a sacred terminus for every carter and porter between the High Street and the docks. By these they waited like surly tribute-bearers before Pharaoh, impatient to unload their burdens and receive their paper saying what they had delivered and what the Committee for Improvements had agreed they should be paid for it. With this in hand they fought their way back against the flow with much pushing and cursing. Their destination was another queue, one that stretched across Milne Square, through the side entrance and down into the candle shadows of Markinch's iron cage where each paper would be sceptically examined and the monies paid. Each of these bore my signature, written as they were issued at first but then, as the flow of goods threatened to overwhelm us, written at night on to blanks until my hand froze and could write no more. These were numbered, gathered together in blocks and distributed to the clerks as required. The task irritated me and I considered how I might pass it on to someone else until a curious incident in a tavern tickled my vanity and quite changed my mind. I had received the impression, on several occasions, of someone speaking my name, but was unable to find anyone who wanted me. I might soon have feared for my wits, had I not looked up one day to see a group of gentlemen rise from a table obliterated by empty bottles and glasses and observed one of them settle their debt with a 'mackenzie'. As the proprietor nodded one of our warehouse receipts was presented and the excess returned in good coin. This strange transaction was soon a commonplace and my name could be heard several times a day, elevated to the grandeur of a common noun.

Without being aware of it the Company had become a bank too, and I the signatory of its notes. I need only have signed my name to be rich!

It was not long before this same thought occurred to another. I first learned of the fraud from Markinch, who surprised me late one evening, setting foot in my office for the first time. He approached my desk without a word and laid two fresh mackenzies before me. They were for different amounts and for different goods: one for four barrels of oil and another for a quantity of cordage. For the rest they were the same, including the numbers. Markinch's finger lugubriously pointed out the twin 867s. I peered at my two signatures. It was well done: I had to look twice to be sure which was which.

It was decided to settle the matter quietly. Whoever this artistic gentleman's associates were, the Company knew it would have no difficulty in outbidding him for their loyalty, and in gold rather than paper. It was put about in the more disreputable taverns of the town that his name and address would be appreciated. It was not long before his betrayal was purchased, and for a sorry sum at that. Two of our mastiffs visited him: an ageing engraver of portraits who had enjoyed little success in persuading customers to part with a few shillings for a slapdash likeness. I felt the unpleasantness of the episode keenly and preferred not to enquire too closely into how they treated him. In any case, the problem did not recur.

Those who made their way to and from the warehouses had already succeeded with the Committee for Improvements, a body that included Mr Vetch, who did me the honour of asking frequently for my attendance. D'Azevedo, also a member, was present on two occasions when his affairs had in any case brought him to Edinburgh. The Improvements was the key to opening Markinch's money-bags and every merchant in the country dreamed of being offered one of its contracts. It published the directors' requirements at the beginning of every week, copies of the sheet being snatched from the hands of a boy on the steps of Milne Square as the clock struck twelve and carried off at a run to every workshop and office in the town. A handful were taken straight to the post inns, whence horses clattered out to every populous part of the country.

Interested parties were required to prove their wares and to this end a near permanent fair grew up along the south shore of the loch. Every day the more assiduous members of the Improvements would process through this encampment of hopefuls and listen to the merchants' extravagant praise of their goods and their equally extravagant denigration of their rivals. Occasionally there would be more spectacular demonstrations such as the shooting contest between three manufacturers of muskets, or the great powder race.

The order for gunpowder was amongst the greatest the Improvements had to place, and as the fate of our venture is likely to depend on this rather more than on the thickness of our shoe leather or the wear of our cloth, particular importance was put on obtaining the best. On the morning of the race three lines of boards were laid near the shore of the loch where it was flattest and extended for a full two hundred paces. Forewarned of what was to happen, I had left business at the warehouses in other hands and joined the few onlookers who had gathered early to watch the work. By noon men in the Company's livery struggled to keep back an excited crowd. Thick lines of powder were poured along the boards. At one end they were drawn together where they would be ignited at the same instant with a pistol flash. At the other, they led up to three flares the size of small cannon planted upright in piles of stones. A flag dropped, the pistol was fired and three brilliant fires rushed forward along the boards. There was a sound like a high wind in trees, floods of yellow and white sparks thrown out in all directions and plumes of smoke as thick and white as clouds. The crowd cheered, each person happily adopting one of the furious blazes as their own champion. Although I stood by the midpoint of the track I could hardly have counted to four when the three competitors galloped past me with a blast of heat and such brilliance that we had to look away or shield our eyes as if from the sun itself. Fumes billowed over us, catching in our throats and stinging our eyes. As I blinked through these tears, I would have sworn that the result was an equal triumph for all three. Plumes of coloured fire shot up from the flares all at once and were cheered to the heavens by every part of the crowd, convinced that the victory was theirs. Referees had been empanelled for just such an eventuality and these, including Mr Vetch and Sir Robert Blackwood, now met in solemn conclave at the far end of the track. It seemed that, whatever their decision, it must be unpopular with at least two-thirds of the spectators. One of the manufacturers appeared to be remonstrating with the referees, and when it was passed down the line that he was from a Birmingham firm, boos and catcalls replaced the cheers. He soon thought better of his protest and the winner was declared to be the powder that had ignited the red flare. This met with a loud shout of acclaim, *nemine contradicente*. The third competitor, a Glasgow concern, was heard later to have spoken churlishly of hidden interests. That Farquhar and George, who added the order for powder to the one they had already received for muskets and pistols, were shareholders in the Company was a coincidence doubted only by minds already black with corruption.

Such were the incidents that disturbed the general eventlessness of my life extending from the middle of my second year in the city to the middle of my third. Save for these occasional surfacings, I led a life sunk deep in the minutiae of grand commerce. I had a curious underside view of the world, one so difficult to interpret that I soon lost interest in affairs in Milne Square, and indeed in all the world beyond my warehouses. Now and again, a strange sinking item would pass and rouse me to look up and learn of some event that had buzzed in the coffee-houses for weeks. Few of these tidbits had retained their savour and I worked on undisturbed. The purchase and recording and storage of a score of long timber saws or of three gross of catechisms seemed more to the point. In two weeks or less I will see them again, cutting out a space for a new Scotland.

As often as I could I continued to observe the Sabbath, and so it was that these surfacings most frequently arose from Sunday-afternoon encounters. On one occasion, after having made my respectful nods across the pews in the direction of Baillie Ritchie and his wife, I encountered James and Douglas in the High Street. We exchanged some sober words, each of us closer to the final admission to our professions and realizing that evenings in the Wilful Willy were behind us. I was asked about the Company and indulged myself in saying that I was not, alas, permitted to tell them what they wanted to know. I had caught them up. Indeed, I had left them behind – a fact that was of no small satisfaction to me. The rest of the day passed quietly save for the abrupt halt of a carriage as I was strolling by the Physic Garden. I recognized Lord Belhaven's arms on the door, but the head that appeared through the window was Vetch's.

'Hail, young Roderick!'

It seemed that some drink had been taken.

'We haven't forgotten you. I hear good things of your work. Can you join us tomorrow at the Improvements? The wandering Jew promises to attend!'

From within, another hand banged on the roof of the carriage and it drove off smartly.

The next day I left my chief clerk in charge of the warehouses and joined the Committee for Improvements in a back room at Maclurg's coffee-house at two in the afternoon. Mr Vetch, Sir Robert Blackwood and two others were already engaged in discussing how they might procure the goods the Court of Directors had declared us to be in need of. I made laborious notes, counting over in my mind the many more pressing tasks from which I was being detained.

Mr Vetch seemed to detect my mood and twice suggested an adjournment, but the idea met with no favour from Sir Robert. Toward the end of the fifth hour, during a discussion of tenders from three wigmakers, something massive collided with the door causing the whole room to shake. Guttural, alien curses were heard. After a brief fumbling with the catch d'Azevedo backed into the room, staggering under the weight of two pairs of saddlebags. He dropped them in a corner before turning to us and raising his hands in a tragic appeal.

'Friends! What can I say? That ostler! May the good Lord shrivel up his daughters before his very eyes!'

He began to tear off a long oilcloth overcoat streaked with a rain we had been unaware of.

'I could have eaten that horse and been here sooner!'

'How good of you to make such an effort, Mr d'Azevedo.'

Sir Robert had not lifted his eyes from the figures he was examining. Under the influence of his chilly greeting I felt obliged to conceal any sign of relief at d'Azevedo's appearance, though it was very great. Did he wink at me? I was never sure. Equally, I never doubted that with a single glance he understood the whole of our situation. He threw his coat over one of the two mean chairs that flanked the hearth and perched his great bulk on the other, shaking drops of water from his hair and beard like a wolfhound returned from a winter hunt.

'We were examining a number of offers from wigmakers.'

'A worthy consideration, Sir Robert. Many a deserving venture has failed for lack of the correct headgear. Had not Xenophon neglected to equip his men with suitable coverings and so recklessly exposed their addled pates to the full rage of the desert sun, might not the whole history of the world have been different?'

'They are for trade, sir, and might I remind—'

'Most certainly it would! Boy!'

He started a brutal raking of the fire, which had been allowed almost to die. There were more Hebraic mutterings, which ended with the phrase, just audible, 'what a country'.

'Forgive me, brothers, but I can be of no use to you until I have restored my wits.'

He started to wrestle with his boots.

'Everyone admires the Scots for living in a country like this. In Seville this very night even the nuns are sleeping naked. A single thread on the skin is like fire the nights are so hot. But here—' He made an exclamatory noise.

A serving-boy arrived and seized a muddy heel. Punctuated by groans of effort and complaint as the boy heaved off first one boot and then the other, the two conversed, the Jew demanding a full list of the delights of the house.

Propping his feet on the hearth he elected for the peppered game pie with a sauce of pickled radishes.

'And bring some coals, and a glass of your cheapest aqua vitae!'

The boy ran from the room and was back in a moment, struggling to balance a bucket of coal with a glass of whisky. While d'Azevedo rubbed the latter on his feet the boy piled up the coal on the grate, all the time glancing at his customer out of the corner of his eye.

'Please, gentlemen. Carry on, don't let me disturb you.'

The boy stopped in the doorway and stared at d'Azevedo for a moment as if making a hard decision. He approached Mr Vetch, who was nearest, and bent to whisper something in his ear, causing him to smile.

'Yes,' said Mr Vetch.

The boy whispered again.

'I think you had better ask him that.'

The boy went to d'Azevedo anxiously and repeated his question which, from all I could hear, had something to do with the game pie and contained the words 'wild boar'.

D'Azevedo put on a solemn expression, tugging his beard in a pose of rabbinical concentration. He put his arm round the boy's shoulder, pulling him closer for an intimate exchange. 'Now tell me, do you think this famous pie of yours contains any of the flesh of the camel?'

'No, sir!' protested the boy.

Mr Vetch did not hide his amusement, while Sir Robert sat stony-faced. I struggled to maintain a neutral expression, hoping to offend no one.

'Hmm,' d'Azevedo pondered theatrically, 'perhaps a morsel of bat?'

The boy became indignant. 'This is a respectable house, sir!'

'Of course it is. Bring on your pie, boy, and may God forgive me for it. In any case, my belly tells me this is one of those cases of mortal necessity that excuses all sins.'

He set to the pie with an unabashed relish, congratulating the boy warmly on the heroic scale of the portion and pressing a coin into his hand. An expression of amazed joy broke over his face when he realized its value. He ran out again, faster than before, to tell his envious colleagues.

'Press on, gentlemen, press on. As soon as the body is attended to the spirit will be with you. A hungry man never yet did good business.'

Sir Robert gritted his teeth and moved on to item thirty-seven. From behind us furious guzzling noises continued with the occasional moan of satisfaction and sluicing of wine. Cutlery clattered on a polished plate. There was a hurricane of belching and then snores.

It was not, if I remember correctly, until item forty-six that food, drink and sleep had done enough to bring Mr d'Azevedo back to us. A comparison of the various prices of lime juice brought an interjection so loud and abrupt that it made Sir Robert start and then wince.

'Leave that to me, gentlemen. I can have it for you by January and at half the price. A man I know . . .' His hand smoothed out an imaginary vista. 'Forests of lime trees. Oranges and lemons too, if you want.'

He made his way over from the fire and took the fifth place at the table. What remained of our business was soon concluded, every second item being settled with a wave of the hand and talk of 'a man I know' in this country or that. From another it would have been preposterous and quite unbelievable, but from d'Azevedo everything was believable. Indeed, five months later, two dozen small barrels of lime juice were signed into my warehouse at rather less than the price we had been promised. It was never clear where they had come from or precisely how the transaction had been agreed. That evening, as I watched him, I imagined I caught a glimpse of the inexpressible mysteries that divide those who make livings from those who make fortunes. I thought of Colquhoun too, in miniature as it seemed, and caught a scent of something for the first time: a consciousness of freedom, raised for a moment to the intensity of a physical sensation.

D'Azevedo was rummaging through one of his enormous saddle-bags, declaring that, as the business was over, it was time for a little pleasure.

'Business, pleasure, pleasure, business! The good life, no?'

Sir Robert managed a weak smile, but looked as if he only half agreed with this prescription.

'Tokay!'

Two straw-covered cylinders were banged down on the table, their coverings pulled off with a flourish to reveal short fat bottles of golden liquid.

'A gift from my brother . . . Boy! Glasses, corkscrew! . . . He'll make a good merchant one day. We may all die waiting, but one day . . . He was going down the Danube with a barge-load of fox furs and turpentine. Whooosh! Biggest firework the good people of Budapest had seen since the Turks came to call on them. Thank the Good Lord for insurance!'

He distributed the glasses and carved the black wax from the necks of the bottles with the end of the corkscrew.

'You must help me unburden myself, gentlemen. I've been carrying them about for months in hope of a worthy occasion. They're tiring me out. Sir Robert, please, I know you are a connoisseur.'

The remainder of the evening passed in a very different spirit. By the end of it even Sir Robert was persuaded to try to learn the Arabic for 'May your daughter marry a Turk.' A phrase which, we were assured for reasons I dare not even commit to paper, is quite the worst thing one can say in those parts but which has, nevertheless, certain uses in the souks of Cairo and Beirut.

The bells counted up to ten and we heard d'Azevedo's name being mispronounced in the raucous tones of a messenger-boy. He placed a message in his already outstretched hand. It was read, turned face down on the table, a reply quickly written on the back. 'Back to where it came from, Mercury.' He looked inconsolable. 'Alas, gentlemen, I must apologize again. The captain of the *Bon Accord* insists on leaving half a day early. He wishes to take the tide at midnight.'

He pulled on his boots and wrapped himself in his vast coat. Wisps of steam rose from it as the heat drove off the last of the rain. He hooked his saddlebags over his arm.

At the door he turned to us and made that gesture that so shocked Sir Robert and so entranced me: the right hand raised in apostolic blessing.

'Prosperity, brothers! Eh? Prosperity!'

'Prosperity!' we returned, and he was gone, slamming the door as if he meant to rip it from its hinges and take it with him. Even Sir Robert's hand was momentarily seduced into returning the gesture. When the door closed it quickly returned to the table, ashamed of its blasphemy. The wait for the next word seemed interminable. Mr Vetch raised his hands from the table in a conclusive gesture. Sir Robert cleared his throat, muttered something about enough for one day and was gone.

Mr Vetch and I stood outside in the street. As we talked, a half-mist, half-rain started again. There was a pause and I thought we were about to part when he asked: 'Tell me, Mr Mackenzie, have you thought what you might do after this?'

'After this?' was all I could ask stupidly.

We were interrupted by the sound of an approaching rider, trotting at first and then cantering recklessly on the cobbles. Sparks struck from the animal's shoes were the first thing we could see. Suddenly, horse and rider loomed and were almost upon us. We both jumped back to avoid being trampled, but as Mr Vetch started to curse him for a fool, the rider raised his broad, concealing hat in salutation. 'Prosperity!' He disappeared in the direction of the sea and the impatient *Bon Accord*.

'A fine mare,' observed Mr Vetch.

*

I RETURNED TO MY LABOURS. Pyramids of barrels, sacks, cloth, rope, of coiled sheets of copper and lead soon touched the roof. Though they honoured no kings, I walked between them as through a dream Egypt. I read every copy receipt and reconciled every ledger page myself. I knew how many yards of cable and canvas, how many gallons of pitch and hogsheads of oil, how many pounds of flints, how many dozen handsaws and reams of paper to the last quarter-measure of each. To these figures I would add what I saw coming in each day. In the small hours I could sit with my eyes closed before the ledgers and know exactly which figure I should see at the foot of each column. It was surprising even to me, but I do not believe I was ever wrong. My clerks were awestruck, something which, I admit, I allowed myself to take a little vain pleasure in. They would ask me for the stock of this item or that. They would check their ledgers with amazement. They would say that I knew the number of grains in each sack of barley, and counted even the hairs on their heads.

We acquired another warehouse and set about filling it as completely as the first. We acquired a third, a small bond house taken over from the Excise who no longer had need of it on account of the continuing weakness of our trade. It was set a little apart from the main buildings of the port, at a safe distance it was thought. Ranks of muskets were soon chained to its walls and barrels of black powder from Farquhar and George stacked on its floors. Some old soldiers, quondam stalwarts of the castle garrison, were employed to guard it.

Intrusions on my attention were fleeting. Baillie Ritchie's eldest daughter was married to a gentleman he had long coveted as a son-in-law. The price of grain soon exceeded the worst levels of the previous year and we extended our guards from the powder store to all warehouses. Requests for a word of support from the King were answered only with silence and the poisonous slanders of the East India Company. These difficulties only strengthened our position. To each of them, the Company was the answer. Each was a further proof of our necessity. For myself, I knew from the last meeting of the

Improvements that Mr Smith and Mr Paterson were abroad commissioning ships and this great fact kept my mind on the future and on what part I might play in it. As I struggled through the black sleets of the last months of the year I was sometimes, while on the road to the warehouses, taken like a pilgrim with a joy so passionate I was forced to stop and look up at the blustering, icy skies before going on. The year of departure was closer by a day.

My mind hummed with the names and quantities of the goods in my charge. The wind about my head seemed to shout about crown pitch and Stockholm tar, Norway deals and turtle line. The clouds in the sky were anvils or shovel-irons. When, for a moment, I tasted a meal, I was at once pulled back into my world of ledgers and stock-books; so many ounces of cinnamon, of nutmegs, mace and cloves, so many pounds of pepper. Sweetness hardly touched my tongue before I was reciting our stocks of sugar – refined, loaf and muscovado, I knew the figure for each. If a man looked at his watch, I counted out our compass glasses. Every ribbed nag that laboured between the shafts told me of our horse hides and glue. I took little sleep, and soon what I did take was of little use. I dreamed of deadeyes and mizzen shrouds, of sail twine, marlin and bolt rope. I dreamed I was awake and, at the noonday bells, wondered if I might be asleep.

This was but half of my mania. At night, despairing of true sleep, I let the candle burn on. I would lock my door, and from beneath my mattress pull the stolen manuscript and pore over its words with the fervency of a Covenanter. Soon, I knew it entirely. It would recite itself through my mind, drifting in strange harmonies through the chanting columns of the ledgers I had reconciled that night. Its opening words were like a prayer, which would release me into a half-sleep filled with brilliant images and scents. I would hardly have read the incantation, *I, Lionel Wafer, late of the* Bachelor's Delight, *having to relate some matters of fact that will seem strange, yet have taken more especial care in these to say nothing but what, according to the best of my Knowledge, is the very Truth*, than I would fancy the touch of a plantain leaf on my cheek, the flash of a macaw behind curlicued leaves, pineapples to be picked from the ground, tobacco-smoke drifting from an Indian council.

Then, our part. I would see a harbour filled with ships under every imaginable colour, and along the newly made jetties a constant traffic of sacks, boxes and barrels. On the wharves were stacked the sawn trunks of the Nicaragua wood I read of, its extracts red as blood and capable of dyeing any cloth a dazzling hue. Behind it all, crowning a hill, stood a governor's mansion or custom house, the front all of white stone with a dome atop and on that dome our proud and honoured cross.

From such triumphs I would wake at four, tensed with cold, with the taint of candle-smoke in the air. Within the hour I was at my desk in Milne Square or pacing in one of the warehouse offices, desperate to set my hands to anything that would hurry time along. The year had hardly turned when I was awoken a hundred times more coldly.

It was a shivering, bitter January, scarcely less cruel than the one before. The directors met early in the month, sooner than had been intended. In my state of mind I could only interpret this positively – our affairs, no doubt, were in advance of themselves, all was in readiness for the next great stage. I hurried to Milne Square, anxious to make myself visible to the directors and to remind them of everything I had done on the Company's behalf. At first nothing seemed amiss. Two or three pairs of minor directors stood about in the council room talking easily, waiting for the proceedings to begin. For the first few minutes there was no one there with whom I had any acquaintance and I busied myself with the elaborate arrangement of the writing materials on my desk. Sir Robert Blackwood came in behind me, looked about the room, and left again without saying a word. Several of the more substantial men came in, but they kept to themselves or spoke only to each other in a manner that soon suppressed all other conversation in the room. Feeling themselves observed, perhaps overheard, they too stopped. We stared at each other in the sudden silence.

Erskine walked in with Haldane, neither showing any surprise at our demeanour. Lord Belhaven entered on his own, then Blackwood again with Sir Robert Chiesly. Mr Vetch came last. Although I did not expect to see d'Azevedo, I did wait to see Paterson or Smith, but neither appeared. Mr Vetch came towards me, evidently bearing a message from Sir Robert Blackwood.

'I'm sorry, Roderick, but it has to be a closed session. I'll tell you what I can later.'

I found myself once again on the wrong side of those weighty double doors. As if that were not bad enough one of our mastiffs, clearly under instructions, placed himself close to my shoulder and with a gaze of stony authority repelled me down the stairs. I paced in the hallway for a while, the mastiff dutifully glaring over the upper banister. I had decided to leave when I heard the sound of a carriage drawing up. The doors opened. Mr Paterson walked past me without acknowledgement, his chin shrunk into the collar of his travelling cloak, face white as one who had already succumbed to the cold.

I climbed to my office by the back stairs and tried vainly to do some work. From time to time I would throw open the door and snap out instructions at my clerks only to forget what I had said and demand the very opposite half an hour later. Every page I stared at was blank, every word I tried to write lost itself in my mind the very moment my pen touched the paper. At one, I despaired and rode to the warehouses. From remembering everything, I then found that I remembered nothing. As my fears grew ever more tyrannous, I stumbled in my speech so that those still in blissful ignorance thought I was drunk or ill. Every argument I used to persuade myself of the absurdity of my thoughts was overthrown by the image of Paterson's bone-white face and its expression of utter disaster. I locked myself in the back office, huddled close to the fire, shivered, watched the clock-hands turn.

At a quarter after four I returned in the gathering blackness, certain that the meeting must be over and nerving myself for the knowledge I wanted and feared in equal measures. As I approached Milne Square

I saw light from the four tall council-chamber windows strengthen through the fog that was settling on the city. Inside, the face that scowled down at me from the first floor was different, but no more welcoming. The council door opened, a lace-cuffed hand pulling it shut again. It was Markinch who stood at the head of the stairs, a sheaf of papers under his arm, the outermost sheet covered in close-written columns. He remained still, pinching his upper lip with his fingers. On noticing me he came down the stairs, favouring me with the briefest nod as he passed. I returned it even more briefly, concentrating as I was on trying to read a figure or a word on the papers he was carrying. Without a pause he continued on his way, descending the unlit stairs to his underground domain and leaving me more fearful than ever.

I knew that Vetch, during his stays in Edinburgh, lodged in the rooms of a Mrs Buchanan at the western extremity of the High Street. I went into Crawford's tavern opposite and set myself to watch through the bleary glass for a sign of his return. At the first glimmer of a lamp I ran across the street, straight up the stairs and directly into his room without the slightest ceremony. He stood up from where he had been sitting by his lamp, still in his heavy cloak, travelling bags already in his hands. It was I who broke the silence.

'You promised.'

'I did not.'

I pleaded.

'The only promise I have made today, Roderick, is that I would tell no one.'

'I am the Secretary to the Company.'

His smile painfully reminded me of my place.

'I have to know.'

He sat down again, letting his bag drop to the floor. He rested his head on his hand, hiding his eyes.

'What has happened, Roderick, must not be known. Do you understand that? Not on any account. The Company might survive . . .'

'Might?'

I had thought I would be equal to any news, but that word drenched me with a sudden cold. I felt behind myself for the other chair.

'The Company isn't in danger. With ships on order, warehouses full to the eaves, how can it be? It's impossible! If there was . . .'

He stopped my pleading with a gesture.

'Forgive me, Roderick. I forget that you have come so far in such an uncommonly short period of time. People give us things because they believe we can pay for them. Many of the goods you mention are liabilities not assets. They were delivered in return for notes signed by you, many of which are still in people's pockets and strong-boxes waiting to be presented to Markinch.'

'Yes,' I said, in a stupid imitation of understanding.

'What would a mackenzie be worth, Roderick, if by some terrible misunderstanding people began to fear that there was nothing left in Markinch's money-bags?'

'Money,' I said, reduced near to idiocy by the paralysing and still incomprehensible horror of what Vetch was trying to tell me.

'Money,' confirmed Mr Vetch.

'You must tell me!'

'I will not.'

'You must! How can—'

'I thought you had company, sir. Mary told me she heard voices.'

Mrs Buchanan came through the door I had neglected to close and busied herself in the preparation of some hot toddy, chattering all the time. She left the door ajar when she had finished and Mr Vetch crossed the room to close it before taking up his glass – both were empty before we spoke again. He looked at me steadily, his gaze, as ever, fixed on some point over my shoulder.

'It's the knowledge, Roderick. The thing itself can be survived. We can make the second call on the capital, say all is well . . .'

'Lie?'

'It was never more necessary!'

The answer was unhesitating, fierce with impatience.

'Our duty isn't to the people, Roderick, it's to their money. The new capital will be enough to pay for the rest of the goods and to meet the contracts for the ships. That's all that's needed. But if they know . . .' His hand cut the air emphatically. 'Fatal!'

'And you think I'm going to tell them?'

'No.'

'So?'

'If you know, the silence is already broken.'

I was now angry as well as frightened. I turned to the window to watch the lights in Crawford's and the last few carriage lamps trot home through the cold. In an agony of frustration I turned over in my mind everything I knew. I envisaged every possibility my imagination was capable of, withdrawing from each as they were contradicted by one or other of the few definite facts I had at my disposal. Slowly, I came to see the one possibility that was not contradicted. The moment I saw it clearly, I was certain. I turned.

'Where's Smith?'

Not a word from Vetch, not the slightest move.

'How much?'

'Newgate prison – we still have some friends in London. The further from Edinburgh we keep him, the better.'

'And Paterson?'

'He trusted Smith.'

'How much, Mr Vetch?'

I begged for another number to add to those that already seethed in my mind.

'Forty-seven thousand, Mr Mackenzie, and eight hundred.'

*

VETCH LEFT EDINBURGH that night, reminding me that he had other affairs to attend to. I made my way to Widow Gilbert's and climbed the stair like a blind man. Susanna, now plump on the generosity of my purse, accepted my presence coldly. Directed by vengeful gods, she filled my cup of misery to the brim by telling me how generous Mr Aeneas Caldwell had been to her the night before. I stared at the roof timbers through a sleepless night.

The directors wasted no time. My first sight that morning was of a printer's boy tacking up a broadsheet on the boards by the Mercat Cross. Even before he ran off to distribute the others rolled under his arm, there was a jostle of curious people. A young minister near the front was appointed to read it out. I listened in amazement and shame as he enunciated, syllable by syllable, in his best Sunday voice, the most honeyed and absolute lie I had ever heard. I often wondered who wrote it – it was such a beautiful piece of work, so perfectly constructed to trick its way into the most sceptical of hearts. By the end, even I was struggling to defend what I knew against its thrilling bombast. In short, our success was greater even than we had dared hope for and it was for that happy reason that the directors had decided to bring forward the second call for capital. As the minister gave himself enthusiastically to the concluding oration I moved away, fearing that I might somehow be unmasked in the midst of that crowd of believers.

If I thought that I could retain a pristine conscience while the remainder of the Company set about this task, it was only another sign of how slowly I was learning. The very desire for such a thing was a vanity, a shameful arrogance – that I alone should be excused my part in the necessary lie. I reflected more calmly on what Mr Vetch had said – the dangers, the necessities. Finally, and not without a certain pride, I arrived at what he had surely meant: that I had given up the right to honesty for something greater. Whether by chance or Providence, I do not know, but I learned a new word about that time which was much in fashion: I understood that I was becoming what men of the world call a pragmatist.

Two days after the revelations of that night a note arrived at the warehouses from Milne Square. As I had some experience of managing the original subscription, would I be so good as to open a second book for the next tranche of capital without delay? Thus, not only was I to acquiesce in this paternal ruse but I was appointed to be one of its chief purveyors. I did as I was asked. Indeed, I was happy to go further and invented many elaborations on the Company's success, which I would share throughout the day with the more garrulous subscribers. At night I went from tavern to tavern like a spy, hoping not to learn of our troubles. My ears strained after the loathed sound of 'Smith'. Once, almost trembling with fear, I edged within earshot of a rowdy table about which that same secret word was mixed with angry talk of thieving and gallows. The story came to an abrupt halt as my interest was noted. I ran out to the street, laughing at myself for having heard nothing but how a man had been cheated by his farrier.

No more than a dozen subscribers failed to pay, and half of those were dead. By the middle of February the exercise was complete and not a word had been heard of the true reason for it – our fragile vessel had held tight.

The shipwrights' bills could now be paid and as I had, in the meantime, acquired the specification that Smith and Paterson had agreed with them, there was a new subject for my night thoughts. I knew something of the process from watching the fishing-boats and pinks being made in the small yards at Leith. It is like the death and decay of an animal, but in miraculous reversal. First the spine laid down and then the naked ribs clutching like hands or the cage of a flensed whale. Next the wooden skin rises up plank by plank and then the flesh and limbs of decks, rails, forecastle, masts and yards.

Across the sea, in one of the great yards of Amsterdam, the same was happening on a ten times grander scale. Every night I dreamed a more complete ship.

My thoughts on this great vessel soon became part of a general excitement. By March, the directors were confident that Smith's betrayal had remained secret and that we would, after all, be able to pay for our flagship. Anxious to offer some tangible sign of the near two hundred and fifty thousand pounds entrusted to them, they announced that the ship was under construction and would arrive at Leith within a few months. The city fathers were prevailed upon to declare the day a holiday.

This event became the dominant anticipation not only of the city but of the nation as a whole. More than the lengthening days or the rising temperatures, more even than a slight relaxation in the price of grain, it raised the spirits of a dreary and hard-pressed people and allowed us to return our eyes to the future without fear. The complete imprecision about when the great arrival was to be only heightened the excitement. The Company artfully refused to give any further information and was happy to allow a short run to every rumour that the day of deliverance was to be in a week or a fortnight. Every report that passed unfulfilled increased the certainty that the next one must be true. On one occasion, the berthing of a large Dutch brigantine caused a panic rush to the quayside from all over the city. The bemused captain refused to disembark into the incomprehensibly cheering crowd that met his ship. There was a good twenty minutes of bellowing from ship to shore before he made himself understood: the ship was his employer's, a cargo of cheese and salt herrings. Were the people starving? Had a new war broken out? The truth was eventually accepted and a few rotten projectiles bounced harmlessly off his timbers. Most absurd of all was that his vessel was nothing to give a second glance to.

In succeeding weeks there were another two or three of these feverish stampedes as the minor vessels of the flotilla arrived. These had been bought rather than commissioned and, although of a good size and substance, they were not above the best of the Dutch or Swedish merchantmen that could regularly be seen along the quay-sides. Notwithstanding this, they were greatly magnified in the eyes of our people and each was extravagantly greeted as our flagship. I took no part in these vulgar millings but looked down on them from the old bond house where we kept our powder and guns. I felt ashamed to see how excited the crowds became on the most feeble pretexts.

I saw, too, how the Company had become the whole hope and faith of the nation. Even when there was no particular excitement at a new arrival, I would come across groups or pairs, very often men with their small sons, and sometimes individuals of all trades and ranks who had stopped in the midst of their business and become quite rapt at the sight of the *Endeavour*, *Dolphin* and *Caledonia* riding at anchor in the Firth.

They became my concern too, though more prosaically. There was little change in the character of my daily work except that it was now in perfect reverse. Having given my all to fill the warehouses, I now concerned myself with their emptying, boatload by boatload into the holds of our ships.

Though I was never conscious of having doubted the Company or the wisdom of Paterson's design, its full reality came upon me in a sudden rush only in those last months. There had perhaps been some deep, unconfessed reserve of pessimism, a silent chanting over and over of the ancient inherited lesson of the man who forgot his place. All that was gone as the boats constantly shuttled between the ships and the quays, and notices were put in the prints to find captains and officers to sail them. With this renewed exhilaration there was also a creep of fear across the skin, as in a child whose dangerous game is ended when he realizes that his stolen pistol is real and no toy.

As we moved into early summer and enjoyed a slight, uncertain relief from another dismal spring there came a vague rumbling from far above our heads. A crumb from the giants' table fell neatly and timely into our laps. I learned of it first in the High Street one morning when I came across a crowd pressing their noses to the news-boards where the latest London paper had been tacked up. I pushed my way through and read in bold that Their Majesties the Kings of France and Spain, the United Provinces and the Holy Roman Emperor had, in the form of their plenipotentiaries, been entertained by the King of England at his manor of Ryswick near The Hague. Conscious, as Christian sovereigns, of the sanctity of peace and the desirability of untrammelled trade for all the brother peoples of Europe, they had come to amicable terms for the settlement of recent misunderstandings. There followed in fine type a list of towns, provinces, fortresses and ports to be exchanged between these gentlemen as earnest tokens of their intentions. I read not only of Strasbourg, Charleroi, Liège and Namur but also of Acadia and even of San Domingo, Pondicherry and the forts of the Hudson Bay Company. I wondered at the vastness of it all, then smiled. While these lions were roaring at each other, a Scotch mouse was getting ready to run between their legs.

Messrs Farquhar and George took to their beds with grief, but for the Company the benefits were clear. Within a fortnight a stream of tattered soldiery began to arrive in the city, straggling through West Port in groups of six or a dozen, stared at by women yearning for a familiar face. It was an inglorious homecoming. The town council regarded them coldly and gave stern instructions to the watch, who soon learned to look for red whenever there was trouble. The remains of disbanded regiments took up their quarters with each other so that one coffee-house became the possession of the Strathnavers, a tavern the province of the Argylls. They clustered about their captains, hardly less tattered than they were themselves, begging for favours or a secret word of where employment might be found. When, in the middle of May, we posted in every tavern, coffee-house and inn in the city an offer of fifty acres of plantable land, fifty-foot square of land in the town and a house thereon in three years, they re-formed themselves into an army as tightly commanded as on any field of battle and invaded Milne Square down to the very last man.

With a groan I received instructions to create a register of all those wishing to become planters, assistant overseers, overseers or gentlemen volunteers. There was soon a list far in excess of our needs and it was decided to conduct private interviews with some of the officers to obtain accounts of the character of the men.

When it was known there were places for only a third of those on the list, the whole jangling mêlée of scarlet and spurs and swords that gathered in the square at every dawn turned on itself in a frenzy of black rumours. Whenever it was believed that one man had been favoured above others, his reputation would suffer a dozen wounds before the end of the day, each one, it was hoped, fatal to his preferment. In the end, all aspersions were ignored, although one was unusually persistent and did seem to have some substance. When too much drink was taken or too many slighting words spoken, a bitter division would always open between some of the officers and the clansmen of the Highland regiments. It was said that those indicted for the great massacre who had found shelter in foreign wars had now returned and were hiding somewhere in the midst of that shabby, eager crew.

I was aware, as I sat there taking down names, ranks and regiments and whatever few words they wished to tell me to persuade the Company of their fitness for the task, of how little I had seen or done and how shallow and safe that little had been. They sensed it in me, and though I could never say exactly how, they managed eloquently to express their contempt for me and my laughable authority. Before some I had to restrain myself from cringeing, imagining that they might attack me at any moment and for no reason. They were men from whom nothing was forbidden, immune to consequences, ready for anything, good or ill.

It is possible, I suppose, that I did see Drummond amongst them but I have no recollection of it. I was aware from the start that there were other routes to the senior positions, which did not pass through my humble hands. Indeed, save for Mr Paterson himself, I had seen none of the men of authority on the expedition until we left land.

We soon recruited all the teeth we needed. We cast our net more widely, telling carpenters, farmers, builders, coopers, smiths, apothecaries, clerks, weavers and bakers of the good encouragement they would have. In smaller quantities we invited physicians, printers, brewers, and two land surveyors to plot the streets and avenues of our new capital and the best route for our highway to the Pacific. We had all the lading for a new, human ark; every breed of man and everything they made.

For me, those last three months were fully the equal of the three years that preceded them. They were a falling, now exhilarating, now terrifying – an ever faster rushing towards the great day. The recruitment not yet over, the directors finally announced what everyone had been waiting for: in four days' time, early in the afternoon, our flagship would drop anchor in Leith road. Mr Vetch was in town and it was on that account, no doubt, that I received an invitation to join the official party.

I worked in the warehouses from early morning, observing the thickening crowds as I signed out lighter-loads of goods to the three smaller ships and to the *St Andrew*, which had arrived a week before. A dense haar had curdled over the sea since sunrise. The boats would push off from the quays and, after only a few strokes of the oars, would become ghostly and then invisible, unlocatable sounds – nothing but the ruck and grind of rowlocks, the repeated phrase of a simple song for the men to keep time by. Above the mist there was no cloud and the day was warm enough. The weakened sun was a clear disc you could look at directly, a guinea in the sky. The end of the Great Quay was similarly faded, but after a pre-dawn breakfast of bread and chocolate I had walked to the end and seen the preparations. A rope of braided blue and white cut off the last twenty yards where the directors' party would gather. Carpenters were already advanced in the construction of a sort of scaffold that would support three ranks of seating. Two men were standing on boxes, stretching up as high as they could to pull an awning over the top.

I paced in my office and adjusted one or two stock lists in a half-hearted way. At noon, I dismissed my clerks and locked the doors, dropping the weight of the great key into my coat pocket. The quays were already full, the earliest and boldest teetering on the very edge of the waterfront, leaning back on the weight of the crowd behind them. At the back, every possible purchase on the walls of warehouses and chandlers' shops had been used to gain a better vantage-point. Mounting blocks supported a half-dozen at a time, each hanging on to the others to prevent themselves from falling. Small boys and their sisters perched on window-sills like starlings. Messengers and young deck-hands from the fishing boats had hauled themselves up to one of the loading beams outside a merchant's stores. The smallest of them swung in the curve of the enormous hook that hung from it.

The density of the crowd took me quite by surprise and I thought it might take me an hour or more to make my way to the directors' enclosure. I had just started on my first ineffectual 'Excuse me' when Mr Miller, my chief clerk at the warehouses, barked out from just behind me, 'Make way there! Make way for the Secretary to the Company! The Secretary to the Company, ladies and gentlemen. Make way, please!'

I was about to hush him up, but such was the immediate success of his demand that I had no time. I received a firm shove from behind into the narrow lane that opened before us.

'Best get on while we can, sir!'

'Thank you, Mr Miller!'

'Not to worry, sir. I'll be right behind you.'

In this way, with the occasional trumpeting of 'Secretary to the Company!' to renew our privilege every thirty paces, the doughty Mr Miller facilitated our passage through the crowd.

At the beginning of the Great Quay he suddenly disappeared. As he unblushingly explained the next day, he had come to the point at which he needed to go another way to meet up with his own party. Too modest to shout out my own position and fearing, in any case, that the claim would seem less convincing coming from myself, I kept quiet and accepted that I would soon become bogged down. To my relief, and to my further embarrassment, the very opposite happened. The space about me was like a wave, rolling on under its own impetus. After another few yards, the people who parted to let me pass had no idea who I was. I was struck on the shoulder and turned ready with an apology only to find a butcher, still in bloody apron but with a face almost tearful with pride. 'Good on you, sir! Well done!'

At once a hail of congratulatory slaps landed on my shoulders, propelling me more rapidly towards the end of the quay. Occasionally, my hand would be seized and vigorously shaken.

'Well done, sir!'

'God bless you, sir!'

I almost stumbled over the rope that marked off the directors' enclosure. One of the doormen from Milne Square was standing guard. He gave me a nod and I stepped over it. I found myself beside Sir Robert Chiesly, his face frozen in amazement as he realized that I was the cause of all this excitement.

'Some sort of misunderstanding, Sir Robert. I don't know who they think I am. I was just—'

'Is that so?'

He walked away to join his equals.

The mist about us began to thin, although over the sea one could still see only a mile or so. The forms of the *St Andrew*, the *Endeavour* and the other ships faded and darkened as the haar drifted over them. I took a glass of wine from a footman. I recognized Sir Robert Blackwood standing under the awning talking to James Gibson, a Glagow shipowner we had done some business with. Mr Farquhar of the gunsmiths and powder-makers joined their conversation. I thought I recognized some of the city councillors and I believe – he had been pointed out to me only once before – the great Fletcher of Saltoun. D'Azevedo, as usual, had been detained in some other part of the world. I feared there was no one to whom I could open my mouth until I noticed Markinch, also standing alone, blinking moleishly at the light. I moved towards him and we exchanged banalities on the weather and on when we expected the ship to arrive.

Behind us, from somewhere beyond the blue and white rope, there was a sudden swell in the noise from the crowd. Markinch and I both looked seaward but it soon became clear that the commotion had some other cause. From the thicket of caps and hats waved aloft or thrown in the air it was possible to detect the movement of someone through the press towards us. This was a greater acclamation, altogether more confident and based on no delusion. The excitement lapped up against the rope and washed back to reveal, in fine knee-breeches and summer coat of grey and blue silk, Mr Paterson himself. I had not seen him since that freezing day of the closed meeting and the revelations of Smith's treachery. I remembered his appearance then with a pang, but felt a thrill of joy to see him in his finery, representing in his own person the recovery and triumph of our Company.

We settled down to wait, our facile conversations constantly distracted by glances out to sea. Only Mr Paterson remained entirely silent, undisturbed by the refusal of any of the other directors to talk with him. He seemed to have selected a spot at which he expected the great vision to appear, and kept his eyes steadfastly fixed to it.

From the slight elevation of one of the benches I looked back towards the wharves and warehouses. Now, not only the harbour was full but also the streets leading down to it. All the higher ground was occupied in a grand arc like an amphitheatre, formed from gaping humanity itself. From time to time the smell of roast mutton drifted over us, accompanied by the sound of a voice coarsely shouting a price. Somewhere, a fiddler played for coppers.

Perhaps an hour passed before there was a general murmur from the people. Everyone turned seaward. At first we could see nothing and it seemed to be no more than an agitation of the crowd, each one setting the other on to see what was not. Those with us on the quays soon returned to their talk and their drinking but the people on the streets above continued to stare out over our heads.

One of our party had come equipped with a glass and declared there might be something there, but he could not be sure because of the mist. Mr Vetch was in one of his rare holiday moods.

'Come on then, Rory. We'll make a lookout of you. Up with him, on his shoulders!'

I protested as best I could, but in a moment was manhandled on to the nearest willing shoulders. Markinch was the surprising volunteer for this task – I fear the effect was a little ridiculous as he is by no means a tall man. Nevertheless, a raucous and good-natured cheer went up from the people all around as the glass was handed up to me.

Questions were shouted from every direction as I swayed on my improvised watch-tower, trying as best I could to keep my narrow circle of vision on the horizon. Although the mists had cleared from the coast and we were by then in almost undiluted sunlight, the miasma over the sea was still so dense and confusing that I could hardly find the horizon. I kept my other eye open fearing that, nine-tenths blinded by the restricting tunnel of the telescope, I might be the last to see her rather than the first. About me the crowd became more and more importunate and I strained ever harder to see something other than mist and water. On the higher ground people began to point so that the mob on the quays became convinced I could see her but would not tell them for some wicked reason of my own.

'You must see her. Where is she?' they demanded.

'Why don't you give that thing to someone who isn't blind,' shouted another.

'Come on, Rory!' growled Markinch beneath me, already resenting his burden.

I was on the point of saying I had sighted her anyway, thinking that if the people weren't satisfied there would soon be some disorder, when one point on the horizon became lighter than the rest. No clear form was visible, but then a tiny hair of darkness appeared, standing vertically above the light. A moment later I could see it was part of the top mast. Out at sea it seemed that the wind changed, or that there was a sudden gust so that the mists sheared away and I saw her all at once as if a cloth had been snatched from over her.

I don't believe I shall ever live to see a more glorious sight. I swear she was proud: she swaggered over the sea to us, knowing her own magnificence. The great sails puffed out, wrenching her through the water with what seemed, through the exaggerations of the eyeglass, a prodigious speed so that I almost feared she might trip over herself and plough down into the sea. I saw that my fears were groundless when I caught sight of her bow cutting through the waters, sending white remnants to left and right, biting at the waves before. I cried out when I saw her: 'Yes!' I shouted. 'Yes! There she is! There!'

A great roar rose from the crowd. The sound swept back along the quay like fire through powder, each person's joy exploding on to the next. Those on the streets above us who had strained their eyes and been unsure, and those on the quays and strands who had seen nothing until the mists had cleared, all of us, we saw her together.

There was a forward surge of people, those behind determined to see as much as those at the very water's edge. A good dozen or so were sent plunging into the harbour although none, I am happy to record, came to any harm, all being hauled into one of the many small craft that were about that day. They were soon shaking themselves like dogs and boasting of their auspicious baptisms.

I was myself so absorbed by the sight that I did not notice for some time the silk clad shoulder beneath me. I had the honour of handing the glass down to him before getting my sweating mount to kneel and set me on my own feet again.

As she approached more closely, we could see men in the ropes and leaning over the yards taking in sail. When almost all that sunny whiteness had been folded up she crept to her mooring by the four smaller ships, dropping her anchor from her bow with a great splash into the still waters of the firth. The cheer that greeted her first sure sighting had died away as she made her slow progress towards us. Now that she was still and we could see her every outer detail there was no reprise of this, but a deep communion silence eddying out from that anchor-drop and quietening at last even the most boisterous and drunken of the crowd.

One by one every man, woman and child on the strands, quays and roads above them fell silent as they gazed on their *Rising Sun*. We had been proud before of the *Dolphin* and the *Caledonia* but now they seemed contemptible skiffs besides this triumph. She clearly overreached even the *St Andrew* and her timbers were so new and pale that she was not only larger than the rest of the ships but brighter too.

The rigging was as white as fine thread and the wood of the masts and rails seemed to have a sheen on it that would have pleased any London cabinet-maker. The casements about the stern-lights were a wonder of carved carmine and gold, and hanging out from them on a bracket the stern-lantern glinted in the sun, its metal as brilliant as if it had come from the coppersmith's shop but a day before. Just above it, wonderful in its capriciousness, in the confidence of its luxury to a people who had lived so long by the simplest necessities, was a large golden globe – the sun itself. To the smallest infant we seemed to have been struck dumb by the sight. Greater even than the sight was the knowledge that this was ours, our great argosy, our gilded India-man. It was more than we had ever thought ourselves capable of.

By now the last of the sail had been furled up and her gun ports opened with a rattle, their edges marked in scarlet. All along her nearside the black snouts of her ordnance were pushed out. Somewhere out of sight a cord was pulled and from the main masthead our standard unfurled into the breeze; a gilded sun rising over the world. At this signal a roar of cannon fire rolled over us from the castle batteries. The *Rising Sun* answered with a stunning blast of fire and sulphur.

For me, the joy of this event was at first crushed and then multiplied a thousandfold. The first blow was swift. The next day was one of furious activity in the warehouses. The flow of goods into the holds of the other ships had been steady, but now it was a flood pouring in spate into the cavernous holds of the *Rising Sun*. I became the subject of constant shouted demands for instructions. Papers were thrust before me for signature. Goods were loaded on to the wrong ships and had to be unloaded and transhipped, bolts of canvas were dropped into the harbour and had to be fished out and unrolled on the quayside to dry. Those who guarded the weapons in the old bond house refused to let a single musket ball out of their sight without my presence. At noon I was confronted by the lightermen with a list of six reasons as to why they should be paid more.

All this would have been nothing more than an irritation if I had not learned a short while before that the full list of those accepted for the expedition had been posted in Milne Square. I did not consider the possibility of my own name not being there but I was, nevertheless, in a passion of curiosity to see the whole list. I made a poor bargain with the lightermen and then sent a messenger-boy into town to get a copy of it. In my liberal mood I overpaid him and never saw him again – no doubt the weight of my shilling in his pocket curved his steps into the nearest tavern.

It was not, therefore, until after seven that I could get away from the warehouses. In Milne Square there was still a steady stream of people to and from the noticeboards. I watched one young soldier dance with delight as his finger stopped over his name. I read the list studiously, starting at the bottom end, as it were – the planters who covered several sheets. Then there were the gentlemen volunteers and then at the top, a sheet of several short columns where now familiar names were divided by their rank and function. Without any knowledge of the meaning of the words I read of Pincarton, Drummond, Mackay, Stobo, Galt, Cunningham, Munro and others for the first time. Samuel Vetch appeared first among the list of councillors, the only one who was not also to have command of a ship. As I was progressing, albeit slowly, in the ways of the world, I was not altogether surprised to find that Mr Paterson's name did not appear.

I realized, calmly at first, that I had gone through the entire list and missed my own name. I re-examined it more closely finding, first with relief and then with mounting irritation, three Mackenzies, but all of them among the planters and most definitely not myself. To make quite sure, I read it one last time, my finger, like that of the young soldier, stopping at every name, my lips miming their syllables. I damned the printer to eternal torment for his carelessness and marched into the Company offices. Sir Robert Blackwood was in, but occupied. I paced in the ante-room for nearly half an hour before protesting the importance of the matter. His secretary, wishing to show that he could see Sir Robert even if I could not, entered the inner room to return a moment later and say that, if I wished, he could convey a note. I wrote a few lines, folded the sheet and handed it over. Another quarter of an hour passed before I could hold my peace no longer. The secretary's mouth twisted with satisfaction. He assured me that he had put the note in Sir Robert's own hand and that, if I particularly wished, he would go and see if there was an answer. Another five minutes passed before he returned with another folded sheet. This he handed to me and stood insolently close as I read it. Sir Robert regretted his indisposition and was sorry to hear of the misunderstanding *vis-à-vis* my position relating to the expedition. He was not aware of any errors in the list of those selected to go and had always believed it clear that my services, for which the Company was grateful, would continue to be required in Edinburgh. There was no signature and the hand was unfamiliar. I looked up into the complaisant features of the secretary. As he opened his mouth to speak, they began to blur and I ran.

I came to myself in the High Street, the secretary's note a tight ball in my fist. I went to Maclurg's, sought out the most obscure table I could find and set to drinking an interminable series of brandies. For hours I struggled to form a single coherent thought out of the empty space before my eyes. Suddenly, I was sure I could hear Colquhoun's voice. Looking back, I think it was some sort of strange daymare brought on by the shock and the spirits, but I believed it at the time and blundered out of the place as if it were on fire. I attracted censorious glares in the street and rolled away into a close. My wise legs carried me to Widow Gilbert's and up the stair to Susanna's attic room. Plumper than ever on her constantly improving business, I was able for an hour or two almost to forget until exhaustion, nervous and physical, brought a sort of sleep.

I awoke resentfully at first light, my mind brittle and seared. I dressed as quietly as I could. On the bed Susanna whimpered like a dog in a dream hunt. I wondered what her quarry might be as I pulled the single sheet from her and looked down at her naked form, still only a vague pattern of white flesh and dark hair. For a minute the image did what I most wanted: filled my mind sufficiently to allow everything else to be forgotten. Her body curled in search of its own warmth and I covered her again, glimpsing as I did so how easy it might have been to live an entirely different life, caring nothing for all that has most maddened and possessed me these last three years.

For a while I had the city almost to myself. At the last quarter before five, the sun rose. I walked through the bread-smelling streets, bought the first paper of the day from an early news-boy, paced like a sentry outside the door of Mrs Purdie's until she opened. She bustled in the back room, yelling out questions and comments through the clatter of dishes and spoons. Whose bed had I come from at such an hour? She knew the town well enough. She was all alone first thing, save for Mr Purdie and what use was he? Hadn't I seen the *Rising Sun* come in and wasn't that a sight? I stayed silent as my eyes bleared before the paper. I fumbled for my spectacles. The paraphernalia of breakfast rained down on my table, the food flooding me with appetite, momentarily cleansing me of self-pity.

'I remember you when you were first in here, Mr Mackenzie, I swear I do. There's a man who'll go far I said, very first time I saw you, and now look. I can tell things like that, and my mother was the same, you know. I can just tell.'

She paused by my shoulder to give me another chance to break my silence.

'Ah, well,' she picked a thread from my coat and patted me on the head, 'I'll get on.'

I ate my breakfast and bought a rum to drink with my coffee as I ran over the columns in the paper. I read of a world I no longer seemed part of and reflected bitterly on the inadequacy of Mrs Purdie's prophetic powers.

I was awoken by the smash of a plate on the tiles and jerked my head up from the table. The place was full, even the other half of my table being occupied by an old man who took his pipe from his mouth to bid me a good morning. I picked my way over the shards and walked out into the full brilliance of the morning.

I was looking up, under the shadow of my hand, to get sight of a clock when a familiar, though at the time unwelcome, voice demanded my attention. Mr Vetch opened the carriage door and signalled for me to join him. 'Take the morning off, Roderick!' He was clearly unaware of my situation and I thought it easier not to explain. 'Come and meet the Duke of Hamilton.'

I took my seat in the carriage beside Mr Vetch and found myself facing Lord Belhaven, John Hamilton by name, on his way to meet his kinsman.

The carriage continued for only another two or three minutes to the western extremity of the High Street where it stopped on the south side. I looked up at the Duke's town house – four tall storeys with confidently large windows, which gave the appearance of being cleaned daily by many hands. I noticed that immediately to the left of it issued the long wynd I had come down on my first arrival in the city. The recognition brought with it a memory of my feelings that day, and lifted my spirits a little as I realized I was about to fulfil an ambition.

It was Lord Belhaven who, disdaining the bell-rope, gained us admittance by banging on the door with the head of his cane. The footman scrutinized me severely and looked towards Lord Belhaven, who looked towards Mr Vetch.

'Mr Roderick Mackenzie, secretary to the Company.'

The footman nodded.

'The Duke thought he would receive you in the library.'

The room, at the back of the house, took its name from two bookcases against one wall. Down the left side was a row of tall windows, the middle one a door leading into a garden so long I could not see the end of it.

The footman left us. Mr Vetch seemed in a strangely high mood, talking volubly about the progress of the Company and asking me for news of the lading from the warehouses. None of his talk was of any consequence, however, and I understood with some surprise that he was nervous. This was something I had never seen before and the thought that there were others as far above Mr Vetch as he was above me almost made me jump.

The footman reappeared, clearly having warned the Duke of my presence. His gloved hand opening the door to the garden – 'Perhaps Mr Mackenzie would care to see the garden?'

I found myself standing on a paved terrace, my whole body burning with indignation. I even cursed Mr Vetch for turning me into such an unwanted guest with his whimsical invitation.

I looked down at a double line of yew trees clipped to the form of enormous eggs. Beyond them, a dense hedge with a single narrow opening blocked any further view. Aware of the presence of the footman behind the glass, I went down the steps and started my slow walk between the yew trees. I looked up to the hills and to the brown thread that ran between them. I thought I could see something small, parasitic in scale, moving along it. I took my spectacles from my pocket and looked again to see a cart drawn by two donkeys led by a man on foot. Behind him a single horseman appeared over the rise and stopped. I felt as if I were looking back in time at that earlier, unlearned Roderick approaching the city for the first time and gazing down at the pleasure gardens of the great town houses as a pilgrim gazes at the first sight of his holy city.

I walked through the gap in the hedge to find myself at the beginning of a maze, still young enough for me to be able to see a little of my way ahead by standing on the tips of my toes or by jumping a few inches. Imagining after several turns that I was very cleverly making a map of the maze in my mind and that I was on the point of understanding its whole pattern, I found myself turning into what I believed must be the centre only to find my way blocked. I was about to turn back when a woman's voice stopped me. The hedge was thin at that point and I could just see the shapes of two figures in pale dresses on the other side. Now, rather than jumping to see over the hedges, I bobbed down to ensure that the top of my head didn't give me away. I was immediately conscious that it made me a spy and I crept backwards shamefully without declaring myself.

'I don't care, Sarah,' were the last words I heard, 'I've said it mustn't happen again and it had better not.'

'Yes, madam.'

I retraced my steps, or so I thought, only to find myself after another half-dozen turns confronting the two women. The older, though I should think not above thirty-five, sat on a bench drawing her needle through a piece of embroidery. Her maid stood beside her, a ball of yarn in her hand. I was about to offer my apologies and an explanation for my presence when her furious stare turned my voice to stone. As the lady was not prepared to break the silence I stood there with my mouth open, looking more ridiculous by the second, but absorbed by the conviction that I had seen her before. Sarah's head was down and her shoulders were beginning to shake. My attempt at a bow was enough to cause her to explode with laughter, turning to the hedge behind with her hand over her face. The last thing I saw as I withdrew in confusion was the Duchess herself beginning to smile.

I wandered for a few minutes more in the maze, searching my memories for that face. The footman appeared before me. 'Her Grace thought you might wish to see other parts of the garden?'

I followed him out until he left me at the entrance by the yew trees. I wanted to leave but could see no way out of the place other than through the house itself. I admired beds of roses, stroked the leg of a stone nymph, heard the clocks strike the half-hour. I walked along the high wall that cut off the filth and noise of the wynd. Trained fruit trees held out their arms in artful symmetry. I guessed that one was a peach, its fruit small as apricots – green and hard as they would always be. A movement attracted my eye to an open window. The lady sat there looking down at me. She turned her head to speak to her maid and a moment later Sarah came to draw the curtain. The sight of her half obscured sparked the memory I had been searching for.

Having lost patience with the situation I re-entered the house and found myself back in the hallway. Loud voices approached from the direction of the library. The one I did not recognize was the loudest of all.

'No, no, no! I tell you, gentlemen, I cannot. His Majesty has a settled view of the matter and there is no . . .'

The three men entered the hallway and found themselves not alone. I saw that the Duke was indeed the man whose carriage had nearly run me over three years before. There was a curt leavetaking.

'John, Mr Vetch.'

'Your Grace.'

Bows were made.

Lord Belhaven, Vetch and I stood in the street, Belhaven's carriage trotting up to meet us.

'You go on.'

Belhaven got in and left us without a word.

Mr Vetch gazed unseeingly at the buildings opposite. 'I'm sorry, Roderick.'

*

IN THE DAYS after that absurd encounter my warehouses seemed like hourglasses, draining their contents into the holds of the ships, my part in the great venture bleeding away with every barrel and bale. I would stay at home and read the letters they sent back. I would check the price of the Company's stock in the newspapers and receive the colony's accounts twice a year and write them up in new ledgers. And yet within a month all this was merely as if I had eaten salt the better to enjoy my drink.

My task at the warehouses ever diminishing, I was more frequently required to attend Milne Square. I forget the particular occasion, but I happened to observe a clerk completing a record of the previous directors' meeting. He wrote Vetch's name, drew a line across the page and put 'absent' in the opposite column. I thought little of it until a week later at another meeting at which I myself was taking the minutes. Sir Robert archly pronounced Mr d'Azevedo's standing apology and then added that Mr Vetch regretted that his illness would once again prevent him from attending. This struck me, as the purpose of the meeting was to agree a departure date for the ships. After taking navigational advice and hearing from me that the warehouses were almost empty, a date eleven days in advance was set.

I stood outside in the hallway, transfixed by the selfishness of my calculations when Markinch walked in from the square. I managed to intercept him before he disappeared down the stairs and learned that Mr Vetch was staying with Fletcher of Saltoun. He added – as if my prayers were being answered minute by minute – that there was even some talk of his not being able to join the expedition.

I hired a horse from Maclean's, and by two in the afternoon was approaching a fine manor house. The name of the Company gained me ready admittance and on this occasion I waited in a real library, three of its walls dark with leather spines from floor to ceiling. I stated my business as a concerned visitor enquiring after the health of Mr Vetch. This was true enough, if a little incomplete. Try as I did to control my prayers, the heavens were loud with my pleas for his recovery to be harmlessly delayed for a mere eleven days.

A door opened after a few minutes to reveal the great scholar himself, the man I had recognized from the end of the pier when we both watched the arrival of the *Rising Sun*. He effused that kindness reserved for immeasurably distant and harmless inferiors. I was complimented extravagantly for my infinite trouble in coming such a very long way to show my concern for Mr Vetch's health. Mr Vetch, nevertheless, regretted very much that he was still under instructions to receive no visitors.

'It's not serious, I hope?'

'His doctors seem quite happy.'

The flow of nothings came to an abrupt halt. I tried quickly to think of what I knew about Fletcher, what his sympathies might be, what it might be safe to tell or ask.

'Does he know about the decision?'

'There was a courier here half an hour before yourself. I'm sure a man like Mr Vetch keeps himself well informed.'

'It will speed his recovery, no doubt.'

Fletcher of Saltoun pinched the spine of a book and seemed for the first time to think about what he was going to say.

'I understand that excitement can delay recovery in such cases, Mr Mackenzie. But, of course, I'm no physician.'

'If it's not impertinent,' I asked, 'does the condition have a name?'

He waved his hand dismissively. 'I suppose it must.'

He saw me to the door himself and there, either because he had decided something or because he had indeed almost forgotten it, he held out a note from Mr Vetch.

'He does appreciate your coming, Mr Mackenzie, I do assure you.'

Once back in my office in Milne Square I carefully snapped the seal on Mr Vetch's letter. There were the conventional sentiments expressed with the careful formality of the old Vetch when I first knew him. The remainder was precisely indefinite: *I shall not obstruct your wishes, whatever they may be, but most strictly I tell you that I cannot and do not give you any advice.*

What did it mean? I read it fifty times, tried to make impossible deductions from the paper, the seal, the writing – was it that of a sick man? How would I know? I lit the lamps and read it again. A failure of heart, perhaps? That seemed the least likely explanation of all. It was with some reluctance that I finally decided to believe what I had been told. Vetch was ill then, quite simply, but still, what did it mean? I wrote a reply: if it was possible for anyone to benefit from his misfortune, I hoped he would remember me. I trusted he would not do anything unwise with respect to his health.

Four days passed until one of my warehouses was completely empty. I paid off six men and set the others to sweeping the dust out of it. Still I heard nothing. I watched the colonists line up in columns, one for each ship. They shortened throughout the day as the lightermen took them out a dozen at a time. Instructions came from Milne Square to begin transferring the arms and powder from the old bond house – other than the ferrying out of the captains themselves, this was to be the last act before departure. Had Vetch recovered? Had he favoured another? Perhaps no one would be sent in his place, or then again, perhaps someone had bribed their way into his boots?

I knew that the next day there was to be another meeting of the directors. I arrived early and looked down from my office windows, tensing as each carriage appeared. Vetch did not come. The noon post brought a packet from him. It was even briefer than the last, but contained a separate sealed note addressed to Sir Robert Blackwood – *Use this if you wish, Roderick, but remember I advise neither one thing nor the other.* I examined the note to Sir Robert, tested the seal with my fingernail, held it stupidly up to the light. What if there had been a misunderstanding? Doing nothing seemed the only truly impossible course. I gave the note to a clerk with instructions to take it to Sir Robert's office.

I lunched at Maclurg's and tried to walk off my nervousness in the city. I returned at three to look at the salver on the side-table that received important internal messages. It was empty. I returned at five and again at seven. Still empty. Agonizing trivialities detained me at the warehouses the next morning, but I managed to return to Milne Square a little before one. I opened the door of my office gingerly, peeking through a narrow gap, frightened to let go of the last moments of ignorance. I saw the salver on the side-table, still empty. I repeated the wanderings of the day before. I returned at four, again empty. Perhaps I should talk to Sir Robert directly? I did not have the courage. My fate was a hair-sprung trap – the merest touch and it would snap shut on my ambitions.

The next morning I entered my office in a sterner mood. I moved strangely about the room, sat at my desk at an unaccustomed angle. The salver had become a gorgon that I must on no account look at. I told myself that it was certainly empty, so why should I bother? There were several days yet. In truth it was that very emptiness that gave it the power of the petrifying eye, the soul-ambition lost, freezing one for ever in the last attitude between recognition and defeat. For all my promises to myself, I soon began to catch its pale edge out of the corner of my eye. Even when I looked in the very opposite direction, its shape began to float before me like the after-glimmer of a full moon. I turned to stare it out and break the spell. The small, folded, unsealed note that lay on it carried my name in Sir Robert Blackwood's unmistakable hand. I eased it open to read a single word, and then a little wider to see a phrase of two or three. As my eye fell on the word 'regret' a cold sweat started to gather on my spine. I closed the letter again and, in the closed eyes, hands together (note crumpled between) and face upward position of the all-believing child, uttered a last supplication to my neglected Creator. Could He please rewrite the words of the letter before I had to read them? I would have made God my forger to get rid of that 'regret'. I snapped the paper flat and read the four pinched lines at a single gulp. I read them again. I put my head down on my desk and wept.

How long I sat like that, I do not know. Time became the feeblest of the universe's powers. It was annihilated absolutely. I trembled as at the onset of a fever, had visions more vivid than those of any opiomane, more real than the damp wood beneath my face and, as I now know, more true. They receded at last. I raised my head from my desk and let it hang over the back of my chair, stretching to see the sky upside down through my low windows. I gasped, lay unstrung as after escape from a literal drowning. I read it again. And then I read it again.

> As Superintendent of Cargoes with rank of gentleman volunteer at the rate to be settled for that rank. Strictly no other function granted save at discretion of senior captain at sea or of councillors on land. Regret no variation of terms possible. Indicate acceptance by return. Immediate effect.
>
> Sir Robert Blackwood

I searched through the dust of old Latin lessons to find some high-flown strophe of rhetoric that would do justice to the joy I felt. It was a hopeless task – indeed so much so that I now despise the emotions of those poets as miserable foothills by comparison with what I experienced in the minutes after reading Sir Robert's note. I resorted to manly brevity, refolded the note and dropped it on the salver on my clerk's desk as I left the office.

I walked as fast as I could to Baillie Ritchie's house, breaking into a run every few steps. There I took twenty pounds from my box under the floorboards and threw myself on the city's best tradesmen. I bought a dozen shirts and as many stockings, three pairs of stout boots and a jar of grease to keep them supple – the latest formulation, I was assured, especially effective in the torrid regions of the world and repellent to all snakes and spiders. We shall soon see. I bought a pocket compass and a folding knife from a chandler, a stout green jacket from a tailor. I saw the envy in his eyes when I explained to him why I could not wait for him to make me one of a more suitable colour. I bought a neat campaign writing box – including this very pen – and finally a waterproof chest. I watched as 'R.M.' was painted on the lid in elegant red letters. All these I asked to be delivered at once to Baillie Ritchie's house.

Once back in Milne Square I wrote my farewells. After an hour of writing to my mother I had covered half a sheet. I decided that she, too, would appreciate concision. I wrote to my brother and Dr Lennox. Because I knew it would vex him, I even wrote to Colquhoun. I wrote to James Minto and Douglas Whyte to let them know what their little drinking partner, whore-fellow and paymaster was doing now. I addressed a businessman's courtesy note to Cohen d'Azevedo. I left instructions for one of the porters at Milne Square to collect my chest from my rooms and deliver it straight to the warehouses.

At Baillie Ritchie's house my purchases had started to arrive and were beginning to cause some excitement. By happy chance all the family, except the married daughter, were present and I was able to make an impressive announcement in the best parlour. At news of my departure, Mrs Ritchie looked wistfully, I thought, at her second daughter and even became a little tearful. Ritchie himself was heartily congratulatory and waxed pompous on the Christian virtues of trade. I declined the evening meal, claiming demands of last-minute business, but accepted a valedictory glass of claret. Ritchie shook my hand again in the street.

I made my way to Widow Gilbert's for my final adieu. There I found Susanna languishing on her draped divan – a present from another worshipper, but enjoyed by one and all – her hand already outstretched to receive my present. She regarded my box of honeyed figs and bottle of muscatel with the gratitude of a sultana receiving tribute from one of her most malodorous subjects. She took the news of my departure with the equanimity I had come to expect of her; after all, business was good. In the last sun of the long day I spent myself in her with the appetite of one who does not know where his next meal is coming from. I lay with her till midnight, never in more than a half-sleep filled with visions so real they would wake me with a start. I had intended to stay till morning, but at the midnight chimes I could stand it no longer. The image of that great ship in the Firth filled my mind and pulled at me as the moon pulls at the tides. Once again I looked down at Everyman's sweet little whore. But in what changed circumstances! And with what changed feelings! No magnetic power in that musky softness now, wooing me to the poisonous ease of a surrendered life. No soft-singing, mooning tug to the lovely, hateful, day-by-day animal compromises. Rather an enticing repulsion, a prickling instinct of danger, a glimpse such as, I believe, is permitted to very few, of the awful banality of pleasure. I drew my hand over her pale, tight skin, cupped the well-fed belly wherein there stewed a broth of sweet wine and all but one of my figs. I knew then, with an entirely novel certainty, that when I commanded my hand to lift itself from that warmth it would do so at once, and without complaint. I left her room for the first time with neither remorse, nor regret.

I arrived at the warehouse at one to find that my chest had been delivered exactly as instructed. A sudden burst of shouting and laughter told me which of the shuttered quayside taverns was still entertaining. After much thundering on the door and loud assurances that I was not the watch, I was admitted and managed to scare up the only two lightermen still capable and willing for business. I lay back in the bow as they pulled on their oars. Above me, Vega glittered. The great swan flew through the endless cloudy band. Never had I been more certain of the world's benevolence. The boat stopped with a bump. I looked up at the mountainous blackness of the *Rising Sun*.

Part Two

Perhaps two pages more, three at most and I would have caught myself up. I left this account with one foot on the summit, but return to find my stone rolled to the very bottom of the valley. One never catches history.

History! The word fills me simultaneously with gloom and elation. Not only have I slipped hopelessly back from the summit of completeness, but my burden now is ten times greater than before. I must give up the lacy vanities of biography for the solemn weight of History. I would not begrudge a share of the laurels to any capable collaborators, but I must report that I have, at best, been able to detect no more than two or three occasional diarists and none of these is a man of substance. Willing or no, I am the historian of Caledonia.

It is Sunday. I have come to the highest point above the landward coast of Caledonia Bay to rest my hands in the unaccustomed and perhaps curative exercise of writing. It is very necessary as they are already more transformed than any other part of me, except perhaps my mind. Palms scaly as lizards, and where not calloused, still smarting with tender blisters. No man is, or wishes to be, above the common task.

This is no mountain, but a hill nevertheless of sufficient height to command all that lies about for a distance of several miles. It has the virtues too of being accessible by a well-worn Indian path and having a jumbled rocky top that keeps it clear of obscuring vegetation. There is an arrangement of these rocks that makes a very serviceable seat for the human frame. Here I now sit under a sun made gentle by a haze of vapours from the heavy rain that fell last night. If for any period of time I remain entirely still, small splinters of rock reveal themselves as finger-sized lizards – very different from the large green ones – and begin to move in short dashes from sun to shade and back again according to their desires. One even climbed my boot to sun himself. A tiny earthquake from me made him disappear, quick as a dream. From the west I can just make out the constant bickering of a type of gannet that crowds the cliffs here with a wondrous thickness – they have already afforded us some excellent, though strangely fishy meals. From time to time there are the calls of other birds for which we have no equivalent and no names. There is the short shrill laugh of a creature we have not yet set eyes on, but which the Indians say is some sort of monkey. They have not even a Spanish word for it and Mr Spense who, like a latterday Adam, has already started a list of their own words so that we may know how to describe our new world, has not yet come to this one. The only other disturbance is the quick double beat of pairs of our men with axes. Every half-hour there is a creaking, a whishing sound like a change in the breeze. There is a tiny tremor in the green tops below as another tree falls and another yard of Paterson Avenue is cleared.

My pen makes a sundial on the page and still I have said nothing! Forgive the disorder, but there is one other thing I must set down first. Namely, a description of the literal foundation of our new republic, which is as perfect a vindication of our scheme as could be wished for. Within hours of our arrival here it became clear that Mr Paterson had planned more wisely than he knew. The good Lord himself, had he wished to enter upon a career in commerce, could not have created a more convenient nor more defensible harbour than we have possessed ourselves of here. The only wonder, and it is truly a wonder, is that we are the first to see this treasure for what it is and to stretch out our hand to take it. Genius is rare!

Caledonia Bay is a long wide loch that runs parallel with the sea and is divided from it, and very thoroughly concealed, by a peninsula. At the innermost end of this loch its form expands to an enormous acreage of still and deep water – the reason for calling it a bay –

which will in time accommodate with ease any number of vessels of the deepest draught. The seaward side of the peninsula presents an aspect of the most hostile cliffs, below which no worthwhile landing of men or weapons could ever be effected. Although the main body of the peninsula is broad it is joined at its root by only a narrow waist of land. Captain Drummond has already declared that a fortification must be built across this and it would appear to be an easy task. A league or so beyond the mouth of the bay a line of small islands trails out from the coast. Together they are known as the Pine Isles. Except for the largest, which is Golden Island, they are too small for any European to have named. On each the saltire has already been raised. At the mouth of the bay the Designer of this happy topography took especial care for the safety and convenience of its holders. The passage is by no means difficult and the water is admirably deep, but it is divided into two channels by an underground rock, which barely breaks the surface at the exact mid-point. For the careless or unwary intruder, or for any vessel manoeuvring to avoid fire from the fort we will build on one side or from the battery that will be established on the other it will prove a fatal hazard. Save for these rocks, the land all about is thickly wooded. Some of the trees are types of pine very similar to those we know at home, but most are entirely strange. Amongst those we have examined, we have not yet found the Nicaragua tree. Around the trunks of these trees is an impassable chaos of vegetation. Much labour with hatchets and machetes has already begun to improve the situation, but for the most part we must still make our way about by water or along the shore. We have found traces of some ancient footpaths, but they are something of a mystery and seem always to connect places of particular uselessness. The land on the southern side of the bay is well supplied with springs which, insofar as we have been able to determine in this short space of time, are wholesome and reliable. In this respect the peninsula is not so well equipped, although there is a small source near where it joins the mainland and a marshy area at its seaward end where we may sink a well.

Such, in the briefest details I can permit myself, is the face of our new capital. I have not lifted my eyes from the page to describe them, so deep is the physical impress they have made on my mind. If tomorrow, or a minute from now, I were to wake from a fever and find myself in my room above the High Street it is this place that would seem more real and to which my heart would yearn to return. I confess that I borrow this idea somewhat from Reverend Mackay who has, if I may say so without too irreverent a smile, some very interesting ideas on the origins of these feelings. But onward, Roderick, onward! What an age you take to say nothing!

When did I first see this place? An age ago, and not yet half a month. My account almost up to date, I rewarded myself with more time on deck, justifying my premature relaxation with the thought that as Fate had appointed me recorder-in-chief I had better be on hand to guarantee the truthfulness of this account.

Gratifyingly, I discovered that as with the scarcity of any commodity, so my sojourn below decks had increased my price. There were solicitous enquiries after my health and gentle probings as to the possibility of my having withdrawn in response to some offence. I did not admit to this and was glad to find that the grumblings with respect to the provisioning had indeed died without trace and that, so far as I was aware, Captain Galt had still not found time to read the envious document addressed to him on that topic. Indeed, these surreptitious attacks I now recognize to have been part of a general bout of mid-ocean backbiting amongst the colonists. The starvation of the landward mind caused by having nothing but a watery horizon to gaze at for weeks on end does little for judgement or charity.

By this time even the feeblest of navigators had realized that land was near and all the five boroughs of our floating town were feverish with excitement. Captain Galt did not appreciate this mood and issued a notice to all ships that the first land would be the island of St Thomas, at which there would be no general disembarkation.

I was woken one morning before first light by the splash of plunging anchors. I fumbled about on deck until the first lightening of the sky – a sultry blanketing of clouds – revealed a darker mound a thousand yards to our starboard. As day broke, the rails and lower reaches of the ropes became crowded with colonists staring avidly at their first sight of living green since we left Madeira. Small guards of five men on each ship were detailed to stand by the landward rail and ostentatiously clean their muskets, the purpose obscurely described as being 'for the protection of our colonists and volunteers'. If the faces of the unhappy musketeers on the *Rising Sun* were honest then I'd say they had treason in their hearts, for they looked as longingly as the rest of us at that tiny oasis of unshifting, saltless earth. Had we still been there at nightfall I dare say some would have tried their luck. As it was, we were there only long enough for the briefest of embassies.

Captain Galt had himself rowed across to the *Caledonia*, whence he collected Mr Paterson and continued into the harbour. This was, I have since learned, one of our guiding genius's early proving grounds. It was here that he learned the arts of trade and left behind a name that is still remembered. How many hours passed, I don't know. Sweat ran down our skin like lice, draining even our appetite for that solid greenness. The clouds trapped us into a bed of feverish heat. There was a wooden thump as one man fainted. Others went below. Those who waited on deck soon looked as if they had been swimming in their clothes. I took my hand from the rail to see a sweaty print on the wood. In the space of a minute I watched it shrink and disappear. All wind had dropped and the water curled like oil.

Early in the afternoon the *Rising Sun*'s boat appeared again, inching its way out from the harbour mouth. When it turned to place Mr Paterson back on the *Caledonia* we could see that, besides the rowers, it now contained three men. Captain Galt soon climbed over our rail and took Mr Cunningham aside to speak a few words with him – and not very pleasing ones at that, if I read our first officer's expression aright. The two men joined the rest of us to peer down at the boat wherein we saw our two seamen with their oars raised, and facing them from the stern a grey-fringed pate, moribundly rigid between a pair of threadbare shoulders. Mr Cunningham's equable expression was, I sensed, the result of some effort on his part.

'Help the good captain aboard, Mr Cunningham.'

With that, our own good captain, having had to endure as much human intercourse in the last few hours as in as many weeks, withdrew to his cabin.

The order required some ingenuity in the execution. After several gruff rejections from the immobile head below, a painful and hardly dignified contraption was improvised from a few lengths of rope. I watched the work intently, but it outpaced my inexperienced eye and quite baffled me until, with a conjurational flourish, a kind of harness was presented, attached to a good length of cable. Hauling it over the lowest spar, two of our stoutest seamen put themselves into a flood of sweat as they heaved up this strange burden. The whole man appeared, dangling in mid-air three feet off the rail, still staring straight ahead, his body retaining a now comical seated posture as if it were quite unaware that it had parted company with the boat. The rope he was hanging from was hooked in, allowing him to be safely lowered on to a chair. Finding himself the sole object of attention of more than a hundred souls, he struggled to his feet. His sword quavered under his weight. His eyes passed over us without finding any point worth stopping at – either that or they were no longer capable of conveying to his mind the distinction between one face and another, or indeed between a man and a mast. The face, as crushed and tanned as an old purse, was of an almost native darkness. Voluminous breeches, patched as desperately as an old fishing net, seemed – from what pictures I could remember – to have been borrowed from a Netherlandish arquebusier of the dying years of the last century. There was a once fine undercoat with a prodigious frequency of buttons indicating the wearer's contempt for convenience. Hardly two of these buttons now bore any resemblance to each other. Over this lay a stiff coat of that universal grey-brown-green dullness that serves as the mortal remains of all colours – I noticed as I observed this coat that he had acquired an immunity to heat. A belt, as broad and as buckled as that on any fashionable cavalier of fifty years since, hung from right shoulder to left hip where his weapon-crutch rusted peacefully in its scabbard. He stroked a beard whose only colour was that of tobacco juice. He decided he had seen enough of us. Muttering something under his breath, which was certainly no compliment, he clambered stiffly up to the quarterdeck and helped himself to Mr Cunningham's quarters, the occupation of which he had negotiated as part of his price. The man's identity was a greater surprise even than his appearance. Here was the night-terror of Spanish children who, if they have not forgotten all about him, must now retail his exploits to their own offspring. One of the most feared predators of the main, the incendiary of Portobello. In short, a buccaneer! No less than Robert Alliston, one of those very men I had read of as a child. And yet, what a pitiful gulf stretched between all the vicious poetry and boy-thrilling enchantment of that word and the careened hulk of a man we had taken on board as our pilot. For those who will never see such things for themselves, and our specimen must surely be one of the last, let me tell you that there are few things in the world as sad as an old buccaneer.

In his time with us – and he is here still, muttering about the decks of the *Rising Sun*, waiting for the first ship to take him back – only one opinion of this gentleman has been reported to me, overheard by the steersman of the midnight watch.

'Trade! If they want something, why don't they take it?'

Hence his humiliation in guiding mere traders to the coast where he had once only to ask to be given. With what a rush the world now changes that such a man could still live and yet be so curious an ancient.

We left St Thomas promptly, our colonists staring sternward at its solidity until the horizon hid the tallest palm. At sundown Thomas Dalrymple, of whom we knew little, was buried at sea.

In common with all the landsmen, I did not anticipate either the length or the difficulty of the journey that remained to us. The sight of land had cheered us and we happily reasoned that our final destination, being made of the same stuff, could not be far off. For a few days after our departure from St Thomas, one or two other islands sustained our optimism. On the *Rising Sun* at least, our captain chose not to disabuse us of these hopes and when the horizon became once again an unbroken circle of water and remained that way for day after day, the ship became solemn. Four or five times in a day violent rain squalls would throw us about and drench the decks. These, already heated till the timbers bled tar, would throw off dense, bitter vapours. There was a great increase in sickness. As reports of conditions on the other ships were signalled to us even Dr Munro's mood deepened. Six days out of St Thomas he added up the figures and asked for the decks to be washed daily with vinegar.

The heat of this zone and the extraordinary humidity of the air, which makes it weigh down on the chest with every breath, turned us all, I believe, a little feverish. This, with the strange light in that vast gulf, wrought on us a most dispiriting deception. From afar, these squalls had such a concentrated darkness that several of us – and even myself on one occasion, though I was too cautious to say so – mistook them for land. Once planted in the mind this concept tinges the rain-sheets with green and makes the cloud-heads wave like palms. So cunning was our desire for land that the delusion would sometimes convince us until we were only ten or fifteen minutes' sailing time from the squall. Disillusionment would be quickly followed by another steamy drenching.

After several more days of this I was woken, half-way through a night of lurid dreams, by the sense that we were no longer moving. There was no moon behind the clouds. The feeble light of a few lanterns was soaked up by the darkness. A tiny glimmer, too faint to be sure of, indicated the possibility of one of our sister ships to our starboard. I looked about, but could find no trace of the other three. From above came shouts and sounds of canvas and rope as invisible men took in the last of the invisible sail. I made my way up to the quarterdeck, which I found deserted save for the watch. I shielded one of the rail lanterns in an attempt to see beyond its glare, but still could not make out anything. When I turned back Mr Cunningham was there. He asked me if I had seen it yet.

'Darien?'

'Close to it. It's the mainland, certainly. We're waiting on Grandfather Alliston's opinion.'

'I can't see a thing.'

At the rail he pointed me in a certain direction.

'Wait.'

The wind began to pick up, making the lanterns gutter. Blood-warm drops of rain landed like flies on my cheek and hands. Alliston appeared beside me, reaching into the lantern to pinch the wick. In the immediate aftermath of this extinction, the old cut-throat was as invisible to me as the supposed coast. My eyes widened to catch the last fraction of starlight that penetrated the clouds. Alliston was there again, darkest grey against black. A colourless trace of a form. He looked up and sniffed the air like a hound. My arm was seized powerfully. I strained my eyes but still could see nothing. Then Alliston's fingers convulsed as the world appeared before us in a brilliant, shimmering flash. I just had time to see a coast of high, brown-black cliffs with a line of white at the bottom as the seas broke over boulders. It disappeared, leaving us more blind than before.

'Is it Darien?' I asked.

If there was a reply, it was drowned by the long, groaning peal of thunder that rolled over us. I waited by the rail, hoping to be able to add some redeeming detail to the discouraging vision of the first flash. The cliffs flickered into existence again, as stark as a skeleton. Alliston was leaning over the rail, trying to recognize a gully perhaps, or one of the tall trees on the tops. I saw the true reason for his snuffing out the lantern. He was wearing the most unbuccaneering pair of spectacles imaginable – small black-rimmed lenses, thick as an old lace-maker's.

The thunder came more quickly, sharply cracking over our heads. As the noise subsided I could hear a low murmuring from Alliston.

At first I couldn't make it out, but as the rumbling of the thunder decreased it resolved itself into a long list of names. 'John Costelloe, Jed Ferris, Billy Preece, Old Man McAnaney, Nat Clark, Samuel Chalk, Cat Casson, Dem Dempsey, Joe Fish, the Quinn brothers, Roscoe, McMinn, a fine cruel man, Nigger Webb, Davy Plymouth, played with the only arm he had left, Peter Pope, Ned with the eye, and the other one too . . .'

And so it went on. I can't say if any of these names were pronounced exactly by Alliston, but I have tried to render as best I can the music of that list. Surnames and forenames would reappear often enough, dancing with other partners so that it all became one, making an eerie continuo under the ever more frequent crashes of thunder. He held his spectacles in his hand and looked more at the sea than at the cliffs. He turned away and spoke to Cunningham. 'A hundred miles westward. Against the wind.'

I could hear the hissing of rain striking the sea and went below as heavy, warm drops began to splash the deck. I drank brandy to help me sleep, and while waiting for it to come, blearily gazed at my coat on its hook, Alliston's lampblack thumb-print marking the arm.

He was right on that last point. The final hundred miles of our journey drained more from us than the first thousand. Alliston's 'hundred miles westward' became two hundred or more as we tacked and tacked again against a sly wind. Every time we found an angle to make some headway it would turn against us, leaving the sails flapping like flags. More than once we were taken aback. A stunning shock would shudder through the whole frame of the ship as it came to a sudden halt. Once, as the light was failing, a gust veered against the *Dolphin* and almost ploughed her under with the force of her own sails. The swell obscured her and I, never having seen the like before, was certain she had been gulped down entirely. Captain Galt, more in evidence at this time and often at the helm himself, looked on stony-faced. Whether he expected it or not I don't know, but she came up again, decks streaming. A count, later reported to us, revealed only two crewmen lost. I had more respect for Captain Jolly after that day.

A lull on the next Sunday allowed us to bury one David Hay, died of a fever, and John Lucason, the printer's boy, the latter not yet sixteen. Reverend Mackay, much concerned of late by the enforced brevity of such proceedings, took rather too much time over these despatches. The wind picked up again before he had finished, and as he tried to return his hat to his head, he had it plucked from his fingers and thrown on the water like a wreath.

For all this time the coast was rarely out of sight and I took comfort from the slow change from the grim, rocky aspect that first appeared that night to a greener, more accessible land. The winds, though still contrary, began to moderate. Three days after the burial of Hay and Lucason the water turned a pale yellow. Alliston emerged from Cunningham's cabin to inspect it. He was pleased. The colour comes from a great river twenty miles to the east of our new home. That evening, for the first time in ten days, the wind helped rather than opposed us. Just before sundown, piled banks of cloud near the horizon broke to let the sun shine straight into our eyes. The silt from the river was now like a wide yellow road leading us on our way. The last direct light from the sun caught certain grains in this silt, which concentrated the light and caused the sea to sparkle with a fire-like brilliance. I turned to Mr Shipp who had joined me with many others to watch this spectacle – but he forestalled me.

'Best not to say so, Mr Mackenzie, even if it does. It can be bad luck, you know.'

We kept our augurizing to ourselves.

The next day we dropped anchor in ten fathoms off the most inviting part of the coast we had yet seen. Alliston had donned his spinster spectacles again and tried to dredge up some memory that would fit a boulder or tree or distant hill. He wasn't sure and a party was sent ashore with casks to get water and more information. They returned at four in the afternoon, casks still empty, much to the consternation of Munro, who had become anxious at the prospect of exceeding the average fatality or, as he put it, wastage for such a voyage. No springs had been found, nor any of the other signs Alliston thought he remembered from thirty years ago. They did bring several brace of gannets and, still alive, a large leaf-green lizard which one of the men had caught basking on a rock. This miniature dragon – fire-red tongue and all – was the subject of much fascination and amusement. One of the crewmen put a twine about its neck and tried to lead it about like a lap-dog, but the beast would not co-operate in this humiliation and had to be dragged across the deck, its claws scratching lines in the wood. Whatever nourished it, it was nothing we had in our holds and it soon sickened and died. As for the gannets, we eyed them greedily, but Munro persuaded Captain Galt that they should be reserved for the sick. He had a broth made from them, which seemed to do some good.

Wearily, we hauled up our anchors again and resumed our attempts to outwit the winds. They slackened and then, without reason, forgave us and settled gently at our backs. Alliston appeared more frequently, putting on and taking off his spectacles as if a blurred image of the coast might jog his memory better than a sharp one. These sightings were closely watched for some sign of recognition but I never detected any change in the strange fixity of his features. I formed the notion – a last trace of romance from my boyhood readings, perhaps – that some deep feeling at this return to his old hunting grounds so occupied his mind that it had no power left to animate the outer man. At night, the winds dropped still further to a stillness we had not experienced for a fortnight or more. The sounds of land tantalized us – the great nations of birds that populated the cliffs and the sounds of the sea breaking about the rocks below. From time to time there was a single, sharper cry from the edge of the forests. On one occasion I saw light from a fire whose maker, no doubt, could see our lanterns with equal ease. I looked about for someone to tell but was alone at the time. In the end, I said nothing. Closer to hand was the coughing and feverish moaning of the worst affected of our colonists whom Dr Munro had brought up on deck to take what benefit they could from the cooler air.

It was on Monday 28 October that this pattern was broken. The coast ahead seemed to move out at an acute angle, almost blocking our way. As we got closer it became clear that it was not part of the mainland but an island separated from it by a narrow channel. As it was known that this was one of the signs we should look for, the decks were soon crowded. All our vessels, sailing close in the light winds, dropped anchor in hailing distance of each other. Alliston was summoned from his cabin to give his opinion. With spectacles on, spectacles off and finally with Captain Galt's spyglass he ignored the island but examined the coastline closely for what, on that day, only he could see – the mouth of Caledonia Bay, all but invisible from the western approaches.

With much shouting between our main vessels a party was got together in two boats. In spite of loitering in the vicinity of the ladders like a dog around a dinner table, I was not favoured with a place. Captain Galt, Mr Cunningham and Alliston – lowered down the way he had been hauled up – occupied one boat along with their rowers and four redcoats. Drummond, Captain Pincarton and Mr Paterson with a similar complement occupied the other. They rowed steadily towards a darker patch in the trees. After a certain distance I noticed the boats begin to shimmer as if they were made of water themselves. They disappeared as they rounded the head of the peninsula that conceals the bay from all but the most informed observers.

Six hours later they re-emerged, the only evidence of their existence in the meantime being the report of a single shot. Captain Pincarton reached his command first and a moment after he set foot on his deck a loud cheer went up from everyone on the *St Andrew*. We were wary, and waited silently to hear from Captain Galt himself. He positioned himself impressively on the quarterdeck before saying a word and sternly maintained his habit of never addressing the crew or colonists directly.

'Mr Cunningham, prepare to disembark!'

We added our cheers to those from the *St Andrew* and soon the whole flotilla was loudly celebrating with the help of double rations of brandy.

One of the redcoats pulled the victim of the shot we had heard from a sack. He held it by the tips of its wings and stretched it to its full span. There was the most brilliant creature I have ever seen – a bird that seemed to have caught the sun like a prism and split it into every possible colour across its wings, breast and tail. Truly, we have come to a land of wonders!

It has been decreed that this St Andrew's Day is also to be the founding day of Caledonia and a holiday from all work. It shall be the hottest any Scotsman ever celebrated and the most deserved too. I would swear that never have twelve hundred souls laboured so passionately as we have this last month. Mr Paterson is the author of the idea and has gained much credit for it as well as sympathy for his sad loss.

I had not seen Mrs Paterson since our encounter on Madeira. My next and all but last sight of her was pitiful indeed. Those too debilitated by the trials of the voyage – and there were no more than a score or so across all the ships – stayed aboard to be tended there. Mrs Paterson was the exception, being brought ashore on the tenth day; the courageous woman determined to be with her husband and to feel our new land under her bones. I was there by chance, sledge-hammer in hand along with a dozen others making a preliminary landing stage on one of the few areas of gravel about the shores of the bay. As a boat came in from the *Caledonia* we continued our work, seeing only crates and bundles of cloth. One of these had almost been carried past me when I noticed with a shock the drained, colourless face of a woman I could only just recognize. We stopped what we were doing as she was carried by towards a new clearing where some tents had been pitched. A man with a shovel hid it behind his back. Two days later we laid our first flesh in our new soil.

The event, by the way, helped one arm of our little state achieve a victory over another. The selection of a site for kirk and cemetery had been made by the Reverends Mackay, Stobo and Borland on the third day from our arrival. On the fourth, the same spot was pronounced by Drummond to be most suitable for an entrenchment. Simultaneous declarations on the impossibility of compromise quickly followed. Only the prospect of being responsible for keeping poor Mrs Paterson above ground allowed our soldiery to beat an honourable retreat. Mr Mackay officiated with triumphant dignity. Drummond has been pacified by the council's acceptance of his plans for the fortifications and for the siting of a gaol. He was most insistent on the latter although, as we have not discovered any good source of building stone, nor yet have any malefactors to put in it, this seems likely to remain merely an ambition.

What next, what next? I hardly know where to turn. Perhaps our compatriots – if that is not too presumptuous a word – should be in the first rank of this account. Compatriots, or at least fellow inhabitants, there certainly are and they very boldly made themselves known to us on the second full day of our presence here.

Two bumps on our hull was the first sign of their arrival. Ropes had been put out for an advance party on shore and in no time they made their way up these like a troop of monkeys and stood on our deck, thirteen in all. They carried weapons, but it was clear that these were more to honour than to threaten us. As we stared at them in fascinated amazement, they looked about themselves with no discernible interest or surprise. Although we had never seen the like of them before, they gave every sign of being familiar with the likes of us and our vessels.

Without a word being spoken we soon understood that one of them, the only one who did not carry a weapon, was different from the other twelve. When Captain Galt came down to the main deck it was curious to see how these two specimens of humanity, as remote from each other as any two beings of the same class can be, recognized with some sort of ancient instinct, the unique authority that each man held. Galt declared that we were merchants, come to settle peacefully in Darien and to trade with anyone who would trade with us, to make ourselves and the country prosperous.

Their leader, the man we have come to know by the more pronounceable name of Andreas, seemed not to hear any of this but pointed up to where the saltire flew from our top mast. Captain Galt said that we were Scots, but this did not seem to have any meaning for them. The man spoke briefly in his own language, maintaining his unsmiling expression, and there the exchange ended. Mr Spense was already being rowed over from the *Endeavour* and until his arrival we contemplated each other in silence.

We are able to look down on the men by an average of three to four inches. The women are shorter still, seldom exceeding five feet. They are round-faced like Chinamen with a nose not so flat as a Negro nor so high as our own. Their eyes are as large as cats' eyes and are all of the same dark brown. Their hair is similarly uniform – deep black and very straight. They allow it to hang down to the middle of the back, the women tying it together behind the head with coloured strings. A few heads are grey, but not many live to that age. Their teeth are notable, being of a particular whiteness and straightness and never, so far as I have seen, with any gaps. The colour of those we have come across varies as little as that of their eyes or hair – all are of a middle brown like a strong Virginia tobacco leaf.

The women, from their eleventh or twelfth year, wear a cotton cloth about their loins but the men as a rule have no such apparel. The thirteen that stood on our deck concealed three inches of their bodies at most. The first two were the upper lip, on which a crescent plate of metal is suspended from the bridle of the nose. It seems to us a curiously inconvenient ornament but it in no way prevents them from speaking and, I understand, is removed only for eating. The third inch is the tip of the penis which is contained in a funnel or cone after the manner of a candle snuffer. The whole organ is pulled back in its natural covering and held upwards against the belly by a string which attaches to this cone and ties around the waist. Save for occasional items of European clothing worn as trophies, these two adornments represent the full extent of their modesty. We have learned subsequently that these cones are made of diverse materials according to the position and resources of the wearer and are as reliable a guide to rank as the cloth and cut of a gentleman's coat. Some are no more than plantain leaves curled to the correct shape, others are made of copper. For a gentleman nothing less than silver will do. We were honoured that day by twelve silver cones while the end of Andreas's yard was encased in polished gold.

Mr Benjamin Spense duly arrived and correctly guessed that his only common language with these men was Spanish.

'This is . . .' He made a garbled attempt at the leader's real name.

'Capitano Andreas,' intervened 'Captain Andreas'.

'This is Captain Andreas. He would like to know who we are and what we are doing here.'

Galt repeated his explanation and Spense conveyed it to Andreas.

'Captain Galt, he wishes to know what Scots are.'

'Do they know where Britain is, Mr Spense?'

Another few words of Spanish.

'That doesn't seem to help, sir.'

'Then I suppose you might as well tell them it's just to the north of England.'

Spense turned to convey this only to find the word 'Ingliterra' already being passed around the group in sudden recognition.

Andreas gave another doubtful glance upward to our flag before speaking again.

'He would like to know if we are enemies of the Spanish.'

'Tell him . . .'

Captain Galt paused and listened carefully to Mr Cunningham, who leaned closer to whisper some advice in his ear. He put on a diffident expression and replied with a quiet 'Very well'.

'Tell him we have no enemies but are peaceful traders concerned only to enrich ourselves and our country by honest labour.'

The message made its way into Spanish and thence to the native language. There was a brief conference among the thirteen, which ended with a disconcerting murmur of amusement. The reply made its way back through the first two languages and brought such colour to Mr Spense's cheeks that several of us took a step closer to be sure we did not miss a word of it.

'He says, Captain, that a man who has no enemies has no friends. He wants to know if we have come here because we have no friends.'

Captain Galt straightened. There were more words between himself and Mr Cunningham which, unfortunately, I missed as I had to listen to Reverend Mackay's opinion on this exchange.

'A very bold and witty people, Mr Mackenzie, do you note it? It is exactly what I would have expected.'

I was surprised to see at this point that Captain Galt was showing some signs of embarrassment. Nevertheless, he declared very firmly that no man had ever harmed a Scotsman and not suffered for it. If the Spanish made that mistake then they would know what it is to have a Scotsman for an enemy.

'Well said, sir,' murmured Mr Cunningham.

'All papists are our enemies.'

'Thank you, Mr Mackay.'

Captain Andreas was conversing with his silver-tipped lieutenants again. He spoke to Spense in Spanish.

'He says that anyone who is an enemy of the Spanish is a friend of theirs.'

'How convenient. Tell him, Mr Spense, I am sure our two peoples will be friends. As an earnest of which we respectfully request the permission of . . . of this gentleman . . .'

'Captain Andreas.'

'Obliged to you, Mr Spense. Permission to live and work peacefully in this country. Do you have the document, Mr Cunningham?'

Cunningham, who had just returned from Galt's cabin, handed over a blue velvet baton, which Captain Galt pulled apart to reveal a scroll headed with our arms and signed by every member of the Court of Directors. He rolled it up again at once, returning it to the baton.

'Don't they have to sign it first?'

Captain Galt, however, was already losing patience with the whole affair. He hissed in Cunningham's ear with uncharacteristic temper. 'I don't think these gentlemen brought their pens with them today, do you, Mr Cunningham? Let's just get on with it, shall we? Get something suitable.'

Captain Andreas accepted the velvet baton with solemn uninterest. Several minutes stretched out unpleasantly before the second mate and Mr Shipp arrived *dona ferens*. A horn-framed mirror seemed to be quite a success. Captain Andreas tested its effectiveness with his own features before holding it up two inches from Captain Galt's nose. There was some comment from him, which greatly amused his followers. The presentation of two campaign wigs was merely baffling and did nothing either to advance or retard our cause. The final gift, or at least the final official gift, produced entirely the desired effect. Two of our older muskets were received with great delight. They became the centre of a circle of fascinated Indians who jostled with each other as they reached out to stroke their every rusting part with awful reverence. For a while we were quite forgotten and Captain Galt took the opportunity to address Mr Shipp, who stood by us, sweating under the weight of a small keg of powder. 'A little too generous, I think, Mr Shipp.'

It was quickly taken below.

One final and spontaneous donation made our guests' joy complete. Throughout the proceedings the colonists and crew had been rapt and silent spectators, but at the last moment a young seaman, shoved from behind with a rough word of encouragement, came forward. A black bottle passed from hand to hand. Captain Andreas uncorked it and cautiously inhaled. He waved it under the nose of one of his men for a second opinion. It was all I could do not to laugh aloud when I saw those black eyebrows rise in that apparently universal gesture of reluctant acceptance I had seen so many times while attending on gouty old connoisseurs haggling over the claret in Colquhoun's office. In a moment they were gone, the slam of Galt's cabin door as their salute.

I stood by the rail and watched them as they paddled back to the coast. Mr Mackay stood by me a while. As always when in his presence, I struggled to find some suitable comment. Not wishing to seem cold I finally, and without much conviction, decided on the suggestion that amongst our gifts should have been some clothes.

'Adam had no need of them, Mr Mackenzie. Clothed in the glory of God's perfection!' He nudged me in the ribs and quite took me aback with a salty wink. 'Perhaps we shan't need them ourselves now.'

He did not wait for a reply. Like the others, I have taken Mackay for a sort of modern holy fool and I still say there is that in him, and an obstinacy besides. Yet there is something else less common, something that makes him occasionally talk a strange, bold sort of sense. For all that, I can't make him out at all.

I returned my gaze to the Indians. When they had gone about half the distance I could hear a low repetitive singing from them, which continued until they were out of sight. Just before that point, when I was no longer sure that I could see them, something brilliant flashed in the sunlight before splashing into the sea. At such a distance it must have been my imagination, but I had the conviction that something blue followed it.

Since that day they have been good and discreet neighbours, coming to us only once in a large party in which we saw their women and children for the first time. They brought a great number of pineapples, which have amazed us all with the goodness of their flesh and have, besides, been very beneficial for those still sick from the voyage. We have learned to find these for ourselves in the forests. Some, having seeded themselves, are found on their own, but the fruit has long been cultivated by the Indians and we have come across old plantations with many hundreds. I saw some once in Edinburgh, shrivelled from a long voyage, but could not afford to buy them. Here we pick them from the ground as big as men's heads, exactly as I had once imagined. They taste of the best of all fruits together in one. They brought several other fruits we have not seen the exact like of before and the visit was a good lesson to us as we are in a hazardous state of innocence as to what is good and what may be harmful. There were red fruits about the size of a pear but clustered together in groups of twenty or more like giant grapes. There is a large stone at the centre and one gnaws round to get the flesh which is astringent like a bitter orange and stains the skin a gory colour. They grow atop a sort of spiny palm so well defended that the Indians cut the whole tree down to get at the fruits. This is a great labour as the heartwood of the trunk is so hard they make arrow-heads from it. 'Pejebay' is our approximation of what the Indians call it and is now our word for it too. There are bananas in great profusion and plantains too, larger than the banana and always green. Some of our people discovered to their cost that it is best boiled before being eaten. They brought also a basket of something small like a bergamasco pear with a skin like a russet pippin. Benjamin thinks it is what the Spanish call the 'sapodillo' while Mr Paterson says in Jamaica they call it the naseberry. In any case, it is very sweet and though sustaining has little character. They brought sugar canes also, which we were very pleased to see as we have high hopes of repeating the great commerce of the West Indies. Mr Paterson has calculated that even the land on the peninsula, if the soil be well suited, could produce ten thousand hogsheads of sugar a year. To all this we responded with two good steel axes, which greatly pleased them.

*

Our own affairs progress apace. We are all conscious of the approach of the last day of the month and of its great significance. The thought of it keeps us to the task like titans racing to produce the first rude sketch of a new world worthy of our saint's day. The time to scratch down another few words in this book I must steal from sleep. Yet sleep is already a beggar grovelling for four hours' alms a night. To take more would be another and wickeder theft – from the common weal to which we are all free and willing slaves. Some work by moonlight and if the sound of an axe or shovel wakes another colonist, there are no complaints but rather two new hands joined to the task. The most reviled accusation is that one has let another man do one's own work. There is a great fear of being thought to pull on a rope less mightily than one's fellows, to dig less deeply or to have cleared less land by nightfall. Idleness is treason, sleep is treason. Every man wishes to settle on his farm or in his house in the town when the time comes and to know that he has paid for every square yard or every brick of it at no less a rate than his neighbour. The sailors, who are paid for their work and have no share in the colony, sun themselves like seals on their decks but are despised. Already, they come on shore only when required. The landsmen are bonded by exhaustion and a hope the seamen have no part of.

Some knew what work was before they came, others have met it, and joyously too, for the first time. I am one of these, and the record of my education is set out as much in this script as in these words. I wrote before of the pain and blisters, but now there is something different. Used to pressing hard against the grain of an axe or pick-handle all day, it is now as if my fingers refuse to acknowledge the contemptible featherweight of a pen. I can hardly feel it at all and must look as intently as a child to be sure that I am writing correctly. I press harder than before, making the lines thicker. In short, my hand is not what it was and I look at a finished page with hesitant recognition as if I were looking over the shoulder of another scribe, or at some old forgotten document of my own, which must be read carefully before memory finally connects and authorship is admitted.

Two days ago, another more general surprise greeted me. I rose early and began to walk round the shore of the bay until I reached the landward side where there is, at the moment, no work being done. Aching from the previous day's work, I took off all my clothes and laid them out on a rock whose day-old warmth I could still feel through the soles of my feet. In the vestigial pre-dawn light I could see a vague outline of my form, its alien whiteness making it just visible against the darkness. Oddly, my arms from the elbows down are now so darkened by the sun that I had only an idea of their presence. I proved their existence by moving a hand to obscure some of the fires I could see across the bay. No doubt the whole of my face and head were covered by the same cloak of invisibility. I plunged out of the hot air and into the water. At first there was an exhilarating shock of cold and I broke the surface gasping and thrashing. In truth though, the temperature is well above any I have experienced around our own coasts and it soon settles on the skin as a luxuriant coolness that I was very reluctant to leave. I swam perhaps for a quarter of an hour, straight out into the bay until I could no longer see the shore. I floated there for a while until the darkness thinned and a crack of red began to glow between the clouds and the horizon. It was half light when I returned to my rock and it was then that I noticed how my whole body had changed – the arms and legs thicker, the bony shoulders smoothed by their swollen muscles, the chest and flanks no longer the anatomist's model they had always been before but approaching something that would not, or so I thought to myself, disgrace a good piece of marble. I must admit to being highly pleased by this transformation – as perhaps only a clerk can be – and was engaged in admiring myself when I caught the sudden sharp hiss of one person strenuously hushing another. I crouched down, suddenly aware of my nakedness. I looked about, but there was still some time before sunrise and the light was poor. I started to gather up my clothes and was about to withdraw a little into the undergrowth when I heard voices. One was undoubtedly Reverend Mackay – the rock in question is close to the site being cleared for his church. Notwithstanding his comments on the Indians, I had a particularly strong desire not to be found naked by Mackay and began slowly to make my way backwards towards the obscuring decency of the nearest vegetation. He, from a position I could still not detect, suddenly shouted some words of Gaelic. Gambling that he had still not recognized me, I bolted a dozen paces or so into the jungle, luckily not encountering anything spiny or poisonous. I pulled my clothes on and, after a wait of ten minutes or so, returned to the rock and thence round the shore of the bay to the main part of New Edinburgh. I was last in the queue for breakfast, but attracted no comment, or none that came to my ears.

The day that followed was like many of those I have spent over the last few weeks, save that it exceeded them in intensity to an extent that left us at the end in a death-like bliss of exhaustion. It started as I was finishing my breakfast when I found myself by chance in the company of a dozen men detailed to clear some land on the peninsula. I happily attached myself to them and we filed through the forest for half a mile until we reached a fresh clearing.

Perhaps a quarter of the designated area had already been cleared and that, I was told in a significant tone, was the result of two days' work. The cleared land, with everything chopped to within an inch of the ground, was admirably level and, judging by the thickness and vigour of the vegetation it lately supported, will be an excellent soil for our first crops. Only the greater trees have been left – which in this very ancient part is the majority – so that the work still gives nothing like the appearance of a field but rather that of an impossibly large building, its remote and dim green roof supported by random pillars.

Where the cleared area ended the vegetation rose like a hedge, sometimes to the waist, sometimes as high as the shoulders. This was our battle-front and I was one of thirteen that ranged themselves across it and waited for the signal. In my hand was a machete – I recall signing two hundred into the warehouses at Leith – a villainous piece of ironwork conceived by a master of destruction. The wooden handles are plain and without any concession to the shape of the human hand. The rest is a straight blade, a foot and a half with a single slashing edge and no point. They have an extraordinary weight, the spine being never less than a quarter of an inch thick and closer to a half near the end so that the whole instrument combines the incisiveness of a sword with the brutishness of a club. When I first picked mine up I feared that, even with my new strength, my contribution to the day's task would end in exhaustion after an hour or two at most. I soon learned, however, that this weight was my friend – although a man must struggle to raise it, for a blessed second his task is over as all that is required is to direct its murderous fall to the desired stalk or creeper.

In the middle of the row stood a giant of a man. He held his machete high like a flag and when it fell the other twelve fell too. The line moved slowly at first, testing the new ground as well as the twelve links in the chain. After a few minutes, a decision seemed to have been taken and agreed as to the proper rate that would keep us together. No one was willing to show any ambition to move ahead.

Almost at once my right arm and shoulder were in agony. I began to miss my strokes, ploughing the head of the blade into the ground or finding nothing but air and letting the heavy blade swing past me, wrenching my shoulder. My neighbour in the line gave me an uninterpretable wink.

'All right, son?'

'Fine,' I gasped.

The humiliation renewed my strength as I watched him out of the corner of my eye, trying to learn from the easy skill with which he scythed through the swarming growth.

The pain lessened only as it was overtaken by a numbing semi-paralysis. I could still move, but without any precision. My arm would faint away in the middle of a stroke, letting the blade fall harmlessly on its side, or into innocent soil or clang loudly on a stone. I changed the machete to my left, but after another few strokes I almost cut off one of my feet. I returned it to my right hand and was almost at the last of my strength when everyone stopped.

'Ho!'

The long wordless cry came from the giant in the middle, a Galloway farmer as I have since learned, Oswald by name. Twelve machetes dropped with a single sound. Some men, myself included, sat on the ground, hunched over their knees, heads down, heaving for breath. Others kept to their feet, either still or moving round in little circles, looking down at the ground or stretching their spines straight again with heads thrown back to suck in more air.

'Hup!'

Perhaps three minutes had passed, though it never seemed so long. Those who were standing bent slowly to pick up their machetes while those who sat used their blades as crutches as they climbed stiffly to their feet. We took our positions, no longer looking to the centre of the line but standing, or rather hanging motionless, over our weapons, calculating the most fatal slash into the strangulating nightmare of stems and monstrous distorted leaves before us. Unwilling even to turn a head unnecessarily, it was now the sound of Oswald's first cut that was our signal. Twelve blades fell after the first as close as the taps on a drum roll.

The pain in that second bout was no less, but it was more endurable. I was learning what the peasant learns from childhood: that physical suffering is a taste he has no choice but to acquire. The cramps of exhaustion raging in my arm and shoulder became in themselves the subject of my labour. Every swing, which always seemed certain to be the last, was an exploration into new and different pains; a scalding agony in every muscle from wrist to neck, a grinding fire deep in the shoulder, the crushing of the palm and fingers on to the edges of the handle to save it slipping from a sweat-drenched grasp. Before the second call for rest I could see the pain. The colours darkened and shapes writhed. Nothing was steady and what I could fix my eyes on would flicker as if illuminated by a private lightning. Had the call come a second later I would not have heard it or taken any further part in the day's labours.

This time I fell rather than sat on the ground and was saved only by the arrival of the water-carriers. The few women we have with us and the boys still too young to do a man's work have taken on this task. All day they cross the bay to fill barrels at the coolest springs and distribute the water wherever work is being done. We drank greedily from a ladle, but twice only in obedience to Munro's fierce prescription. A sack of salt was passed about, each man thrusting in a wet finger to collect his measure. I lay on my back, struggling for air, and looked up at the dense, baffling canopy of green that denied us the faintest breath of wind. As I closed my eyes and ground the salt between my teeth I found myself back in Lennox's schoolroom. It was the old story of the Roman soldiers dying from too much water after a desert march. We didn't believe it. '*Sitire*, gentlemen. What is *sitire*, please?' Now I know.

'Hup!'

And so it went on. Ten minutes of fire, three or four of rest. Water every rest break, salt every five. The exhaustion reached its limit and stayed there. I learned the limit, and having learned it, forgot my fear of it. The knowledge that I could go on was in itself a new strength. Save for Oswald's calls for rest and work, a word was never spoken between us. Each man was alone with his ordeal, sealed into his own furious solitude. Speech could only have been an intrusion, especially any that required the wasted energy of a reply. Worse still, it would have diluted the force of that especially silent bond that strengthened between us with every blow.

The world was everything within reach of my blade. Whatever was beyond it was not worth a glance, nor even a thought. Towards the end of each period everything beyond my reach ceased to exist. A black hood of exhaustion and pain would shrink around me until I could see nothing but what I could reach with my machete and destroy. The call for rest would come – hands would wipe sweat from filmed eyes, eyes would close on their own fiery redness and open again, restored.

At first there was little reward for the work. At the call for rest I turned, hoping for encouragement, only to find that our efforts seemed to have been entirely without effect. But as the day went on, and became timeless to us, the cleared strip at our heels widened like an afternoon shadow. It was a field of slaughter, a stubble of severed roots and stalks. Some bled white and one plant we encountered very often gave out such a volume of fluid it was as if an artery had been cut rather than a stalk. It congealed quickly in the air and stuck to our hair and clothes in strings. Two small specimens of the plant were dug up and put to one side, it being thought that some sort of rubber might be got from them to add to our trade. Other plants gave up their lives with a colourless ichor that sometimes had a heady fragrance and sometimes the stench of green meat. During one of our rest breaks we noticed that our forearms, faces and necks were spotted with brown where one of these gory fluids had settled and dried to a solid gum. When it is scraped off it leaves a clear stain beneath, making us look as if we had all at once taken a pox. Two men, one of them still under Dr Munro's care, awoke the day after to find themselves not only with the brown marks but with red ones too, which have tortured them with a rage of burning and itching and a fever that, at one point, was dangerous.

At midday we dropped our blades for an hour. There was a campaign meal and when the water-carriers came we drank them dry and sent them away for more. Few words were exchanged and some even slept, though I could not. I lay on my back looking up at the motionless leaves or with my eyes closed making a tour of New Edinburgh in my mind using the sounds that came to me as my guide. On the north shore of the bay saw-pits have been dug and one of these was in use. I heard the rasp of the long saw – one note for up, another for down. I could see them doing it – one man on the log inching his feet back from the cut with every stroke, the other in the pit, his head, shoulder and arms heaped with the sawdust. Drummond's voice was there too, shouting orders to his men as they dug out the ditch for Fort St Andrew on the point. I began to drowse to this music and imagined that the sound of the saw was in reality that of a great clock approaching the hour. As the plank lengthened, each stroke of the saw let out a lower note and I became stupefied by fatigue and the sound of this ever deeper droning. Time passed unnoticed until a sudden acceleration of the beat returned me to my senses. There were shouts of encouragement, the clang of the saw as it dropped and then, all at once, a chorus of triumph and the slam of a fresh plank falling on the trestles. I raised my head to look at my fellows. As if we had heard the resurrection trumpet itself, we rose from our graves and returned to work.

We continued as before, finding almost at once those private cells of vacancy and concentration that made our endurance possible. The strokes of the machetes fell like a chant or like an endless peal of bells, passing in and out of an infinite variety of rhythms. Rarely they would fall as one, then separate into chaos. Phrases would form and dissolve and bring to my mind their attendant images with an intensity coloured by the feverish extremes of exhaustion. Sometimes the blades would fall like hoofs – a single horse, a pair, a coach and four, the formless clattering of a whole street. A new picture would emerge – smiths at work. I thought of the vaults under Milne Square to which the profits of our labours will return. Other rhythms would intrude – shipwrights chiselling tenons in the great beams of a ship, coins being counted, the refrain of a drinking song. These images became as complete as dreams. It was my hand on the drawstrings of the money-bag as the last coin dropped. I answered aloud through labouring breath to questions from smith or horseman. Then my blade would fall on stone and the shock would wake me. I had just enough time to see what ground we had covered, to check that I was still in line and to observe how my grim-faced fellows were dreaming as deeply as myself before returning to that necessary stupor.

'Ho!'

We straightened, grimacing, coming back to the world with amazement to find that it was nearly full night. We dropped our machetes and turned to receive the applause of thirty or so of our fellow-colonists who, unnoticed by us, had gathered to mark our achievement. We looked back on two and a half, maybe three acres of cleared land. It was four times what anyone could have expected of us and our clearing of it has already become a famous victory. I have already heard tell of three and a half acres cleared and confidently expect soon to hear of four and then of five. Even so, for the thirteen authors of the work there was but a tempered triumph, knowing what a hard bargain the land had driven us to, and that such an expenditure cannot often be repeated.

For the fellowship that had grown between us we were not yet willing to part, and so we ate together around a fire in the middle of the land we had cleared. We had bread – the return to his craft of the single baker amongst us being one of the chiefest joys of our landfall – cheese melted on to it by the heat of the fire, beer from the ships' stores and, from my officer's allowance, a good measure of brandy for each man. In outward show we must have seemed a melancholy gathering, for we remained as taciturn as we had been all day. Of our labour, there was a perfect community of knowledge so that on that subject no one of us could tell another what he did not already know. As for whatever, in other circumstances, might have seemed interesting to us or worthy of exchange across the light and warmth of a fire, this had been somehow diminished by what we had shared so that no one dared speak for fear that, by intruding upon the company with some foreign matter, he would be blamed as the breaker of that strange enchantment. So we sat in silence, in the midst of the largest and heaviest mark the hand of man has yet made on our new-found land, three-quarters dazed without even the energy to decide between a cautious glorying in the extent of that first field and more sanguine reflections on what lay beyond it. The bread, beer and brandy found us in such a condition that it was like milk to infants, bringing on sleep so fast we knew not how or when it came to us, but slumbered where we lay.

How much later I awoke that night, I cannot be sure. I heard the sound of a machete again. Not the shifting rhythmic peal of thirteen blades, but a single stroke, heavy and regular as the death toll. For a long time it seemed a dream, but when at last I was sure I was awake the sound was still there, as clear as before. Bodies lay asleep around the embers. I stumbled to my feet and looked behind me, towards the edge of the clearing. The sound was clearly coming from that direction, but my eyes could do nothing to confirm it and I began to tell myself that it must be a delusion brought on by the excesses of the day. I was about to lie down and go back to sleep when I heard the ring of steel against stone. There was a grunt and a heavier, angrier blow before the steady rhythm resumed. That momentary human sound was enough to tell me that this was no dream, but Oswald insanely returned to the task in the middle of the night. I staggered drunkenly over the stubble of severed roots and stalks until I could see in the barrier of the uncleared growth a darker patch, like the entrance to a tunnel. By a pale filtering of moonlight I was just able to see the white of Oswald's shirt. His head, and the arms below where his sleeves had been rolled remained invisible, but it was an easy matter to guess at their motion as I listened to the bite of his machete, each blow accompanied by a grunt of monstrous effort. He dug himself deeper into his tunnel until there was nothing for my senses save for the fall of the machete and his wordless explosions of strength. The rhythm suddenly quickened, momentarily seemed frantic so that I was about to call out to beg him to stop, but the next blow never came. I strained my ears, but heard nothing. Above the trees, a cloud cleared from the moon and I saw him more clearly than before. He stood at the end of the path he had just cut for himself, facing the wall of dense, tangled growth. His great arms he held rigid above his head, one hand a fist, the other holding the machete. He stood still and silent as stone, and I believed, in my half-dreaming state, that he might triumph there for ever.

GIVEN OUR REMOTENESS from all the restraints that civilization has laboured to build up about our baser natures, it could be said, by a generous man, that our inaugural day passed decently enough. Although it seems to me, as I gain experience of this task, that a chronicler may, in good conscience, draw a veil over this lapse of character or that indiscretion, it is not for that reason that my account of these celebrations must have a more stringent economy than of late. Rather, it is because I have returned from – indeed I might say 'survived' – events of such a colour that if I do not hurry on, I will soon be able to write of nothing else and must leave Posterity an even more faulty history.

I have retreated for the purpose to the *Rising Sun* and occupy once again the cabin intended for the good Mr Vetch. There has been much to do in adjusting the ledgers, principally deductions from our stocks of powder and small shot. After accounting for the last of Mr Shipp's tallies, I permitted myself two hours' sleep before the current midnight. The sea is still and my lamp full.

From the events I have already described to the end of the month there was little of note on land. Work on more substantial shelters, on Fort St Andrew and the battery across the bay, on the kirk and on further dignifying the council's meeting house and on the clearance of more land continued steadily. Mr Paterson, having failed to prise off any of the redcoats from Drummond's work parties, retained some men from the ships' crews to start another clearing on the landward side, half-way between the site of the battery by the mouth of the bay and the rock from where I went swimming some time ago. Though not privy to the discussions, I know there have been harsh words on this work and that Mr Paterson is paying the men from his own pocket. He has always struggled to raise men to his own level and even here, in the very wings of this great achievement, they will not raise their eyes.

More significant is what came to us from the sea. At the point of the peninsula that hides the bay from the offing, now known by us all as Point Look-out, we have a sturdy tower a good twenty feet in height and a man atop every hour of the day. From here it has become clear that there is a very encouraging traffic in these parts. Most seem unaware of our presence, an ignorance that, until we are more established, suits us well. Others, perhaps, have heard a rumour and, without caring so much as to delay their journeys, have come a little closer into the shore to see if there might be any truth in it. A Danish trader came within signalling distance a fortnight ago. We fired one gun in welcome, thinking she might be ready for some business, but she went on her way carrying only a report of us back to her masters. I am pleased to say she had a good sight of the *Rising Sun*, which will, no doubt, have conveyed the seriousness of our intentions. Other ships have approached without colours. The mariners amongst us are sure that one of them was an English Sixth Rate – a suspicion strengthened by the fact that she gave every sign of wanting to retain her anonymity. When she lingered a mile off the mouth of the bay, Captain Galt took out the *Caledonia* (himself in command rather than Drummond), and the *St Andrew* to ask her a few questions. She was too shy for such an interrogation and made off sharply Jamaica-way, to Admiral Benbow's office we don't doubt and thence to the Admiralty in London. Another appeared in the same fashion – no signals, no colours, but by the style of her clearly a Spaniard, most likely out of Portobello. This we took more seriously, it being our first opportunity to impress ourselves on our least amiable neighbour. The *St Andrew* and the *Caledonia* went out again, but this time in a file of three, the *Rising Sun* leading the line, all her ordnance at the ready – a double row of black teeth around her hull. The whole colony crowded together on Point Look-out save for a party of thirty or so on the opposite side of the bay who had been working on the battery. We parted to let through a procession of the Reverends Borland and Stobo, led by our capital minister himself, Mr Mackay, who stood very graciously at the edge of the cliff, blessed our ships and reminded us that the followers of Antichrist were as assured of suffering and degradation in this life as they were in the next. The outcome was a victory to be sure, but a bloodless one. Before our ships were in range, the *señorita* gathered up her skirts and fled. Suddenly, cones of white smoke blew out from the side of the *Rising Sun*. I was amazed to see some of the shot skip in the water throwing up great plumes of spray. One of the balls bounced twice off the sea and hit the intruder just above the water-line. We gave it a great cheer, but it was already spent and bounced harmlessly off her timbers. We hoped for a chase, but it was soon clear that Galt had decided against such an adventure. The gap between her and our ships lengthened and she was allowed to run for home unharmed.

In all these comings and goings our first true visitor was a creature of quite another character – 'Captain' Richard Long, a swaggering, tall-tale-telling braggadocio of a fortune hunter, whose only service to us was the bearing off of our redundant pilot, the gloomy Captain Alliston. He appeared on the nineteenth, creeping upon us in the hour before dawn and causing an alarum. I witnessed a smirking apology for this, delivered to Mr Paterson, to whom he declared himself and his business as he stepped on to our territory. His ship, the *Rupert*, is a Frenchman of very modest dimensions, a 'prize', if that is the right word, in the late war and in a condition that seems likely only to have attracted men who care not overmuch if they see home again. This vessel is the measure of the Admiralty's confidence in him. They have provided him with it and with the money for crew and provisions on the grounds, we are to believe, that he alone knows the location of two plate wrecks of exceptional richness and is willing to allow His Majesty the lion's share of their bounty if he succeeds in recovering them. These wrecks are to be found somewhere off the northern shore of the isthmus, but we have never learned any more than that.

It is doubtful that we would have entertained him at all had it not been for his knowledge of the area and for our desire to find out something of his true purpose. He was, he assured us, 'an old hand' along the coast and was quick to demonstrate a knowledge of the Indian leaders. This earned him the hospitality of the *Rising Sun* where he dined with certain of the officers and councillors of the colony. Mr Cunningham was generous to me in his account of the evening, the general tenor of which I gathered at the subsequent reconciliation of the ledgers when it was revealed that stocks of our two best wines have been dealt an almost fatal blow. Throughout the evening Captain Long was fulsome in self-praise, informing us that he had been busy in the area for some time before our arrival, making peace amongst the Indians and uniting them against the Spanish. It was to this diplomacy that we owed our warm welcome from Andreas – he took us for Englishmen and consorts of their good friend. Mr Paterson remarked that it was strange that for such a renowned figure we had, to that point, heard nothing of him except from his own mouth. This, according to Long, was due only to the innate discretion of the people, especially with those whose intentions they were not yet sure of. As to the purposes of his peace-making we were informed – 'unblushingly', as Mr Cunningham put it – that Captain Long is a Quaker whose principles bid him make peace wherever he can.

After a few more glasses of good Bordeaux wine had warmed his goodwill towards us he was reminded of another of his achievements. This relates to the great Darien river, which empties into the gulf of Darien and is reputed to have its source deep in the southern continent near Peru. The mouth of the river is populated by another petty tribe of innocents whom he has, but three months prior to our arrival, persuaded to consent to a charter giving the entire sovereignty of their lands to the Crown of England. Our side upped its game from claret to Madeira and was rewarded with a full exposition of the richness of the river in gold, its usefulness in navigating close to some Spanish mines which could easily be seized, its inevitability as a conduit for trade up-country and the readiness from that spot with which one can pass over the mountains in a mere two days' easy travel to reach the South Seas and the whole other half of the world. In short, what an excellent place for a colony. Such was his simplicity that he was put quite at a loss by the silence with which this speech was greeted. When at last something of the situation penetrated to him he was determined only to wade deeper into the mire.

'Consider, gentlemen, if there were ten thousand English settled up that river, what harm would that be to the Scotch? Or if there were as many Scotch here near Golden Island what harm would it be to the English? None at all, surely. For like loving friends they would surely assist one another against Britain's common enemies.'

The brandy arrived and, although the evening went on for some time, nothing more of any value was got from him. It is Mr Cunningham's view that after a certain degree of drunkenness he can talk of nothing but gold. We can only be thankful that the colony on the Darien river, having as its promoter such a vainglorious and addle-pated fantasist as Long, is most unlikely ever to trouble us.

The next day he was very amiable. He professed great admiration for our work here and a desire to see all that we have done so far. This led to a very brief private conversation with Captain Galt, whence he was briskly escorted back to his vessel and carefully watched until his top mast sank beneath the horizon.

Alliston went with him, happier in his company than he had ever been in ours. In all we felt half flattered that we were of such interest to the Secretaries of State in London, and half insulted that we were not worth a better spy.

Ten days passed before our next visitor, during which we made good progress in all our endeavours. Sufficient work was done on Fort St Andrew to allow the emplacement of the first three cannon, the hauling of which engaged a tenth part of our whole population.

Three days later another three were added to the battery across the bay so that whoever approaches us now is presented with two strong jaws with six good iron teeth between them.

It was these teeth, perhaps, examined through her captain's telescope, that kept the *Santiago* a generous mile offshore. At our first sight of her we made ready to go out, everyone abandoning their part in the preparations for the festivities. As our ships are always manned, the *St Andrew* and the *Caledonia* were quickly out of the bay to make a line with the *Rising Sun* who, on account of her size and capabilities, remains permanently on the seaward side. No sooner had this manoeuvre been completed than it became clear that the Spanish ship was taking in sail. She fired one gun and a moment later a runner came from Point Look-out where Benjamin Spense, whose turn it was that day, reported no other ships in sight.

A group of us gathered on the cliffs to watch the proceedings while others ran to the landing-stage in the bay to see what would come ashore. By the time I reached my vantage-point, the *Santiago*'s boat had already splashed into a light sea. Six oarsmen, like a flock of parrots in their scarlet uniforms, made way with unhurried dancers' strokes, the narrow blades of their oars cutting the water, rising from it and pausing at their height for a moment of immobility before cutting into the waves again with precise obedience to the taps of an imaginary drum. They had made about a third of their journey when the *Rising Sun* dropped her boat too. This pulled quickly, if less elegantly, into the bay, bearing Captain Galt to where the other councillors had gathered. As the Spaniards approached, I could see two black-clad worthies sitting between the lines of red. Our ships' crews hung from the rigging and leaned over every part of the rails to gape at them, but they made an excellent show of passing by without the slightest awareness of this interest.

Realizing that he would soon be needed, Mr Spense climbed down from the tower. I accompanied him through the woods to the main part of New Edinburgh, where we anticipated the meeting would take place. There was a large assembly there, which we pressed through to find Mr Paterson, Captain Drummond and the other councillors standing in a line. To the right of them the Reverends Stobo and Borland stood shoulder to shoulder, Reverend Mackay in front of them. Captain Galt's boat arrived first, Mr Cunningham also aboard carrying a portfolio. They jumped ashore and had time for a brief conference with the others before the Spaniards came into sight. They approached with an unvarying rhythm, pulling harder on their oars for their final stroke before raising them high above their heads and letting the bow of the boat bite into the gravel. Throughout, all six of the oarsmen remained with their backs to us, not a single head turning. The black-tailored dignitaries stepped on to the land in a manner that suggested they had been taught to walk by the same school that had taught their oarsmen to row. The lesser of the two carried a leather wallet with elaborate arms impressed in gold. Mr Cunningham shifted his more modest portfolio as it became clear there was to be an exchange of documents. Mr Spense went forward in response to a nod from Mr Paterson. The first Spaniard strode forward and, with a deft turn of his rapier to one side, gave a dancing-master's bow.

'That sword's seen nothing but ink,' someone shouted.

There was some laughter, abruptly cut off as the Spaniard started to speak. Mr Spense conveyed the meaning in the same booming crier's voice that the gentleman himself had used – which was taken as an excellent joke. We learned that this was Don Miguel Ximenez, principal secretary to the Conde de Canillas, president of the province of Panama. His familiar, who opened his wallet at this point and handed a letter to Don Miguel, was to remain anonymous throughout.

Don Miguel expressed the very great extent to which he would be honoured if we were to receive this letter. He presented it to Captain Galt, who indicated to Mr Cunningham that he should take it. This he did, presenting in return a copy of our founding Act setting out all the powers and privileges of the Company. The nameless one accepted this expressionlessly and placed it in his wallet.

'We come as peaceful traders,' began Mr Paterson, 'to a deserted territory, to do the duty of every Christian in enriching the world by . . .'

He stopped, Mr Spense's Spanish rendering coming to an equally sudden halt. Don Miguel lunged towards Captain Galt, seized his hand and pressed it firmly to his lips. He took three steps back to the prow of his boat from where he seemed to notice the crowd for the first time. He addressed us in English. 'Gentlemen, you are far from home. God grant you a safe return.'

Despising us with a final bow, he vaulted elegantly into his boat, which rowed out of the bay with the same sinister precision with which it had arrived.

'Papists!' exclaimed Mr Mackay.

The Meeting House being still in too primitive a state to afford much privacy, the councillors made their way out to the *Rising Sun* to read the Conde de Canillas's document in Captain Galt's cabin. Through the remaining two days until the eve of the thirtieth, the incident was very nearly the sole substance of our conversation. There was soon a hundred variations on what the letter must contain and the councillors seemed happy to allow them to flourish. Even Mr Cunningham, who, although not a councillor, is often very well informed on all such matters, was in complete ignorance as to its import. I got some idea of what use they intended to make of it when I noticed that a man by the name of Carlaw, our only printer, was ferried back to the *Rising Sun* where our press is stowed. I soon received a note asking me to adjust my ledgers by deducting four reams of paper from the balance.

In all, the timing of this delivery could not have been better for us. The spirit of the colony, suffering of late under the extremity of the heat and, through the few days prior to St Andrew's Day, under a most inconvenient quantity of rain, was greatly lifted by having our enemy present himself to us in flesh and blood. The incorporation of all that threatens in human form with a cuttable throat and a breakable head seems to have restored, in particular, the rougher members of our state to full confidence in what we attempt here. It was, then, in the highest of spirits that we met the dawn of our saint's day.

The main area of our ceremonies was just above the best natural landing point on the peninsula (one of the many places yet to be christened and which we must tiresomely describe to each other rather than name). This is the widest expanse of entirely flat land we have, extending perhaps to three acres and now very thoroughly cleared. Already, it is taking on the features of a town square. To the left, as one looks from the shore – perhaps I will add some drawings to this book if have the time, and the skill – is a line of good sturdy huts made partly from our cargo timber and partly from that we have sawn ourselves. These are progressively replacing the tents we originally relied on and are now enough in number to make a true street. The occupants, all gentlemen volunteers, take a great pride in these dwellings. In the evening they stroll up and down the boards that have been laid outside, smoking their pipes and exchanging pleasantries. They entertain each other in their parlours, and reveal the secrets of their characters by displaying the one treasure they were least willing to leave behind. In one, I have been served claret from a silver jug and in another just glimpsed through the smoky light of a tallow lamp a miniature painting of a seated lady hanging from a ship's nail. I have heard that one of the occupants of these desirable addresses, having been unlucky at cards, has already been forced to sell his hut to another who now charges him rent. A month old and New Edinburgh has her first landlord! Going to or coming from the day's work, groups of Highlanders pass by these gentlemen and growl at them in their barbarous language.

Adjacent to these huts is the building that confronts one most forcefully when approaching from the shore. This is the councillors' Meeting House and our only construction so far that goes beyond the simplest necessities. Built of the same planks that make up the huts, it is a little taller and the length of about eight or nine of these huts put together. For about two-thirds of its length it still goes bare-headed, but it will have a good roof of shingles cut from local wood when all is done. Almost all our supplies of flat glass have gone into making six tall windows, three on either side of the door, which is what passes here for a grand affair, befitting our seat of government. There are pairs of columns on either side of it surmounted by a heavy architrave. In reality, the architrave is a block of rough-hewn timber and the columns lengths of a spare mast got out of the *Dolphin*, but they have all been whitewashed so that one can imagine them to be marble.

The third side has no permanent structure yet, but is still the home of a row of tents, which make up Dr Munro's infirmary. Thank God, it is but sparsely occupied. From it, only six men have been sent to join Mrs Paterson in their graves, and all of them sick before we arrived. Needless to say, this is a cause of great concern to Dr Munro, who would be happier by far if his expectations of twenty or more had been despatched. The last time I congratulated him on the health of his patients – and it will be the last time – he explained that it was nothing more than a sinister conspiracy of the Afflictions who, in accordance with all the proofs of science and history, only stay their hand to gather strength for a more fatal strike. The last edifice in this scene, and as worthy of note in a civilized history as the others, can just be seen behind Munro's tents. These are the latrine pits, bounded by a simple canvas screen stretched between poles.

Thus the modest amphitheatre of our celebrations. By dawn on the day itself this space was equipped with five rows of improvised tables, two roasting pits, each with three spits, a large area paved with deal boards for the dancing, a small dais just before the steps of the Meeting House and a mile of red and white and blue pennants made up from cloth from the ships' stores and strung about the huts and the Meeting House, the infirmary tents and the trees. Anxious to put myself in a position to give a first-hand account of as much of the day as possible, I had risen early and was able to look on this in complete peace. The only movement was from the four peccaries, gifts from Captain Andreas, straining at their tethers as they rooted under the spits on which they would soon be roasting.

With the exception of the sentries, the look-out and myself, the colony rose slowly from its holiday beds. Such has been our labour in this first month that the rest was very necessary. Many walked stiffly from the aches in their bones and others seemed even a little dazed at the sudden release, like draught horses relieved of their harness but still standing stupidly between the shafts, wondering what to do with themselves. This quickly lifted as people happily involved themselves in the final preparations, hanging lanterns along the paths and enjoying the first of the day's many distributions of beer and brandy. Two boats left early to see what fish they could add to the feast. Another went across the bay to some of the workings there, but when I asked what they were going to do I was told with an air of great importance that they went on the instructions of Mr Paterson and I would just have to wait to find out with everyone else.

By midday all the remaining small tasks had been completed and everyone, saving those who in some way were to be masters of ceremonies either by manning the roasting pits or by setting up – and guarding – the barrels of wine, brandy and beer, was lying idle in groups about the square. There was drowsy talk, now and then a few notes on a fiddle from amongst the Highlanders where they sat together under some trees. The peccaries, scoured and gralloched, hung by their heels from a spar where a boy chased flies from the long gashes in their bellies. A good many bottles were already being passed round and a sudden spell of sleep was cast over the whole assembly.

I was awoken in the late afternoon by the sound of half a dozen muted cheers – many were still asleep or stupefied by the heat and the unaccustomed idleness. The first of the roasting pits had just been doused in oil and set alight. Tall flames ran along its length sending dark smoke straight into the motionless air. I got up and was going to see them light the others when there was a loud bang from the first sending up clouds of sparks and causing people to scatter. The cries of alarm soon turned to indignation and laughter as the culprit broke from the group of spectators, was chased and wrestled to the ground to be punished with a few mock slaps to the head of which he complained very loudly.

I watched the second and the third pits flare up and noticed with surprise that one of the men hurling wood into them was Reverend Mackay, his face red with effort and his shirtsleeves rolled up over burly arms.

'Don't look like that, Roderick! It's all hands on feast days.'

I am not alone in remarking that the tropic air has had a very beneficial effect on Mr Mackay, on whom I am increasingly – and quite happily – having to revise my views. Sadly, this cure for clergymen is very capricious in its effects, for it appears to have had no benefit at all on the Reverends Stobo and Borland. Rather, it seems to have deprived them of what small capacity they ever had for appreciating God's gifts. Or perhaps there is a law that in any three true Scots clergymen there shall only be so much of human kindness so that if one gain more than his natural share, it can only be by stealing it from the other two. In any case, let it be noted that by the feast day of St Andrew the Apostle Reverend Mackay had become more popular with his flock than any of them had anticipated, and his juniors no less unpopular.

I freely confess to digression, but the thought of him has reminded me of something that will be as well recorded here as anywhere else. For all Mr Mackay's softening, the reprobates amongst us have not lost their appetite for telling stories to his detriment and one such came to my ears not two days before these events. It would appear that the site chosen for the kirk was favoured before us, indeed since time immemorial, for a very particular purpose. Though the Indians here are mostly a people of superstition, there are some respects in which they have achieved a degree of practicality which our own society seems unlikely ever to match. They are of the view that a man and a woman should enter into no obligations to each other before ensuring that they are, as it were, of a suitable fit. All things being well, the arrangement is solemnized immediately after the non-appearance of the first menses after the fact. The custom with such preliminaries is for the intended, typically no more than two or three years out of childhood, to leave the village at night to go to a place hallowed by tradition where they do with each other as frankly as beasts in the field. In the case of lovers from Captain Andreas's village, they go now to a doubly sacred place, for it is the very same as that chosen by Mr Mackay for his church and is now known by one and all (for the story has travelled fast) as the Shades of Love. As for what ancient scent of holiness drew our clergy to the place, I will not speculate. In any case, it was never likely to be long before two such ill-matched tenants in the same property came into conflict and the story goes that when the kirk was nothing but a few frames of timber, Reverend Mackay, who had gone there to pray one evening, detected a young Adam and Eve at their carnal devotions. He rushed out shouting, lantern in hand, and thus appearing to the young and tragically interrupted Indians as the most terrifying of devils, sent them fleeing into the safety of the forest. Here comes the Archangel, they say now whenever he approaches, here comes the fiery sword barring the gates of Eden. I am bound to record that our new, warmed-up Reverend Mackay has not failed to see the humour in the matter and has borne all disrespect with admirable patience.

As the light started to fade and the mood to rise as more people came into the clearing, I noticed a group clustering around one of the tables. Dr Munro was walking towards them from the infirmary and carrying his instruments with him. I stood on my toes to look over shoulders and saw several lines of fat silver fish already gutted. The attraction, however, was not these but an enormous grey-brown bulk that lay on the ground, blood seeping from one end of it. At first, I took it to be a seal or perhaps, though I have never seen such a creature, a walrus. As the group parted to let Dr Munro through, a seaman from one of the ships answered the unspoken question.

'It's a sea cow, a manatee they call them. They say it's bad luck.'

'Nonsense!' Dr Munro was kneeling down by the enormous corpse. 'It's the very best of luck – I've never even heard of someone who has seen one of these before.'

'I've seen one before,' said the seaman.

'Besides, it looks as if it will feed a hundred people.'

I moved round to the head of the creature to find a strange, leathery old woman's face, bright blood seeping from the nostrils of a flabby nose that looked like the root of an elephant's trunk. From where the shoulders would have been grew two impracticably small limbs, like swans' feet with which, presumably, it directs itself in the water. Stranger still was the swelling between these limbs of disconcertingly human breasts. Dr Munro squeezed one of these and was clearly pleased when he succeeded in making a drop of milk run down his finger. He picked up one of his instruments and ran his hand down her belly. Suddenly she was open, a mass of still warm guts slithering out over the ground. At once Munro was all blood to the elbows as he sorted through this slop of offal. Absorbed in his task, there was the occasional noise of confirmation or surprise and at least one exclamation of 'Fascinating!' He heaped a pile of coiled, greyish gut to one side and with a deft movement pulled out from the resulting hollow a glistening oblong, which I recognized as a kidney.

'It's like a pig's,' I ventured.

'It's more like one of yours, Roderick. Fascinating, quite fascinating!'

He dropped it in the pail his infirmary assistant had just brought him.

'This one for science, if I may. One of you can make a good meal of the other.'

I thought I recognized the heart and the lungs but was baffled by a distended mass towards the creature's lower end. Munro squeezed and prodded it with his fingertips. 'Yes,' he mused to himself, 'yes, I think it . . . Pass me that, will you?'

His assistant passed him an instrument. The vessel, like a stomach I thought, except that I had seen one of those already, was opened with a stroke. Fluid gushed out, not blood as I had half expected but clear, like water. I decided this must be the bladder, but was at a loss as to why Dr Munro was finding it so interesting. His hand slipped inside, up to the wrist and then half the forearm too as he probed the contents, looking away from the creature to concentrate on what his fingers were telling him. Suddenly he stood up and held out for our inspection the most strangely, beautifully revolting trophy. There was a perfect miniature of the sea-cow: the odd half-trunk, half-snout of a nose, tiny eyes bulging behind never-opened lids, the limbs like webbed baby's fingers. It was in colour that it differed most starkly from its mother. While she was encased in a leathery coat of brown, her infant was red as if no skin at all had formed over it, or one so fine and translucent as to reveal the pure flesh beneath. Dr Munro held it up with an expression of great satisfaction on his face. 'There'll not be another like it in all Europe.'

It was early evening and the red light from the sun caught the strange, half-formed substance of the unborn sea-cow and seemed to illuminate it from within. It glowed like a jewel and brought to my mind the irrelevant memory of a cheap trinket I had bought for Susanna – a little fish with a ring in its mouth, carved from cornelian. Munro slapped it into the bucket that contained its mother's almost human kidney and went back to the infirmary. The great carcass was skinned and spitted over one of the fire pits alongside the peccaries, whose fat was already dripping into the flames. Much later in the proceedings, I had a very well roasted slice of that creature. It had a powerful restorative effect, but I suspect its part in some strange dreams I had later. As for its taste, I thought it no great prize.

The clearing began to fill more rapidly and soon the whole colony was assembled there. A boat came in from the *Rising Sun* carrying Mr Shipp, Carlaw the printer and two boys. These four distributed a paper amongst all the colonists. As I watched the boys hand out the sheets I experienced a sudden emotion – half of pride, half of poignancy. I wondered that in so short a time our New Edinburgh had grown to such a resemblance of the old as to have news-boys running amongst an evening crowd. I thought I knew what this document was and saw I was right when I drew near a lantern to read it. 'The Popish King of Spain to the True Men of Caledonia' ran a bold title, which had, I assume, been added by one of our own. There followed a rendition by Mr Spense of the letter brought to us by that most sedulous servant of Spain, to wit:

> Don Miguel de Ximenez, principal Secretary to the Conde de Canillas, President of the Province of Panama, begs to intimate that the President, loving the service of God and his King, His Most CATHOLIC Majesty, Charles II, and guided by the true Christian brotherhood and love that exists between His Most CATHOLIC Majesty and King William of England and all his subjects, wishes it to be known that, desiring only peace and concord between their two peoples, the Scottish brigands and pirates lately arrived in Darien, notwithstanding their many offences and encroachments against His Most Sovereign and CATHOLIC Majesty Charles II, may withdraw entirely and absolutely from the aforesaid Darien with all their property, trade goods and weapons, excepting only the warship *Rising Sun*, by the Feast of the Purification of the Blessed Virgin next. In this instance and in this instance alone, His Excellency the Conde de Canillas, President of the Province of Panama, undertakes on his honour that the said brigands and pirates shall not be harmed.
>
> Begging to remain your ever-willing servant,
>
> Don Miguel Mastrangelo Ximenez del Rio de Cariñena
>
> I kiss your hand.

This paper was variously received with guffaws of laughter, bellows of indignant rage, curt, snorting harrumphs of contempt and in many cases gaping incomprehension as the bearer sought the nearest man who could read. Don Miguel's extravagant valediction was a particular source of amusement, as well as causing many outbursts of pantomime hand-kissing throughout the evening.

'Kiss your hand?' demanded one burly, bearded soul I did not know.

To loud encouragement, his breeches were soon about his ankles and the paper being treated to that time-honoured gesture of which the worldly reader will require no further details. It quickly joined some others that were already blazing in the roasting pits, though most were kept, it being understood that they would have their allotted place in the ceremonial to come.

As darkness thickened, parties of lamplighters came in from the paths leaving behind them lines of light connecting us to the shore, to the battery and Point Look-out and on the other side to the kirk. Torches were lit in the square and more lanterns hung from the trees, some borrowed from the ships, others made for the purpose from coloured paper or cloth. In the bay, the smaller ships, the *Caledonia*, the *Endeavour* and the *Dolphin*, rode at anchor. Although populated by the seamen rather than the colonists, and in spite of having taken on something of the character of a neighbouring and rather different town from our own, the ships took full part in these illuminations. Lanterns were hung from the rails and spars and each top mast carried a coloured light – red, yellow and blue from east to west. As the sky turned to moonless black and the masts became invisible they hung there amongst the other stars, the newest and most brilliant constellation.

A fiddler struck up a familiar tune behind me, and those who had stood guard over the barrels all day turned happily into tapsters. Finding myself still more reflective than social, I found a quieter spot and spent some time with my thoughts looking out over the bay. The ships were mere suggestions of the lights in their rigging and on their decks. I saw lamps moving on the *Dolphin* and one go down her side until it stopped and seemed to hover above the water. The sound of oars approached. As the boat carrying Captains Jolly and Malloch and their first officers bumped into the jetty another light approached from the direction of the *Caledonia*. Jolly and Malloch and the others made their way up towards the dais. Several from the crowd greeted them warmly as they went and there was a hearty cheer as they passed a large group that had travelled with them on the *Endeavour* and the *Dolphin*, grateful for having been safely delivered. Drummond was standing on the jetty now, firelight glinting on a splendid uniform I had not seen before. Others from the *Caledonia*'s boat disembarked and stood behind him, waiting for his lead. Darkness obscured their faces but I could still see that they were all garbed as soldiers. This was enough to identify them, for there are half a dozen lesser men who, linked by ties of common experience in Flanders or elsewhere, one-time membership of common regiments or merely a common cast of mind, are now rarely seen except in Drummond's company. As this group followed the first past the tables and the roasting pits towards the dais (the air now thick with burnt pork fat), they had their welcomes and their well-wishers too, but perhaps not so many nor so hearty as before. As they passed some turned away to speak to neighbours or moved off to another part of the ground. The foundations of Fort St Andrew and the battery across the bay are Drummond's work, but he has won no friends in the making of them. Some of the Highlanders have a particular dislike of him and on that night they were sullen as he passed. The rumours regarding the old northern business first indicated to me in the earliest days of the voyage have flourished in men's heated imaginations and have been still further magnified by the resentments harboured against a hard taskmaster. I still decline to take any position on the precise truth of the matter, though I must admit that recent events have made it seem less improbable.

As Drummond took his place on the dais, leaving his companions on the ground like hounds at his feet, attention returned to the bay. Lights appeared round the point as the pinnace from the *Rising Sun* approached. Captain Galt, Captain Pincarton of the *St Andrew*, Mr Paterson, Reverend Mackay and Mr Cunningham were soon standing together on the jetty. Their procession towards the Meeting House was accompanied by the roar of a general acclamation. Men shouted themselves hoarse, every pipe, fiddle and drum was added to the clamour, the short jumped and jostled to see past the tall as they went by, blessings were warmly pronounced on all sides. They seemed a little confused by their reception, but by the half-way point it could no longer be ignored. Mr Paterson acknowledged the crowd with regal gestures and was rewarded with still greater hurrahs. The others followed suit, though failing to give the impression, as Mr Paterson did most forcefully, that they had been born to it. Mr Mackay caused some amusement with a highly excited expression, which suggested he believed a good portion of the cheers were for him. Of the whole party, only Captain Galt remained determinedly unmoved. He was very warmly received none the less, especially by those who had put themselves in his care since they had last looked on old Edinburgh. Like myself, they would, no doubt, have been disconcerted if he had behaved in any other way.

The chief men of the colony all being assembled on the dais, it fell to Captain Galt to create a sudden hush by stepping to the fore. He spoke in his shipboard voice.

'Men and women of the *Dolphin*, the *Endeavour*, of the *Caledonia* and the *St Andrew*, and of the *Rising Sun*.'

He measured the names of the ships steadily, allowing a swelling response to each, from the tiny complement of the *Dolphin* to a great roar from the hundreds who had voyaged on the *Rising Sun*. Only at the mention of the *Caledonia* were there some half-humorous calls of dissent from a group of Highlanders already deep in their cups. The matter was resolved between them and some more loyal members of Drummond's command with a sporting scuffle and a round of laughter. Captain Galt raised his hand and silence was restored.

'Much good work has been done here in a very short period of time. Much good work by good and honest men . . .'

There was a lengthy pause here, very nearly long enough to be embarrassing.

'. . . good and honest men in the like of which our country has always excelled.'

He was rewarded with a few tremulous cheers. They quickly drained away, leaving the crackling of the roasting pits the loudest sound in the square.

'It has been an auspicious start . . .'

I was close enough to witness (but not to hear), the giving of a few quick words of advice from Mr Cunningham.

'It has been a good start and bodes well for an excellent success.'

A cup was passed to him just in time to save the situation. He raised it.

'Good health and fortune to you all!'

The invitation to drink was received as the finest eloquence and he was allowed to retire from the light of the torches as a fine, companionable fellow. Some of the gentlemen volunteers were disappointed by this performance and others a little baffled by its hasty conclusion. On the evening itself, I felt the same way, but now, after more considered reflection, I realize that I would have been even more disappointed had our good captain shown too great a familiarity with the cunning arts of the rhetorician.

Now the dais was a pulpit. What parish Mackay ministered to, or what rank he held before he was rowed out with Paterson at the last minute, I have not yet had the curiosity to enquire into, but here there is not one above him of his own sort and never did he enjoy his new supremacy more than on St Andrew's Day.

'Scotsmen and Christians!'

'And Mr Spense!' shouted some wit, ignored by Mackay.

'Never, since his bones were first brought to our shores, nor through all the centuries that our forefathers have followed his sacred symbol as soldiers and pilgrims, has our saint been more honoured than he is today. By our labour – which the Lord loves and rewards – and by the boundless generosity of His Providence, we have come to a New Land, an unsullied land, a land as if but freshly drained of the purifying waters of the Flood and which now receives its first impress from our feet and hands under the inspiration of our holy cross of St Andrew.

'This is a rich land. It has welcomed us with its soil, its fruits and the fishes of its seas. It has welcomed and protected our ships with this fine natural harbour. Can any man here believe that this virgin treasure has lain fallow until now because every other nation, only by some strange chance, has remained in ignorance of it? Can it be nothing more than a coincidence that we have now landed on this blessed spot that has been denied for so long to other peoples? I tell you that the Lord God does not permit coincidences. If, embodied in you, the talents of our people have blown across the ocean like a seed to land on this good and fertile place at this time, it is no chance, but the hand of God!'

An emphatic thump on the rail before him demanded a response and the crowd, heads swimming in the heat and stomachs still empty – of anything solid, at least – were happy to give it in full measure. The Reverends Stobo and Borland, who stood uneasily at the foot of the dais, patted their palms in approval but declined to add to their voices. Too much, I fancy, of virgins and seeds for their liking.

'Friends! Please!'

The crowd returned to a restive silence.

'Some authorities tell us we were of old a voyaging people, as the ancient predecessors of the Christians were in eastern lands. Scotland, the old Scotland, may not have been our first home and I know that I am not alone in feeling for this dear place a strange and ancient sense of familiarity.'

I thought I saw Captain Galt stir from his stony passivity as if a violent wave of itching were passing over him and he was struggling against the temptation to scratch at it. The Reverends Stobo and Borland exchanged looks of exasperation and bafflement. Reverend Mackay lowered his voice as if his next remark should not be generally overheard. 'Who is to say whether or not this is the first time the Scottish people have trodden this fruitful land?'

Attention was passing to the peccaries on their spits and the powerful aroma of new-baked bread, which just then seemed to waft over us. With the experience of many thousands of Sunday mornings at his back, Mr Mackay knew precisely what to do.

'We bring all that is best in our country with us, and of that store of riches the finest pearl, as you all know, is the true faith, truly practised. It has been the misfortune of the so-called New World for the last two centuries to have so many of its fair acres soiled by the idolatry of papism!'

The crowd growled and hurrahed and hissed and waved Don Miguel's ultimatum.

'As in the first Eden, in this one too there is a serpent creeping and we have already seen his minister. But now, the true, pure and original faith is planted here and, through our increase, will spread its goodness across the land.'

A muted approval suggested that some at least had embarked on this venture with other aims uppermost in their minds. Sensing, perhaps, that he had already passed the high point of his congregation's patience, Reverend Mackay concluded with a vote of thanks for all the labour expended so far on the kirk, adding, slyly, a special appreciation of Captain Drummond's generosity on conceding the site. After leading the Lord's Prayer, skilfully balancing speed with decency, he stepped back into the shadows.

Now the reins were taken up by a surer hand.

'Caledonians!'

Mr Paterson was there, one hand aloft with the Spanish ultimatum. We all roared, and waved our own copies back at him. There was a thrill through us, a sudden rush of feeling in our response to this greeting.

'Let no man mistake what we do here. What we are about to achieve will be remembered for a hundred generations!'

His voice was stronger and deeper than I had ever heard it before. Stronger even than when he had sent it echoing across the High Street in front of Mrs Purdie's an immeasurable age ago.

'We are the people of a great and a greatly despised nation. We are a giant chained! A people abounding in all the highest virtues of our kind – ingenious, resolute, intrepid. And yet, for all that, we have been forced to watch generations of such skills die away unexercised in a country that affords little for men of calibre like yourselves. We have pleaded against the iniquity of the English Navigation Acts, we have sent petition after petition to our common king, we have requested the most modest of concessions, but to no avail – they hardened their hearts. Oftentimes a Scottish merchant in New York or Kingston has had to play the smuggler, slipping out of port at midnight so as not to be charged as if he were nothing more to an English harbour-master than an Italian or a Portuguese. More often, that merchant has not been able to trade there at all, and for want of these freedoms our people have shivered and gone barefoot. In all forbearance and humility we returned to our simple request – let us trade with the English colonies, we will enrich them, ourselves and you too. Who could object? But no, they were deaf to reason. We were sent away, and we said, "Enough, we shall not ask again. If we will not be given, we will take."'

He paused to take a glass from someone and to pluck the cuffs from his wrists.

'Perhaps, gentlemen, the news, the very bad news has already reached the Admiralty. Picture it! The red-faced runner gasping up flight after flight of stairs, the secretary pacing in his office. He is anxious, perhaps he has had some intimation of what has happened, an alarming rumour plagues his mind as he listens to those clattering steps as they labour up the last flight – but surely it can't be true. At last the despatch is in his hand, he cracks the seal and reads, his deputies crane round his shoulders. They go to the map that hangs on the wall – it can't be true, surely – but watch now as the finger traces down the coast and stops at Darien. Watch very closely, gentlemen, as they see it – one of the world's great oceans to the right, the other to the left and that miserable thread of land in the middle – Darien, a possession of Scotland! Watch their faces as they understand it at last and their hearts turn to ice.'

He bellowed in a sudden, triumphant fury, 'They could have had us at half the price! But no, they wanted it all for themselves and now they're going to have to watch the greatest prize of all being seized from beneath their very noses.'

There again was that captivating fist I had first seen closing around the neck of the Americas in the directors' chamber in Milne Square. I caught Mr Paterson's eye and received a gratifying nod of recognition. I was, of course, the only one there save Paterson himself who had seen that particular detail of the performance before. I did not object to seeing it again, nor to witnessing the effect it had on the audience standing behind me.

'The entrepôt of the world, gentlemen. Now they'll do business with us, and at our price.'

Mr Paterson calmed the cheers, pressing the sound back with both hands.

'Of course, none of this will fall into our laps; nothing of value ever does. But I know you don't expect that, and I know you've realized that if what we have here is worth keeping, others will try to take it from us. The Spanish have already obliged us by declaring their intentions. Here it is . . .'

He took the ultimatum from a pocket and unfolded it with just a touch of exaggeration. He held the sheet up in the torchlight. A rustling wave surged behind me as the crowd held up their own copies.

'. . . and a bold and pretty letter it is too. What reply shall we make to this? Shall we argue or excuse? Shall we plead? Shall we talk of our nation's great needs? Shall we threaten and defy? No! They'll come all the same and we'll contend with them then, with our muskets and swords. For now, let this be our answer!'

He moved the paper into the flame of the torch, letting it flare up and brilliantly illuminate his face. The crowd roared like a single, terrifying beast. At the same time, it transformed itself into a wave of fire. It ran backward from near the front where the most torches were. Everywhere fingers were pinching the ultimatums by their last corners as flames fluttered down towards them. The cheering and roaring went on in full voice as the flames were passed from paper to paper until they ran up against the rearmost part of the crowd like a wave against a breakwater. Such sudden combustion in an air already so hot had the effect of making all the space above us a chimney. I looked up to see dense clouds of squirming embers being sucked into the night by their own draught.

The flames and the shouts of triumph died away together as our attention returned to Paterson, arms outstretched in the torchlight to plead for silence.

'I think those hogs are about ready, gentlemen, don't you?'

Had he not been so quick, I believe the movement in that direction would have proved unstoppable. He promised to detain us for only two minutes more.

'A day of rest and a night of feasting and dance was rarely more deserved but I would like, if I may, to tell you one more thing. Perhaps I shall not see it myself – at least, not in the flesh – but I know that most of you will, and as an earnest of this great future I want to tell you tonight what you will see from this spot in twenty years' time. No canvas, gentlemen, no deal shacks and no bare earth under our feet, but hard cobbles to rattle against carriage wheels and a square of fine town houses as good as any in the old city. Behind me will be not this shed with two lengths of mast painted to look like stone, but as solid, tall and well-proportioned a public edifice as anywhere in the New World. Up and down its broad steps you will see captains coming to pay their harbour dues, and many foreign merchants, perhaps a few English amongst them, coming to settle their trade licences or to pay tolls for their goods to pass over the road to the Pacific. To the left and the right you will see not these simple paths, hung with a few coloured lanterns, but wide thoroughfares thronged with men and women. Some of them, admittedly the greyer heads, are standing here now, others will be your sons and daughters, perhaps those you have left behind for now, others still the new natives, as yet unconceived. Behind you . . .'

Many of us turned to follow the vision, already convinced that it had, at the very least, a real location.

'. . . there is no longer a rocky shore, but there an esplanade for pleasant walks and moorings for the many boats that go to and fro the ships. To either side of it . . .'

Heads turned, my own very willingly included.

'. . . and across the bay not pleasure but seething commerce fills the wharves with men and goods. One hundredth of every sack of wool, loaf of sugar, bushel of grain, yard of rope and tun of wine making its way to the customs house and thence to all those who hold a share in the colony. And what will make this possible? Indeed, what will make it a necessity, as certain as the rising of the sun or the setting of the moon, what will draw this tide of trade here as a force of nature? Our industry, certainly, but our industry applied to the simple, central heart of this enterprise, gentlemen, which you can see now already begun.'

Captain Malloch let off a pistol shot. Slowly, without instruction, the colony followed Paterson's gaze, above our heads now, across the bay to the opposite shore. A flicker of light appeared, hovering about the shoreline. It expanded quickly, illuminating the billows of its own black smoke. Over a minute or so, the smaller lights moved about, giving birth to these greater ones until there was a curving line of blazing tar barrels. Beyond the last clear light, a smoky glow could be seen through some trees, hinting at the extension of the line to that other ocean, infinitely near.

'Gentlemen, the road to the Pacific, prosperity, Caledonia!'

Paterson raised the brimming glass to his lips and everything happened at once. The crowd cheered mightily, but the sound was as nothing to the celebratory blast from the cannon of our three lesser ships moored in the bay. The gunners had double-charged their ordnance and laced them with copper so that they sent blue and green rods of flame across the water like horizontal lightnings. The guns of Fort St Andrew exchanged ceremonial fire with those of Drummond's battery. The sky beyond the peninsula flickered orange. In a second, these lesser instruments were counterpointed by the rolling, thunderous roar from the *St Andrew* and the *Rising Sun*. I would venture that there has never been such a noise in this part of the world, which violently awoke as if at the call of a new creation. The air seemed to fill with birds, detectable from their squawks and shrieks, the applause of their wings and occasionally by the sight of a pale belly or turquoise tail close enough to be caught in the lamplight. The rightful citizens of the night air, the bats (here three times the size of our flittering mice at home), seemed greatly confused by these intrusions and could be seen hovering about the torches and roasting pits contrary to their nature. From the forest too came an angry chorus, and just beyond our clearing, the sound of something rushing away in panic.

The colonists, detained too long by words, fell upon the roasting pits, the beer, the wine, the brandy and the rum, and the tables laden with a good portion of our best stores. Unwilling to join in the hottest part of the battle, I walked apart for a while. Standing by the shore, I watched the flames from the tar barrels and wondered at their suggestive inland curve. I thought over Mr Paterson's speech and, though the elements were familiar to me, felt again the intoxicating power of his vision. The tarry blaze that now lighted the way to the Pacific fused in my mind with the light from the tall windows at Milne Square and all my hopes and fears for what was being decided behind them. I seized upon the word 'Prosperity' with a sudden and unexpected poignancy – Paterson's toast, but a still greater word when it was d'Azevedo's battle cry. I heard it then, cutting clean through the triumphant, celebratory din coming from behind, but fading so fast that the last syllable escaped me. A woman's voice was briefly heard from amongst the dancers, high and wild. For me, it was Susanna's. There is, it seems, no end to wanting what one doesn't have.

My untimely reverie was broken by the sound of oars and excited voices. I barely caught sight of the boat before it ran up on the shore. Four men, the secret missionaries I had encountered earlier in the day, tumbled out in high spirits. Being the first piece of humanity they encountered, they clapped me heartily about the shoulders and imposed a mouthful of rum on me before going up to join the rest. I stood a few minutes still, letting the rum mingle in my lungs with the cloud of tar fumes that had followed them back across the bay. I had turned to rejoin the feast when something in the corner of my eye stopped me – a dim red light like a half-shuttered stern-lantern. I noticed it because it was moving. As soon as it had my attention, my senses were able to add the slight sound of an oar shifting in its rowlock with, it seemed to me, a deliberate quietness. For a moment my mind raced fancifully with thoughts of an attack. Then there was a familiar voice.

'Make straight for the *Sun*, boatswain.'

'Sir.'

I smiled. Captain Galt had already had his fill of our ceremonies. I made my way up towards the revels, mindful of my duty as a recorder and in search of a more fitting humour.

Though we have fed ourselves adequately since our arrival – and with fresh supplements from the land, much better than during the voyage – our desire to conserve stocks until we are better established meant that this was the first occasion on which we could eat our fill. When I arrived at the roasting pits one of the peccaries was already stripped to its frame and another was fast disappearing.

'Here you are, young Mr Mackenzie. You'd best take that while you can.'

It was Mr Shipp, braced in the centre of the maul, who thrust out a wooden platter of bread and meat, the fat still boiling on the blackened crust. The beer not yet having run out, it was an easier matter to get myself some wine. I pulled out the spigot myself, letting a good measure rush into one of the many thousands of horn cups I remember being entered into the ledgers at Leith. I recalled confident talk of them being excellent trade goods, but the Indians have no interest in them and I hold to my view that our great abundance of these things has more to do with one of the directors' quarter share in a workshop that makes them than any consideration of trade.

It was while making my way to observe the dancing and moralizing in the above-mentioned fashion that I enjoyed the most exquisite revelation of my own hypocrisy. I paused to taste the wine and experienced a shock of recognition as I swilled the watery sourness round my mouth and swallowed it with a grimace. There was no mistake, but I returned to the barrel none the less to see the inevitable initials burned into its end – C.V. that is to say, Colquhoun

Vintners. There I was, once again at my first encounter with the man, being introduced to the eighteen shilling and the twelve and the nine. In my throat was the unforgettable caustic signature of the five shilling. A memory of Colquhoun whispered in my ear: 'Not all our customers are gentlemen, Roderick, but they know what they like . . .'

And why is this odious fluid here? Because, of course, I recommended Colquhoun to the Company. It was the price he demanded and the price I was very willing to pay for his generous lies on my behalf. Little did I think I would have to drink the stuff myself. I held the cup high and toasted the old rogue for what he was worth. 'Your health, sir!'

A figure stumbled past me in a onesome reel.

The horn cup has its reason for being here, as does the wine I poured out of it, and this meditation led me to consider the many hundreds of tons of other goods we have brought with us. How many of them could tell similar stories? Two redcoats passed me. Would the powder in his pistol fire when it was needed? Would the flints in their muskets spark? Or was one in every twenty slate dull because a director's cousin told his brother that the receivers in the warehouses never checked – as we did not. We have trusted greatly to ourselves and this thought puts a strange shudder through me as, perhaps, a gambler must feel when the light of dawn touches the table and he reaches forward to turn the last card. I shook myself angrily out of these gloomy thoughts and, now equipped with beer, which proved excellent, resolved to put myself in better spirits.

Two fiddlers and a fifer stood under one of the great trees at the edge of the clearing playing, I realized after some time, their complete repertoire of four jigs. At the other extreme of the dancing area, almost under the eaves of the Meeting House, a wilder Highland band competed with an endless succession of whirling reels. At one point I thought I noticed an ambassador go between the two, but he must have failed in his commission for they fought each other until dawn – a southern Apollo against a hyperborean Pan. The dancers divided according to their allegiances so that the whole formed a crude figure-of-eight, each ring dominated by its own music. In the middle was a wild cacophony where traitors to both camps went their own way.

It was in that territory that I first glimpsed a dash of clerical black. I looked again and stared open-mouthed as I watched Reverend Mackay emerge from the centre of a reel to spin round its rim, wig-tails flying. A sudden acceleration threw him off and he came to rest by me, bent over, hands propped on his knees, gasping for breath. 'Roderick, oh . . .'

I handed him the dregs of my beer, which he drained at once.

'Bless you.'

He pressed a handkerchief to his face, scarlet and drenched. 'Roderick Mackenzie, has there ever been such a night?'

I agreed there had not and, thinking that I might gently test his humour, expressed my surprise at seeing him in the thick of the dancing. He feigned horror with such an unexpected theatrical talent that he had me in violent laughter. I was informed that the angels danced in heaven, hand in hand with the blessed, and was forced to admit that there was, therefore, no more suitable place for our pastor.

'The other two . . . ?'

He shook his head in a humorous, humane sadness. 'Oh, no. Not at all – but that's just between us, Roderick.'

I marvelled at the completeness of the metamorphosis and half expected to see below the edges of his wig not the hairless lobe of a human ear but the golden pelt of an ass, or perhaps, protruding from the cuffs of his coat, not the thick, ruddy hands of the actual Mackay but the paws of a friendly and fabulous bear, which, any moment, would run off to the forest leaving a man's clothes dropping to the grass behind him.

'In fact, Roderick, you're the very man.'

'Oh, yes?'

'You remember what we talked about?'

A moment's blankness from myself brought forth the manuscript from his coat pocket – he seems to carry it with him everywhere.

'Wafer's Journal?' I said.

'The white Indians, my speculations – you remember?'

I admitted that I did and he told me of his still greater certainty in the truth of his theories. I had not thought such a thing possible and smiled benignly on the information, but without encouragement.

'I have seen them!'

Here I could not conceal my interest, and I saw the triumph in his eye.

'Without a doubt! One only, but there must be others. I was coming from the kirk one evening, walking by the far shore of the bay, when I heard some splashing in the water. I went forward quietly to see what it might be, hoping to see a new creature or, if we were under attack, to give the alarm. Then he pulled himself on to a rock and I saw him in the moonlight not ten yards away. A young male, a perfect Adam. Like a fool I rushed forward and called out to him, but it frightened him and he ran into the woods.'

'Fascinating,' I said, hardly daring to move.

'And I tell you, Roderick, he was as white as you or I.'

An enormous force seized me by the arm and dragged me off, stumbling across the boards.

'You'll not stand there all night, young master. I'll not have it!'

There was Mr Shipp, much the better for drink and much lighter on his feet than I would ever have guessed. I was swung round him for a couple of turns, hardly touching the ground at all, before being flung off at a dizzying speed. I staggered through the field of dancers, only then remembering the notorious potency of Colquhoun's five-shilling. I seemed to bounce from one group to another, happily without volition, like an erring minor planet before I was caught up in the gravity of another eightsome. As the world started to spin into mere colours and sounds, I remember a last glimpse of Mackay, still standing on the edge like a man on the shore seen from the stern of a departing boat. I have not seen him since. Whether I should have told him what I knew or not, I still cannot decide, but wherever he is, God keep him safe and return him to us soon.

Drinking every cup that made its way into my hand and taking a turn on every arm that passed within my reach, I remember little of the hours that followed. The world spun about me in firelight and lamplight, dancing to the mad and ceaseless contest of the two bands. My senses spun too, counter-wise it seemed so that never was a man so dizzy. When I stopped, the world took no notice and whirled on as if I were no longer a part of it but merely a neighbour to its speeding sphere, seeing it quite apart as one man sees another.

At some unknown hour before dawn, an irrefusable physical urgency finally made itself heard. I broke off from the thinning ranks of dancers and ran to the edge of the clearing, arriving not a second too soon. As I stood there, listening to the noises of the animals beyond the light, I became aware, much to my consternation, of a row of three round, brown faces staring at me. Our eyes met and they were gone.

I made myself decent and returned to the centre of the square. I looked over the wreckage of the tables, felt the heat of the ashes in the roasting pits. Bodies lay strewn as on a battlefield, dropped by the deadly fire of Colonel Beer and General Brandy. Some lay singly, one on a pathway where oblivion had surprised him, others snored in heaps. Those past dancing but still awake sat around in circles talking quietly or in exhausted silence.

I noticed a light through one of the Meeting House shutters and made my way towards it, thinking perhaps that Mr Paterson might be there and that I could congratulate him on his great achievement. Anxious to ensure that I was not intruding I first looked through the slats. It was not Paterson I saw, but Drummond surrounded by several of the young officers that now dog his every step. The meeting was over and I stood hard by the steps as they filed out into the clearing. They stood together without speaking, easy with each other – the men almost everyone now refers to as the Glencoe Gang. No one seemed to notice them, except for one group whose heads half turned in their direction as if in receipt of a private signal. The soldiers started to walk across the littered ground towards the shore where they would take a boat for the *Caledonia*. A single bass voice started to sing in Gaelic, slow and clear. The song was taken up by the eight or so men sitting around their own fire and was a throbbing funereal chorus by the time Drummond and his party drew level. One of them slowed his pace, but Drummond's hand was quickly on his elbow to advise against. They moved on with no other sign that they had heard or seen their accusers.

Every time I have returned to this incident it has grown in my mind, but at that hour I could not keep a thought in my head and I dismissed it all in favour of sleep. My last memories of our inaugural day were the receding oars of Drummond's boat, his voice hailing the watch on the *Caledonia*, and over it all that sonorous, alien threnody, as strange as anything I have yet come across in this new world.

14

DID I PROMISE BREVITY? I see that I did, and a mere eight hours ago. It was when the lamp guttered that I broke off. The wick started to smoke and I examined its empty reservoir with surprise, waking from an absorption as deep as any sleep and with only the completed pages before me to prove that I had written and not dreamed.

I emerged to first light, hearing the hissing of the rain on the sea before I felt the impact of its heavy droplets on my head and shoulders as I came on deck. The sea was as calm as before, but opaque now, etched by the rain's relentless corrosion. I saw the hunched back of the watch as he made himself small under a makeshift awning. There was no other sign of life. I stowed my clothes behind the bulkhead and stood naked in the downpour for several minutes, letting the stink of sweat and burnt lamp-oil run off me.

In the mess and the galley the same viscous torpor held sway. I helped myself to some biscuit and a measure of water and crept round Cook's sleeping form to steal a handful of dried peaches. With the benefit of this breakfast and two hours' sleep, I have now returned to my table and refilled my lamp. A few minutes ago I heard Captain Galt ordering the boat to be made ready. He goes to meet the other councillors in the Meeting House. As it has been decided that whatever they have to say to each other would be best unrecorded, my services have been dispensed with and I shall, God willing, have an undisturbed day.

*

HARDLY HAD OUR HEADS CLEARED the next morning when six Indians, Captain Andreas to the fore, appeared in our midst. I did not witness their arrival, but think they could not have been with us more than a few minutes before I awoke painfully in my damp bed by the Meeting House and saw them trying to communicate with a few of our number.

Mr Spense was roused from the table on which he had been sleeping and quickly conveyed the meaning of their excited talk. A village of the neighbouring people had been attacked by the Spanish and many people in it killed. One man who had escaped and come to Andreas' village said the Spanish officer had demanded knowledge of the new foreigners. While hunting, one of Andreas' own men had seen the soldiers and they would soon be very close. If our 'great captain' was an honest man, now was the time to prove it.

Before this story was told Drummond made his entrance, demanding all the details again and barking out further questions as if they were orders.

'How many?'

'Thirty at most.'

'How armed?'

'Muskets and swords.'

'Every man with a musket?'

'Yes.'

'You're certain?'

'Yes.'

'How much do they carry with them?'

'Only what is on their backs.'

'Have they come from Portobello, over the isthmus?'

'We don't know.'

'From a ship?'

'We don't know.'

'Are there any forts, encampments near where your man saw them?'

'No.'

'You're sure?

'Certain.'

'How many days are they from the nearest fort?'

'Eight, maybe nine.'

'How many days ago was the attack?'

'Three.'

'Where your man saw them – how many days from here?'

'Two, but they were moving.'

'Your men can find them?'

'Of course.'

Captain Drummond scratched his jaw and looked away from us as he considered this testimony. He came to his conclusion and smiled.

'Good. Excellent!'

A signal had been sent and the pinnace from the *Rising Sun* was already coming in. Captain Galt sat in the middle facing Mr Paterson whom he had collected from the *Caledonia*. The other captains were summoned from where they slept and took part in a short conference under the dripping eaves of the Meeting House. We waited at a respectful distance, hearing one voice raised and then another, but never enough to let us follow the debate. The outcome was clear when Drummond exited almost at a run. He addressed a waiting officer, a young man with the trace of a poorly aimed musket ball on his cheek.

'Jardine! Twenty men – you know the ones – ready for five days.'

He turned abruptly to me. 'Mr Mackenzie, you are what passes here for a quartermaster. You will supply Lieutenant Jardine and his men with the requisites.'

He had started to turn away when he suddenly stopped, as if remembering some essential detail. 'Mr Mackenzie . . .' He caught the eye of Captain Galt as he walked by us on the way back to his boat. 'Perhaps you would care to join us? It might give you something interesting to put in that book of yours.'

I too looked at Galt and found no objection.

I soon had a list from Lieutenant Jardine and took a boat with Mr Shipp to the *Rising Sun*, where most of the weapons were stowed.

With the help of two grumbling crewmen, who extracted a shilling each from colony funds for 'business not in our agreements, sir', we spent two hours fulfilling the list and loading the boat till the gunwales scarce stood an inch above the water. Twenty muskets and twenty-two pistols with ten pounds of shot and a full horn of powder for each and a thirty-pound keg of it besides went in first. Twenty bayonets too. Two compasses (unnecessary as it proved), three tinder boxes (almost as unnecessary), a prodigious quantity of meal and an iron pot to cook it in, a pound of salt, ten quarts of brandy, a waxed canvas bag containing three tourniquets, a mile of bandages, an instrument borrowed from Dr Munro suitable for extracting musket balls and two phials of tincture of laudanum.

Shortly before eleven our twenty men were marshalled in the centre of the square and received their muskets, shot and a small quantity of powder each. I was taken aback when Lieutenant Jardine handed me one of the pistols. 'For your own protection, sir. When we meet them, the rest of us will be busy.'

This established my place in the expedition, or in the first half of it at least – I was to be the despised one, outside the soldierly brotherhood. The joke was that when the fight came they would have to go slowly so that I could see all the details for my account of it.

'You've used one before, I take it?'

'Never.'

'Private Miller, take Mr Mackenzie down to the shore and let him have some practice with that writing finger of his – ten shots at twenty yards.'

Private Miller was an earnest teacher. He started by commanding my full attention for a lesson that was as like to save my life as anything I had learned to date. I fumblingly shook in too much powder and rammed home a wad and the ball.

'You can forget about that in an emergency. For all that you can forget about the ball too – if a man's close enough you can blast out his eyes with some powder alone. Now prime the touch-hole and the pan.'

I hesitated.

'That bit. Just a shake of powder on it.'

A small block of wood was tossed into the water.

'Now, sir, let's say that's a foreign gentleman intent on opening you up like a pudding. I suggest you stop him. Arm straight, sight along the bead so you can just see the top of it and no more.'

I pulled, winced as the powder in the pan flared up, felt the pistol kick in my hand and opened my eyes again in time to see a small plume of water settle back into the bay so far from my target that it was not even disturbed by the ripples.

Private Miller put on a disconsolate expression and tried to explain the situation in terms suited to the most elementary of military understandings.

'I would suggest, sir, that after such a shot the foreign gentleman would be alive and you would be, as we say in the soldiering trade, dead.'

Miller loaded his own pistol and took casual aim. A spray of splinters shot into the air as the block ducked under the water, bobbing up a moment later with a pale blaze of fresh wood showing where the ball had struck. 'Now there's a man who won't be troubling you again.'

I privately resolved to stay behind my tutor in the event of any trouble. The lesson continued for another half-hour during which I gradually learned to compensate for the pistol's kick and the rightward pull of my over-eager finger. Finally, by aiming considerably below and to the left of the block, I managed to knock one of its corners off.

'Between the eyes!' declared Private Miller, a little generously. 'As for the theory, sir, it's straightforward. In close work, such as this is likely to be, you only get one shot. Make it count against the closest man who still has a firearm like yourself. For the rest, use your blade. You'll not have time for anything else. When you've fired your pistol, don't forget it has another end.'

He flipped it over neatly, catching it by the barrel. 'See this?' He ran his thumb over a brass knob on the base of the pommel. 'Not just for decoration, sir. Do you play golf?'

'A little.'

'Take a good swing with it, both hands on it like a club and land it just there.' He pressed his finger against my temple, level with my eye. 'Behind that little ridge there. Do you feel it? Land a good blow on that and you'll smash the eye-socket. If you get behind your man, go for the very centre of the back of the skull, there. Not too low, you'll just hit a fleshy part and make him angry.'

A wave of dizziness made me stagger and my sight haze over. I stepped backwards and sat down heavily on a rock. Private Miller sympathized with my weakness. I got back to my feet and excused myself.

'Think nothing of it, sir. The first time takes us all differently. My old sergeant said it was like your first time with a woman. One minute before it all seems quite a task, and one minute after you can't remember what all the fuss was about. You'll know what to do when the time comes. We all do.'

I accompanied Miller in a state of some confusion back to where the other members of the expedition were readying themselves. I am afraid I did nothing for his estimation of me by asking if he had himself killed. He seemed so young that I did not think the question unreasonable, but it was received pityingly and as a sign that I had understood nothing of what he had tried to teach me. 'I would hardly be here otherwise, sir.'

He returned me to Lieutenant Jardine, reporting that I had found the target with my last shot, but would be best kept well to the rear all the same – an opinion from which I in no way dissented.

A quantity of shot and a flask of powder were issued to me along with a belt from which to hang them. By the time we left I looked at least half soldierly. Drummond was in a pitch of impatience, pacing about us like a dog about his flock as we made do with a hurried standing meal. The rain, hardly noticeable to that point, started to strengthen and another half-hour was taken up in sending a boat to collect two bolts of oil-cloth from the *St Andrew*. These were cut up and lengths handed to each of us to use as improvised capes or crude shelters to crouch under at night.

Captain Drummond went into the meeting house and came out again almost at once, tucking his formal orders into his jacket. Formed up in four lines of five, the soldiers gave the impression of formidable force and pleased the crowd that had gathered to see us off with four fusillades from their muskets, fired rank by rank. Reverend Borland, accompanied by Reverend Stobo, confirmed divine support for all just wars. It was as he drew breath to develop his theme that Captain Drummond lost the last of his patience. 'That's enough of that. Shoulder arms! Single file from front rank, march!'

The four ranks peeled off into one long line.

'Put yourself in there second from last, Mr Mackenzie, please.'

I ran to catch up and squeezed into my allotted place. As we approached the edge of the clearing, the single Indian who had been left behind from Captain Andreas' party rose from where he had sat motionless all morning and led the way into the forest. As I pushed my way between the first dripping leaves, day turned half to night.

For four hours we moved along a well-defined path, though as it had been made for smaller persons than ourselves we were constantly lashed by foliage or having to bend low in the denser parts where it was as gloomy as a tunnel. The incline was upward though not steep, and the route so twisting that I could never see more than three or four men ahead of me. The ground was as soft as flesh and sucked at the feet. In places the footprints of the man in front would fill with water before I reached them. On the few occasions that I could see any distance it was clear that a heavy mist hugged the ground, so still and cloying that it might have curdled there for centuries before our passage through it. The air was heavy as lead and I got the notion that it was the very same air that had been breathed by every man in the line ahead of me. Certainly, the unwholesome steam I pumped in and out of my lungs would have hardly sustained a mouse, let alone a man.

The path was suddenly steep and after a few minutes we emerged on to a cleared knoll of scorched earth and rock. A small patch of sky revealed that the day was almost done and there was general relief when our guide indicated that we would stop there for the night. Another half-pint of water was distributed as we stood about, reassured, I think, by being all in one another's sight for the first time since leaving New Edinburgh. My own realization of our situation was confirmed as I watched Lieutenant Jardine take out one of the compasses and exchange a few words with Drummond. There was a smile of some sort as it was put back in Jardine's pack unconsulted.

Our guide slipped away and we were alone listening to the birds and to some monkeys chasing each other through the treetops. To my surprise, and somewhat to the embarrassment of the rest, Captain Andreas appeared with a dozen or so of his leading men – by and large the same party that boarded us when we first dropped anchor off Caledonia Bay. With the small amount of Spanish we had in common we soon learned that our prey was some six miles off and heading in the direction of a small, unoccupied fort. We would be closer to them the next day and would meet them before the end of the day after that. We were informed that it was safe to make small fires and that, if we wanted to sing and dance like the night before, no one would hear us but the birds and the monkeys. Sentries would be unnecessary. With that, they left as unaccountably as they had arrived.

Throughout the expedition the Indians were either present or entirely invisible and how they moved from one state to the other remained a mystery. All the more disconcerting was the fact that we were never unobserved by our allies, who would appear to provide for our needs without a word from us. That first evening we were allowed to struggle for an hour to achieve nothing more than a wisp of smoke from some sodden tinder before one of Andreas' men appeared with a small clay pot of glowing charcoal and a load of wood on his back from a type of tree sufficiently resinous to flare up in a moment despite the universal dampness.

A sleepless night was spent. Some lay under their lengths of oil-cloth against a rain weakened again till it was hardly more than a heavy mist. Others, like myself, lay with the cloth under them, more fearful of what would come up from the ground. This had a warmth of its own, constant throughout the night. I would drowse and start from time to time, thinking I had fallen asleep on the flanks of a vast animal that breathed beneath me. In more wakeful moments, I could not escape the thought that it was in fact a dunghill that had been chosen for our rest, steaming with the heat from its own repulsive ferment. Then it seemed not breathing that moved beneath me, but the oozings and scuttlings of all the venomous horrors that hide in every crevice and under every leaf of the forest and that cluster at night towards any living body still with blood in its veins. More times than I can remember, I leaped up in fright, shaking off some crawling thing. Soon my skin prickled and twitched and insisted, in a general alarm, that every inch of me was being swarmed over by some nightmarish insect. Often I was deceived – I thought I could read from my forearm the scratch of all six brittle feet of some monstrous beetle or fly but then, as I laid my other hand down on it, there was nothing but my own hair and fear-tightened skin. Just before dawn I did the same again. A furious buzzing exploded against my cheek and ear, and wings the size of spoons battered against my hand. I leaped to my feet and let out an uncontrollable shriek of fear and disgust. An order to 'Shut up, man' was the only sympathy I got. I sat up for what remained of the night, straining my eyes at the darkness and feeling a burning pain swelling on my face.

A sweltering, leaden dawn brought a hideous confirmation of these fears. Nothing seemed amiss at first. We got a good fire started and a pot of meal over it for our breakfast. Light made the place less hostile, its attack on us less pressing, or at least in abeyance. We soon discovered that it was only less obvious. One soldier went aside to relieve himself and found five inches of fat black slime sucking at his groin. He rashly pulled it off, causing himself some harm and the creature to burst, drenching his fist in his own blood. We were ordered to examine ourselves, particularly between the legs and under the arms. Not one of us found less than half a dozen of them, hidden away in the warmest and most intimate corners. It was impossible to pull them off without tearing at the part they sucked. Some one suggested brandy, another salt, thinking they might shrivel up like the slugs we know at home. Both were applied, but neither was effective. We heated dirks in the fire. A touch from these caused them to drop off at once, but given the places in which they were hidden away, the method was as much a hazard to ourselves as to the leeches and there were several yelps of pain as men burnt themselves. There was some co-operation in burning off those under the arms or on more open patches of skin, but for the parts where they gathered most, every man was his own surgeon.

It was in this state, half naked and wholly undignified, that Captain Andreas and four of his men came upon us. The confusion could not have been greater if they had been a party of Spanish soldiers. Some leaped to cover themselves, but only appeared the more ridiculous being, even as we were, the most clothed men there. Captain Drummond decided that blaming the sentries would help. He pulled his breeches up and screamed at the hapless pair, demanding an explanation for the lack of any warning. Our position was all the more painful for the supreme dignity of Andreas and his men. They behaved with the aplomb of a party of ambassadors who, having coming upon an emperor in a moment of indisposition, affected with absolute conviction to be unaware of anything that might cause embarrassment.

They did not come empty-handed. Two of them carried gourds filled with a white fluid the thickness of whale oil. Another laboured under the weight of a larger vessel and carried on his back a net filled with things like small loaves. After a few Spanish solecisms and a bit of dumb show we gathered that this fluid was the solution to our problems. We were ordered to take off the rest of our clothes and sit in line to wait our turn. The thick fluid was applied in drops from the end of a stick. One touch on the back of a leech makes it contract like a spring. They curl into balls and drop off within seconds. Once on the ground, a very curious thing happens. The creature seems truly animate for the first time, uncurling and curling itself, writhing with an energy quite astonishing for such an undifferentiated length of jelly. After a minute or so, it is still. For all their simplicity and loathsomeness, their expiry seemed such an agony that I had some pity for them.

My own turn came. I did as I was instructed by the Indian's hands – sitting, standing, turning this way and that, finally lying on my back, watching the raindrops as they fell down towards me. He went over every inch of me, methodical, gentle, as licensed as a lover until the last and smallest leech was dislodged from between my toes. The second part of our treatment involved the thinner fluid, which I took to be a dilution of the stuff they had applied with a stick. This was drawn up into the things in the net which were, I think, some sort of dried vegetable matter, but which acted exactly like a sea sponge. Each man was given a thorough washing in this fluid, which dried to an odourless second skin which I was aware of only as a slight tightness in some parts of the body as I moved and as some premature wrinkles on the backs of my hands. We were told that this would protect us from leeches for five days, and so it proved. I received a special consultation on account of the bite on my cheek, which was now generally swollen with a hard aching welt in the middle, big enough for me to see for myself without a mirror. Two of the Indians palpated this and discussed it with all the solemn incomprehensibility of the most expensive physicians in Edinburgh. A gesture of refusal, three fingers and a smile indicated that it would come to a head in three days' time and they would deal with it then.

Divided once again into the clothed and the naked, we hurried a simple meal as Drummond fretted about lost time. I reflected on the curiousness of these events and, in particular, how the Indians might have come across and refined such an effective remedy. Mere good fortune, perhaps? Or, as with us until so recently, many centuries of chance and blundering until the oddest of coincidences made the virtues of some plant clear to one who had the wit to understand and pass it on? In our state of dependency, and in the apparent infallibility of the Indians in all matters to do with living in these wildernesses, I found it easier to believe that there was a more precise guiding principle, another calculus that would tell the uses of a plant or the part of some animal according to its colour, shape, smell and habits of growth. To them, no doubt, it is their A B C, but to us as obscure and inconceivable a mystery as the workings of Mr Cunningham's chronometer would be to one of their number.

As before, our day was spent with a single guide at the head of the line. Captain Andreas and his party, we assumed, were somewhere close and though we had no more evidence of their presence than on the first day, the belief that they were there reassured us.

So far as our march was concerned, the day passed without any incident of note. Twice we had to wait for two of our soldiers, but I was never one of the stragglers and earned myself, through this feat, a partial reprieve from the comments that had been constantly aimed at me since before we left. Once again, we stopped as the light was fading and this time waited expectantly for someone to arrive from our invisible parallel force. It was not Captain Andreas this time, but four of his leading men and in a state of some excitement.

After the usual struggle we got the necessary information out of them – the Spanish had reached and settled in their fort, which, we gathered, was nothing more than a small earthwork and a few felled trees. When they told us that they had not posted guards and that some had the fever and others were already drunk, there was such an expression of keenness on their faces, of appetite for the killing to come, that I knew not one of those Spaniards would see the next day out. I appended to the thought a silent and unheroic prayer that I would not meet the same fate. They told us also that we had made better progress than expected that day, and if we wished, we could continue for another half-hour (they show five fingers for a period of time that roughly equates to this), to a place good for us to spend the night and which would allow an attack tomorrow within three hours of first light. This was agreed and at the end of a short extra march we arrived at the site of our eerie vigil.

As we approached the place I could hear expressions of surprise ahead of me in the line. All the same, I was unprepared for the shock of suddenly passing between the dim masses of crumbling gateposts and feeling under my feet the ridges of a fallen iron gate. To move from such desolation to the courtyard of a building one might once have admired in the finest of European cities was such a violent contradiction of all my assumptions that I felt, in an alarming moment of vertigo, quite unsure of where I was. To the left was a wide building of two storeys, white plaster still adhering to enough of its walls to make it the most visible thing we could see. Two rows of empty casements broke its form with rectangles of perfect blackness. The lower row centred on a doorway – no door now – approached from the courtyard by a flight of curved stone steps of breathtaking pretension. A balustrade on the left remained intact, the one on the right arbitrarily tumbled away to rubble on the courtyard floor. Through one of the casements poked the timbers of a roof long since fallen in. Something fluttered out for its nocturnal hunt.

From one of the Indian's ember pots a fire was quickly kindled and makeshift torches lit. We were reassured about the dangers of this – the density of the vegetation stifling the most brilliant light within a few paces – but were sternly admonished to make no smoke beyond first light. Captain Andreas with more of his senior men joined us. There was a conference apart with Drummond, Jardine and a man named Black, our third in rank. This – and a similar meeting the next morning before we moved off – was, I assume, to determine our tactics. They left after a few minutes, refusing once again to share our company but staying that night close enough for me to detect the occasional voice as I nodded over the fire and drifted nervously around the edges of sleep. They left a fat, fresh-killed peccary as they went, dropping it beside our contemptible pot of meal. Private Miller's joke, *The Lord is my shepherd; I shall not want,* was grimly received.

The ruined house contained such a quantity of debris and was so tangled with creeping and climbing plants that it was decided to spend the night in the courtyard. Here, flags half the thickness of millstones pressed back the century-long attack. Even so, for all their weight, the battle was being lost and the final result was quite beyond doubt. Around every stone a furious thicket had pushed its way through the cracks. Twisted, woody stems emerged here and there, throwing off the stone above as if it were the lightest of coverlets. Others were in twenty pieces or more, having been pressed from all sides until they had shattered like glass.

The men lit other fires and cleared themselves patches of stone on which to sit or lie back on their packs to rest. They now seemed uninterested in their surroundings and I was the only one to examine the building and its environs more closely while they busied themselves with gutting and spitting the peccary.

Being paved all about with these stones and bordered by a wall, it was still possible to walk entirely around the house. At the side, the light from my torch could just show a single row of windows along the upper storey. Small, elegant and one time promising coolness within, they further enlarged the mystery in my mind. At the back was a more intimate courtyard where a fountain once played into a scallop shell basin. A toppled cupid now lay almost hidden in the riotous growth that spilled over on to the pavement, his right arm drawn back, fingers pinching the string of an absent bow. Here was a gentleman's house, a refined essay in taste, a confident building, open, in no way disposed to defence, restrained in its grandeur, occasionally playful and unmistakably made for pleasure. Such a gesture, such an expression of a man's hopes and nature dropped impossibly in such a place almost made me want to laugh. What mad don had made his stand here where no road passed or ended, where no town was near and in the midst of land that would take a people a generation to subdue and cultivate? Did he think he could make good all such defects by his own efforts – be the author, entirely, of his own paradise? I looked up at the dimly firelit mass of the house from the back and caught the dark shimmer of bats leaving their roosts. A new thought made me kinder to his memory – how amazed he would be to see his house thus, more even than I was to find it already ruined. Who could, after such a triumphant assertion of their will, walk those corridors and rooms for the first time, smelling the plaster as it dried on the walls, and not be certain of success? I became aware of a sense of intrusion and, forgoing my curiosity to see what lay within, returned to my fellows.

The Indians, no doubt, thought we would be pleased to spend an evening in at least a half-familiar environment, but whatever their intentions, the company was solemn. A bellyful of pork and double rations of brandy made us sleepy, but not talkative. The house and its miserable dilapidation depressed our spirits. The reasons were not articulated but I feel certain that, like myself, the soldiers thought again of the vision given to us by Paterson and felt uneasy in the ruins of something that had once been almost as great.

In the hour before silence finally descended on us, I witnessed a strange sacrament. Captain Drummond took two small silver plates from his pack and two small pairs of tongs, miniatures of what a farrier might use to heat a shoe. One set was handed to Lieutenant Jardine and the other he held himself. The nearest soldiers knew the ritual well and handed over their powder horns to the two officers. What they did with them seemed very madness and I know I would have doubted the story had I heard it from anyone else. The contents of the horns were tapped out on to the plates and then toasted over the fires! I drew back involuntarily, my caution attracting smiles of contempt. The purpose of the exercise soon became clear. The slate-grey powder caked, forming a crust that both men would occasionally break with a prod of the finger. When at last it had been warmed to a perfect dryness it was funnelled back into the horns and returned to the owner. The process was repeated for every man and was clearly something that Jardine and Drummond relished. The flames never touched the plates, but the unspoken rules of the game demanded that they be allowed at least close enough to risk an explosion. When dry, the smallest grains would catch in the updraught and burst silently into minuscule puffs of smoke. I was the last and received my powder back from Drummond as solemnly as a communicant. I tucked it under my shirt and felt its warmth against my belly, dust-dry and deadly.

The last of our talk subsided and was replaced by the double click and snap of flintlocks being tested and of whetstones on steel as the soldiers tried to find the last infinitesimal of the killing edge. I drowsed and counted my heartbeats as they pushed the blood past the hardened swelling on my cheek. Sudden fears snatched me back from sleep – that I had forgotten the most essential part of Private Miller's lesson, that I would be killed because I had no sword (I never did find the courage to ask for one). Perhaps because of what Miller had said, or perhaps because it is really true that love and killing are man's twin virginities, my mind accepted the suggestion of the flames and conjured a vision of Susanna exactly as she lay when I took my leave of her. Calmed by this, I was at last able to conquer my pride and offer up a prayer for my life.

I awoke to hissing and steam to find one of the soldiers relieving himself on the embers of the last fire recklessly close to my head. When I objected, the barely visible form explained: 'No smoke, sir.'

True to our instructions from the Indians, the other fires were scuffed out before first light. From the last of these a flame was kindled and carried to a small lantern. A man appeared, hunched over it, and as the flame took hold the whole company emerged from invisibility. We waited quietly for dawn. I waved away the insects that continually cloud the air and felt the occasional raindrop penetrate the leaves above.

A small amount of meal was prepared.

'Half rations, now,' ordered Sergeant Black, 'we don't want you falling asleep.'

A delegation of Indians appeared and seemed very content with the situation. The Spanish had not moved or been reinforced and were clearly unaware of our presence. We would follow our guide as usual. Captain Andreas and his force would precede us by another route and when, as they put it, a stick showed no shadow, the attack would begin. Captain Drummond said he would give a single shot as his signal and both sides left believing they had understood each other.

As soon as the light permitted we started to move, myself in my accustomed place of second from last. I looked back, over the shoulder of the last man, to catch a final glimpse of the ruins. Though we had hardly taken a dozen steps it was already all but invisible. In that early-morning light the walls and gateposts had a colour strangely close to that of the plants that rushed in on them with such intent. It occurred to me that every step I took equated to the passage of a year, or perhaps five or ten at a time. What I was seeing was the future of that building, its repossession, or rather its accelerated digestion by its offended environment. I was amazed at the speed with which it lost all semblance of itself, how, without protest, it returned to the elements from which it had so pointlessly been raised up.

Concealed, as we supposed, thirty yards or less from the edge of the earth and timber rampart that formed the Spanish position, I remember my heart slowing for a moment as I stumbled on the thought that I knew quite well what was about to happen because I had read about such things often enough and imagined them as a boy in colours more lurid than can be found in any reality. As with my earliest conceptions of women, my understanding of war was to be quite disproved by its first contact with reality.

Our belief in our invisibility was brusquely disproved as a dozen musket barrels were thrust out at once. Without pause, I saw seventy to a hundred Indians run towards the rampart from our right. Save for their feet and the clatter of their pitiful weapons – long-bladed spears, a few cherished swords, here and there a stone-headed club – they made no noise. My first sense that something had indeed begun came from a volley of Spanish musket fire. Three or four men fell, all silent save one who screamed long notes between short, convulsive breaths. It was a sound I had heard before, and I knew it was one of the last men make. Drummond bellowed something and I heard Jardine and Black echoing it further away. We stayed where we were and watched the musket barrels retract and reappear as fresh-charged weapons were seized. Another volley dropped five from the continuing charge – this time none of them moved again.

'They're not bad,' said the soldier lying closest to me, in calm appraisal.

A dull but enormous thud came from somewhere. The ground jerked and my head felt for a second as if it were under water.

'Mortar!' cried someone.

I had just enough time to question the fatuous vision of cement that entered my head, and to wonder what my companion was doing pressing himself so fiercely to the ground when there was a detonation above us straight from the heart of a thunderstorm. Whistles and sirens filled the air before the shock punched me flat and snapped my teeth together like a trap. Something hissed and spat all around us. The sapling in front of us leaped in two as an invisible force sliced through its trunk. I struggled to my feet, drunken, blurred, and saw in a strange moment of silence – or of deafness – an odd white cloud drift away and disintegrate, like a sea urchin of smoke, spikes protruding from it in every direction. I realized that a shell had exploded and that those spikes traced the paths of a swarm of steel blades. I looked down to see shattered fingers clasped about the back of the head and a paste of blood and brains slopping from a lifeless mouth. I knew that at any moment my own life might be as easily extinguished and that there was nothing I could do about it. I was recalled to my senses by the sensation of my water running helplessly down my legs.

The shell accounted for another six or seven Indians, but in no way delayed the rest who quickly reached the rampart. There had been no time for the Spanish to recharge their muskets, and there was now nothing to prevent Andreas and his men clambering over the defences, spears, swords and clubs flailing. As they met the Spanish hand to hand, their silence was replaced with a shrill ululation like hounds giving tongue when the scent of their fox becomes too rich to bear. Still we kept our positions – for fear, I suppose, of another mortar shell. There was now not a single living Indian outside the fort, all of them having thrown themselves recklessly on their enemies within. I saw one fall directly on to a bayonet. Already launched on his course from the top of the rampart, he suddenly found it beneath him and fell resistlessly on to its steel, which I could see emerging from his back before defender and attacker toppled together out of sight. With that exception the rampart prevented any view of what was happening, leaving us to deduce the progress of the battle from its sounds. Spanish commands indicated that they were not yet in total rout, but it was impossible to believe that the fight could go on for much longer. I was beginning to think we might have no part in it at all when, after a full minute without any sound of musket or pistol from within the fort, Drummond gave the command to advance.

There was no charge, but an orderly progress at fast walking pace in a single long rank of nineteen men – my poor neighbour was, as yet, our only loss. I interpreted my own orders loosely, breaking cover with the rest of them but keeping a clear ten paces behind. In response to an order I did not understand, the four men in the middle of the line split into two pairs and started to busy themselves with something I couldn't see. It was an extraordinary scene; the others came to a halt and stood as calmly as at a parade while the most hideous sounds of carnage came from beyond the rampart only a few feet away.

'Grenadiers?' shouted Lieutenant Jardine.

'Ready!' was the reply from both pairs.

With a glance to Captain Drummond, he gave the order. 'Grenades!'

All four men, from crouching close to the ground, leaped to their feet and pulled apart from each other. Slings of canvas snapped tight and two black balls flew over the rampart, trailing thin cords of smoke. A period of time passed by at the end of which I was quite certain that the devices had failed. A further period passed in which it seemed incontestable that the grenades would be sent back over the wall to land at our or, as I saw it, my feet. I started to take reasonable precautions but was chagrined to hear Captain Drummond growl with evident satisfaction: 'No need to alarm yourself, Mr Mackenzie.'

I retreated no further and contemplated the thought that I was about to die principally as a result of pride. A shattering blast from within the fort put an end to my misery. The sound of battle immediately diminished by half and was reduced almost to nothing by a second similar shock.

This was the signal for action. A chorus of orders and responses started to be shouted, which I found impossible to follow. The result of them all was that five of our men clambered to the top of the rampart and started to discharge their muskets and pistols into the chaos below. The remaining fourteen, led by Drummond and Jardine, ran round the back and charged straight into the mêlée roaring like madmen. A feeble barrier, which hung from a single leather hinge, had been one of the casualties of the grenades and was easily brushed aside. I followed the fourteen, conscious of my duty as an observer, yet anxious also not to disobey too grossly Captain Drummond's instructions to keep well to the rear.

I need not have hurried, for the scene I came across was so infernal that it quite overbore my senses. For some time I stood immobile, receiving everything my mind could convey of what lay before me, but with as little understanding as an infant looking for the first time on such a wholly unprecedented world. Parts of it have returned to me since, most often at night in the quarter-hour before sleep or in the morning before full wakefulness. It is at these moments of vacancy that whatever obstructed my mind at the time weakens and lets the wildest visions of horror break through. I see the tip of a Spanish sword slash through an Indian throat and – most pitifully – how he clutches at the gash for a second as if he might hold his life in even as his terror forces it to flood through his fingers all the more quickly.

I see a Spaniard wandering in the middle of it all, ignored as one already dead. He stumbles towards me, causing me to cock my pistol and step backwards. I just have time to wonder about the importance of the coils of rope he holds before he almost collides with me, seems to excuse himself and, if I understood him correctly, asks for water as he collapses at my feet letting his intestines slither from his belly like a butchered pig.

When I woke a few hours ago to take up my pen once more, I had to shake from my mind the image of an Indian whose open mouth was the only clue as to how he had come by his death. The rest of his body was unharmed and he might merely have been asleep until turned over by the toe of someone's boot to reveal the obscene absence of the whole of the head behind the ear. Whether it happened on the day or not, I cannot say, but in my half-dreamed memory it was the sound of my own screaming that finally shook me out of sleep.

If anyone had asked me about this ten minutes after Drummond ordered the cease-fire, I could have told them nothing. It was only as the chaos died down that I came back to myself and was able to take in the horrible results of the battle. Some twenty to twenty-five Indians remained alive, though several of these were sufficiently injured to put their survival in doubt. Captain Andreas and most of his leading men were uninjured – protected during the battle by those of lower rank whose bodies lay about the fort and greatly outnumbered the Spanish. It was clear from their injuries – jagged tears or large holes as if something had exploded from within – that many had died from our grenades. Whether or not Captain Andreas understood this was never clear: I heard no reproach from him, and no regret from Drummond.

Our opponents had also been careless of their own safety. The mortar they had fired stood exactly in the middle of the fort's small enclosure and pointed directly upwards. Its shell had exploded over their heads as much as it had exploded over ours and it seemed all but certain that it had taken Spanish lives as well as some from our own side. An inspection of the fort's pathetic contents revealed neither powder nor shot to fire it again. Its use had been a last desperate act, sent up with the bitter prayer that their destruction should be as costly as possible to those responsible for it.

As the smoke lifted, I saw the awful thoroughness of what our soldiers had done. Only a single Spaniard seemed to be alive and that one with his wrists already tied behind his back. I say 'seemed' because the grenades and the mortar had had a second effect I had not anticipated. Four or five of the bodies, some Spanish, some Indian, lay as if dead but had been merely stunned by the shock of the explosions. The soldiers, who must have seen such a thing many times, made no effort to see who was alive and who dead, but busied themselves in picking over the fort's supplies, keeping an eye open as they did so for some sign of life. The first to stir was one of the Indians. Several of his comrades ran over to him from where they had been separating their dead from the enemy. They had shown no emotion in this task, but welcomed their reawakened brother with great joy as if he had indeed come back from the dead. Three came back to them in this way. Otherwise unharmed, they were confused by their resurrection and by the joy with which their doubting fellows shook them and examined them to see if it were really true before helping them to their feet. Two Spaniards in the same state were treated very differently. The first was on the opposite side of the fort from where I was standing. From amongst three or four dead there was a moan and an arm rose up before flopping back on to a comrade's shoulder. Sergeant Black dropped some piece of worthless booty and went over to him, quick as a spider feeling a twitch on its web. His own body obscured what he did as he knelt over the man, taking a firm grip of his head. A sickening coldness ran through me as I saw a quick movement of the elbow send him unprotestingly back to sleep. Another stirred, almost at my feet. 'See to that one too, Sergeant.'

It was Drummond's instruction. Black approached the half-conscious Spaniard with an appalling calmness, quite without any sign of wishing the man harm. I prepared to look away, but rather than the quick despatch there was a pause and some words. I realized Black was speaking to me and had to struggle to stay on my feet as I grasped the meaning of his appalling courtesy.

'Would you like him, sir?'

Amongst our own men, all activity stopped. Every eye was on me and on the disgraceful pistol by my side, still loaded after so many opportunities had been let by. The Spaniard stirred again and mumbled something – a name, I think. My heart raced at an impossible speed and my whole body seemed about to melt under its own heat. I am sure that the final humiliation of collapse was almost upon me when Drummond gave the order. 'Get on with it, Sergeant.'

He knelt over the man as before. I could not move and saw only the Spaniard's hand over Black's shoulder. He tried to raise himself, thinking perhaps that the day had been theirs, that he was being embraced by one of his own. A slight twitch of his fingers indicated that the job was done.

Black was standing beside me again, wiping a dirk on his sleeve. 'I shouldn't worry, sir. They don't feel it.'

I decided that I ought to look at him and found a man a little older than myself, thin, neglected – though a gold ring in one ear suggested that was not his nature – the skin yellow-greenish where it was not stained with the blood that had flooded from his ruined eye. My emotions disappointed me – there was no redeeming pity, only disgust and a selfish regret that I had looked and seen something I would never be free of.

I had declined to kill, and though everyone returned to their tasks as if nothing of importance had happened, I had put a barrier between myself and the others that I don't believe can ever be taken down. I am glad of it now and would not have it any other way. The decision which Drummond spoke of and which, until that day, I had hardly understood, has been made for me. I feel the easier for it and am sorry only that I stood too close to bring my own skin off entirely clean.

I went outside the fort to where our injured had been gathered together to be tended to. We had done well – only three were not on their feet. One of them was Private Miller, who had taken a ball through the thigh while firing from the top of the rampart. He joked with me about his wound and my unharmed state – how the pupil had done better than the teacher. A fresh bandage was already blood-soaked and his face white with pain as he raised his head to take another mouthful of laudanum. A little way apart our two dead lay waiting for their graves.

Faint with exhaustion, I sat down on my own and was ignored by one and all for two hours or more. In this period Drummond and his men completed their examination of the fort and its contents. The result, above all, was surprise that such determined resistance had come from such a hopeless situation. It was decided that only three pistols and four muskets were worth taking. The few swords and bayonets to be found were left for the Indians, who made no visible objection to such a poor bargain. The mortar was too heavy to take back and so was hauled to a nearby incline and allowed to roll down out of sight. The graves were dug and filled, the ceremony of interment nothing more than a moment of silence. The Indians collected their own dead and took them into the forest. Three processions were required. We were not privileged to see their rites, but half an hour before we left, some time in the latter part of the afternoon, thick smoke rose from the high ground a mile away.

Those Indians who were not engaged in these preparations remained in the fort and busied themselves with stripping the bodies of the Spanish for trophies. Soon the dead were mostly naked and the Indians more clothed than I had ever seen them before. Like the man Black had killed, all the Spanish bodies were sallow with fever and had the ribs and shoulders of starvelings. As one emaciated corpse was moved in the hope of finding something of interest below, I saw black bile as well as blood drain from him. If we had delayed a week, we could have come as gravediggers rather than as soldiers and won an altogether cheaper victory.

Whatever could not be worn, or was not a weapon or made of

gold or silver was of no interest to the Indians and accumulated in a pile. It was from these rejects that I picked out a letter, carefully sealed, elegantly addressed and just a little bloody on one corner. I put it inside my shirt and have it now at the bottom of my chest. As I straightened from this theft, two of our soldiers appeared and started to douse the whole fort with oil.

The men having been kept hungry before the fight, a meal was prepared to set us up for our departure. They fell to with an untroubled relish. I, by contrast, had no appetite and was the subject of some close and rather surly attention when it was noticed how easily my fastidious stomach had been turned by such a simple piece of work. Copious quantities of brandy were handed out in celebration, as Captain Drummond put it, of the first battle honours of the Caledonian Foot. While Drummond and Jardine planned the triumphal ceremonies, the wounded were helped to their share and with further doses of laudanum were soon very content.

We had proved expensive allies for the Indians. Nevertheless, they still provided us with a guide and we set off with about two hours' light left. The three wounded were carried on makeshift frames and, because of the nature of the terrain, were greatly shaken about. Our single prisoner, his hands still tied and his ankles roped together by three feet of cord, stumbled along between two of our men. I was again the last but one in the line and could feel the heat on my back as the remains of the fort and its occupants blazed. A curious detail formed my last impression of the place. The barrel of oil our soldiers had found was olive – its aroma pursued us into the semi-night of the forest and sharply reawakened my hunger.

When we camped for the night the wind began to pick up. The rain became heavier, drumming on the dense ceiling of foliage, which bowed under the weight of the deluge, gathering huge drops the size of musket balls to fire on our heads, down our necks and into the bowls of our pipes with unerring marksmanship. Some huddled under their scraps of oil-cloth, but moisture came at us from all directions and most attempts at staying dry were soon abandoned.

Our guide stayed with us on the return journey and I was able to watch him, cross-legged on some leaves in nothing but his skin, and wonder what he could possibly make of these strange visitors to his world. It was by his craft that a fire had been started earlier in the evening. Though never healthy, it outlasted my predictions by far. Much later, when the winds had risen to a storm that thrashed violently through the tops, a whirling gust penetrated to the floor and threw its embers in our faces. Our only light then was a shuttered lantern.

For periods we were protected from the worst of the wind by the closeness of the trees, but at other times, when it veered, a part of it would become detached from the main body and would dive down to the forest floor where it would surge about, furiously seeking escape. Sometimes it was funnelled between the trunks and would gain a terrifying force. Under such attacks I would dig my fingers into the earth to avoid being plucked off it altogether and would hold my oilcloth in my teeth as the wind tried to tear it from me. It was in that state, deafened by the roaring, hands and face lashed by debris, that I approached a delirium of exhaustion that was as close as I would get to sleep either that night or the next three.

Perhaps it was because of the occasional howling of the wind, or the groans from Miller – already feverish when we made camp – that I was able to ignore that third sound for so long. Perhaps in my semi-wakeful state I had just enough sense to know that I wanted to ignore it. Whatever the reason, I am sure that the sounds of a man beyond all words with pain and fear must have been impinging on me for some time before a horrifying shriek snapped me out of my stupor. The lantern had gone and in the near blind-blackness of the night I could only guess at the shapes of two or three of the men nearest me and of the three wounded lying side by side. Several of the others who had been there when I last had my eyes open were gone. Another scream cut through the storm and from the same direction I caught sight of a feeble glimmer, flashing as leaves were blown to and fro across its path. I stumbled towards the light and was on the point of reaching it when I had my right arm seized and found one of our soldiers breathing hotly down my neck. In my foolishness I thought at first he was there to help me, but he pulled me backwards roughly as if I too might be a prisoner. Even as I looked ahead and saw what he was trying to prevent me from seeing, I did not understand. There was the sound of a man sobbing and then another appalling cry. Several men stood close together, their outlines made clear by the light of the lantern. They were looking down at something on the ground and I could just see the legs of a man lying on his back. My intrusion was noticed and one of the men sprang up from where he had been kneeling. No faces were visible, but I knew from his bearing it was Drummond.

'I'm sorry, sir,' said the soldier, who once again took hold of my arm.

'This is no place for you, Mackenzie. Take him back to the camp.'

That's where I stayed until dawn, more or less under guard, every muscle rock hard and quivering with revulsion and shame. By morning I still had the courage to ask Drummond what had become of the Spaniard – and in a tone that surprised even me and made everyone stop to watch the exchange. Drummond shouted through the wind, 'He has gone away, Mr Mackenzie.'

He and Jardine moved towards the head of the column to start the day's march. Jardine looked back and with his parting words all but accused me of treason.

'He was a Spaniard, Mr Mackenzie. There is a difference, you know.'

My question had put me beyond the pale and not a word was spoken to me from that moment on – except a few from Miller, who had become too confused to know better. For two and a half days more we waded through the storm. Part of our way was across more open ground and here the wind would sometimes drop and a drowning deluge of rain fall straight on our heads with the force of a summer hail. At other times it would blow so hard and the rain be so horizontal it was a wonder it ever reached the ground at all. The mud was never less than ankle deep and often rose to the middle of the calf. The burden of our three wounded delayed us even further.

It was Miller's condition that pushed us on. Towards the end of that day he changed from quietness to meaningless volubility. When his bandage was changed it was found that a great quantity of pus had already collected in the wound. The torn flesh about it was strangely livid, redder than blood. We endured another night quite as bad as the one before and though I heard his groans throughout, he was quiet all the next day and very pale. At dawn we started again with the expectation of reaching Caledonia by noon. It was perhaps an hour before our arrival, while stopping to take advantage of a spring, that someone noticed he was dead.

On the borders of the colony our guide stopped and indicated he would take his leave. Before doing so, he offered to perform a last service, which his fellows had promised and I had quite forgotten. Namely, the treating of the swelling on my face. He examined it carefully and seemed to approve of what he found. He held my head tightly – Drummond and his men observing the injury to my dignity with evident pleasure – and prepared for the operation. A brief, intolerable pain caused me to cry out and was followed immediately by the nauseating sensation of the matter contained in the swelling spurting out. He grinned and held his palm in front of my face. Something like a small mound of yellowish rice lay in the middle of it. I just had time to see how the grains squirmed before rushing to one side to give myself up to a fit of vomiting.

I staggered into New Edinburgh half blind and drunk with fatigue and found, by good fortune, a boat on the very point of casting off for the *Rising Sun*. I have no recall of how I actually made my way aboard, nor how my legs carried me below, but do remember that at the time I had the firm conviction I had started to float rather than walk. I descended on my bunk like a feather, kissed its heaped blankets and fell into a day-long sleep without the slightest concern for the meaning of the incomprehensible question posed to Drummond by the first sentry we came across: 'The Reverend, sir – is he with you?'

I HAVE BEEN A FORTNIGHT AWAY from these pages and as I return to them now would be only too happy to say, 'All's well,' and lay them back to sleep in my chest for a fortnight more. Alas, it is not so.

Why so long, then? Because it has taken me this long to decide whether I should write another word here and whether, should the answer to that first question be 'yes', I should do so as a true and loyal patriot or as an honest man. I covered the last dozen pages with the speed and obliviousness of a court clerk, content with the precision of his letters and the form of his setting out until, when the advocate pauses for breath, he reads one of his well-written words and finds his own name there in the very heart of the indictment. When I was finished, I broke my habit and read them over. The corners are still brown where they were singed by the candle flame, but I reprieved them at the last instant, telling myself that if I was to commit such a crime it were best done coldly.

Once again, it was Drummond who made the decision for me. I thought his invitation to join the expedition had been nothing more than a whim, a joke that might amuse his men in the quieter moments. It was a remark from Captain Galt that made me see more clearly. By chance we were returning to the *Rising Sun* at the same time and on our way to the boat were passed by two redcoats or, as I should now refer to them, soldiers of the First Caledonian Foot. Although neither man had taken part in their regiment's first victory they had, no doubt, been fully informed of what had happened and this was enough for them to look ostentatiously the other way as they passed me. I had already become accustomed to such slights, but was surprised and disturbed that they would dare to include Captain Galt in such an insult. According to his habit, Galt said nothing either at the time or when we were being rowed out to his ship. It was only when we took leave of each other on deck that I received, instead of his usual nod, his considered judgement on the whole affair. 'I see Captain Drummond has not persuaded you, then.'

I pretended not to be sure of what he meant, but a single sentence is as much as he spares any man these days and his cabin door closed on my question without another word. In reality, I saw it at once. My presence on the expedition was not something Drummond thought would benefit me, nor was I there to ensure his proper place in this history – the only truth that matters being Drummond's own; rather it was a touchstone against which he might test my nature and determine if I were worth any further attention. In short, our tendency to faction, but briefly subsumed by the common efforts of our first month here, is once again to the fore. If any further proof of this were needed, it is to be found in the attitude of Mr Paterson who, even before our agreement, was exceedingly solicitous and thought nothing of enquiring after my health twice in the same day.

Immediately after our return Drummond was preoccupied with the exploitation of his victory. A colour was made up and trooped about New Edinburgh with much fanfare. The first wholly dry day any of us could remember was devoted to the festival, which was preceded in the morning by the burial of Miller and one of the other wounded soldiers who succumbed to an infection in a similar manner. Mr Borland officiated and gave such an affecting account of the miseries of poor sinners' lives that by the end of it few of his listeners felt the two men had lost anything of consequence. In this way, he prepared his audience excellently for the lighter spirit of the afternoon. Even though the parade had sometimes to pick its way over the storm wreckage of our little town, the collection of which had been neglected for these triumphs, it was met with an unequivocal approval on all sides and restored us to full confidence in our fortunes. A triple measure of brandy and a glass of claret for our few ladies, all at the expense of the regiment, further assured us of the excellence of our success.

It was, no doubt, these pleasures that distracted Drummond from conceiving of the little awkwardness that might, at any time, arise from my having been on the expedition – namely, the fact that he had returned irreversibly estranged from the person who would write the most meticulous and credible account of the whole affair. Gaining as I am in my understanding of men's natures, it was clear to me from the first that this would occur to him before long and that, once planted in his mind, the thought would grow from the merest imperfection to something entirely intolerable. Indeed, having suffered so much from the rumours of his connection with the infamous Massacre of some years ago, I thought it impossible that he could fail to move against me. After all, what would be the point of leaving behind the sins of the old world only to allow new ones to be laid at one's door here?

It is a matter of some satisfaction that it happened exactly as I expected two days ago on the conclusion of the council meeting. I was with Mr Shipp in the hold of the *Sun* verifying adjustments to our ledgers when a note was delivered to me. It was from Captain Jolly who, by rotation, is the current president of the council. I could almost feel the words burn with embarrassment as I read them. There seemed to be nothing but excuses and apologies save for two entirely predictable facts. Firstly, owing to the delicate position of the colony, the multitude of its enemies, the uncertainty of who they might be and the potential problems arising from inaccurate information about certain things, the council required to know if I had written anything of the late expedition against the Spanish, and if I had, they required to see it. Second, and I could not help but wonder if Captain Jolly were hoisting a friendly signal here, there was the suggestion that I would be pleased to learn of and congratulate Colonel Drummond on his promotion. The note ended with an expression of the good captain's great regret at having to convey the council's insistence that there be no delay.

It is one thing for an author to consider destroying his own work, but quite another for someone else to threaten the same thing. I felt a passionate indignation at the idea and resolved at once to frustrate it. Pleading faintness, I left Shipp to finish the work on his own and went to my cabin. I gave the boy who was waiting for my reply a crown to say that he had found me unwell and asleep and that he had left the note under my door. As fast as I could, I made a copy of everything I had written about the expedition. When it was finished and hidden, I sat gloomily in my cabin, expecting a knock on the door at any moment and reflecting that the effort had been wasted as Drummond would surely ask for the whole journal and would find as many reasons as he wished not to return it. I needed an ally in the council, and one who could gainsay Drummond even while his glory was still fresh on his shoulders. I turned to my master in such affairs, and even as the boy drummed on my door with a second message Colquhoun's voice tolled in my head, damning me for a born fool and telling me what to do.

For a second crown the boy agreed that he had not been able to wake me and took a message of mine to Paterson, which brought him to my door in less than a half-hour. He greeted me warmly, as is his manner with all men, shared a glass, enquired after my health once again and exchanged opinions on the weather. He then unfolded my note, placed it before me and raised an eyebrow.

'"Re my Journal. Anxious to avoid embarrassment to yourself. Your servant, R. Mackenzie." Admirably terse, Roderick, I must say.'

'I thought it best not to put any details on paper.'

'But you have not always been so discreet, is that the problem?'

'Precisely. It is a private journal. I never thought—'

'Words are promiscuous things, Roderick, they'll let themselves be read by anyone. You should have thought of that.'

I apologized fulsomely and refilled his glass.

'What exactly is my interest in this?'

I explained that Drummond would no doubt insist on seeing the whole thing and that it went back quite a way.

'You have said something about me you now regret?'

'Not really about you, and certainly nothing but the truth. It's just that it might be taken the wrong way and I don't think anyone here knows.'

I thought this would be enough for him, but he insisted that I spell it out.

'Smith.'

'What about him?'

'Your recommendation of him, the fraud, the amounts involved, Newgate, your being here in lieu of your share in the Company to make good those losses.'

He looked down, twisted the stem of his glass. I saw that I had hit hard but was determined to press on.

'People were surprised that you joined the expedition in person, and at the last minute. They don't know why.'

He held up his hand.

'I know the story, Roderick, thank you.'

'I guessed most of it and Mr Vetch told me the rest.'

'How odd. He was the one who insisted we take a formal oath of secrecy. There you are. And you now propose to tell everyone else?'

It was a flash of what his detractors have often said about him – a certain petulance, a rush to make an enemy rather than a friend, a need, almost, to be conspired against. I had dismissed it all before, but must admit to being unsettled when I saw it for myself. I rejected his accusation passionately and made lengthy assurances to the effect that he had quite mistaken me and that my purpose was, above all, to ensure the protection of his good name.

I didn't believe it myself and as soon as I had spoken I knew that the last claim was too much. Naturally, Paterson saw it too and for the next few minutes I played mouse to his cat.

'Surely, Roderick, it would be a simple matter to excise a few pages, submit the innocent part, receive it back in a few days and put it back together again as you please.'

I argued that the omissions would be obvious, claiming (inaccurately) that the pages were numbered.

'Does that matter? It's enough to frustrate one's opponents. Whether or not they know they've been frustrated is neither here nor there.'

I pointed out that the context of the omissions would make it clear that it was something particularly relating to Mr Paterson that had been cut out. 'It could only arouse suspicions, sir. They might do more harm to you than the facts.'

'Hardly, in this case.' He smiled as he sensed himself getting the upper hand. 'Then simply dispose of the whole thing, Roderick. I can understand that you have some attachment to it, but it has no material value, surely. It is only an amusement, albeit a very imprudent one. Make up some lie about it falling overboard or something. Obvious, of course, but it doesn't matter if a lie is obvious as long as it serves one's purpose.'

I saw nowhere else to go and angrily asserted that I would submit it to the council entire if that is what they wanted. He was too pleased at having driven me to ground in this way to be angry himself.

'You could have told me that at the start, Roderick. Let me see if I have you right: you feel the need of an ally and think you have found the means to buy one.'

I made to protest.

'I know, I know – you would not put it that way yourself, but that's what it amounts to all the same.'

I feebly suggested that we had a common interest.

'You have created a common interest, Roderick.'

'Circumstances have created it.'

He waved the remark aside. 'Whatever. Let's do business. I unhook you from this little awkwardness and you, let us say, will remember whose side you are on should that ever be necessary.'

'Agreed.'

How clever it was! I had started by offering Paterson a favour and ended by receiving one from him at an unspecified price. I am still at a loss as to where the balance swung.

His side of the bargain has already been met. There was, so I hear, much shouting and banging of the table at this morning's council, but I have heard nothing more about my journal, which now resides under lock and key whenever I am not here.

Midnight already, and I have written of nothing but myself!

*

THE STORM THAT TORE at us in the forest struck New Edinburgh with a still greater force. No building was undamaged and several of the simpler structures were blown flat. The half-covered frame of the church suffered likewise, its timbers scattered across the Shades of Love. Partly because the buildings were new and not yet settled, and partly no doubt because our joinery was not of the best, most of the timbers were pulled apart at their joints rather than broken and this allowed a more rapid reconstruction than at first seemed possible. In three days the wreckage was reconnected with such speed that it was as if the storm itself had been put into reverse. I assisted directly in the reconstruction of the kirk, which was done with great spirit. At the end of the day, exhausted, steaming and black as Moors with mud we stood back and regarded our work with exultation. The rebuilding and the victory together have, in spite of everything, put the colony in an excellent temper. As one of my fellows declared, 'We've beaten the Spanish and now we've beaten the weather.'

Two other facts confronted me that day and combined to give an impression of such changes that I felt I must have been asleep for weeks rather than for a mere twenty-four hours. The first was the presence of another ship in Caledonia Bay and the second was Mackay. What the sentry had said to us had become entangled with my dreams and seemed so implausible that I readily dismissed it as an anxious fantasy of my own. But after an hour of inspecting the damage from the storm and taking instructions as to what supplies were needed I still had not seen him. I asked a man on the roof of one of the huts where he was. He took the nails from his mouth and asked me another question. 'He's back, then? They've found him?'

Opinions vary on who was the last to see him, but no one claims a sighting after daybreak on 1 December. While we were away, patrols went out a short way along all the established paths but found no trace of him. Since our return, Lieutenant Jardine has led parties of soldiers in more extensive searches, and Indians from the coastal villages on either side of us have been questioned. For the last week, however, there have been no further efforts and the matter is no longer much discussed. Reverend Borland assumes his position and has confided to me that, although he is determined to leave a considerable interval, he has already given some thought to the placing of a memorial in the cemetery. He maintains that Mackay must have fallen victim to a beast of some sort and spoke very morosely last Sunday.

The second change in our little world is the arrival of the *Worcester*, captained and owned by Thomas Green, an excellent fellow. Running from the storm that swept over us in the forest, she put into the bay three days before our return. As she had already been harshly treated by the weather he has careened her on the opposite side of the bay and will be with us for a fortnight yet as her crew makes repairs to the hull and rigging. The ship is about the size of the *Dolphin* and very trim. In spite of the damage she is a pretty vessel and clearly carries a proud crew. The gunwales are painted in blue and have a design of ivy running right around them. Above it, the rail seems newly varnished and the balusters shine like bottles. Such a quantity of gold has been put on the decorations around the bow that one might fear she would plough under in a heavy sea were there not an equal extravagance at the stern. She is sailed by a flock of peacocks even more brilliant than herself. If one stood them in the right order with their jackets and breeches there would be a perfect rainbow. Green himself, on account of his rank, dresses entirely in black. Several have a year's hard work in gold hanging in their ears and there is neither a hole nor a patch on any of their clothes. The explanation for this, it seems, is that the *Worcester* is a sort of commune or partnership in which each member of the crew bears the costs and enjoys the profits according to his share. The arrangement gives every sign of being a great success and is looked on with envy by our own crews and a certain suspicion by some of their officers.

The men of the *Worcester* are assorted as humanity itself. There is a Turk, a Chinaman, a Russian, several Europeans (though no two from the same country) and a branded Negro, who cannot be much less than seven feet tall. There is even one of our own, a man from Kelso, who knew nothing of our Company and is most amazed to find us here. There is no common language among them and, according to Green, the attempt to agree on a *lingua franca* some years ago was the closest the company ever came to civil war. Since then, they have developed by default a strange and disconcerting tongue of their own consisting of equal parts of every native language on the ship. At times Mr Spense can understand a good amount of it, but when they choose to be incomprehensible they talk more in Chinese and Turkish, which defeats even him. When in dispute they revert to their mother tongues, having to go home, as it were, before finding the full force of their obscenity, the effect of which is happily lost in mutual incomprehension. Questions about the *Worcester* and its crew are usually met with friendly but unhelpful answers, but it occurs to me that they must have quite a history together as a new language, granting even the effects on men of a life at sea, cannot be made quickly. As confirmation of this, I might mention the newest member of the company who has yet to learn to communicate with any of his fellows. This is a parrot, which resides mostly on the Chinaman's shoulder, cracks hazelnuts like eggs and every half-hour or so favours the company with a lengthy and totally obscure speech. The explanation, as far as I could understand it, is that he was acquired only two months before from an embarrassed merchant who was a Jew. The bird has stubbornly refused to adopt the *Worcester* babel, no doubt because each member of the crew seeks to make a friend of him and teach him his own language first. As these men put a greater store by colour than by truth I was unsure as to what to believe. However, as the bird's speech contains one particular word more frequently than all the others put together I was soon able to parrot this myself and ask Mr Spense for confirmation. He confirmed that it is indeed Hebrew, but would on no account be persuaded to translate.

Being in need of repairs and replenishment, the *Worcester* has been our first opportunity to practise the vocation that led us here – that is to say, trade. We have supplied over two hundred pounds of rope, tar, sailcloth and tools, taken seventy pounds more for a replacement main top mast and sold fifty pounds of comestibles. Their Turkish sailmaker bought thirty yards of scarlet damask and with his own money, or so it seemed. Green is also very interested in our stocks of powder and asked with an easy smile if we would part with as much as three hundred pounds of it. In spite of an excellent offer it was decided that the sale only of fifty pounds would be prudent. The request has, of course, caused no little speculation about the true nature of the *Worcester*, which some think may not be entirely as Green presents it. The crew spend most of their time with their own ship engaged on her repair but occasionally wander through New Edinburgh of an evening. They make jovial company and have been warmly befriended by our bolder businessmen who, very disappointed by their lack of custom so far, are determined to sell them whatever they can. The Worcesters, as they are now known, are happy to part with their money and some considerable success has been had in the trading of brandy allowances. However, they have a fiendish skill at cards and by the time they row back across the bay it is very doubtful who has the profit and who the loss.

I learned more of the *Worcester* and her men when Captain Green and his first officer dined aboard the *Rising Sun*. He shares his men's taste for gambling and claims he won the ship from a Frenchman in a game of dice and renamed her after his home town. Sure enough, the trace of another name can be seen where it has been scorched off the bow, but I wouldn't like to swear as to whether he came by her honestly or not. We were regaled by a succession of tall tales of how each member of the *Worcester*'s extraordinary crew came to join her. We heard how the Negro, in flight from his possessor with fifty pounds on his head, made a pact with a printer in New Orleans to make up and post a bill of reward exactly describing his master as the most notorious arsonist, ravisher and stock-thief whom the governor of New York would be glad to have hold of for five hundred guineas. He had the pleasure the next day of seeing the man seized before his own eyes and borne off from the middle of the street, all his protestations laughed at. Green was in port at the time and, viewing such shameless cunning as the highest of recommendations, offered him a share in the ship there and then. This was ten years ago and the printer still receives a tithe of the Negro's profits every six months. We heard of how the Turk, once a merchant in Marseille, responded one night with a stroke of his sword on hearing an insult to his religion and would be hanged on the spot if he ever set foot in the place again. It was explained that he is the sailmaker out of remorse – every stitch is a prayer for forgiveness. We heard also – and how Reverend Borland's cheeks burned at it! – that one of their number had been a priest and had suffered terribly, as Captain Green put it, from the cruel tortures of the most beautiful woman man had ever had the misfortune to set eyes on. She confessed to him every Sunday, recounting piteously her every surrender to the young bloods of the town before going out to blaze with sin even more brilliantly than before. Alone of all the men in the town, he fell in love with her soul and conceived an intolerable passion for her salvation. After a year of such agonies, in which his whole theology bounced harmlessly off the purity of her godlessness, he changed his tactics. In the heat of August and finally driven mad with desire, he tore off his robes, demanded her for his wife and did with her what every man must in full view of a queue of pious widows waiting to drop their dust in his ear. The town was as full of hypocrites as it was of fornicators and he was driven from it by a yelping crowd, outraged to find another man sharing their weaknesses. When Green found him he was in Naples selling Virgin's milk to innocents transhipping for the Holy Land. With his profits he would forget himself in the city's innumerable bordellos, forever seeking and failing to find an impossible likeness. It was a chance meeting in one of these oubliettes that allowed the two men to recognize in each other whatever essence binds the crew of the *Worcester* together. An offer was made and gratefully accepted. Father Crivelli became Seaman Crivelli and let his burdens diminish with the coastline.

Captain Green refilled his glass, highly satisfied with the silence that descended around the end of his stories. Borland pressed back the table with his hands, confused as to whether it behoved him more to welcome the fall of a priest of Rome or to deplore the manner of his falling.

'And the thing is,' Green concluded, 'he makes such an excellent pastor.'

This was enough for Borland to attempt an oblique insult.

'I am surprised, Captain, that the pursuit of money can hold such men together. Are they not tempted to seek an even greater profit at each other's expense?'

'On the contrary, Father . . .' I noticed Cunningham and Galt exchange a glance of appreciation at this barb. '. . . money is our common master. For money we have forsaken all others.' He raised his glass to chime with that of his first officer. 'And what else could achieve this wonderful harmony? Nothing I know of. I keep an ounce of gold to remind me of its magic. There it is.'

He placed it on the cloth, a heavy, polished, unstamped yellow disc, which we all stared at as he evangelized its properties.

'In the same market, on the same day it is entirely as it is. Other things can change from beautiful to ugly, from friend to enemy simply by being looked at, but not gold. It is a fair master, worth exactly as much to one man as to another. It is our common ground, the value we all agree on. We see it clearly. Everywhere, men shake hands over it.'

'Quite a preacher, aren't you?'

It was Drummond. Until this point he had been doing his best to repress the occasion with his silence.

'Forgive me,' smiled Green, 'I am so in love with my vocation that I sometimes forget others don't share my interests.'

Drummond drained his glass brusquely, but it was Galt who spoke next.

'An excellent philosophy, Captain. I would say it's a shame more people don't think likewise. It's the very neutrality of gold that makes it such an honourable ambition for a man – if I've understood you aright.'

'The very word I was about to use myself.'

'It's a quality that doesn't satisfy some men, and taken all in all they're the sort that could be charged with more than their fair share of the world's trouble.'

I rejoiced that a word from Galt was still enough to put Drummond to flight. Reckless with wine, I made no effort to conceal my smile. Not wishing to leave the field in disarray, he stayed for another quarter-hour but was the first to excuse himself, an indignant Jardine at his heels. I could hear their voices outside, momentarily loud as they climbed down the ladders to be rowed back to the *Caledonia*.

There was little of note in the rest of the evening. Captain Green showed a courteous interest in our project which Mr Paterson outlined to him with as much enthusiasm and persuasiveness as ever. There was, I think, a genuine misunderstanding when Green received Mr Paterson's suggestion that he buy stock in our Company as a jest and in the general good-humour the awkwardness was quickly passed over. For me, the most unexpected aspect of the evening was the highly agreeable manner of Captain Galt. I approached the meal thinking it was no more than a matter of courtesy on Galt's part and an opportunity to find out more about Green and his crew. As I have indicated, many officers view the *Worcester*'s unusual arrangements with distaste, fearing it will make their own crews dissatisfied, and I assumed that Galt would have similar views. The reality, however, proved to be very different. He attended to Green's stories with a more lively interest than I have seen on any other occasion. The taller and more teasing these stories became, the warmer his appreciation of them. He would frequently solicit further details – or inventions, as I suspect many of them were – and was highly delighted when Green responded to his encouragements with the most nonsensical embellishments. The opinions of the two men accorded with each other precisely, or at least Captain Galt was pleased to give that impression, and very soon after the start of the meal Green was able to sail on without the slightest hindrance from anyone else at the table. For some awkwardly long periods the rest of us were no more than an audience to their dialogue and it was impossible to say whether Galt was unaware of such a breach of courtesy or was revelling in it. Certainly, it is very clear that he finds Captain Green more interesting than any person he has spoken to since his departure from Leith. I watched the other members of the party closely and saw that I was by no means alone in my surprise. Only Mr Cunningham seemed familiar with our new Captain Galt – he gave me the assured smile of one who had always known.

While the Worcesters busy themselves with the repair and beautification of their ship, Caledonia has at last settled to a number of projects for her security and enrichment. Parties have been sent out into the nearby forests to bring back samples of anything we might exploit in the way of commerce and in particular to find specimens of that Nicaragua tree of which we have such good hopes. The description we have of it from Mr Wafer's journal, however, matches every tree equally and the task is made no easier by the fact that it is not of a natural redness to the eye but requires boiling for many hours before a useful dye is produced. The Indians have been questioned about the tree, but claim to have no knowledge of it and say the few items they have that show any evidence of red dye have been traded. We must find it by good fortune, therefore, and have set up six large copper pans, each over a constant fire, to boil logs from each of the multitude of different trees to be found within a mile or two of our position. On account of the frequent rain, the whole business has been gathered together under a tarpaulin which, having no chimneys or even holes occasionally becomes so full of smoke and steam it strains against its ties like a mainsail in a brisk wind before letting out a great belch of fumes and sagging back. Such importance is put on the matter that there are two groups of men whose task is to maintain the process at the fastest pace possible; one cuts fuel and stokes the fires, the other fetches the constant supply of fresh water needed to boil in the pans. To date we have produced nothing more than a dull ochre and even this fades after a day or so to something that could most honestly be described as the colour of wood.

'Excellent!' declares Mr Paterson with every new failure. 'There's another one we don't have to bother with any more. We must be getting close now.'

One ingenious fellow has collected the slops from the bottom of the pans and made several sheets of surprisingly good paper from them. These were presented to the council with a petition for the setting up of a manufactory. Not wishing to discourage any efforts, the proposal was received with courtesy, but how the poor fool imagines a living can be made from travelling a third of the way across the world only to return with a hold full of paper, I don't know.

Elsewhere, similar efforts maintain our spirits against conditions that continue to be very wet and excessively hot and, if truth be told, must soon begin either to moderate or take a greater toll. On the cleared ground a variety of crops is being attempted. Wheat and oats have been sown and both give us good hopes, sprouting almost as soon as they touch the ground. Pineapples have been transplanted from where they are found in the forests and there is now a quarter-acre or more of them with experiments under way to find how we may propagate them from seed and improve them. Dr Munro puts great store on their revitalizing qualities and in my own view they would, in dried form, make a most profitable commodity. To this end I have the flesh of one here in my cabin and enjoy the scent of it as I write. One half I am trying simply to desiccate – though the weight of the air makes it as likely to rot before it dries – the other I have boiled briefly in sugar to see if it gives any advantage.

On the matter of the cleared land, it is now apparent that it is not entirely flat as it first appeared, but slopes very slightly to the east. This is enough to cause part of the land to become a marsh or even a temporary lake when the rains are heavy enough, which is often. Some crops and much effort have been wasted as a result of this, but as flat land is scarce on the peninsula, rather than abandon it ditches are being dug to drain off the excess. I passed by the place the other day to see the work and to make a list of what equipment might usefully be signed out of the holds. There was an infernal sight of men struggling in black water and semi-liquid mud, trying to dig channels through an oozing paste that closed in on every space as soon as the shovel had made it. They were all covered entirely in the stuff and seemed to be made of mud, like sketches of men attempted by a juvenile divinity, at risk of slipping back at any moment into the general formlessness. They were indistinguishable save for Oswald, whose huge bulk and furious energy marked him clearly from the rest. I found it dispiriting at first, but stayed long enough to see one of the trenches connected to the main channel at the edge of the clearing. I was a little heartened by the time I left, having watched the flood begin to pour away and the area of inundation begin slowly to diminish.

These projects are but satellites to our main ventures which I would say take up eight-tenths of our present resources. The first of these is, of course, the road to the Pacific, which has begun slowly to penetrate the resistance of the forests. The other is the completion of our security by means of a fortified ditch across the narrow neck of the peninsula where it joins the mainland. Mr Paterson insists on the primacy of the first and Colonel Drummond on that of the second. Harsh words have crossed the council table more than once, and I am now almost daily the recipient of notes from these two champions demanding the same score of shovel-heads or the same half-dozen saw-blades. Mr Paterson has already visited to remind me of 'where I stand'. The perfect mid-point would be my choice, but it is a choice that is no longer there to make. Drummond is no fool – what I tell him one day is not to be had, he or his men see the next in the hands of Paterson's volunteers.

The mere thought of it exhausts me extremely.

*

I HAVE HARDLY set my pen down these last few days, and yet have not had a moment for this journal. I am ever more pressed from all sides by demands on our stocks, which I must sign out and account for, and I have also been greatly plagued by the business of the letters. As if this were not enough, certain members of the council are becoming nervous and ask more frequently for reports, the composition of which is very onerous.

Christmas Day passed gloomily enough. The sermon from Reverend Borland showed considerable theological originality. It dwelt principally on the remorse to be felt by all sinners that Our Lord should ever have had to soil himself by descending into the loathsome sty of humanity in the first place. From the sour, acrid edge on his voice and the damning glares he cast at his flock, I deduced that this is a crime for which we are directly culpable. I freely confess it to be a fault, but the truth is I can hardly bring myself to be civil to the man. I have noticed that men become more fully themselves here and this, I believe, is why Borland has been hardened as much as Mr Mackay was softened. The intemperateness of the service set me thinking about that unfortunate gentleman for whose formal memorial a date has now been set, but whose fate remains as dark as ever.

The *Worcester* is now fully repaired and has been waiting to sail for four days, prevented only by the persistence of contrary winds which make it all but impossible to manoeuvre out of Caledonia Bay. Her departure has been anticipated for some time and has begun to have a most unsettling effect. The main interest in her is as a carrier of letters, of which a great number have been scribbled of late – I have signed out four reams of paper – and most especially in who is going to be the courier for these letters and for the report of the council to the Court of Directors. The thought of walking up the High Street and into the comforts of Milne Square in a very short space of time has been playing on the minds of some of our fellows, and there has been a most unseemly number of candidates, all of them most distressed at still not being rich after so many weeks here. One William Carmichael has been chosen on the grounds that he is a man of probity, a second cousin of Sir William Blackwood, and that he has expressed no interest at all in the commission. I chanced to have a few words with him shortly after the council made its decision. I would say that he is very solid and mostly sincere when he says he regrets leaving the colony so soon and hopes to make a speedy return with the second fleet. He has, nevertheless, become the object of a biting envy and I have heard at least one grossly unjust rumour about how he came by the appointment. I can't help but think that it might have been better to use the opportunity to dispose of one of the less stalwart.

I, too, have become involved in this business of the letters, firstly as an honest scribe – more or less honest – and secondly in an altogether more delinquent fashion, which I will describe without any favour to myself. Many of our number are illiterate, but are as anxious as the rest to communicate with the parents, siblings and womenfolk they have left behind. To facilitate this, both myself and Mr Spense have been deputed as public scribes. We were installed in two of the huts belonging to the gentlemen volunteers and sweated there for three whole days like Romish priests in the confessional. We were frequently sworn to secrecy before a letter was dictated and gave assurances of our absolute discretion, passionate and worthless in equal measure. While we heard every hope, fear, disappointment and intimacy, they did not all reach the paper in an entirely pristine form. We had both received orders from the council, conveyed to me in a hushed conversation with Mr Paterson, that given the importance of maintaining the keenest support at home we should not hesitate to correct or improve on whatever might cause alarm or be liable to 'misunder-standing'.

Thus began a farcical deception in which relentless rain and ubiquitous mud became our well-watered soil and where the diseases of the minority were inverted into the health of the majority. When the fact – noticed as yet by very few – that our harbour may prove hard to exit for several months each year was described by one of the sharper correspondents as a foolish error, which has made of our ships nothing more than flies in a bottle, I recorded his opinion as praise for its many natural protecting virtues. I decided that when a man criticized the arrogance of Drummond and his soldiers, it was his true intention to commend their hardiness and resolution. Likewise, when another spoke bitterly of breaking his back with toil in a hellish furnace of heat, I helped him to his real meaning by writing of the great fellowship of labour by which we have already achieved so much.

Of all the forms of lying practised by men this must surely be the most difficult. A double deceit is required, firstly in the sincerity of one's expression and in the ready acquiescence in whatever is said, however necessary it may be to change it. Secondly, there is the conjuror's art of making the hand lie so that there is every appearance of coincidence between what is said and what is written. In part this is a manual skill – breaking the normal rhythm of one's hand to mimic that of the instructor's speech even though one sometimes has to write more than he has spoken, and sometimes less. Unnerved at first, I would make a play of pausing to consider the spelling of a word or would pretend that I had not heard correctly and ask for a phrase to be repeated while I thought of what to put in its place. By the second day, however, I had gained a greater fluency. I was beginning to learn the vocabulary and syntax of deception and was able to interpret truth into lies as easily as Mr Spense can render Spanish into English. If a man grumbled on some point in fifteen words I would write, without any hesitation, a sentence of praise of the exact same length. When I felt myself to be under particular scrutiny, I even took pains to ensure that the pattern of longer and shorter words resembled that of the speaker. Indeed, as my skill improved this was often the only likeness between what I heard and what I wrote. It would not be fair to myself to suggest that I did not spare a thought for the questionable nature of the exercise, but no truly honest man, I believe, would deny that he could get pleasure from some venial wrongdoing if only it could be done with sufficient virtuosity. On the third and most poetic day of my letter-writing, this was precisely the state I fell into. I escaped my qualms by taking a simple pleasure in the task, and as the day wore on amused myself by letting all restraint fall away. In the last few hours of the final day there was no dross of disillusionment, complaint or back-biting I could not instantly transform into a tale of harmony and happiness in an easeful paradise. As I indulged these fancies, I even had time to consider my defence at the outraged bar of decency – namely, that I had lied with such extravagance that I had made the whole affair into a harmless comedy that no sane man could mistake for reality. It was, no doubt, my unhappy conscience that pressed me to think of such a thing, but I confess that it seems now a wholly worthless argument. The more I see of such things the more I am convinced that there are few if any restraints to man's credulousness, especially when his appetites are hard upon him. I doubt that many of these forgeries will ever be detected.

For all this, I found it a strangely exhausting experience. A deceiver can never be at ease, knowing how effortlessly one can get past a man's defences and that practising the art confers no immunity from becoming a victim oneself. I was steamed like a pudding in that hut, the laden air overburdened with breath, sweat and lamp smoke and my own never-conquered fear of being found out. There was always a moment when the finished letter was handed over for approval when it seemed certain that it would be thrown back at me as a worthless counterfeit. Some were marked and handed back without so much as a glance, others were regarded with an innocent curiosity to see the mysterious shape of their words, others still were scrutinized with obvious suspicion and my heart raced as I was asked what this or that word meant and I struggled to remember what had been said. By the end not one had been rejected – my credit was good.

At the end of it all I was gathering up my pens and paper when the weak evening light from the open door was suddenly cut off. A man was bowing his head and shoulders and stepping sideways to get into the tiny hut.

'Excuse me, sir.'

I recognized at once the voice that had told me when to work and when to rest. The stool on the other side of the table creaked under Oswald's huge weight and sank another inch into the ground. I prepared to write another letter, saying it would be a pleasure and relaxing in the knowledge that on this occasion I had decided to take a true dictation.

'It's not that,' he said. 'I've saved you the trouble.'

He placed a neatly folded and sealed letter on the table. I could just see the address in a hand at least as well schooled as my own.

'You wrote it yourself?'

The last syllable had hardly left my mouth when I realized the idiocy of it.

'That must surprise you, Mr Mackenzie.'

I apologized and hurried on. 'You know you can hand it in at the Meeting House? There's a sack there that's going straight to the *Worcester* as soon as she's ready.'

'So I've heard.' He looked down at the table, pinched the letter by one of its corners. 'I just thought that perhaps you would oblige. See it on its way . . . personally.'

Our eyes met and broke off again.

'There's nothing in it that the Company could regret.'

I stared at the letter as if it might tell me what to do.

'Of course, Mr Oswald,' I said. 'I give you my word.'

I emerged from my three days' scribing to see New Edinburgh for once without any rain at all. Clouds broke near the horizon, letting a brilliant, deep red light glance across our settlement until the shadow of the forest cut it off prematurely. Here and there damp fires clung to life in braziers. Clothes were quickly hung round them in an attempt to dry them before the next rain and to smoke out the vermin. From near the shore, the awning over the boiling pans filled and collapsed sending a perfect ball of steam rolling across the clearing. Such was the feverish sluggishness of the air that it hardly rose at all before dissolving into the trees.

All work for the day had ended. The last boat carrying the workers from the Pacific road crept exhaustedly back across the bay and nudged into the shingle by the landing stage. More mud men got off it. Some of them shed their clothes on the spot and waded into the bay to stagger back to the land moments later, fully human again. They stood naked, fiery red in the last of the light until the tree shadows reached them too. Something was passed from one to another. At that distance and under that strange light I had the sudden fancy as their hands met that they were captives chained together. The vision was broken by a bout of splashing and laughter. They put on the fresh clothes they had been brought and began to come up in search of a meal, emphatically free again.

As I saw how much the appearance of New Edinburgh had changed since the jubilation of St Andrew's night, I smiled coldly and wondered if I had not myself breathed in too much of the thick air of delusion. The rain that began so gently to fall on us that night and intensified until it raked us like grape-shot has wrought a dismal transformation on our little capital. Like too many cattle in a drenched field, our own feet have churned the place into a slough of mud. We are now restricted to picking our way along boards, inching past each other sideways to avoid sinking into it knee-deep. In some places the boards themselves have sunk and quite disappeared. On the level parts there are patches of standing water, stinking and thick with contagion. In the evenings they spawn clouds of mosquitoes, the whining and biting of which is a constant irritation. One consequence of the deluge is that there are now very few places where a tired man can lie down to rest. The benches that were used for our celebration have been brought back so there is something to sit on in the evenings. But even some of these have sunk so low as to be of little use. Men have taken to sitting on the rocks near the shore like the pelicans who, now fully acquainted with these human perchers, make their way among them without the slightest concern. That evening I saw one man who had found a hard point to one side of the clearing in front of the Meeting House. He sat there on his own on a pile of sacks smoking his pipe. He sat with a serene stillness, only the puffs of smoke from his pipe indicating he was not a statue or asleep. It struck me as an odd sight because I could not see how he had got to his rock nor, given that he was surrounded by fifty yards of stinking filth on all sides, how he intended to get off it.

The onshore winds that delayed the departure of the *Worcester* had died away so completely that the smoke from the braziers rose straight as plumb-lines. Its scent blended with the tannery smells from the boiling pans of wood and with those of labouring humanity and the latrines, which have overflowed twice since the rains began. It is now said that New Edinburgh at least smells like its old namesake and it is indeed remarkable how forcefully this odour can transport me back to the High Street in the first festering warmth of a spring day. We take the rapid onset of these difficulties as a hopeful sign, reasoning that they must diminish just as rapidly and that all that is required of us is endurance until that time. There is also increasing talk of the second fleet, which will be despatched as soon as the directors receive confirmation of our successes so far. The councillors, Mr Paterson in particular, have encouraged discussion of these matters. They are now heard everywhere and are so inexhaustibly repeated and picked over like an old prayer that one might think they indicate the advance of doubt rather than hope.

These problems have not been made any easier to bear by the presence of the Worcesters. Their wealth has become ever more maddening to our men especially, I think, because its mysterious generation is not linked to any one place. As I found myself later that evening closeted with Mr Paterson on the *Caledonia*, I did not see it, but an incident was related to me that shows how timely their departure will be. Their skill at cards was (once again) the beginning of the dispute, but the true *casus belli* was the way the sailmaker and the cook mocked the poverty of our men. There was a muddy brawl from which the two Worcesters extracted themselves with black eyes and one with a torn ear where a gold ring had been. Captain Green put it down to drink and heat and is happy to say no more about it, but it has had a sombre effect on some of our men. They are not ashamed to be seen by each other as they are, but to be intruded upon by others is painful to them. When I heard the story I thought of that terrible and ancient question: *Who told thee that thou wast naked?*

I made my way along the boards towards the shore, hoping to find a boat leaving for the *Rising Sun*. I passed the infirmary tents from which desperate seizures of coughing could be heard. One of Dr Munro's boys sat outside smoking on a stool, his apron stiff with gruesome stains. Munro himself appeared carrying a large glass jar with something black and appalling floating in a urinous fluid. I kept trying not to look at it as he gave me a nod and placed it carefully on the ground. Munro is probably the happiest man amongst us at the moment, relieved that his enemy has shown itself at last. In doing so it has proved to be, so far at least, a familiar enemy and one that he has greeted with the pleasure of renewing an old acquaintance. Private Miller and Mrs Paterson now share their resting place with twenty-three others – a figure that is regarded by Dr Munro as cause for much satisfaction. A violent, clacking hiccuping started from within the tent.

'Give him a smoke of your pipe, will you, Rob? And bring me another bottle while you're at it.'

The boy glared at his master and sulkily dragged himself into the tent.

'They can't die quick enough for him,' said Munro. 'He'd rather be in a red coat than a surgeon's apron.' The hiccuping became more furious and Munro winced. 'That's the flux that does that to a man. It's a misery, like trying to cough up a razor. It shakes them so hard they can't sleep and I've seen some die of exhaustion just for that.'

The boy stuck his head out of the tent and handed Munro a bottle of brandy. Munro lowered his voice. 'In his case it won't be troubling him much longer – day and a half at most before he goes to his eternal reward. There's two others in there you can't hear. They're not so bad.'

He took a mouthful of brandy as he considered this judgement. He swallowed and let his expression turn doubtful. I declined the bottle and asked him if he thought the situation bad.

'Could hardly be better! A mere twenty-three under the sod, twenty-four by tomorrow, a couple more by the end of the week – who could complain? And there's nothing I haven't seen before. Flux mostly, some of it bloody. If I was on a ship anywhere south of Biscay and this was all I had I'd think my luck was in.'

He knelt down to empty the brandy into the jar, filling it to the brim. When he stood up he stretched his back, let out a heavy sigh and looked over the scene I have just described. I thought I could see the old creases of suspicion returning to his face.

'Still not happy, Doctor?'

'I don't know. Look at it. It must be capable of more than this. I feel like a man in a strange town with too much money in his pockets.'

He put a lid on the jar and held it up for my admiration. A leathery nightmare peered out at me, hideously magnified by the glass of the jar.

'I'm no expert on bats,' he said brightly, 'but I think perhaps they won't have seen one quite like this.'

'Munro's bat?' I suggested.

'Who knows?'

He returned to his infirmary, greatly cheered by the thought.

A boat had just come in from the *Caledonia* and I joined her for the return journey. We rowed out over motionless water. I lay back in the stern sheets and looked up at the lantern gently swinging on its pole. As the stink of New Edinburgh was cleaned out of my nostrils and everything but the rowlocks and the blades churning the water faded to silence, the exquisite beauty of the bay impressed itself on me once again. Near the mouth we passed the *Worcester*, busy with preparations for sailing at first light. We rowed on past the sunken rock, only the slightest of disturbances on the water suggesting its presence, and out to where the *Caledonia* and the *Rising Sun* rode at anchor. Those who were for the *Caledonia* had clambered up her ropes and we were about to push off for the short journey to the *Rising Sun* and, for me, some blessed rest when Paterson hailed me from the quarterdeck rail. 'A word, if I may.'

I was half-way up the ropes when one of the oarsmen asked if they should wait. My heart sank as Mr Paterson answered for me: 'No need, thank you.'

He beckoned me up to the quarterdeck and took me to one side. 'I can't apologize enough, Roderick, for imposing on you like this – Forgive me, you are well I hope? Good. The calm has caught us out, as I'm sure you understand. The *Worcester* is certain to leave at dawn and must take the letters with her. You understand what an effect it could have on the spirits of certain members of the colony if they felt that such an opportunity had been missed?'

I protested that I had just come from exactly that task.

'I'm very grateful, Roderick. I do hope you accept that.'

'Of course,' I said quickly.

'And now, to have to ask even more . . .'

He let me see how much this distressed him. He caught something in my face and put a more urgent cast on his own features.

'It's just one of the burdens of being above the common man, Roderick, as I know too well myself. You see, there really was no one else I could turn to. There's Mr Spense who has already been so, well, indispensable – excuse me – but when such absolute discretion is required one has few choices.'

He made that sharp, pecking motion of his head which, I have learned, precedes the delivery of a particularly choice opinion.

'So few these days have any understanding of the sort of sacrifices demanded by the service of the common good. The road to success in worldly affairs is by no means a straight one. Sometimes one must deviate, sometimes one must even get a little muddy before crossing the threshold and . . .'

The intensity of his vision forced him to pause and gaze for a moment over my shoulder.

'. . . receiving the thanks of one's grateful fellow men. Besides, you will have noticed, I'm sure, that while failure is a story everyone insists on hearing to the last syllable, few men enquire too closely into the causes of success.'

How Colquhoun would have understood all this! I could not help but wonder if the two men would ever meet, and if so what that moment would be like. A recognition perhaps?

'You agree, no doubt?'

I admitted that I was familiar with the mud of expediency.

'Excellent!'

Paterson was already holding the handle of the door to Drummond's cabin.

'The esteemed Colonel,' he pronounced it in the French manner, 'drinks ashore tonight. We will not be disturbed here.'

Inside, there was a thick haze, of brandy, tobacco smoke, burnt paper and sealing wax. Paterson walked over to the enormous map table and turned up the lamp.

'As you can see, I have already started. But it's simply impossible for one man to get it done by first light.'

The table was littered with opened letters and the debris of broken seals. Amongst them I saw a crushed flower, a lucent fragment of shell and even a lock of hair from a dead brother.

'There you are.'

I sat where Paterson indicated.

'All straightforward. If it's acceptable reseal it with the Company seal there and put it in this pile. If there is anything that could discourage, alarm, give rise to question, criticism, doubt, disparagement, anything at all that might turn someone's mind against the Company's great purpose, it goes there.'

He placed a basket between us, which was already half filled with ash. He rubbed his hands together in a brisk gesture of readiness.

'Right then! Off we go.'

Inside my waistcoat, Oswald's letter burned against my chest. I eyed the pile of resealed letters and made myself ready for the first opportunity.

*

THE *WORCESTER* has finally left us, charged with £500 of trade goods to sell on consignment – Green assuring us he will be back within three months with the proceeds – and with William Carmichael as supercargo, guardian of a sealed leather sack of letters. She did not, in the event, sail the morning after the calm, and Paterson's haste, therefore, was quite unnecessary. By the time I had condemned my last letter for heresy and solemnly committed it to the flames the winds had risen again. It was enough to put the cork firmly back in the bottle of Caledonia Bay and to give me a rough and wet transhipment to the *Rising Sun* where I made my way directly to my cabin, fending off an anxious Mr Shipp bearing a sheaf of demands on our dwindling stocks.

It was a week after my last duties as censor that the *Worcester* finally sailed. It was my turn to be on Point Look-out and it was from there that I watched her manoeuvre cautiously out of the narrow mouth of the bay. She moved imperceptibly before the feeble coastal breeze. Several times the swaddling closeness of the heat and the pattering of rain on the roof of the tower dragged me down into three-quarter sleep from which I would start guiltily only to find her almost exactly where she had been before. Eventually, she caught a stronger wind, swinging briskly northward for Kingston and firing three guns as she went. I observed her through a telescope and was able thus to get an excellent view of the purpose to which the sailmaker had put his damask. The top mainsails now proclaimed the true nature and nation of the ship. I saw the designs only briefly and, as I discerned each one through the glass and understood their meaning, experienced a leap of half-forgotten joy, disturbing and oddly intense at the sight of such a trivial thing. From bow to stern, where no flag flew, in huge scarlet letters that stretched before the wind, I read 'L. s. d.'.

'What is it?' my companion asked. 'What have you seen?'

I denied that I had seen anything at all.

Now that we were not overlooked by any outsider, another deception could be revealed – a deception of which, I am happy to say, I was a victim rather than a perpetrator. Four days before the *Worcester* sailed, five men went missing. I knew none of them, but soon heard that they had a habit of associating with each other and were held, depending on who I was listening to at the time, in middling or little regard. Comings and goings from the Meeting House were noted, Drummond and Paterson to the fore, and there was talk of a boat carrying a message out to Captain Galt on the *Rising Sun*. By midday, when the first rumours were hardly half spread, we heard that these men had been sent into the forest to find further types of tree that might yield the red dye. It was understood that those who didn't believe it, which was most of us, should keep their counsel to themselves. When it was rumoured that Lieutenant Jardine and half a dozen soldiers had left New Edinburgh without any announcement, the last doubt was quashed. Whether these efforts kept the Worcesters in a state of innocence as to our affairs, I cannot say, but what is certain is that there was a universal expectation among ourselves that as soon as Green and his crew were out of sight, we would learn the truth about these wood-hunters.

So it proved. At five in the afternoon, three of Drummond's young protégés lined up and made an inexpert essay at a drum-roll. The business had the colonel's stamp all over it. The five men were marched in under guard, their hands bound, and were paraded in front of the Meeting House while Jardine shouted out a parody of an indictment to the effect, merely, that they had traitorously abandoned the colony and had been led in this crime by the carpenter Jason James. They made a pitiful sight, James especially. All were bruised about the face and James was trembling with fever. The drums were rolling again and a noose swung out of nowhere, dangling from one of the Meeting House beam ends. It seemed that it was only a matter of carrying out the sentence when Mr Paterson appeared on the Meeting House steps in a highly alarmed state. He ran over to Drummond, one arm waving in an ungainly panic. Drummond tried to ignore him as long as he could, but the drums withered away and the whole miserable comedy came to a halt. While James stood there with the halter round his neck, his fate was urgently discussed not ten yards in front of him. What is more, it was discussed before the whole colony to whom it was now clear that there had been no judgement and no sentence, except perhaps in Drummond's own mind. I could see Captain Jolly peering out around the half-open door of the Meeting House. He stepped back into the shadows. Heads were turning towards the shore, including Drummond's and Paterson's, their conversation having come to an angry impasse. There was Captain Galt, wearing his uniform and sword, striding up the boards through the field of mud followed by Mr Cunningham and several other crew-members. Drummond, Paterson, the three drummers, the redcoats guarding the prisoners, all the colonists and the wretched James himself stood frozen and silent at his approach. I almost believed he was about to strike Drummond, but it was an absurd idea. Instead, he marched straight into the Meeting House without slackening his pace and without so much as a glance to left or right. Although he gave no order, two of the men with him went straight to James, took the noose from his neck and helped him down from the block on which he had been tottering for the last five minutes. No one raised a finger to stop them. From the Meeting House we could hear the heels of Galt's boots stamping up and down the boards.

Paterson submitted to this summons at once and left Drummond standing on his own, so petrified with rage that I swear I could hear his teeth grinding themselves to dust. The Meeting House had been left open and after a minute he too stamped up the steps and slammed the door behind him.

The details of the debate could not be made out, though its temperature was not in doubt. Every voice was raised in turn until they all clashed together in that brutish tone which never means anything except 'I will be heard!' The only words that could be made out were the decisive ones. One of the general bellowings was just subsiding when Captain Galt, in a voice made to compete with hurricanes rather than mere men, made his ultimate declaration.

'I will not countenance it!'

I remember it as if he were shouting directly in my ear and, in my fancy at least, I was sure I heard the words twice, their confirmation rolling back across the bay. A long, dragging silence ensued before the bickering started up again. I could hear enough only to know that it was Drummond speaking, but less furious than before – Galt had won the day and this was the coming to terms. He appeared in the doorway a few minutes later, hand on sword, and strode back along the boards and straight to his boat in which the rowers sat, never having taken their hands from the oars.

There were, therefore, no hangings. Instead, the men were to be imprisoned indefinitely. This has presented a practical problem as the prison, Colonel Drummond's first enthusiasm, has seen no progress since he allowed himself to be distracted by his project for fortifying the peninsula. Consequently, it consists of nothing more than a square of rocks half sunk in the mud with a gap where there might be a door one day. None the less, it is all the prison there is and that is where these five unfortunates now sit, having first sworn on the gospels that it is indeed a prison with four solid walls and a stout iron door from which they may not escape. Only this promise, and perhaps a less noble fear of retribution, keeps them where they are. Without it, they would be as free as any of us to walk away.

THE FATE OF REVEREND MACKAY is a mystery no longer, though it might have been better had it remained so. In itself, the mystery did us no harm, but the solving of it has been a great blow, and I fear that many will not find their feet again. The effect has been very great and has spared no one – those who had little love for him being no less disturbed than the rest of us. Outwardly, New Edinburgh has struggled on, but within, our dejected citizenry has been able to think of nothing else. Men become vague and break off in the middle of conversations, or when sitting quietly take on a sudden expression of alarm and shake their heads. It baffles us. We are overborne by it and find the whole world around us strangely changed. We have had a glimpse of what this place is capable of. It goes beyond us, has incubated a black miracle that none of us could have conceived of. I found myself contemplating it by the shore a few evenings ago and by the force of these thoughts alone fell victim to the terrifying conviction that the rocks, the forest and even the clouds were all slithering towards me with an unmistakable hostility.

Some time ago light was also thrown on another lesser mystery, that of the 'treasonous deserters', as some call them, though I have not the energy to use such language myself. It was first put about that they were taken on their way to Cartagena to sell what they knew to the Spanish and find themselves some more comfortable employment. But this has proved to be nothing more than Drummond's hanging charge and the men themselves, well able to tell their own story through their promissory prison walls, have given a more corrosive explanation. They were found by the banks of a small river seven miles up the coast sifting for gold and though they came away with nothing for their trouble, they remain convinced that only a little more time or a little more luck would have brought them their fortune. The belief has spread faster than the flux, particularly amongst our cutpurse tendency who talk of little else and find their axes and shovels becoming heavier and more contemptible with every stroke. Some say the story started with Alliston, which seems likely enough, and that the current excitement is nothing more than a descendant of one of his tall tales of buccaneering days – itself, no doubt, a very remote relative of the truth. Confirmation has been found in the gold worn by the Indians, though in reality everything we have seen could have been beaten out of three guineas. As well as gold in the rivers there is talk of old Spanish mines which have, we are to suppose, obligingly been abandoned by their original proprietors in spite of still being rich in ore. The most damaging fantasy of all is that it was the Company's intention from the first to seek gold as well as a trade route to the Pacific and this has been concealed from the ordinary volunteers to deprive them of their share of the riches. James was the chief author of this idea, showing such little gratitude for his reprieve that he made a pulpit of his prison and orated at length to all who would listen about the greed and deceitfulness of the directors and councillors of the colony.

'Tell me, then,' he would ask, 'what other reason could there be for coming to a place like this?'

It was the only string on his fiddle, but he played it incessantly and our difficulties are such that some of us, at least, have been persuaded. Mercifully, the bloody flux carried him off to the infirmary after only a few days. It was suggested to Dr Munro that he make no particular effort in his case and he was quickly moved on to the cemetery.

I have noticed a sharp division between those who are helplessly attracted to such romances and find relief in them, and those who despise such beliefs and see them as nothing more than a sure sign of an idle nature. In general it is those who, before they came here, were of a better standing who do the despising and those who were in more difficult circumstances who do the believing. No doubt these groups would condemn each other in any case, but the matter of the gold has provided a reason for doing so and has made the division all the greater. Be that as it may, a close inspection of the matter shows that men have chosen their opinions more according to the solvency of their lives rather than by any form of enquiry.

These reflections lead me on to a more general problem, which will test us severely until our external conditions improve – as they surely must in time. The constant hot rain, the growth of flux and fevers and the disturbing absence of traffic – though our presence here must now be generally known – press us hard and all the suspicions, estrangements and even hatreds that seemed to have been put away on the night of our great celebration begin to itch again. Men are recalled to their true and poorest natures and seek out their own sort to the exclusion of all others. Those who worked to cut down the same tree a week ago now pass on the mud-boards like ghosts, only a brush of the shoulder to tell each other they exist. Everywhere, our difficulties eat away the compromises that made us acceptable to each other and return us to our old animosities, only here, heaped up on one another as we are, they are a hundred times more dangerous than in their native land. I have spoken of a sense of hostility and though I know this can be nothing more than a daydream, the idea has a hold on me and threatens to become a mania suggesting connections everywhere I look. I have even asked if it is by the same invisible principle that the powers of corruption are so fantastically accelerated. Though the ships remain clear, a side of meat, however well salted, cannot be hung in New Edinburgh for a day without becoming green. In three days it swarms with vermin. Men turn sour with the same speed.

The Reverends Borland and Stobo have suffered particularly in this process. On account of the piteous fate of the latter I have struggled with myself as to whether I should say anything here, but I am sworn to tell all and have decided to risk whatever charges of harshness might be laid against me. Besides, these pages are now the only place where honesty can show its face and I would be loath to stain them with a pretended respect I never felt while the man was alive. In describing these events, I will speak as if I had no knowledge of the terrible incident I have already alluded to, but which I cannot yet bring myself to describe.

Though no one would have guessed it before his disappearance, Reverend Mackay was a restraining hand on his two colleagues. There was some human warmth in him, and never more so than on his last night with us when his removal rendered that quality entirely absent from our clergy. Stobo and Borland, it was remarked, were more disturbed than saddened at his demise and it was thought that their grief was lessened by the prospect of ministering to Caledonia according to their own lights. This they set out to do with the ice of damnation as their sole instrument. On the first Sunday our souls were under their care (*Isaiah 1:4: You sinful nation, a people weighed down with iniquity*), they surprised the congregation by naming a man for his drunkenness and ungodly language. On that occasion he was left to his shame, a hundred others as bad only too happy it was not their name that had been read out. The next week (*Genesis 19:24: The Lord rained upon Sodom and Gomorrah*), there were eight names, one of them a gentleman volunteer, and two days after that a summons to one man to attend the kirk to be rebuked. In this way they quickly made allies against themselves and the congregation began to decline. Word reached Captain Galt and he sent a note to the man who had been summoned. This quickly became one of the chief treasures of the anti-clerical party, its wording their fundamental law, cited every bit as often as Stobo and Borland resorted to the Old Testament: 'I note that I have not asked you to attend kirk. No doubt you will consider your own best course of action.'

Reverend Stobo proved to be a sufficiently poor judge of men to dare to address a reply to Captain Galt, demanding a meeting. His note, by some unknown mechanism, also became public knowledge and astonished everyone who read it. The poor man sealed his fate with a line of Scripture: *Correction is grievous unto him that forsaketh the way, and he that hateth reproof shall die.* It was a particular characteristic of Mr Stobo that he could never make use of the Bible without also making an enemy.

Captain Galt granted his request. As a foretaste of his intentions he sent his boat with its full complement of six rowers in their best uniforms. As Mr Stobo blithely stepped aboard, one of those who had travelled on the *Rising Sun* from the beginning turned to me with an almost indecent relish and said simply, 'Lamb to the slaughter.' Precisely an hour later, from which it can be deduced that the interview endured for ten minutes at the most, the boat returned. A blanched, trembling and speechless Stobo was forced to splash through the shallows before walking round the long shore of the bay to the Shades of Love and the sanctuary of his church.

'Aye,' said my shipmate, looking on with satisfaction. 'That's Captain Galt for you.'

When the process of their defeat was well advanced, the two ministers would still occasionally walk through New Edinburgh, determined to show themselves. As they went they had to endure pretended conversations reminding them of Galt's first note. There were a thousand variations, but the form was always the same.

'What o'clock is it?' one would say.

'Well, you've got a cheek,' the other would reply. 'Has Captain Galt asked me to tell you what o'clock it is?'

'I don't suppose he has.'

'Well, I'll have to consider my own best course of action!'

Their tormentors never tired of it, and Stobo and Borland never tired of being subjected to it, continuing their evening walks through the settlement until the return of Mackay so brutally put an end to their bitter partnership.

Apart from these regular martyrdoms, the rest of the colony saw little of the two men in the fortnight before Mr Stobo's sudden illness. They preferred to remain in the kirk, which had finally been completed and was the only building apart from the Meeting House to keep its occupants' heads tolerably dry. One or other would make a daily visit to the infirmary until that service, too, was no longer required. I knew that doctors, like sea captains, were not as a rule well disposed to the clerical profession, but Munro had tolerated their interference with cynical equanimity.

'I don't know if it does harm or good,' he told me once. 'I sometimes think half an hour on the torments to come helps them to cling on, although it all comes to the same in the end.'

It was Stobo who changed his mind for him and I don't think I have ever seen him angrier.

'I could have hit him!'

There was no rhetoric in what he said.

'I tell you I could have knocked him down. I raised my hand to him!'

He had overheard Stobo talking to a young man who had been working on Paterson's road. He had slipped in the mud and had his toes crushed by a blow from a hammer. The wound had festered and although Dr Munro had already amputated, his blood had been poisoned and a secondary gangrene was eating around the sutures.

'Stobo couldn't see me. I was with another patient, trying to bring down his fever, but there was only a sheet of canvas between us. I heard every word. He was on and on at him, had his teeth in him. One of his congregation – those Pharisees! – had seen him drunk on several occasions. Did he deny it? Perhaps he had gambled with the Worcesters? No? But he was sure someone had told him otherwise. He must think. There was little time left. Had there been licentiousness on Madeira? Really, had there not? Many sins had been committed there; perhaps one of them had been his. A young woman in the street – you looked after her. The thought is the same as the act in God's eyes. Of course that was long ago and he was young. Perhaps he had a friend in Caledonia, a special friend, a particular one apart from the others. Temptation was strong, was everywhere. Could he really swear that not even the thought had ever been in his mind? If it had the Lord would know. Had he dreamed wicked thoughts? The Lord knew the sins of our dreams. Then he changes tack. "Let me recite the thirty-eighth Psalm with you", he says. I don't mind telling you, Roderick, since attaining my majority I have had neither the time nor the inclination for Bible-reading. I had no idea what was coming, but this was a pretty piece of poetry. You know it?'

I shook my head.

'I'll not forget it. *I am feeble and sore broken, for my loins are filled with a loathsome disease and there is no soundness in my flesh. My wounds stink and are corrupt because of my foolishness. My heart panteth and my strength faileth me. My lovers and my friends stand aloof from my sore . . .* I couldn't listen to any more. The boy was weeping. I got a hand under Stobo's arm and had him out of there so fast he didn't have time to say amen. I told him what I would do if I saw him in my infirmary again. The man's a coward, did you know that?' He smiled at the thought. 'I could feel him shaking.'

That rude expulsion completed the rout of our first estate. In the three weeks since Mackay's disappearance, the apprentices had succeeded in turning Caledonia into a largely irreligious community. Borland and Stobo viewed this result as irrefutable confirmation that they had been right all along – namely, that we are an incorrigibly godless people that deserves every punishment from which we are currently suffering. The congregation dwindled to about twenty and has stayed there. Known as the 'caterpillars', these men now lend their hand to nothing and content themselves with creeping about the place and noting down the names of the most dissolute for their great project of disapproval. Every evening, they can be heard singing hymns of abasement in the Shades of Love.

Though in each part it takes a different form, it is becoming all too clear that something similar afflicts many of the other organs in Caledonia's distempered body. Except for the day of Reverend Mackay's memorial, Captain Galt has not been on shore since he took the noose from around James's neck and even I, who still spend all my nights here in my cabin, have seen very little of him. Two or three times, when he has been inspecting his ship and I my stocks, he has brushed past me on his way from one hold to another, his only acknowledgement of me a wordless grunt. Save for these encounters I have, for a fortnight or more, seen only his back as he stands at the rail just by the door to his cabin, sometimes alone but more often with Mr Cunningham conversing in that quiet, indistinct tone that would not be overheard. For the colonists on shore he has become an incorporeal authority, revealed twice a week in the form of the *Rising Sun*'s boat when it calls to deliver or receive some message from the Meeting House.

The Meeting House sees little business, these days, having become, for want of objection from any other quarter, Mr Paterson's private residence and office from where he directs the work on his trans-isthmian road and sends daily requests to me for tools and materials we do not possess. The other supposed councillors have shrunk almost to nothing. Captain John Malloch has kept to his ship with even more discipline than Galt. Though the directors in Edinburgh must have found some virtue in him, it can fairly be said that his weight has never been felt. If he were to step ashore now, it is very doubtful that he would be recognized by those who had not themselves sailed under his command. Likewise, it is not clear what persuaded Captain Jolly to seek employment with our Company. Mr Paterson, anxious for my favour in the matter of supplies, speaks very freely with me, these days, and let me know that Captain Jolly even proposed sailing back to Scotland in the *Dolphin* on the grounds that he had delivered his cargo and that the Company could require nothing more of him. He persisted in this so far as having the terms of his engagement placed before him and his own signature on them pointed out. He excused himself for his forgetfulness and equably reaffirmed that he was, as ever, the Company's good servant and very willing to do what he ought. Although Mr Paterson recounted the incident to me with several additional terms, which I really cannot put down here, I have not noticed any rift between them. Captain Jolly does not seem capable of being the object of anyone's dislike for very long and he continues to frequent the Meeting House for a hand of cards in the evening. It is an entertainment to which he has a great commitment, thinking nothing of the inconvenience of coming in from the *Dolphin* and making his way through the hazardous air of New Edinburgh, his handkerchief pressed to his mouth.

As Galt keeps to his ship, Reverend Borland to his church and Mr Paterson to the Meeting House, so Drummond keeps to his fortifications. He aims to dig a ditch until the waters of the bay break through to those of a sluggish inlet that runs to the sea. A light bridge will allow our men to come and go as they please, but can easily be defended or, if need be, destroyed on the approach of any enemy. The project is his own, a necessary successor to Fort St Andrew, the artillery battery, the victory at Toubacanti and the retrieval of the wood-hunters. As with all these, it has an ostensible purpose, to which there could be no objection, as well as Drummond's own purpose, which is nothing less than the advertisement of himself as our indispensable man. Strictly speaking it is unlawful, insofar as we have any laws here. There was no decision of the council to do such a thing, and by setting himself up there night and day in his own tent he is in breach of one of our founding articles, which forbids anyone to remove themselves without permission. With Jardine's tent now standing beside Drummond's the offence is brazen. Sentries are organized from there and the patrols return their reports to him while Jolly and Paterson play cards in the Meeting House. Only Galt's authority could have pulled him back, but no such note was ever rowed in from the *Rising Sun* and with that silence Drummond's licence has become complete.

Walking near the head of the bay last Sunday, I saw the disposition of the camp for myself. Several tents and even a few deal huts are arranged around a patch of trampled mud. In the centre an improvisation of posts and leaves keeps the damp off their fire. It is a miniature of New Edinburgh and perhaps in the future – admitting the absurdity of the comparison – a Carthage to our Rome. Most of the men were resting, one was preparing something by the fire. Three redcoats were taking their ease on a felled log, a cloud of brandy and tobacco keeping the usual plague of insects at bay. After a minute of staring at me like Grassmarket drunkards, one of them found his voice. 'Here's a road-builder come to borrow a shovel.'

'What's it like, then?' asked another. 'That Pacific Ocean – you must have seen it by now.'

They looked over my shoulder and I turned to find Jardine standing by the entrance to Drummond's tent.

'You shut up,' he told them, before addressing me hardly more courteously. 'You have business here?'

I started to explain that I had been walking by the shore and had heard the sounds of men working, but he retreated within the tent before I was finished. The flap was pulled back and Drummond himself stepped out. For the first time since I made his acquaintance, he made me smile. He was in his breeches and shirt, so white it made me wonder who had boiled it for him. A pistol had been casually tucked under his belt and he held a map in one hand, letting it unroll half-way down his thigh. He held it for a moment, just long enough for him to betray his self-consciousness. He was ready for the gilt frame and the drawing-room wall. This was the man he wanted to be, and a very fine picture he would make when all the world around its golden edge was cut off and safely stowed away in oblivion. He spoke: 'Well?'

I repeated the explanation I had started to make to Jardine.

'You needn't bother,' I was told. 'You're welcome to look and tell them what you see.'

That is how it is with us now: you cannot walk from one end of the peninsula to the other without entering a foreign country and becoming a spy. Nevertheless, spy I did and found the work more advanced than I had expected. Two large mounds of spoil indicated the scale of the work already done. Behind them I found the trench, already twelve feet deep, the bottom cut into the rock, and some twenty feet in length. Groups of men worked at either end of it, slowly pushing towards the point at which the waters can break through. The weakest sections of the sides are shored with planks and stout props. On the surface, its projected track has already been cleared of all vegetation so that one can see straight from the bay to where the ground slopes down towards the inlet on the other side. I watched the men work with a spirit I have not seen in New Edinburgh for weeks, encouraged by a goal that is close at hand and beyond any doubt. And yet if they think that in any way they work for themselves, I am sure they are deceived. Everything I saw there appeared to me solely as an expression of Drummond's will, not least the two small, disregarded mounds on the other side of the ditch, only their human dimensions suggesting what lay below. What surprised me most, given all that is said about Drummond and the suspicions about his past, was the four men resting beside them. One of them raised an imaginary glass to me and wished me good health in Gaelic. I looked again and recognized all four as Highlanders.

Once back in New Edinburgh I did indeed tell Mr Paterson what I had seen, not being able to find any reason why I should not. I had fallen into conversation with him on some other more pertinent matter and when that was concluded turned to Drummond and his ditch quite casually, merely to show myself willing to prolong our talk. Paterson took it quite otherwise, thanking me earnestly for these 'valuable confidences', though I told him nothing he could not have found out for himself with a little walking. Eager not to allow myself to be drawn into any new conspiracies, I described how Colonel Drummond had appeared to me and tried to change the tone by making light of it. The image had dominated my thoughts as I walked back, no doubt because of the great novelty of having seen Drummond, however fleetingly, as ridiculous. Mr Paterson was highly appreciative. 'There you have him, Roderick. The man himself! I hope I will not embarrass you if I say you have a most impressive insight into these things.'

I made to demur.

'No, no! Please. I speak as one who has learned at first hand what a very rare quality it is to see what really lies under a man's skin. Accept a compliment from one who knows. Yes, indeed, friend Drummond is a disappointed man. Ever since his name got caught up in the Commission report about that unpleasantness up north he's had some difficulty making much of himself. Bathed himself in blood in Flanders but still came back a captain.'

'And then the Company,' I said.

'Quite so. And who's to say it wasn't a good choice? Better than some of the others. What I mean is, it would be possible for a reasonable man to take that view without being, well . . . overly . . .'

'I am beginning to think that way myself.'

'And as for this ditch of his. The matter of resources is irritating, but I suppose it will be finished soon and if he's needed here in the meantime he'll come. Drummond can't resist being needed.'

'Perhaps it's a good thing,' I opined, 'that such enterprises as ours give men the chance to slough off their pasts and give their better natures another chance.'

I had intended merely to make a general comment that would place me in a good light with a man of experience. It was only after a few seconds of silence and an ambiguous smile that I realized my blunder. I began to protest the innocence of my meaning but was interrupted.

'How well you see into me too! I forget that you know it all. Nothing escapes you, Roderick Mackenzie.'

He drew the sting from my remark by amusing himself with my embarrassment. I exchanged a few trivialities with him today and am happy to record that relations remain cordial, notwithstanding my indiscretion.

The hour is very late and my mind so crowded with anxieties that I can write nothing more for the moment. As I have it in my mouth right now, I shall end with my pineapple. The sugared piece I threw over the side three days ago. In this liquid air it never dried and its sweetness quickly drew in corruption, which turned it black and stinking. The other fared much better and has lost none of its tartness. This fruit would be a rare delicacy in Scotland, in Europe no less, and when dried would, I believe, easily last the voyage in good condition. At threepence a piece a ship could carry six thousand pounds' worth and still have space for other goods. I am considering submitting my calculations to Mr Paterson. In spite of everything, we are so close to success here. If only we can outlast the rains I do not doubt we will prosper.

*

FIVE DAYS of slow depletion have passed. Our fortunes have not improved, but neither has their downward track become any steeper. I have sent similar notes both to Paterson and Drummond informing them that our stocks of saws, picks and shovels have all been issued; that we have no nails above four inches and that what rope is left must be retained on the orders of Captain Galt.

Today was my duty-day on Point Look-out. I used to go to this task reluctantly, but now I look forward to it as a rest from the many disputes with which our people occupy themselves. There are no mere mischances with us any more and no innocent errors – should a load be dropped or a hammer miss its mark it is no accident but a crime, the blame for which must be endlessly haggled over. When the wind is right a day on Point Look-out also allows me to reacquaint myself with the smell of clean air. The stench in New Edinburgh has become so intense that the senses quickly despair of conveying its awfulness and leave one with nothing but an unnerving but tolerable greenish bitterness in the mouth somewhat like the taste of a rotting tooth.

I recorded three vessels today and my companion saw another while I was asleep. Even though the mouth of Caledonia Bay is marked with beacons, which burn all night and smoke all day, three of the four sailed by without any sign of curiosity as to what we might be. The fourth was very curious indeed. She took in sail and came in close, almost to within hailing distance of where the *Sun* and the *St Andrew* are anchored. In the past the *Sun* has put down her boat to approach these shy visitors, but they have always withdrawn. This one made a slow pass through the inner channel between the coast and the Isle of Pines. Like the others of her type she had taken care to remove all insignia. I looked her over carefully through the glass and saw her so clearly that I would recognize several members of the crew if I were to meet them again. They had been thorough and wore not a single item of uniform that might betray their identity. Mr Paterson has speculated loudly that they might be Danes from St Thomas or free traders not yet sure of our peaceful nature, but I thought there was something English about this ship.

It is not, however, such trivialities that have brought me back to these pages tonight, but rather an attempt at exorcism, which I hope will restore some peace to my sleep. After watching the ship until her stern drifted into the invisible, I passed the glass to my companion and settled down to enjoy the main privilege of look-out duty – namely, spending half the day asleep. Sadly, belief that the cleanness of the air and relief from the burdensome heat of my cabin would give me some untroubled rest proved unfounded. The dream was, in essence, the same as before but through endless and cunning variations I was prevented from ever preparing myself for it and was jerked awake every quarter-hour by fresh alarms. I was leaving Mrs Purdie's coffee-house in good spirits when I had my arm seized by a man at a table. Mackay's face looked up at me blankly, his mouth opening and closing, mindlessly disconnected from the words that repeated themselves from every direction. The nightmare has many disguises, coming to me sometimes in the form of Colquhoun and once even in the features of Mr Vetch. Every time I hope to meet them in themselves, but every time I am deceived. Their jaws move grotesquely as if by some outside force and the voice is always Mackay's or, to be more precise, my sleeping conception of how his voice would be changed by death. Finally, I see him as we all saw him in his last, incomprehensible state. The corpse speaks to me: 'You know it all. Nothing escapes you, Roderick Mackenzie!' It eats at me like an unconfessed crime and I can think of no way of freeing myself from it other than by voiding every detail on to these pages.

Reverend Mackay's memorial day was windless and as dry as this season permits. It was bright, but sunless. Although there were no clouds above, a thick sea mist oppressed us all day. By good fortune it came at the end of the longest period without heavy rain since St Andrew's Day and the mud had stiffened sufficiently to allow some dignity to the procession which ran from the main clearing to the church. I spent the night before on the *Rising Sun* and arrived in New Edinburgh off the first boat in the company of Mr Shipp and several others. I wore a shirt and breeches, which alone had been preserved from the general filth for whatever occasion required them. A small group had already gathered just above the shore and I noticed that some of the gentlemen volunteers had done the same and that others without such resources had been at work with patches and thread and at scraping the mud off their coats and boots. The general brownness that has been advancing on us for several weeks was temporarily pushed back so that we made a pleasingly colourful group. Indeed, up to that dreadful moment, which I must shortly describe, the solemnity of the occasion, the efforts it demanded of us and the brief return to a common and dignified purpose all served to raise our spirits higher than they had been for a long time.

An hour after my arrival the second boat came in from the *Sun*. It had picked up Captains Jolly and Malloch on its way and included, of course, Mr Cunningham and Captain Galt for what is still, as I write, his last day on dry land. By mid-morning very nearly our whole complement had assembled. It was a body, therefore, that included many who had thought little of Mackay when he was alive but who attended merely out of curiosity, want of other distractions or of an unconsidered sense of propriety. Another motive was clear from the sullen quietness that came over us as soon as Stobo and Borland emerged from the Meeting House to lead us to the graveyard – namely, a desire to show that notwithstanding the scant regard in which Reverend Mackay had been held, he had at least been more tolerable than these two gentlemen. I cannot deny such feelings myself, but hope also that I was not alone in having witnessed the beginnings of that other Mackay whose memory deserved a sincere respect.

Reverend Borland stood at the top of the Meeting-House steps, his presence marshalling us into a long column in preparation for making our way to the kirk. As Reverend Stobo and Mr Paterson joined him there, a rather unnecessary few notes on a bugle announced the arrival of Colonel Drummond, the recently elevated Captain Jardine and a selection of soldiers from where they had been working on the ditch. I found myself a position in the back row of the vanguard, immediately behind Captain Jolly. He was speaking to his first officer, whose shoulders were shaking.

'So she said she'd give one price for all six of them and they thought their luck was in. So there's the boatswain already giving his arse an airing when one of the others says he's not paying his sixth unless he goes first and then the Chinaman says he'll go last but only if he doesn't have to pay at all. They start such a row over it the lady goes off to make her living elsewhere and they bring the port guard down on their heads. So next morning it's me who has to . . . Hold on, I think we're off.'

He spat in his pipe and put it in his pocket, still hissing. Borland and Stobo, with Paterson immediately behind them, descended the steps of the meeting house and made their way along the boards to the head of the column. Trailing them came a quartet of grim-faced caterpillars bearing between them a large plank perhaps two and a half feet wide and a little less than true coffin length. On this there were two attempts at wreaths, which someone had tried to fashion out of a refractory plant that had already half uncoiled itself and lay in a formless heap of greenery. At the top of the plank lay Mackay's bands, constantly in danger of being thrown off by the disintegrating wreath to which they had been pinned. In the middle lay his Bible and at the end, a curious choice – Stobo's perhaps? – a pair of black shoes, highly polished. Captain Jolly leaned closer to his first officer and whispered loudly: 'How are we changed in death!'

The column began slowly to shuffle forward. We passed the infirmary, in front of which Dr Munro stood to acknowledge the procession. He would stay with his patients until summoned in haste to the kirk. We thinned out to fit ourselves into the narrow shore path and made way at such a dreary pace that I should think a full three-quarters of an hour were required for us to reach the kirkyard. To the fore a determined silence was maintained, but behind me the rumble of general conversation gradually rose. From far back in the line a loud laugh burst out and was cut off. Captain Jolly took his extinguished pipe from his pocket and chewed it frustratedly.

At length we assembled round the memorial situated on the highest point of the graveyard's slope hard by the boundary stones. The area these stones enclose has twice been extended and at that time contained some one hundred and twenty of our fellow colonists, the place of each marked by a wooden board save for Mackay who, even after Mr Stobo's sudden passing, still enjoys the unique privilege of stone. The bearers manoeuvred their board and laid it down on the unbroken ground before the memorial, inscribed by one of our number once apprenticed to a mason in Dunfermline. The caterpillars stepped back to form an honour guard of dismal black on one side of this bizarre trencher of relics, while on the other Reverend Borland assumed his preaching stance and prepared himself for what promised to be a lengthy epicedium. As it was, we were to be spared all but the opening notes.

It is still hard to believe that what happened next had not been calculated, that it was not intended as the cruellest possible thrust against what remained of our confidence. Nevertheless, however well aimed the blow, calm reflection insists that this could not possibly have been the case. Not only could they not have known what we were doing at that moment, but the weird embassy that was about to intrude on us presented itself with an unquestionable innocence and simplicity. They had come to fulfil an obligation. In doing so at that precise moment and in that way they could only have been directed by savage chance or by some blacker power unknown to us both.

The first evidence of disturbance came from behind me. I could hear suppressed complaints, someone breathing hard, then a loud objection followed by a chorus of demands for silence. Even when a sentry pushed through to the centre and went straight to Colonel Drummond, Borland pressed on with his laudation of Mackay's academic achievements and early signs of virtue. Drummond listened to the report expressionlessly before stepping over the boundary stones and walking up to the edge of the forest to get a better view. Jardine followed him and both men stared towards the kirk. I followed their gaze and, through the mist, could just see something moving towards the shore of the bay. It stopped, turned and began to come directly towards us. As the form approached, a group of Indians resolved very gradually from the mist as if materializing directly from its nothingness.

'Shall I get rid of them, sir?' asked Jardine.

Drummond stayed silent. The whole assembly began to turn in that direction and to murmur questions to each other. Reverend Stobo shifted uneasily but staunchly refused to turn with the crowd. Borland, who had moved on to the first stirrings of Mackay's calling to the ministry, was becoming strident. Jardine was sent to find out what they wanted and confronted them about seventy yards from where I was standing. The mist was not overly dense by this time and over such a short distance I could still see Jardine very clearly. I thought at first that the Indians must be much further off, but then I saw him go amongst them. Beside his dark head and shoulders they had a ghostly paleness, which made them hard to tell apart and suggested that they might, at a change in the wind, lose their momentary humanity and drift away.

Jardine started to walk very quickly towards us and then to run as he noticed the Indians resume their procession. Mr Paterson, being of modest stature, sidled round to me and demanded to know what was happening. There was an urgent conference between Jardine and Drummond of which all I could hear was the latter's assertion, 'It can't be!' and then Jardine saying something very insistent.

'Shall I stop them, sir?'

The mourners were already parting to let them through.

'No,' said Drummond, 'let them come.'

The Indians came on with an unvarying pace and our people struggled to get out of their way, some of them falling over each other in their anxiety not to be touched by this extraordinary visitation. In every respect they resembled the Indians we have been familiar with since our arrival, save for the startling fact that their skins were chalk white, and their hair too. Their eyes had either the last dissolution of colour or else none at all save for the pinkish residue of the blood within. The caterpillars looked on aghast. Reverend Stobo seemed utterly confused. Borland, eyes closed in concentration, misinterpreted the silence as a victory for his sermon and moved on to the deceased's distinction as a scholar.

The two foremost Indians held themselves as men of authority. The elder was further distinguished from the rest by being a blue-grey colour from ankle to neck on account of a dense pattern of tattoos relating an epic of plants and forest animals, which he wore like a garment under the skin. This man took a step forward, revealing what others had already seen – four Indians, carrying a bier the sapling shafts of which bowed under a great weight. Between the slight bodies of the front bearers two huge feet stiffly protruded.

The head man drew himself up and began to address us in a loud, steady voice. Mr Spense was present but was not able to enlighten us as to the meaning of this great oration, part chanted and part sung and, to me at least, deeply affecting. In recalling that moment later, I unexpectedly found myself connected with a day of youthful misery long ago when, after many hours of fruitless struggle with a passage from Homer, a sudden flush of understanding released me into a daydream world so brilliant and simple it made me weep.

The speech had, needless to say, a quite different effect on Mr Stobo. He strode up to the man so quickly and with such an enraged expression that it seemed certain he would hit him. The colonist standing closest took a step forward to prevent this violence, but Stobo's arms stayed by his side. Having failed to perturb the Indian in the slightest by this menacing approach, he found himself stranded face to face with him as his ancient chant-song intensified. It would be presumptuous to speculate on how such a confrontation impressed itself on Reverend Stobo's mind, but I will say that of all the colonists then surviving he was the quickest to call strangeness evil and I believe it was whatever that innocent primitive's song brought up from within himself that was the cause of his undoing. Although the second and immeasurably greater blow was yet to come, he was already almost unrecognizable, in features as well as voice, when he began to shout uncontrollably. 'What is this? How dare you? What are you?'

Mr Borland, who had to this point been ploughing on, thinking he could see off this new interruption as he had seen off the first one, was finally silenced by the sound of Mr Stobo's voice. He opened his eyes to see for the first time the inexplicable scene. He quickly went to Mr Stobo's side. 'In God's name!' he demanded. 'What in God's name are you . . .'

A final long note from the historiated Indian concluded his song. The four bearers advanced to the memorial stone and gently lowered their burden to the ground. Now everyone could see the huge mound of flesh, from the calloused, soil-coloured soles of the feet to the tight, swelling belly, distended by the onset of putrefaction, to the serene, yet unmistakable features of Reverend Mackay. As with his praise-singer, the only thing we could understand of this Mackay was on his skin. He was even more painted than the little Indian – to be sure, the artists of his tribe could never before have had such a generous canvas as this. The toes and tendons of the feet had become roots. They broke the soil at the ankle and flourished over the whole of the body, the last tips of the leaves stretching up the neck to brush the ears. A bird flew across the chest towards its young, which looked out from the pit of an arm. At the centre of it all a monkey balanced on a branch. A navel for an eye, its tail hung down straight extending wittily along the length of the carnal member.

'Oh, God! Oh, God! Oh, God!'

These were the last words Reverend Stobo spoke. His face twisted, the eyes yawned wide, invisible fingers pulling at the flesh. With a moan he fell to the ground.

Questions were shouted from further back where the cause of the commotion was still a mystery. Some men began to push forward, some fell and protested angrily. A riot threatened. Reverend Borland emerged from stupefaction to furious activity. One of his adherents was sent running for Dr Munro. Two others gave up their coats as a covering for Mackay's body.

'Get this out of here!' he ordered. 'Get this obscenity out of our sight!'

The four men who had carried the wreaths from the Meeting House heaved up the bier and made off through the mist as fast as their strength would carry them.

'Put it in the kirk,' Borland shouted after them. 'No, outside it!'

He turned to the tattooed Indian. 'Do you know what you've done?' he shouted into his face. 'Can you? You . . .' He struggled with himself. 'You benighted . . .'

He forced his way through the ring of colonists and ran towards his church. A cracking noise drew everyone's attention back to Mr Stobo. He lay flat on his back, eyes staring up into the mist, teeth grinding mindlessly. The wreaths, bands, Bible and shoes were swept off the board so that it could be pressed into more practical service. Three of the caterpillars and, as I was closest to the remaining limb, I myself laid hold of Mr Stobo and placed him on top of it. Being without handles, it was raised awkwardly and far too short for the task, leaving his head dangling off the front and his legs trailing from behind. My fears that this rough treatment might do him some further injury were not shared by the caterpillars who bore him off at all possible speed. It is a wonder they reached the kirk without throwing him on the ground.

During these several minutes of disorder the Indians had been ignored and had merely stood by as amazed spectators. Throughout the entire episode, whenever my eyes were on them, they had maintained the utmost impassiveness. At one point I caught the eyes of the head-man. He clicked his tongue and jerked his head sharply upwards. If it is true, as some say, that however scattered man's languages his gestures remain universal, I am sure I cannot have been wrong in feeling myself and all my fellows to be the subject of his rankest contempt. His delegation re-formed itself and processed back into the mist with the same steady formality with which it had arrived. As there was nothing more that could be done in the graveyard, I followed them at the distance of a few dozen paces. They went by the kirk and turned to the right to re-enter the forests. Before passing into their obscurity I saw them meet with a far larger group of their own kind whom no one, I believe, had noticed. A movement among the trees distracted me and as I looked to see what it might be my eyes made human forms of the mist that curled about the trunks. With that first recognition I began to see them everywhere, as far back into the forest as the light would permit. There were women there and even, if the gloom and the mist did not deceive me, a few children. It seemed that the whole tribe, if that is what they are, had come to return Mackay to his own. The head-man and the leading group made their way into the forest. The other Indians waited until they passed, then turned and were drawn after them. I felt very strongly that I should say something, but as I searched for words and rehearsed in my mind the actions of my better, braver self, I let the moment slip away with relief. I followed them some way into the forest, wanting to believe that I still might do it, but knowing the meaninglessness of it. Unable to direct my thoughts, let alone my will, I let my tiredness decide for me, dropping back until I could see only a single straggler – a woman, or girl rather, perhaps sixteen, perhaps less. She walked unevenly, delayed by the burden she carried carefully in front of her. She stopped and turned to see what was pursuing her. She looked uncertainly to the left and right of me as if I had become as pale and mist-formed as she was to me. I took a step and her head moved an inch to fix me with colourless eyes. She spoke, quick and sharp, the same phrase repeated twice and with a tremor of fear that made me ashamed of whatever I thought I was doing. With a breath of air the mist thickened between us and all that was clear to me was the beaded string that curved from hip to hip and the infant asleep at the breast. Startling in its brownness, it hovered, supported by the merest implication of its mother. It disappeared when she turned her back and I honoured her instructions to follow no further.

Dr Munro attended on Mr Stobo with all possible diligence, though it was characteristic of the man that he refused to admit to the sincerity of his motives.

'Imagine if I had saved his life!' he said to me later. 'Just think of him waking up to find he had me to thank for his existence. I dare say it would have killed him all over again.'

The triumph was not to be. Reverend Stobo died of an apoplectic stroke on the afternoon of the third day after the events I have just described. Mackay, declared by Munro to have died not more than a day before the return of his remains, was interred that same evening without further ceremony. His memorial stone, or gravestone as it now is, has been allowed to stand – a concession that consumed the whole of Mr Borland's tolerance. He was disturbed by one of the sentries that very night, soiled and exhausted as he moved the last of the whitewashed stones that mark the limits of consecration. As these approach Mackay's grave they now make a neat U-shaped detour leaving him on the heathen side and ensuring, no doubt, that he does not whisper corruption into the ears of the virtuous dead within. His stone is inscribed according to instructions found in his chest on the *Caledonia*; a few words from Matthew: *The kingdom of heaven is as a man travelled into a far country*. Mr Stobo, it would appear, revealed his views on the matter of epitaphs to Reverend Borland some months before. The New Testament, in my hearing at least, is a text that never passed his lips in life and neither does it grace him in death. Deuteronomy was more to his liking and it is from the thirty-second and, in more prominent letters, the twenty-ninth chapters that his board remembers his virtues to the world:

after my death ye will utterly corrupt yourselves.

Nor have ye taken strong drink these forty years.

And now, sleep.

*

THAT WISH, at least, was satisfied. Indeed, for all the twelve nights since I last wrote in this book I have slept like a dead man. I wish I could record some cheering reason for this, but can only think that there is a limit to what can affront the sensitive mind and that it is because my days are nightmare enough that my nights are empty. We still await our change of fortune. 'It must come soon,' is the sentiment on everyone's lips. There is a second part to this incantation, which would be blasphemy to speak aloud but which I have seen in several faces. 'It must come soon, or not at all.'

I had occasion to visit Dr Munro in his infirmary several days ago on a difficult matter. We conversed for a long time on many pleasingly irrelevant topics, which, I would like to think, did us both some good – he has been looking very exhausted of late. We touched on the Mackay affair, but added nothing new to the infinity of opinions that can still be heard on the subject in every corner of New Edinburgh. I did, however, mention my encounter with the Indian girl in the forest and the colour of the child she was carrying. This interested him greatly.

'Now wait,' he said, 'that reminds me of something – but what? What is it? You must be getting on?'

I said no and extended my glass.

'That's it! The fighting-cock man.'

I looked mystified.

'The fighting-cock man – it's the only thing I've ever seen that's remotely like what you describe. In fact, it's precisely like it. It's something I remember from my old navy days. There was a character in Portsmouth known as Jedediah – the only name he would ever give – or Jed the fighting-cock man. He sustained himself by breeding cockerels for all the pits in the town that provided entertainment for the sailors. The hens and the defeated birds – those that lived, that is – were sold on to the ships for meat and eggs at sea. The champions were traded at vast prices and sometimes Jed would buy one back and breed from it. He told me once that for one of these birds he could get two hundred times what it had cost him to rear. He was a gentleman then. But the point is that from somewhere, a new cock perhaps, or a new hen, he started to get pure white birds appearing in his flock. He sold a few as fighters – "They're game enough," he told me, "but not much skilled on account of them not seeing too well." He started to wring their necks as soon as they appeared until, according to his own version of the story, a liveried footman appeared at his door and said that his master had seen one of his white birds and had taken a fancy to it as an ornament for his estate. In only a year there was no petty squire within five counties who wasn't desperate for the same just to show he wasn't behind the times. Jedediah soon saw that he could make more money out of the whites than he could out of the real fighting cocks. So now black was white – he put the whites together and tried to breed a flock of them, only now there was a minority of dark birds hatched and it was their necks that got wrung. As time went on there were fewer dark birds and more and more white. This is what he was telling me in a tavern just before I took ship for a tour in the Mediterranean. He was telling me that one day soon he would wring the neck of the last dark bird and his flock would be pure white from then on, generation after generation. Pure gold, as he put it. When I got back six months later he was in the poor-house.'

'Fashion changed?' I asked.

'Not as fast as Nature.'

'All his birds turned black again?'

'He wasn't so lucky. For three months he hadn't had a single dark bird and then, in the space of a week, almost every clutch failed to hatch. A few monstrosities chipped their way out only to die on reaching the light and the rest were left to go cold in the nest. He was ruined.'

I was taken aback by the miserable implications of this ending and would have been happy to leave them unexamined. For Munro, however, whose curiosity, I believe, can be repelled by nothing under the sun, they were the whole interest of the story.

'As for your white Indians . . .'

'Surely the same thing couldn't happen?'

He shrugged. 'Who's to say? What takes a few months for chickens might take centuries for men and women but if, as some say now, the propagation of all creatures is governed by the same laws, their end must be the same. If that infant was really hers they might have generations still to come – I don't know. One thing I have learned is that everything strong in Nature comes from mixture. Purity is a perversion to her and she always destroys it in the end.'

A thought came to me then that I would not have expressed to anyone other than Dr Munro. It made me smile before I had the confidence to speak it aloud.

'Well?' enquired Munro.

'I was just wondering if in all the time he was with them Mackay might not have . . . well . . .'

'What?'

'Mixed, so to speak.'

'Ah, I see. Well, I suppose he might have done. From the state of him when they brought him back I'd say they'd certainly put some life in the old dog. And there was no illness that I could see. Heart probably.'

'Overflowed?'

'Possibly. It's not a medical term.'

I suggested that, according to his theory, it might have just the required effect.

'It certainly would! A drop of ink in their whey. That might fend off purity for God knows how long.'

We both laughed, indecently no doubt, but surprised by our

capacity for such good-humour and altogether too pleased to worry about its cause. We drifted away to more remote subjects, Munro telling me the obscenest possible anecdotes from the life of a ship's surgeon and all with the most refined mock delicacy, while I made what I could from my poor stock of experience, telling him of Colquhoun's roguery and of my own venial sins along the road of my ascent. Each of us spoke with needless detail and convolution. Several times the conversation was about to falter but was picked up by one or the other at the last moment and carried forward with a new, if fragile impetus. But neither was a true Scheherezade and no more than an hour had passed when we had to return to New Edinburgh and the real reason for my visit.

'So,' said Munro, 'there's none at all?'

'None. Each ship had a pint in its own stores. Some of that was used on the voyage and the rest is what Mr Shipp brought you last time, though it was no easy task to persuade the captains to give it up.'

'And there's a discrepancy in the colony stores?'

'Yes. According to the inventory there should be six pints still.'

'But there isn't?'

'No.'

It was laudanum we were talking about. I had come to explain why we could not fulfil the most recent request for supplies.

Dr Munro rubbed his eyes and the impression of great exhaustion returned.

'Well, then,' he said quietly, 'how did that happen?'

I reminded him that the original figures had been taken from his own memorandum.

'Please, Roderick. I wasn't looking to blame anyone.'

His disappointment was real and shamed me.

'I'm sorry.'

'They'll be hoarding it. The captains will have held some back. Colonel Drummond will have some if he has any sense.'

'I could ask them.' I said it without conviction and was relieved by his answer.

'There's no point. They'd only lie about it – I would if I were them. There's always something a man won't willingly give up. It depends on the situation – usually it's gold, sometimes water or a warm coat. Now it's laudanum.'

He drank down his brandy and refilled the glass.

'It wouldn't have saved any lives. That surprises you? The one thing we have that works, the one thing that everyone has faith in? Well, it doesn't work. It just eases the inevitable. Doctors like it because it makes it seem as if they can do something. Naval doctors like it particularly. Do you know why?'

I shook my head glumly.

'It was one of the first things I learned about naval medicine. The purpose of a naval doctor is to help maintain the fighting strength of the ship. The ship is his patient not the men who sail it. The purpose of laudanum is to keep the sick and the wounded quiet so that their cries don't strike fear into those who can still fight. I'm sorry, Roderick. I'm poor company today.'

I insisted that I should be the one to apologize.

'If you like,' was his diffident reply. He indicated the bottle on his table. 'How much of this left?'

'It's the only thing we're not short of.'

'Good. Set some aside for me, will you? A good amount – ten gallons or more. Sometimes it's better than nothing. You remember I told you I thought I hadn't seen everything yet, that this place was holding something back? The waiting's over.'

He pointed over my shoulder along the length of the infirmary.

'Three bays that way a man died this morning of what looks to me like all the world's diseases put together. In the main it's a type of yellow fever, but not like any I've seen or heard of before. Yellow fever is a well-crafted disease, Roderick, but this is a masterpiece.'

In the short time since that conversation Dr Munro's admiration for this fever has been horribly vindicated. Of the twelve people affected ten are already dead, all within two days of the onset. The remaining two became ill yesterday. Although we are now well accustomed to disease, the malignity of this new contagion and the hideousness of its effects have spread a new fear amongst us. It begins moderately. At first there is an unexceptional fever, which develops into one that swings suddenly from chills to heats. Nausea and pains in the head and neck follow within hours. At this stage it might still be one of the less pernicious fevers, which many have survived, but if it goes on to show its true character, with pains in the loins and back and a tormenting burning in the stomach, then the sufferer cannot hope for more than two days. The fever becomes ardent, the sweats extreme and are followed fast by violent retchings and vomitings of green bile so offensive that the stench of it oozes through the canvas of the infirmary tents and infects the air all around. Next a black bile is vomited up, so caustic that when poured on the ground there is a visible effervescence as if it were the purest vitriol. From this stage death comes quickly, sometimes with convulsions. From the moment of death the body is as corrupted as one lain in the sun for a week. I witnessed the remains of one victim being carried from the infirmary to the shore for burial at sea, it no longer being possible for us to dig graves fast enough. Fluid drained from the corpse, which collapsed and shrivelled before my eyes. Although the soul had departed only an hour before, what they dumped in the boat was nothing but an empty bag of skin.

The fluxes and dysenteries that have afflicted us since shortly after our arrival are now haemorrhagic without exception and are never survived more than a few days. There is more blood than stool in the latrines and every time a man goes there he must look behind himself to see whether he will outlast the week or not. Too many are sick now to be properly cared for and as a result the mud of New Edinburgh is fouled with their excrement, greatly adding to the progress of these attacks. This aspect of our condition is one of the cruellest for few die without being humiliated first. It is more than some can bear to be seen in such a state and they make their way into the forests with their last strength to die unobserved. Under this pitiful cover the desertion of healthy men has resumed. For them, too, it is a desperate, or at least a foolish act – this country is too rich and subtle in its malice for them to get far. Deserters are encouraged also by the knowledge that Drummond and his soldiers are no longer inclined to pursue them. All their energies are employed on his scheme of defences, which has now grown in ambition to include a second ditch and a rampart. It was Mr Paterson who told me this during yet another discussion about resources for his Pacific road.

'The colonel wishes to make his mark. It seems to be very important to him that in certain eventualities at least a ditch will remain. It puts me in mind of those ancient fortresses of which only an earthwork around the top of a hill remains – "There was once a man and he commanded me to be built." That's what they say. As for whether they were lived in for a thousand years or for a month, there's no telling.'

I was the only one to hear this remark and feel sure that he would have spoken differently had we been in company. It was not his opinions about Drummond that struck me – their enmity is no secret now – but the open talk of these 'certain eventualities'. It came as a shock to me, but on reflection as a relief too. I can no longer conceal my own doubts, not from these pages at least, and to hear a word of this from Paterson himself acquits me of any disloyalty.

I have enumerated all the assaults that intolerant Nature makes on us, but it is with a still heavier heart that I must describe how our own hand has recently been raised against ourselves. I have already said that our efforts, such as they are, have become dominated by the two main projects of Drummond's fortifications and the road to the Pacific. For some time the demands of the respective champions of these projects for all manner of tools and materials put me in a very uncomfortable position. For the last fortnight, however, I have been able to excuse myself from this contest on the grounds of exhaustion – there is simply nothing more to be issued. Since the raid on the Spanish, Drummond has been so convinced of my opposition to him that I had to waste half a day in the surly company of Captain Jardine going through the holds of all our ships to convince him there was not a contraband shovel somewhere that I was holding back as a special favour to the road-builders. The whole business was a calculated insult to my honesty and I took my leave from Jardine sharply, observing that if they needed an extra shovel they would be better asking Paterson for one in a civil manner.

A few days after this several tools made their way by night from the road to Drummond's fortifications. Two nights after that an equal number travelled in the opposite direction. Most recently, five road-builders attempted another raid on the land of the ditch-diggers. There was a skirmish and after the confusion it was found that only four had returned to our end of the peninsula. There being so little intercourse between the two groups, no one from Paterson's party was willing to make a personal enquiry as to what had happened to the missing man. Instead a note was sent and Drummond's reply brought into New Edinburgh by Sergeant Black. Mr Paterson showed it to me that evening: 'Regret to inform you labourer Alan Caldwell found guilty of theft. Hanged this morning on my authority.'

'Cannibal!' exclaimed Paterson furiously, as I read the note.

There can be no pretence any more of our being a single colony: Caledonia is divided. Drummond's fortifications and the small camp that has gathered around them are now quite separate from New Edinburgh. Our people do not care to go near them on their own and whenever any of Drummond's men come through New Edinburgh a hostile silence spreads around them. In truth, our unity was brief. The ships kept us apart and flattered us by this separation. In the first few weeks of our being here hope and strangeness made us easy with each other. Perhaps it was for a single night only that we were truly one and seemed to have brought away all that was best in us and left what kept us low and despised. At least, that is . . . But what a childish vein! Too much brandy, I fear – and if I go on I will have to tear this page out when I read it sober and throw it in the sea. I fear I am not wholly well.

To bed then, and to dream of letters. Is that not a curious thing – that I now know in advance what I will dream of? For some time I have had presentiments, and for the last week all my predictions have been perfect. It is not that I say to myself, 'I shall dream of this tonight,' and then carry this intention over the border to my sleeping life. Rather it is as if the dream crosses to me and announces itself, vaguely at first, but now with complete exactitude. The knowledge is not at all like the dream itself – no more than knowing the taste of an orange is the same as eating one. It is quite useless, therefore. What I know will terrify me will still terrify. What I know will surprise me will be no less surprising.

Tonight it is to be letters – they are already hovering in my mind. They are the talk of the Colony – have they arrived yet, how have they been read? Have they spurred the despatch of the second fleet? I overheard some banter today: 'I hope they don't read your whining jeremiad, Tom Johnston, or they won't bother. They'll leave us to rot where we are.'

They needn't worry! I remember Johnston well – he was one of the last to dictate to me. When his wife and sons read his letter they won't be able to wait to join him in the earthly paradise he describes with such uncharacteristic eloquence. And if they should come on that second fleet, and if he and I should have survived that long and if they should stumble into this cess-pit bearing the said treasured letter – what then? The thought is no more than an amusement – no one contemplates the possibility of so many ifs.

In my dream I will see the letters fluttering down. Some land in front of the directors in Milne Square. Another is slashed open by Colquhoun – as he reads his eyes dilate with greed. Vetch receives one too. I watch over his shoulder and see a blank sheet. He reads all the same, making an occasional nod before placing it in the fire. Susanna's lies on a tray of sweetmeats, the seal unbroken. The last is my mother.

'Don't lie to me, Roderick,' she says.

Before waking, I dream that I wake, hot, fearful, hand on heart, wondering if the fever has started.

I LIVE. In fact, I have had to suffer nothing more than a little looseness and pain in the belly and a few days of mild fever. I think the culprit was a piece of bad meat and have resolved to inspect my food more carefully in future. The episode gave me three days of more or less complete solitude and rest which, I am sure, has done me considerable good. It would have been quite complete had it not been for the need to rouse myself every three hours to reassure Mr Shipp. He was jocularly unconvinced of the seriousness of my illness but would, nevertheless, insist on knocking on my door and demanding, 'Not dead yet, young master?' I cannot say that my absence from normal duties was much noticed, but Dr Munro at least enquired after the reason. I dismissed the illness as trivial and said I was glad I had not wasted any of his time. He made a show of being very angry and insisted that I tell him of the slightest upset in the future – it was not for me to decide what was a trivial symptom and what was not. I might have said that I did not call him because I knew there was nothing he could do, but I was too pleased at his concern and held my tongue. I was similarly pleased to discover from Mr Shipp that Captain Galt has once again become aware of my existence – he drew Shipp aside one morning for a few words on my condition. Of course, Shipp refused to allow that there was any solicitude in this – 'Lucky I told him what I did, young master,' he said to me, with a very solemn expression. 'He was going to have you thrown overboard before you infected anyone else.'

I might add that Mr Paterson, normally so concerned for my well-being, did not notice my temporary absence.

I would not speak of myself at such length if my own situation did not mirror that of New Edinburgh as a whole. A new arrival to our shore would no doubt find it hard to believe, but there has been nevertheless an improvement in our affairs. Not a reversal of our fortunes by any means, nor even a stoppage of their previous headlong downward plunge but perhaps a slight decline in speed, a first sense of a pull on the reins.

Such fragile hopes have been aroused by five clear days entirely without rain. The heat has become more intense, but it is easier to find shade than it ever was to avoid the endless dousing we have had since last November. Vapour rises from every part of New Edinburgh's sodden and miserable plot, returning a small part of this watery bombardment to where it came from. As it goes, the universal mud thickens and crusts. Parts of it can now be walked on quite cleanly, and new, more practical paths are being established as people leave the boards for the first time in weeks. Lines have been strung between the huts and clothes hung on them to catch the sun. Shoes steam on the roofs. Linen is spread on the rocks by the shore. Warped wooden chests are brought out to have the mould scraped from them and the moisture roasted out until they close again. Across the bay, the solitary Reverend Borland lays his theological books out on a table and turns their pages in the sun. Following his trick, I have had Mr Shipp arrange our ledgers on the quarterdeck, which shimmers with a terrible heat. In only a couple of hours they were all returned to me, warm as loaves, their rippled pages crackling as I turned them, no longer fearful of pulling damp corners away in my hands. As we have had no wind, the ships have taken the opportunity to do something similar with their sails. Every one has been let out and the ships turned into the sun to receive its full force. A newly unfurled sail, when fully warmed, gives off such clouds of steam that a distant observer might think we were on fire. The air is thick with the smell of canvas and mould. The sails are spotted brown and grey like huge slices of old bread and some have lines of green across them where stagnant water has gathered in the pleats. One can almost see them pale and tighten as the water is driven off. Their state is a scandal to the crew, who are at pitch of frustration at having been detained for so long in semi-idleness and far too close to land for their liking. There has been much sad gazing at these sails and shaking of heads and passing of gloomy comments. This happens particularly in the presence of Mr Cunningham, when they mutter together like farmers over the indecency of a weed-choked field and how someone should set their hand to it and put it to its proper purpose. The sight of all this canvas, impressive enough to me but a sacred image to seamen, was enough to bring Captain Galt out of his cabin. He stood with his great hands grasping the quarterdeck rail and looked up at the limp, steaming sails. 'There's a sight,' he said quietly to himself, 'there's a real sight.'

I cleared my throat, unsure if he had noticed me. After a few seconds he turned and greeted me with his usual economy. 'You have recovered?'

I said that I had.

'Good,' he said distractedly, and returned his attention to the sails. He stood there for a good half-hour or more, as did I at the side rail looking at the water and at the shores of Caledonia Bay. The ship had been turned so that the quarterdeck was in the shadow of the sails, making the temperature tolerable. Twice I looked round to get the impression that Captain Galt had been looking at me and had turned away at the last moment. I walked across to the other side and then back again to where I had started, trying to think of how I might open a conversation without it seeming too contrived. No one else was with us the whole time we were there and the silence was verging on the ridiculous when at last we turned towards each other at the same instant. My mouth was already open, ready to deliver some banality about the weather, when Galt forestalled me.

'Well, then,' he said, and with another quarter-inch nod returned to his cabin.

Though none of this amounts to evidence about anything I was, inevitably, left with an even stronger impression that there is some misunderstanding between us.

The health of the colony, when examined closely and with a hopeful eye, shows signs of responding well to the end of the deluge. It would be unjust, however, to ascribe the changes here solely to the mercies of the weather. Dr Munro's efforts have also begun to take effect and deserve every praise. Having obtained from me a list of everything edible in our stocks, which has not yet mouldered or rotted, he noticed two hogsheads of raisins, which were recorded as trade goods. These have been transferred to the colony's own supplies and there is now a dole of three ounces of raisins every morning before the work parties are despatched. Every evening the one other commodity we have in plenty, namely brandy, is pressed into service. To allow for a good ration for every man, which can be sustained over the next two months, the officers' allowance has been cut to the same level as for the other men. We all now receive one gill per day and have been sternly admonished not to trade our allowance but to take our medicine with good heart. Although dice and cards still give some too much and others not enough, the patients are happy with their regimen on the whole and the conviction that this simple remedy has begun to turn the tide has done much, in alliance with the weather, to relieve our spirits. Curiously, it is Dr Munro himself who has the least confidence in his measures. He described the treatment to me as a mere conjuring trick – nothing but the attempt to make something happen simply through the belief that it is happening. He swore me to the closest secrecy over such remarks, warning me in a whisper before returning to his infirmary, 'Hush! If the Fever hears us, it will all be for nothing.'

Trickery or not, I believe there is a definite decline in the rate of new infections and it matters not in the least whether this is because of raisins and brandy, or merely because we swallow them with a desperate faith. If Dr Munro tends toward the latter view I would say that it is not out of cynicism but from a sincere belief in the healing powers of delusion.

Of those who sicken with the bloody flux or the black vomit none has yet survived, and Dr Munro's admiration for the latter is now unrestrained. He tells me that in a thousand years men will die of it as quickly and hopelessly as they do now. He described to me with enthusiasm the results of an autopsy he carried out on one of its victims. There was hardly anything left of the liver, the kidneys were inflated and pustular, the intestines could be pulled out in pieces and the heart, as he described it, had shrunk to something more like that of a sheep than a man. He has named the condition hepatophagic, or liver-eating, yellow fever. A detailed description has already been addressed to the Royal Society and awaits our next despatch of letters, whenever that will be.

It was a few days before the change in the weather that Dr Munro despaired of ever winning a victory against either of the two diseases that afflict us most. Giving up all hope of physic, he changed his strategy and started on a series of measures that have brought him much credit. In a day and a half of hard labour, the boundary of the forest behind the infirmary was cut back and then the infirmary itself moved some fifty yards to this more remote and enclosed position. A light pale has been set up around it and painted red to emphasize the effect. No one may go beyond it, but must ring a bell attached to one of the posts if they wish to speak to Munro or his assistants (it has been standing by that post that I have had all my most recent conversations with him). No visitors are allowed to those who lie dying inside, with the single exception of Reverend Borland who ministers to them once a day. At night, sulphur candles are burned between the pale and the canvas sides of the infirmary, marking it out with faint blue lights and filling the air with acrid fumes that catch on the throat. Munro has shut himself up in this underworld, sleeping in a small tent of his own inside the pale and trusting to that old-doctor's immunity he once told me of.

After a meeting of the council (Drummond absent and Galt present in writing only), it was decided that the colony as a whole should be arranged according to Munro's instructions. New Edinburgh has therefore been divided into two parishes. The more westward, and furthest from the infirmary, is now occupied exclusively by the eight hundred who, at the time of the division, showed no symptoms of any but the most trivial ailments. The second, and very much smaller, is the province of the sickening in which some one hundred or so have been persuaded to live apart from the rest in the interests of the common good. Since the institution of this division five men have returned to the larger healthy group. A greater number have been moved on to the infirmary from which, at the moment, none return. It is characteristic of Munro that he describes this arrangement as a failure, a surrender, an admission of impotence, and affects to regard it with the deepest possible gloom, particularly when he hears others praise it. In fact it has had more success than anything else he has done, with not a single one of the larger group becoming seriously ill since the division.

Drummond, his soldiers and excavators are not party to this and continue their own remoter isolation. Although they are only a mile away, we have been so hard pressed with difficulties and so preoccupied with our own affairs that we know relatively little of how it goes with them. To be plain, there has been no inclination to enquire. A wit has christened them and their project Ditchville, and the word is now common parlance amongst us, confirming the separation. The meaning has something of opposition, of despised foreignness about it. It is pronounced either with a dismissive shrug or an offended wrinkle of the nose.

The change in the weather has also put an end to the contrary winds that kept our smaller ships in the bay for many weeks. As soon as this was noticed Captain Galt ordered the *Dolphin* to be manoeuvred out of the bay and anchored in open water by the *St Andrew* and the *Rising Sun*. His intention, I believe, was purely precautionary, but the move was interpreted as preparation for a project of some sort and it soon became a widespread conviction that she was to be used as a fishing boat. The thought was enough to spread a passionate hunger for fresh fish throughout the colony and Dr Munro spoke strongly in favour of it. Although, on investigation, no one could be found who claimed authorship of the design, nor anyone who had given any thought as to how it might be carried out, it was universally agreed to be an excellent idea and one that would do much to continue the improvement in our conditions. It had, as it were, proposed itself to our appetites and forcefully persuaded them of the merits of its own case. A number of men presented themselves as having some knowledge of the craft, though none was a master of it. A party of eight was selected including the Highland whale-fisher. He came in from Ditchville on hearing rumours of such an expedition and joined the others on the *Dolphin*, though no one, myself included, expected his particular expertise to be needed. The *Dolphin* has been five days at sea, leaving on the first day of dry weather and returning at dawn this morning with few fish on board but a true leviathan dragging in her wake!

I must leave off now – outside the sun must nearly have set and the thought of fresh roasted whale has driven all other matters from my mind.

*

IT IS THREE WEEKS and two days since I have written in this journal – the longest silence since it was begun, and by a good margin too. I have glanced over the preceding pages, contrary to my usual habit, and found there evidence of a state of mind so foreign to me now that only its description here persuades me that it was once my own. I see a few words of caution, but they were mere courtesies, penny-charms against disappointments I was quite sure would never come. Hope is a distemper for us, bred in the bone, the very salt of our nature. Whatever else afflicts us, it is this that burns most in our sores and raises our suffering to a pitch that is all our own.

Forgive me, I am out of sorts again – something like the last trouble with a little dizziness but not so taxing as before. I have exaggerated it and on that pretext have withdrawn to my cabin to do what I can.

Our hopes grew for several days after my last entry. The whale made optimists of us all. Our minds were refreshed by its novelty and our bodies by the rush of nourishment that flooded into our blood, grown thin from too many weeks of plain meal, ship's biscuit and green beef. Sinclair, the whaler, professed contempt for his catch, telling anyone who would listen that he had brought whales three times the size ashore. I am sure this was nothing but bravado for the mountainous scale of this creature astounded us all and would have fed the colony five times over. Wishing to complete my work in this book and then being detained here and on board the *St Andrew* in checking stocks, I did not get ashore until late in the afternoon when the butchery of the whale was already well advanced. For forty yards around the landing stage, the water was all blood red. Closer in, it was a thick broth of oil and fat and a heavy scum formed from the contents of its stomach, the slashed remains of which lay on rocks nearby amid piles of other offals, the most extraordinary part of which was the intestine, heaped up like a great mound of cable. As we rowed through this effluent, I noticed that the surface was constantly disturbed by fish gorging themselves on the blood and digesta. Flies clouded the offal piles while gulls and other birds squabbled in the air and fought over morsels snatched from the shore or from the waters of the bay. The whale itself had been unseamed from head to tail and when I arrived a man was standing, almost to his full height, inside the bloody cavern of the belly scything away from a rib another slab of the dark meat that was to make us such a good meal that evening. A pile of white blocks lay nearby and it was explained to me that this was the blubber or outer fatty layer, which had been cut off the exposed part of the animal before my arrival. Under Sinclair's supervision this was being boiled down in the pans that had been used in our search for the Nicaragua wood – a search readily abandoned in favour of this more certain profit. The resulting oil filled six brandy barrels.

All this business was watched by a large and growing audience. The day's work projects were gradually abandoned so that when I came on shore an unproclaimed holiday was in full effect with the whole colony either drowsing under whatever shade they could find or milling round the whale like dogs at table. As the roasting pits used last November were still waterlogged it was decided to turn the whole of the apparatus used for boiling wood samples into a kitchen. The remaining pans not being used to boil down the fat were scoured and set over high fires. Two spits were improvised so that the meat could be cooked all the more quickly and that evening the whole colony gorged on whale – boiled, fried and roasted – with an allowance of beer and a double ration of brandy and an extra handful of raisins for each man. It was a diet of which Dr Munro highly approved. A portion of the liver was taken directly to the infirmary where it was pulverized and fed raw to those who might still benefit.

The meat was as dark as old venison, with a taste rather like it, or, where it came from just below the blubber, so shot through with fat that it was pinkish, more tender and with an almost creamy richness. We soon got ourselves into a deplorable state – hands and chins glistening with fat and no one caring what a show they made of themselves. A gluttonous hush settled on the colony as every mouth was filled. The sound of voices rose again slowly as one by one we could eat no more. Snores came from bloated, unbuttoned forms asleep under leaves. Chins were wiped on sleeves and hands on breeches. Brandy aided the travails of digestion as cards were dealt and pipes lit and problems forgotten. Music was even heard again. A fiddler struck up, slowly at first but then a jig, which provoked an attempt at dancing that soon fell apart in drunken hilarity. At the mid-point of the evening Dr Munro relented from his self-imposed quarantine for a few hours and joined the main body of the colony. He brought with him something he was very proud of – William McMaster, one-time joiner of Arbroath and fellow Caledonian. This man, although already known by one and all, was given an extravagant introduction to us. Everyone listened with the greatest attention and looked on as if witnessing something truly amazing. I noticed his wasted frame and alarming pallor, clearly yellowish even by lamplight. And yet I also noticed that he was on his own two feet and that the beer Munro had procured for him was held in a steady hand. Here was the first man to have survived the yellow fever. He was welcomed warmly by friends who had never thought to see him again and made much of all evening by men with a keen sense of personal interest in this victory over death. Someone suggested that the day be set down as Caledonia's second holiday and commemorated every year as Salvation Day. There was universal approval.

Dawn confronted us with the remaining bulk of the whale. Sinclair said there were many more barrels of oil to be had from it and the meat would preserve if dry salted. Mr Paterson, however, anxious to make use of the new strength the whale-meat had given his men, would not hear of them doing any more work on it. He had them ferried across the bay to start on the road particularly early to ensure that they would not get caught up in any distractions. As the gangs waited for boats to return from the other side, they stood right by the carcass of the whale, but refused to see it. The gentlemen volunteers insisted on their right to attend to their own allocations of land and argued that if they neglected to take advantage of the only good planting weather since our arrival we would all starve in the long run, whale or no whale. The score of Drummond's men who had come the night before to eat their fill (neither Drummond nor Jardine had been amongst them), had returned to Ditchville and no one was willing to run a fool's errand to ask them for help. The crew of the *Dolphin* said they had never signed on as fishermen and in any case it would be better to go out and catch another one, such an activity being more to their taste. By ten o'clock the carcass was black with blowflies. Sinclair suggested that he and two other men would take off the remaining blubber and boil it down for two-thirds of the proceeds whenever it was sold. At the time Captain Malloch was president of the councillors by rotation. As this position has never become a reality, despite being much discussed in our constitution, he was embarrassed by actually having a question put to him. He didn't know if it would be a good idea, and as Paterson was across the bay supervising his road, Drummond had not set foot in New Edinburgh for some weeks and Captain Galt had not expressed an opinion on anything in a similar period, he was at a loss as to how he might shift his responsibilities on to the council as a whole. Captain Jolly went ashore about noon, hoping to find Mr Paterson in the Meeting House and ready for a game and a glass of something. Privately, he thought it an excellent idea, but was quite against any arrangements being made on his say-so. By mid-afternoon the whale was already so foul that a decision was no longer necessary.

Such was the general shame felt at this turn of events that the whale remained invisible for the next three days. By the middle of the fourth day, the battle between the colony's refusal to acknowledge the existence of this monstrous corpse and the overwhelming power of its stench was finally lost. After an unspoken agreement between all parties that no one was to blame, it was accepted that something would have to be done about it. It was agreed that cremation was the solution and ten men were detailed to spend a day collecting the driest wood they could find. This was piled around and over the whale, the men wearing moistened cloths tied over the nose and mouth and rousing with their every movement clouds of flies so dense that it seemed already to be smouldering. A barrel of oil was added to the pyre and the whole burned furiously, quickly clearing the air and leaving a much reduced, but still whale-shaped pile of ash. We averted our eyes from this for another three days until the reek of decay arose from it once again along with another and yet more numerous generation of flies. It was clear that a great amount of unconsumed flesh remained under the black crust. It was decided this time to roll the whale into the water (the foulest work I have ever seen – merely looking on turned my stomach), tie a rope around what remained of the tail and row out to sea with it. This plan succeeded only as far as the middle of the bay where the carcass disintegrated and slipped the rope. We have had no direct evidence of it since but sometimes, when the wind changes, a faint scent of it still wafts over us as if one of the pieces has come to shore nearby.

Notwithstanding this sorry business, our fortunes continued to enjoy a general improvement. The rain held off save for mild showers at night such as we would have wished for ideally. Crops were put in that for once were neither pelted into the ground by volleys of rain, nor rotted by the liquid mud out of which they struggled to grow. Oats and barley sprouted with an incredible speed, the first shoots breaking the soil only three days after being sown, vindicating all our hopes about the richness of the land and what we might do with it if only the elements would relent. A small plot of tobacco leaped out of the ground with the same vigour. The process of cleaning and patching after the long assault continued and we were once again able to look at ourselves without contempt.

One effort in which I had a particular interest was not successful; namely the cultivation of pineapples. Several of these were transplanted from glades in the forest where they occur naturally. They prospered for a while but with every plant, as the fruit began to swell, something fatal intervened causing it to corrupt and soften from within then collapse entirely to nothing but a patch of brown slime. Mr Spense questioned one of the Indians on the matter, hoping to find some simple error we could put right. The gentleman saw at once where we had gone wrong and told us that if we went to the pineapple instead of making the pineapple come to us, all would be well. Mr Spense patiently explained the benefits of agriculture hoping, perhaps, to be the source of a great revolution in the lives of these simple people. The old man replied that it was always interesting to hear of other tribes. I remained determined to find some way of exploiting this plant and had every confidence of success.

Those days of hope were presided over by McMaster. A chair was put outside the infirmary for him in which he could take the sun in the early mornings and the evenings when it was not too hot. He wandered through New Edinburgh breathless and unsteady, but nevertheless a miraculous token of all our hopes. Everyone had time for a word with him, had tobacco for his pipe or spare raisins and brandy to fortify him. Every day we were sure he was a little stronger, the pallor of his skin less deathly. Even so, whenever someone spoke with him they examined him closely for the small signs they hoped not to find. When he was in his chair or sitting by the shore or eating with the laborious, zestless appetite of the sick, men nearby would stop what they were doing to glance at him. If he coughed, everyone who heard it would shudder, say a prayer and pretend they hadn't noticed. His life was a violation of the rules of this place, still too new and good to trust in.

I was on shore one evening, confirming the quantities of some stores brought in from the *St Andrew*, when I noticed McMaster hunched on the rock that had become his habitual seat. Having just arrived, I saw nothing strange in it – even a hushed conversation in the middle of the square and anxious stares in his direction did not seem unusual. I finished my business in twenty minutes or so and was walking back towards the shore, intending to get a boat for the *Rising Sun*, when a colonist I was passing spoke out. 'That's three hours now.'

'What's that?' I asked.

He nodded towards McMaster on his rock. A cold lurch of fear went through me, but then I gathered myself and dismissed it all, arguing that the chances of a still man being dead rather than resting or asleep were surely small. I saw that no one was prepared to go near him and decided that I should be the one to go down and give him a shake to reassure the onlookers and to show that I was a bolder fellow than themselves. And yet when it came to the moment of putting this confident thought into action, I found myself prey to the same anxieties and was as unwilling as the rest to let myself become the discoverer of the grim fact which, without any further evidence, had turned in my mind from most improbable to almost certain. Someone rang the bell at the infirmary pale. Dr Munro's assistant came out and had the situation explained to him. He reappeared after taking Munro's instructions and started to saunter down towards the shore. Only when he got within a few yards of McMaster did his arrogance abandon him. He craned forward cautiously, trying to see the man's face without standing full in front of him. He crept forward, said something we could just hear. Everyone watched his hand come to rest on that motionless shoulder and then the shocked recoil, the panicked run back to the infirmary. Munro came out and hurried to McMaster as if it still might not be true, as if there still might be something he could do. But he carried a blanket with him nonetheless, and it was under its decent concealment that he and the boy carried the corpse up from the shore and into the infirmary.

For McMaster, the custom of burial on land was restored. Not since we buried Mackay had there been such a crowd. Even the men from Ditchville were there, Colonel Drummond and Captain Jardine included. We waited while the pinnace from the *Rising Sun* rowed the length of the bay and was moored by the kirk. Mr Cunningham took his place by the graveside and murmured Captain Galt's apologies to Reverend Borland. We listened dejectedly as Borland pronounced the familiar words. As clods of earth struck the thin boards of McMaster's coffin, the first warm, heavy splashes of rain started to fall.

Since that day our affairs have moved with a terrible speed. The rain that fell on the funeral did not at first cause any alarm. It lasted only an hour and was followed by a sunny, humid afternoon. It was declared to be just what the new crops needed. We had more of the same the next morning, but again there seemed to be nothing sinister in it. That night I was awoken on board the *Rising Sun* by a familiar sound – the sharp hiss, like air being blown across a blade, that indicated heavy rain falling on to a still sea. I strained my ears to gauge how serious it was and drifted back into sleep with a confident prayer that the morning would be better. So it proved – dry, with dense mists boiling up from what had fallen the night before. By midday the whole colony was looking skyward. The clouds were familiar, ominous. Optimists prayed, pessimists held their tongues. At four o'clock – if I may use such a term here – the heaviness of the clouds eclipsed three-quarters of the sun's light. With a distant, digestive rumble the deluge began. I was by the shore when it happened and I watched the rocks there, dried to paleness by the heat, darken in circles the size of crowns as the huge drops slapped down. I felt them pelt my head and shoulders, each impact distinguishable until it became a general drenching. The ground blackened in a minute. Paths became gutters with a swift flow of water towards the shore. I got in the boat and hunched on the thwart, staring down at my feet. The rain ran down my back, dripped from my ears, nose and chin and, by the time we bumped into the side of the *Sun*, had risen to the top of my ankles.

Since that day we have been the victims of an ever more extreme assault. The crops did not have time to rot. They were either submerged entirely or flushed away by streams that had not existed a day before. Many of the huts have been undermined. Some have disintegrated, the flotsam drifting shoreward on a steady stream of mud. Trees seem to move from one day to the next, floating in mud. We have even had gusts of hail that dent the boiling pans and ring the infirmary bell. Some men were caught out and had to crouch with their shovels over their heads like shields, and even so one was knocked senseless. The sea has turned brown, and a mile out the water is still fresh enough to drink. The land is being beaten down and dissolved and I wonder, if it goes on much longer, whether it will not achieve our work for us and wash away the whole of the isthmus.

All our difficulties, from which we had such a brief respite, returned and multiplied. We have had to resort to burial at sea once again and it has become an honourable last act for a man to make his way into the forest before dying to spare his fellows the labour of disposing of his remains. Desertion no longer has any meaning – men are seen one day and not the next without it giving rise to any question. Lulls in the rain give way to a rising smell of death, which oozes in on us from all sides. We no longer know how many of us are left. The bloody flux and the black vomit have redoubled their efforts against us. New ways to death have joined them with so little apparent cause or form that Dr Munro cannot even think of how to oppose them. The slightest breach of the skin is enough to admit a violent fever that can carry a man off in two days. One man was found without the slightest mark, lying on his back, eyes open and mouth too, full up to the teeth with rainwater. For want of any better explanation it is assumed that he was drowned by the rain. I believe it myself and if this account should survive and ever be read I ask you not to doubt it, nor to think that you understand anything I have said about rain. What constantly beats down on us here is something quite different and unique. It demands a new word that our temperate language has never had need of.

The moral effects of this flood have not been slow to appear. Many have abandoned their belief in mere misfortune and have decided instead that there must be a guilty party. Several of the gentlemen volunteers who relieved their boredom towards the end of the voyage by making accusations against me have survived – a sure sign of the indiscriminate nature of our afflictions. After two days of particularly intolerable downpour, I received a request from one of them for two reams of paper and a pint of printer's ink. The next day Mr Shipp knocked on my cabin door.

'You're in the papers, young master.'

He handed me a sheet of their work wherein I read an odious diatribe against Dr Munro, which ended with some charges against myself as his 'ally and associate'. That Caledonia is without laudanum became known as soon as the effects of the last drop wore off. They have hung their case on this fact, returning to their imaginings about my behaviour in Madeira and insinuating that I sold some of our supply there. The rest of it has been drunk by Munro while listening to the screams of his patients. He is, although I wonder how this was not noticed before, hopelessly addicted to it. I knew already that my position rankles with them, but why they should attack Munro was a mystery to me until I went to speak with him that afternoon. The motive proved to be nothing more than the scavenger's instinctive draw to what is already wounded.

I ignored the bell and came upon him unannounced, hunched over the two chests he uses as a table. In a dish by the lamp there was something bloody and pitted. He waved a fly from it and returned to his writing. He looked round as I coughed.

'Roderick! I'm sorry, I was . . .' He paused and looked away from me as if trying to recall something that had just escaped him. 'I was concentrating on something. It's not important.'

He apologized again, and I was concerned that he was not himself. His hand trembled as he gathered up the sheets he had been writing and turned them face down. He wiped the perspiration from his face. I reassured him, not entirely truthfully, that I was well and made my own apologies for disturbing him.

'Nonsense! Take a seat. Oh, excuse me . . .' He remembered the thing in the dish and covered it with a cloth in a gesture of unaffected respect. He began to fill a glass with brandy and nodded at another already on the chest. 'Only brandy, I'm afraid. As you may know, I've already drunk all the laudanum.'

'Ah. You've read it, then?'

'Oh, yes. Just a piece of nonsense, of course. It's one of the things that happens in situations like this. I've seen it before.'

'Of course,' I agreed. 'I just came to say that . . . Well, obviously I don't believe a word of it. It hardly needs saying, it's just that . . . well . . .' I trailed off in confusion.

He handed me the glass he had just filled and picked up his own. 'As you say, no need. I always had you down as a sensible fellow. Let's take our medicine.'

We drank and consoled each other in silence. It occurred to me that apart from Mr Shipp, Munro is the only person in the colony whom I trust and to whom I might speak. The unmentionable idea began to crystallize in my mind and I became nervous as I contemplated expressing it. Dr Munro was agitated too, for his own reasons.

'You didn't ask me what I thought you would,' he said, with an odd noise like a sort of laugh. He took the broadside from his pocket and unfolded it. 'Where is it? Yes, there – "knowing that he can't expect much of a welcome at home".'

I protested that I had not come to ask him any questions, but he would not be interrupted and went on quickly, 'You don't believe that either? Well, perhaps you should. You knew I had served in the English navy? I was an impetuous fellow then. It happened in Portsmouth – I heard my captain expressing some views I didn't care for about a lady I knew. He was disinclined to apologize and I had drunk too much wine. I drew my sword. He thought I should be hanged for it and so did the Court of Admiralty. As far as I know that's still their intention.'

I toasted him with the rest of my brandy and declared I was sorry he hadn't run his captain through. He thanked me and laughed, but was immediately sombre again. 'Perhaps I could do something in Jamaica . . .'

'Or New York?' I suggested, trying to sound bright.

He took up the paper he had been writing on when I came in.

'These are intended for an old friend of mine in London. We studied together. He's a fashionable doctor now and a fellow of the Royal Society. He made the right decisions.'

He folded one of the sheets and tore a strip off it. He started to write on it, continuing to talk as he did so. 'Descriptions of the conditions I've seen here, a list of the things I've collected. I don't expect it will be necessary but . . .' He suddenly came to a halt and stared at what he had written. He thrust it towards me. 'If I can't manage it, perhaps you'll see that it gets to him.'

I hesitated, reluctant to accept the implications. The paper quivered in Munro's hand as he stretched forward another inch. I took it, glancing briefly at an address in the Strand before folding it and saying casually that I would be happy to do it, but was sure that I would not have to. It was all the licence I needed to put my own question. 'You think Caledonia will be abandoned?'

He shrugged. 'All it needs is for someone to say so. It's what we're all thinking, isn't it?'

These were the words I turned over in my mind as I stood outside the infirmary again, tucking the address of Munro's friend into my waistcoat pocket and surveying the unutterably dreary scene before me. I seemed to feel that paper pressing against my chest – Strand, London! Without any knowledge of the place I felt sure that it was lined with coffee-houses and busy with carriages and newspaper-boys. I could buy my lunch there – pheasant with onions and apricots – drink a glass of claret, read about the hangings and the price of wool, exchange intelligence with another merchant. As I gave way to these fancies, I tried to believe that at that very moment real men were doing exactly as I imagined. My reason told me it must be so, that nothing could be more ordinary. But no argument could convince me. It was too strange, inconceivable! A planter stumbled past me through the mud. He glared at me furiously for no reason I could think of. Is it true that even then we all wanted to leave, but stayed only because we could not admit it to each other? Perhaps that is what he was saying to himself – 'We'd have been gone from here already if it were not for the likes of you, Roderick Mackenzie.' For a brief and guilty moment, failure seemed like a blessing. My aversion to it was all that stood in the way of everything good and desirable. It smelt of coffee, roast beef and dry sheets. It smelt of Susanna. I desired it as avidly as the long-dying man desires his death. An instant later, I hated and feared it with the same intensity and committed my last strength to fighting it.

When Mr Shipp first handed that libellous sheet to me he, like Munro, was dismissive. He chose to call it 'madness' and suggested, as we all like to think in such circumstances, that it would do more harm to those who wote it. In the event it did no one either harm or good. I never heard a word on the charges it contained and never detected any change in anyone's attitude towards me. It was as if it had never been printed. This silence, however, was not the result of the natural discretion of our people but simply of the preoccupation of each chapter of our fractured society with its own enemies. The appearance of this first broadside proved such an inspiration that everyone was soon too busy composing their own attacks to spare a thought for what the gentlemen volunteers had said about me or Munro. I had soon dispensed half our stocks of paper and in the course of an account of our stores came across the printer who had made a workshop of an empty hold at the bottom of the *Caledonia*. Recriminations were stacked about him and he was still labouring furiously over his tiny press. He wiped his forehead with the back of an ink-blackened hand and greeted me amiably. 'Well, then, Mr Mackenzie, you see what those gentlemen friends of yours have started?'

I picked up one of the sheets from a short stack. It carried a single long paragraph in Gaelic. 'What's this?'

He grimaced. 'How should I know? One of them dictated it to me letter by letter. Took best part of last night. There's only one word in there I know. If you'll excuse me . . .'

He returned his attention to his press, kneading ink into the plate with a huge leather pad. 'If I'd been as busy as this at home I'd never have left.'

For the next few days, New Edinburgh was littered with charge and counter-charge. The road-builders blamed the ditch-diggers for their poor progress. The latter explained that the very opposite was the case – the fortifications were incomplete only because the road-builders would not spare any labour from their own preposterous task. The stealing of tools and the hanging of Caldwell were raised again and refreshed the bitterness of both sides. The gentlemen volunteers regretted the ignorance and roughness of the planters, while the planters, with no lack of eloquence, expressed the view that the gentlemen volunteers, for all the precious little they could turn their hands to, would have been better left behind in the drawing rooms of Edinburgh. One sheet, signed 'Centurion', blamed all our misfortunes on the lack of a purely military government for the colony. Even Reverend Borland joined the fray. He wondered that any from such a company of blasphemers and self-intoxicators had been permitted to live so long. He called for reflection on God's infinite mercy. The sheet of Gaelic remains a mystery. The word 'Drummond' appears three times, but every speaker of the language has been sworn to an unbreakable covenant not to reveal its meaning. The best I could obtain from one of them was a slight and very superior smile and the prediction, 'You'll see.'

These papers fluttered about New Edinburgh, each one disregarded except by the faction who wrote it. Within an hour of their passionate distribution they lay pelted and trodden into the mud, melting into nothingness as quickly as the hailstones. Some groups collected their opponents' broadsides and placed them in the latrines where they disappeared almost as quickly. As for Carlaw, the printer, the Fates waited only for him to perform his allotted function. He lived to print the document Captain Green brought us, but in doing so caught his hand in the press. The small wound was quickly gangrenous. Fever followed and he died three days later, which was yesterday. Burial at sea.

In those three or four days of the broadsides we were close to surrender and I – the hand hesitates, but why not say it now? – I half hoped it would come. The common and unspoken thought that Munro had guessed at spread and strengthened. Men looked longingly at the ships. They thought how easy it would be. They asked themselves if they did not deserve to survive. Mr Paterson caught the mood early and understood its implications. He knew, I believe, that the unspoken was on the point of becoming the spoken. He knew that if that happened there would be nothing anyone could do. He called the council. Captains Jolly and Malloch came because they had no reason not to, but the colony only started to take notice when Drummond came in, showing himself for the first time since McMaster's funeral. Like Paterson, he too understood that the only stage on which his ambitions might be played out was in danger of collapsing beneath him. Drummond and Paterson became allies.

Hours passed. At first Captain Galt remained on the *Rising Sun*, notes being carried to and fro. When at last he arrived in person, the inexpressible hope that they were discussing withdrawal grew. We awaited the announcement, tense and guilty. When Mr Paterson spoke from the Meeting House steps, his face pale and drawn, and announced that the council proposed to overcome all our present difficulties by mounting a trading expedition to Jamaica there was nothing but silence. I thought he was about to speak again, but he seemed confused, unnerved. His hand twitched before being steadied behind his back. He spoke briefly to Drummond and went back into the Meeting House.

Had it not been for Drummond we might, even then, have made the decision to come away. There was a sullen rebelliousness in that silence, a bold unwillingness to call the matter settled that might easily have carried the day if someone had spoken up. It was enough to drive Paterson from the field, but Drummond was another matter entirely. I recognized the expression I had last seen in Madeira – a certain set of the jaw and a smile, just visible under the edges of his discipline, such was his pleasure at knowing himself the master of the situation. I can believe all too easily that he had been waiting for just such a moment, that he had seen it coming in every detail. With relish he set about making us forget that there had ever been the slightest possibility of withdrawal and in doing so he became, at last, the ruler of Caledonia. A constant stream of orders occupied the colony for the next three days. These had the aim, firstly, of preparing and provisioning the *St Andrew* for the voyage to Jamaica and, secondly, of achieving this task with the greatest confusion, repetition and laboriousness possible so that every man's hands and mind were fully taken up with an enterprise that soon seemed very much larger than it was. As the recipient of many of these orders and, on account of my position, the supervisor of the loading, I looked on with cold admiration as bales of cloth and boxes of shoes were brought to the *St Andrew* by one gang, taken away again by another and returned by a third, all convinced of their contribution to the common cause. In these three days I encountered Drummond directly only once. I was leaving one of the holds of the *St Andrew* when I collided with someone. We simultaneously held up our lanterns and were about to ask each other to take more care in future when recognition stopped us short. He praised me brusquely for the efficiency with which I was handling the transfer and loading of the goods. Throughout the whole exchange he took great pleasure in treating me like one of his soldiers and made no attempt to conceal his satisfaction at having me at a disadvantage after our long antagonism. For all that, I received his instructions with indifference. Even his demand that I report to Captain Jardine failed to touch my pride.

I decided to cultivate the habit of taciturnity in all situations except the giving of orders. Very soon, I was as silent as Captain Galt himself. Though there is nothing extraordinary about the loading of a ship I experienced a growing sense of astonishment at everything I saw, however commonplace it might be. Everything became bizarre and strange and the effect of it became stranger still as I observed that I was the only one to suffer this new, distorting fever of the mind. I constantly expected a word or an expression, a confidential glance or press of the hand from a fellow sufferer, but it never came and I began to understand that in some new way I was alone.

Sometimes the effect took the form of an almost insane hilarity. The most unremarkable statement or action would strike me inexplicably as the finest witticism. I would burst out laughing and have to excuse myself and pretend my mind had been elsewhere. I found I had to concentrate on every word I spoke or heard, to calculate carefully before the slightest move. Conversations I overheard became more difficult to understand, as if they were more distant, or were being conducted in a language of which I had only an imperfect knowledge. My estrangement from the colony was accelerated by the very different changes that came over my fellows. I watched in disbelief as those who had teetered on the brink of mutiny and who had then dragged themselves so doubtfully to this new deliverance became so quickly convinced of its power to put an end to all our problems.

As the mood changed, Mr Paterson became more his old self. He spent much time bustling around the jetty, getting himself into the boats as they transhipped the goods and stationing himself on the decks of the *St Andrew* being genial and talkative at every opportunity. By the eve of the ship's departure he had brought about a general conviction that she carried ten thousand pounds of the most desirable cargoes, and that she would return with their full value in gold and silver within the month. How such desperate vendors as ourselves were to extract this bargain and who would live to receive its proceeds were scandalous considerations to be entertained by only the lowest scoundrel.

I was doing my work and Paterson his when we encountered each other on the main deck of the *St Andrew*.

'Well, then, Roderick, is this not more like it?'

He applied a handkerchief to his pale, perspiring face. I noticed how his eyes glittered and brimmed, as if always on the point of shedding a tear.

As the boatswain moved further away to attend to something, Mr Paterson squeezed my arm and adopted his confidential tone. 'It was a close-run thing, you know . . .' He looked round, ensuring that I was fully prepared for the importance of what he was about to tell me. 'Of course, this mustn't be known.'

I put on an acquiescent expression.

'Our colonel was all for making himself an admiral and going out against the nearest Spanish ship.'

He smiled to indicate the pitiful naïvety of Drummond's idea.

'Colonel Drummond has never been much of a one for buying and selling. He seems to think that we poor merchants exist only to provide the wherewithal for the armies of the world. I had to have a word with him about the way the world works these days.' He clasped his hands behind his back and turned to survey the ship. 'It was agreed that he could put ten of his redcoats on board when she goes. He was happy with that.'

Once again I was having difficulty in understanding my fellow men. I fixed my eyes on Paterson's profile but found no trace there of anything but the plainest sincerity. Memories collided in my mind and I became conscious for the first time of referring to some of them as my 'former' opinions of the great man.

His information explained one thing at least: it was only the danger of Caledonia becoming a base for buccaneers that got Galt out of his cabin, and I don't doubt that it was his presence in the Meeting House rather than any words from Mr Paterson that put an end to Drummond's plan. As for the soldiers that were to go aboard the *St Andrew*, there could be no doubt as to their true purpose. For all I know, it might have been Mr Paterson himself who asked for their presence. He turned his feverish smile back on me. 'It does the heart good, doesn't it? Everyone working together at last. We'll be all right now.'

I felt the jarring halt at the end of the tether.

'Do you think ten will be enough?' I asked. 'I hear Kingston is a pleasant town. It would be a shame if the *St Andrew* were not to come back.'

He could not have looked more surprised if I had struck him. He collected himself and spoke very slowly. 'I wouldn't say that, Mr Mackenzie. In fact, I would advise very strongly against saying that.'

Then, without any interim, there was another tone by which it was conveyed to me how remorseful I should feel for having caused him pain.

'I'm so sorry, Roderick, to have heard something like that from you. I was always sure that you were one of the most . . . well . . . never mind.'

He sighed and waved the thought away, unable to continue. I remained impassive and he made to take leave of me, saying as he went that he would take up no more of my time. Just before descending to the main deck, he stopped abruptly. I could see what was coming. I knew it already – the third Paterson in the space of a minute. How many are there? He advanced to within a few inches of me, finger raised, beating time to his words. His face creased with malice.

'I'd say you've been spending too much time with Dr Munro. It has been noted, I warn you. You're using up your credit, young man.'

We have not spoken since.

I retired to my cabin on the *Rising Sun* as soon as my duties permitted, omitting to attend Reverend Borland's blessing of the expedition. I swallowed three glasses of brandy and lay on my bed, trying to empty myself of all thought. I swallowed three more until the hook above my head swam to and fro. I began to drowse, but was plagued by items from the lading bills of the *St Andrew*. Their quantities and values chanted through my mind in a contemptuous caricature of my great days in the warehouses. They became meaningless – three yards of lamp-oil at eight guineas a month, fifty bushels of canvas at three farthings a pint. I found the effect curiously distressing to my clerkly nature. I sat up, opened this book, wrote a line, scratched it out. I became aware of something easing within me. There was something I was determined to resist, but could feel helplessly slipping away. I imagined a man in a city street, walking smartly along, pleased with himself, sure that he will win this time, congratulating himself in advance. And yet, even as he insists on his own rectitude, he feels it crumble with every step. At last, at the moment of truth, he looks over his shoulder as he always knew he would, and nips in through the red door he has not passed once in twenty years. Just so, I returned to the brothel of hope and spent myself there. Possibilities swelled into probabilities and probabilities blossomed into certainties all within a few minutes. Why could it not work out in the end? What was there to prevent the *St Andrew* selling her cargo in Jamaica, even if it was worth only a third of what Mr Paterson had pretended? Had the rain not moderated that day? It had already relented once and the season must change sometime. Was it not mere superstition to suppose that because yesterday had been a failure, tomorrow must be a failure too? Isn't despair contemptible as well as sinful? Finally, and more persuasive than all the others put together, was the thought of how outrageous it would be to surrender now after so much has been endured and when our eventual triumph was, assuredly, so close.

At five o'clock the next morning an approaching ship fired two guns. The noise woke the watch at Point Look-out and they signalled twice with muskets. I dreamed the first three of these blasts and heard the fourth as I was struggling drunkenly into my breeches. I blundered on to a pitch-black quarterdeck, the order already having been given to damp all lights. I heard Captain Galt's voice, and a hushed response from Mr Cunningham. After a few minutes, the general alarm raised at the prospect of an attack began to subside. I strained my eyes into the darkness and listened to every breath of the middling breeze to find some clue as to where the ship might be. Suddenly there was a light, then another beside it. I saw the lights climb up into the blackness and caught a momentary glimpse of sail. More lights appeared and within seconds there was the unmistakable constellation of the masts, spars and ropes of a large ship dangerously close to us. There was a shout from Galt and the few members of the crew on deck scrambled to show our lights, Galt and Cunningham unshuttering our quarterdeck storm-lanterns and the binnacle light themselves. From the direction of the invisible ship came a proficient series of orders and responses. All at once she loomed out at us and we were amazed to see that, although so close to the shore, she was running under full sail. She heeled away as sharply as she could, but it was too late for a collision to be avoided entirely. Her gunwales clashed with ours and there was a terrible screech as the timbers of the two vessels tore against each other. Several yards of our main-deck rail were ripped away. Spars clashed above and one of their crew, desperately trying to take in sail, was dislodged and fell into the sea whence he was recovered by ourselves without injury. As her sails strained above me, I could see a great red S. It was the *Worcester*.

By taking in sail with all possible speed and dropping anchor to drag herself to a halt, she just managed to avoid running on to the cliffs. Not content with one dangerous manoeuvre, Captain Green ordered boats to be put down without delay and had himself piloted past the sunken rock and into Caledonia Bay proper. He thus ensured that, when dawn rose, observers from the open sea would not be able to find the slightest trace of him.

It would have been preferable by far if we could have received them on the *Rising Sun*, which still retains some decency, but his anxiousness to enter the bay made that impracticable. Captain Green himself, the sailmaker and the one-time priest were therefore greeted on the shore by New Edinburgh where the full extent of our degradation impresses itself most horribly on all the senses. At first light a boat made off from the *Caledonia* where Mr Paterson once again spends his nights after having abandoned his long and determined tenancy of the Meeting House. It was summoned by our signal to collect Mr Cunningham, who was to attend on behalf of Captain Galt. I loitered with a well-prepared story about having work to do on shore, but was invited in any case by Mr Cunningham in a very friendly manner. As we waited for the *Caledonia's* pinnace, he enquired ordinarily enough after my health and then surprised me by saying that Captain Galt would be pleased. I could think of no tactful way of asking what he meant, but was sure from the deliberate manner of the exchange that it was no mere pleasantry. It was, I can see now, the first inkling of what Captain Galt had in mind. In the boat, Cunningham kindly sat beside Paterson while I sat behind. We had an awkward and silent journey in.

By the time the sun was fully up Drummond, Paterson, Cunningham, Reverend Borland and the other sea captains stood in a line as Green and his two crew-members rowed in. I stood nearby, disregarded, as is now my preference. The visitors shook hands and exchanged the usual words, but they could not conceal their wonder and pity at the state they found us in. They had the stern, fixed expressions of men exerting every effort not to give way to their natural reactions. Only this dignified and considerate impassiveness indicated their shock at the desolation before them. As the colony began to rouse itself, the piteous smallness of our number completed the story. The sailmaker made a play of tugging at his whiskers, but kept his hand by his mouth for the rest of the interview. I was convinced that his ear-ring was even bigger than before, and in the same vein I noticed Captain Green's waistcoat of brilliant new scarlet with silver buttons and patterns of silver thread about the hem. A gloomy silence began to stretch as we took in these details. Crivelli – the former Father Crivelli – handed a large purse to Green, who presented it in turn to Paterson. 'Proceeds from the sale of your goods,' he explained. 'Only three hundred and twelve, I'm afraid. We lied as well as we know how, but their origin was still suspected. We think we were seen leaving after our last visit.'

'They were worth four hundred,' said Paterson flatly.

Two or three men on our side shifted with embarrassment, but Green paid no attention to this rudeness. No doubt he could see how ill Paterson was and in any case, given our respective conditions, it was hard to see how any of us could have insulted him.

'We've been followed all the way from Curaçao. There are never any insignia, of course, but we're sure they're English. Frigates from Admiral Benbow's fleet most likely.' He nodded towards the mouth of the bay and smiled. 'They're out there now. Hence our unusual mode of arrival.'

He took the fateful paper from his waistcoat pocket and unfolded it. 'I pulled this off a noticeboard in Kingston. I don't know if you've seen it.'

There was something regretful, consoling even, in the slowness with which he handed it over. We were forewarned by that gesture. Mr Paterson read the short printed paragraph with the same disciplined absence of emotion as was being displayed by the men from the *Worcester*. He handed it along the line. It was read by each man with the same frigidity, as if all their honour depended on its absolute unimportance. Only Drummond allowed himself a weary smile. The paper was passed at last to Mr Cunningham. I stood a few yards further off but he turned to me anyway and held it out saying, 'You might as well.'

This is what I read:

To all Governors and Lieutenant Governors of His Majesty's Loyal Colonies, in His Majesty's Name and by command, they shall not presume on any pretence whatsoever to hold or permit to be held any correspondence with the Scots of the pretended Colony at Darien on the territory of His Majesty the King of Spain, nor to give them any assistance of arms, ammunition, provisions, or any other necessaries whatsoever. Neither shall they receive goods from them for money, nor allow their own goods to be transported in the ships of the said Scots, else they shall answer for contempt of His Majesty's command at their utmost peril.

James Vernon,
Secretary of State

This cracked and sun-bleached notice was further subscribed by the King's faithful servant Sir William Beeston, Governor of Jamaica, and dated three months prior to our receipt of it. The document was hastily printed and distributed on Drummond's orders – Mr Paterson, whose illness is now a matter of the most serious concern, has not to my knowledge spoken to anyone since reading it.

It was the plate for this document that trapped Carlaw's hand and started the fever that put an end to him this morning. In a matter of hours its words were committed to the memory of every one of us who could still read and think. Its phrases were confirmed in endlessly repeated exchanges until at last we believed that the words were as they appeared to be and meant what they appeared to mean. We now understand the lack of traffic, and the mute and flagless ships we have observed so often taking an interest in us from a distance. Some of us, seeing a mention of Spain, have even been persuaded to turn their startled minds back to an outside world which, long ago, even before we left Leith, had been excluded from our thoughts. A few, a very few, have had the honesty to ask themselves how it was not foreseen that such a simple checkmate would be played against us and our inconvenient ambitions. How did we come to believe that we alone could slip through the millstones of power unscathed? Others can think only of the date of the document and have given themselves up to fruitless reflection on the expense of so much hope and life on what could never have been. But the most general reaction, I would say, has been for men to hear in their souls the whole sorry story retold in the unmistakable tones of a scrawny, whining, gloating, English accent. For this sullen, intractable majority we have not been condemned by Mr Vernon's letter, but exonerated by it. It has met a need that has been growing for some time in the hidden, unconscionable depths of their minds – namely, to believe that whatever has happened and whatever remains to happen in this business is most certainly none of their fault. All at once, on reading that paper, they experienced the relief of knowing that even in the least of their misfortunes they are the victims of another's injustice.

It was Captain Green who broke the silence. Wanting to avoid the embarrassment of having to decline an invitation, he let us know that he would spend the rest of the day on his ship and that his affairs demanded an immediate departure, that night if possible. It was understood that disaster hung thickly about us and that he had no desire to share it. The company began to break up. Drummond's hand was peremptorily extended towards me and I gave him the paper we had all just read. Mr Paterson turned and began to walk up the squelching boards towards the Meeting House. Several colonists, as yet unaware of the precise nature of our situation, regarded him casually as he went by. As Mr Cunningham went forward to speak with Captain Green, I noticed Dr Munro approaching us from the direction of the infirmary, untying and folding his apron. He came over to me and as I was answering his questions, I tried to hear what Cunningham was saying to Green. I had to make what I could of the terms 'Galt', 'seamanship' and 'congratulations'. Green and the sailmaker had already clambered into their boat when Munro took Crivelli by the arm and said something inaudible to him. Crivelli nodded. I did not learn the subject of this exchange until later, after a painless silence had been restored to the infirmary. The *Worcester*'s boat had returned immediately to deliver two pints of laudanum and a note from Green regretting it could not be more.

There was, then, to be no more of this contemptible buying and selling. Drummond was quick to celebrate by making news-boys out of his men and distributing copies of the embargo by noon that day. From what I hear, these messengers were well schooled in how to put a useful gloss on this hopeless news. It was a declaration of war by Spain and England. The law allowed reprisals, and justice demanded them. It was time for all men of true heart to defend their own. Reactions were noted and names communicated. Lists were drawn up – those for and (for what purpose?) those against. By the end of the afternoon a hundred of our slender remains gathered by the shore to accept the colonel's hospitality and to burn paper. They cheered bravely in the direction of the *St Andrew*, their chosen instrument of revenge.

These details I gathered from conversation. I spent the day occupied by my own role in Drummond's plan. The labour of the previous days was now reversed. All the trade goods that had been added to the *St Andrew*'s holds were removed. Even what she had carried from Leith was cleared out and reassigned to other ships. Then the traffic turned and a stream of boats came to her with muskets and pistols, cutlasses, round- and grape-shot, musket-shot, ingots of lead and a smelter for them, moulds, flints and keg after keg of powder. A platoon was sent to the battery and another to Fort St Andrew to take two guns from each to make up her complement. They rubbed the rust from the guns and rowed them out one at a time, hauling them over the side with a great cheer as they rumbled down the plank and thudded on to the deck. By nightfall the *St Andrew* was a warship.

None of this was done with authority. A good cause for objection perhaps, except that there is no authority now. No one will say a word against Drummond and I have had too much of futility already to be the first to step out of line. Throughout the day, I followed his and Captain Jardine's instructions without question. I made it harder than it needed to be, checked everything twice and did what others could have done more easily themselves. I sought the mindlessness of exhaustion and thought only of the perfect sleep it promised.

When I climbed aboard the *Rising Sun* that night, I stopped when I heard voices. I recognized Captain Galt's straight away and then was surprised to hear Green's voice. Clearly, the *Worcester* was still with us and I had been too tired to notice as I had been rowed past her in the darkness. I crossed to the other side of the quarterdeck where I could pretend to be taking the air by the rail, but could also hear more clearly. The voices became confidential and I in turn became more ashamed at my eavesdropping and looked about to check that I was not observed. From within, I could hear a bottle chiming on glasses and then a sudden explosion of laughter that made me jump. The voices were abruptly cut off, as if their owners had just remembered they were attending a funeral. Low conversation re-established itself. There were long pauses and I heard the rhythm of certain phrases repeated and emphasized. Everything indicated some serious business, but without applying my ear directly to the door, which I was not even willing to contemplate, it was impossible to divine its substance. I heard mention of the Chile coast and Peru and then Captain Green was declaiming loudly, as when he gave us his opinions on gold – 'It's absolutely true! Not once was I asked who I was or where I was from, only what I wanted to buy or had to sell. And then, further north . . .'

Someone hushed him. I was becoming angry with myself at my ungentlemanly behaviour and was already moving away when I was alerted by a squeak from the cabin door-handle. I tiptoed across the deck as fast as a bilge rat and descended a few steps before turning. By the time the door was open and Galt, Green, Cunningham and the one-time Father Crivelli were coming out, I was able to make a convincing show of having just arrived on deck.

A glance in my direction acknowledged my presence. Something unspoken passed between the four men and they began to take leave of each other. Captain Galt put his hand on Mr Cunningham's arm and moved him forward, indicating that he should see his guests off the ship. I was about to apologize for the inopportuneness of my arrival, but was stopped by Galt with a greeting of such uncharacteristic warmth that I didn't know what to make of it. He asked how I was and regretted that we had not seen more of each other over the past few weeks. I was aware that I was in a situation I did not understand, but was too exhausted to marshal my thoughts as to what it might be. I blundered at once when I tried to explain my late return to the ship and said that I had spent all day provisioning the *St Andrew* for war.

'Ah, yes,' he said slowly. 'Yes, of course.'

I cursed myself and offered an excuse that only sank me deeper into the mire. 'On Colonel Drummond's orders. There don't seem to be any others.'

I began to feel faint with tiredness and tried to work out whether or not I had just insulted Captain Galt. I remembered how, from my first day on board, I had feared him and how I had sworn to myself that I would find a way of earning his high regard. I desperately wanted the conversation to continue, but was concerned that I would say something that would make matters worse and could not stop my thoughts from wandering in the direction of my bed.

'I mean . . . What I meant to say was . . .'

Galt held up his hand. 'A moment, please.'

He went into his cabin and returned a moment later. 'I was right. There's just enough left. Would you care for it? Perhaps it will restore you.' He held out a glass of wine. 'It's something I've been keeping back. There's a story behind it that doesn't matter now.'

I held the glass reverently, catching a faint, startling suggestion of its contents before bringing it closer. The odours of sweat, hot mouldering canvas, tar, death and, from my fingers, the relics of ink, gunpowder and the just discernible tang of lead were all eradicated in a moment and replaced by the scent of the wine. I took a drop into my mouth and it filled my mind. For a few pointless moments I chased after its elements, trying to separate and find names for them that most certainly do not exist.

'Weren't you in the trade?'

He was leaning on the rail now, facing out to sea. To my tiredness was added the flooding intoxication of the wine and a dizzying, dislocated sense of strangeness.

'Very briefly,' I answered, 'and without distinction.'

'I would like your opinion.'

My thoughts were unexpectedly turned back to Colquhoun. I smiled. 'It's like nothing I've ever known.'

'Precisely,' said Galt, turning and looking at me with a disconcerting intensity. He began to pace the deck and develop his thoughts aloud as if I might listen to them or not as I pleased. 'It surprised me. One gets used to being disappointed. Adjustments are made. But then, it may be many years later, those adjustments are contradicted, perhaps in a very trivial way, it doesn't matter. Quite simply, a promise is kept and one is surprised, reawakened almost. Perhaps you have felt that yourself?'

The intimacy of the question took me aback and I was still too baffled to find a timely answer.

'Perhaps not. Or not yet.'

I took more wine, lingering with my nose in the glass to avoid his stare.

'It's not as good now, am I right?'

'No,' I confirmed.

'Perfection is momentary, unrepeatable.'

This thought threw up in my mind only an image of Susanna, lying asleep on her bed as I sidled out of her room for the last time.

Captain Galt returned to lean on the rail. A clatter of an oar and an angry curse from over the side indicated that the *Worcester*'s boat had still not pushed off. He held out a palm to check the absence of rain. 'Small mercies.'

I mumbled my agreement and watched in fuddled incomprehension as he took off his jacket and hung it over the rail, rolled up the sleeves of his shirt and started to fill his pipe. There he stood, as if there were no one on that deck but captains.

'I don't suppose this has been what any of us expected.'

'No,' I said.

'I don't suppose it ever could have been.'

'No.'

Moths batted against the lamps. Their wings against horn and glass were the only sound.

'Do you think much about loyalty, Mr Mackenzie?'

Silently, I returned his stare.

'It has been troubling me. It's a sort of promise, is it not? Sometimes spoken, sometimes understood. Should men make promises? Some say not. They say that only the gods can make a promise and know they will keep it. Men are too weak and too blind. They are faithless by nature. They either intend not to keep it, or if they do intend to keep it they are thereby delivered into the hands of those less faithful than themselves. No man ever lived who was not prepared to break a promise without a second thought. All that is needed is a good enough reason. Promises are a commodity – they are bought and sold, they have their price. One is always released by a higher bid. Shocking? I suppose it is, especially for those who cannot conceive of the circumstances in which they, too, would happily betray. Do you not think that must be the case, Mr Mackenzie? Not to know the length of one's tether, just when and how it would snap – in such a blessed state one could think oneself an honest fellow.'

I finished the wine and remember only being aware of how much it was confusing my exhausted senses, and of how little I cared.

'I'm sorry,' I said dully, 'I don't understand.'

'Well, then,' he smiled, 'perhaps I'm not such a philosopher after all. Men always find reasons for their betrayals, good or bad.'

He paused – to make a decision, I thought.

'And you?' he asked.

A minute of silence passed.

'I'm sorry. I was trying to make it easier. I can see that I haven't.'

'I don't know,' I said.

'There's another way of saying all this.'

A ripple of cold crept over my skin as I listened to him.

'I can't stop Drummond now. You know that? As you said, Mr Mackenzie, there were no other orders. The illusion by which one man holds sway over others depends on their consent. There is never really any compulsion. How could there be?'

He relit the taper and applied it once again to his pipe.

'No doubt you experienced that for yourself today when you did what you were told?'

I flinched.

'If I thought I could stop him it would be different, but I can't. I've seen it before, how a man loses command and how pointless it is to try to turn it back. You can't put the illusion together again. It's Drummond's colony now and I never made him any promises.'

The *Worcester*'s boat bumped our hull again and I heard Mr Cunningham clear his throat.

'And you?'

At last it had come, and I failed as I had always known I would.

'I don't know,' I repeated. 'I'm sorry. I'm so very tired.'

'Of course,' said Captain Galt, 'forgive me.'

He climbed quickly down to the main deck. In the gloom I could just see him swinging his leg over the rail before descending to the waiting boat without a backward glance. I heard Cunningham's question – 'No?'

And Galt's reply: 'No.'

The boat pushed off and I listened to the diminishing sound of its oars. Perhaps half an hour passed before I was able to understand that he was not coming back. I stood in the light from his cabin and turned to stare blankly into it, just grasping the candles on the table and the empty glasses. I stared at his jacket hanging over the rail. I picked it up and took it to my own cabin. I hid it in the bottom of my chest and went to sleep.

*

THE NEXT DAY was a Sunday. I left New Edinburgh early, determined not to be caught up in another day's activity on behalf of Colonel Drummond. If challenged, I had decided that a sudden conversion to sabbatarian principles would be my excuse. I took my breakfast with me in a wallet and did not stop or even think until I reached that high rock which I had found in the first days after our arrival. There I sat, absorbing its stored warmth, recalling the lizards that had so delighted me on my first visit. I struggled to swallow some damp biscuit, raisins, brandy and water. I looked down on the few meaningless brown scars amongst the trees, which are all that we have achieved since coming here. Fires smouldered in the wetness and clouded the windless air. Sulphur and filth were detectable even at that height and were joined from time to time by the scent of rotting whale-meat.

As the morning wore on I became aware of another source of smoke to my left. I considered the possibility of a new Indian village, but there seemed to be only a single fire and I thought it unlikely, in any case, that they would establish themselves so close to us. From below I could hear the Reverend Borland ringing his handbell outside his church. As its tiny sound eased away, I began to hear the steady chip, chip, chip of the machete's bite. It came from near the source of the spreading smoke on my left. The rhythm broke and restarted with an unmistakable grunt, which confirmed that this was where Oswald had chosen to make his stand. His absence had been noted a week before and many rumours have been surrounding his fate. No one supposed that he had died under some bush, and as tools and food disappeared at the same time, Drummond briefly intended pursuing him before he was distracted by higher stakes.

I fell asleep to that sound and woke several hours later, around noon, to the same slow, inexhaustible chip, chip, chip. Tiny shouts drifted up to me followed by the ragged crackle of musket fire. All I could see of the *St Andrew* was her top masts standing over the peninsula, but by the puffs of smoke that lifted gently into view after every volley, I knew that Drummond had already taken his volunteers on board and was making soldiers of them. I looked also at the spot at which the *Worcester* had been anchored until the night before. I looked to the mouth of the bay and could just make out the slight and sinister disturbance of the water around the sunken rock, past which Green must have guided his ship in the darkness. I heard Captain Galt's words again, in Mr Cunningham's voice, 'Congratulations on your seamanship.' These sights and sounds coiled round each other in my mind and forced me out of the vacancy I had sheltered in all day. I began to feel that almost physical discomfort which attends on the hopeless worrying away at an insoluble puzzle. I lay flat on the rock and gazed up at the clouds. Mild rain-showers drifted over me, spotting the rock with darkness and causing it to steam gently. My puzzle followed me into sleep.

It was late afternoon when I woke again. Oswald's machete ticked like a clock. An odd coldness troubled my stomach, as if I had swallowed ice. My hands trembled. I took a mouthful of brandy and began to scramble down towards the bay. I pushed through the dense growth until I broke on to one of the paths. I was confident I knew where I was until I reached an unfamiliar fork and was uncertain of which way to go. I chose the steeper path, reasoning that this would return me more quickly to the shore. Once there, I found myself further round the bay than I had expected. I set off smartly, only to stop within a few yards when I came upon a large clearing that cut straight into the forest. I realized that this was the gap in the trees I could see from the New Edinburgh side of the bay. Here was the heart and soul of Mr Paterson's dream, here was the beginning of that fist with which he had wrung the neck of the Americas before the directors in Milne Square, here was the road to the Pacific.

Remarkably, I had never closely examined this most essential part of our project. At the moment of recognition I felt something like fear and my indisposition suddenly worsened. I would have preferred to walk by, but knew there was no point in pretending that I might come another day. Would I return (if that is my destiny), without even having looked at this central fact? My anxieties were altogether too ridiculous.

Even in the middle of the workings there were many plants breaking through the soil. At the edges, thick growth surged up almost obscuring the ditches that brimmed with earth-coloured water. I recalled the ruined house that had provided us with such dubious shelter the night before the attack on the Spanish, and experienced the same conviction that the forces of this place, which have refused to harbour us from the very first, are as intent as ever on the obliteration of every human effort. As I went further in, the banks of spoil on either side grew taller until I could no longer see over them. The road was not merely a clearing, but an ambitious earthwork, deeply cut into the terrain to ensure that the merchants of the new trans-isthmian highway would not be troubled by too severe a gradient.

I went on and turned a slight bend (an outcrop of rock was the cause of the diversion) to see where this fine beginning led. I quickly found solid rock under my feet and could read in it the whole of our brief history. For a few yards the ambition had been maintained. The hard rock had been cut away to the same gradient as before – this was to be no ordinary back-country road. I felt its pick-marked surface and understood why our holds had been emptied so quickly of every iron tool and why the stealing between Drummond's men and Paterson's had ended in death. Over the next few yards the compromises had started. The track became steeper, and narrower too. I stepped over a blunted pick, bright with fresh rust. Nearby lay a heavy chisel, hammered to less than half its original length, the blunt end spread flat and split like a flower. Everywhere the effects of fever on human muscles were palpable. A recent landslip had flooded tons of earth and gravel over half the way – two days' work, perhaps four now, undone in seconds. I scrambled over this and travelled the last few yards to press my hands against a ragged, eight-foot face of rock. The entire road is not more than ninety paces.

I walked into the centre of New Edinburgh an hour later. A new noticeboard made from fresh-cut timber had been put up during the day. A single sheet of paper was pinned to it. It was obvious that this was Drummond's work and I knew at once what the notice must be about. Two of Drummond's soldiers loitered nearby, scarred old confederates from his Flanders days and before. They glared at me as I approached with a look that said, 'Just in time, Mackenzie. Another hour and we would have been putting a notice about you up there.'

It had been carefully hand-written – Captain Galt and Mr Cunningham were declared traitors. They were said to have fled to the enemy in the knowledge that their conspiracy with the spy, Captain Green of the *Worcester*, was about to be exposed. I read every malicious, gloating word of it with the most perfect equanimity.

SEA AGAIN. How it tortures me! I am filled with vitriol and it burns me from within, first on one side and then the other with every roll. My eyes burn their lids when I close them. I spend my time either vomiting or trying to vomit. My belly feels full, though it is entirely empty and rejects even water. I have lain in my bed three days until this morning when I let a third of a pint of blood at stool. I know very well what this means and have defied Mr Shipp's every advice and warning to haul myself up to this table to see if I can at least complete one thing in the day or two left to me. In the event that I should be unable to say what little more remains to be said, the letter in the top of my chest should be opened. I will be very grateful if the instructions there are honoured, most especially those relating to this present volume.

The end was swift, though in other respects not out of character. Colonel Drummond left the stage a little earlier than the rest of us and it was his departure that set the scene for the final collapse. Without a doubt, the details are sensational, but only a fool could have been surprised by the murder itself. It was a disciplined revenge, and an artful one too. Masterly in its brutality, it was a homage to the man it destroyed. Above all, it was patient.

It is seven years since Drummond insisted on the letter of his orders in Glencoe, pressing on even when his superiors no longer saw the point. Out of obedience to these orders, it is said, he shot two McDonald children whimpering at his feet. The expected promotion did not come. Instead, there was the burden of that reputation that Mr Shipp could not fully bring himself to tell me of when we were first rowed out across the Forth towards the *Rising Sun*. It led into exile in Flanders and the prospect of a long, perhaps endless, search for rehabilitation. The outrage of the scrupulous and the Commissions of Inquiry kept him there for years. The second and marginally less deceitful of these commissions reported in the year of my arrival in Edinburgh. It was none of my concern – I didn't understand the conversations I overheard on the subject and could see no profit in making an effort to do so. The matter soon gave way to more exciting prospects. News of these no doubt reached Drummond from time to time as he plodded through his unrewarding foreign service. The Company presented itself to him (as to many others) as the perfect device for shedding an undesirable past. At the last moment he crept back and with the help of a certain Major Wariston, one of whose indebted acquaintances occasionally dined with one of the directors, Captain Drummond, who did in any case seem well suited for desperate ventures, was granted his second chance. Such is the story as I have been able to piece it together, omitting the many wilder claims. Whatever the truth, all that time and all these thousands of miles did not serve in the end to put a single extra day between Drummond and his fate.

The timing was perfect and (it is difficult to believe otherwise) perfectly deliberate. While in every other respect Caledonia was at its lowest point, Colonel Drummond approached his greatest heights and appeared to have no doubts at all about his ability to reverse our circumstances. The removal of Galt and Cunningham gave him everything he wanted. Mr Paterson was already too ill and disappointed to be able to exert any influence, and even if that had not been the case, the victorious Drummond would not have hesitated to brush him aside. Caledonia would now be a military venture as, in his view, it should always have been. To crown this triumph of survival and to take full advantage of Galt's absence, Drummond decided that his privateering should now be conducted from the *Rising Sun*. Everything that had been done for the *St Andrew* now had to be done again for the *Rising Sun* and I faced the miserable prospect of having to watch Drummond strut on the very spot from which Galt had commanded. At first I feared that I might be compelled to assist in this travesty, but the completeness of his control made that unnecessary. Of course, I knew that for a long time I had not been trusted, but now I was informed that I was no longer necessary. Sergeant Black came to my cabin and demanded my ledgers, informing me that henceforth my responsibilities were to be carried out by a more satisfactory appointee of Drummond's. I surrendered them without regret and offered up a prayer of thanks that in the excitement of victory this volume was overlooked.

Drummond's accession to the *Rising Sun* was his undoing. It seems clear now that the final result could never have been any different, but when he climbed up to the *Sun*'s quarterdeck and occupied Galt's cabin he fixed the date of his demise. From that point he could fall a very long way and that was precisely what they had been waiting for. Exactly how they did it remains a mystery. On his last night I was in my cabin, feverish and a little drunk admittedly, but quite capable of knowing what I heard. Drummond was in Galt's cabin and received Jardine at about ten o'clock. They spoke for about half an hour before he left. I lay in abject misery as I listened to their voices in place of the more accustomed tones of Captain Galt and Mr Cunningham. I recall nothing unusual after that, not a single sound.

There was some surprise the next morning when Drummond was not already at the centre of things, finding tasks for everyone who was still fit. After half an hour and the discovery, made by Jardine, that he was not in Galt's cabin, there was evident fear in the faces of his dependents and for the rest of us a lively, if disinterested curiosity. Interrogations yielded no clue. When someone stumbled in from Ditchville (by this stage neglected for the last ten days or so), white with shock and incoherent in his desperation to tell us what he had seen, everyone seemed to know what the message would be.

That he was dead was one thing, but the manner of it was quite another. The messenger had been unable to give any details, responding to every question only with the demand that we go and see for ourselves. Without being heard or seen, they had managed to remove Drummond from the *Rising Sun* and take him to the site of his abandoned fortifications. There we found his remains – his feet had been nailed to the top of a post so that his shoulders and head just touched the ground. His arms were stretched wide and his hands were fixed with tent spikes through each palm. His belly had been slit open from his groin to his sternum and his tripes had tumbled down over his chest and face. The throat had been cut through to the neck-bone. On either side the flesh had been carved off the lower ribs and rolled back, leaving a bloody comb of bone exposed. A man beside me used the word that was to be repeated many times.

'Aye,' he said, 'they've flensed him.'

I looked on this atrocity coldly, and when I consider it now, it has no more effect on me than an event of Homeric remoteness. My capacity for those feelings of compassion and outrage, which are generally referred to as 'decency', have long been in abeyance. Indeed, if I have any sympathies, they are on the other side. It was an act of savage justice. In some way I cannot fully explain to myself it was entirely in keeping with everything we did there.

New Edinburgh was in two minds. It was agreed that the murder was barbarous. That is to say, it was the sort of act that only people very different from ourselves would be capable of. News of Drummond's removal, and of the painstaking butchery with which it had been effected, roused Mr Paterson to his last protracted period of lucidity. He quickly fixed on the idea that it must be the work of some outside force or, if it were not, that it was of the utmost importance to say so anyway to protect the colony from the demoralizing effects of its own guilt. By noon that day, after a hasty interment of the remains – much being read into who attended and who did not – it was announced that an investigation had clearly shown that the Indians were to blame. Caledonians would rejoice to learn that a reprisal would be led by Major Jardine tomorrow. This brought out the opposing tendency, who read the proclamation with angry exclamations of denial, weary shakings of heads, exhausted cynical shrugs and from one fellow a belly-laugh of unanswerable contempt that revealed more than anything else how little time we had left as an organized entity.

The difference was not over the truth, but simply over the advisability of admitting it. It was widely known that Drummond had a past of some sort and that it probably had something to do with the Massacre. The presence and separateness of the Highlanders was obvious to all, and many had also noted that none of them claimed to be a McDonald or in any way related to that breed. This never seemed probable, and I shared the assumption from an early stage that some of them were with us under other names. Most obvious of all was the attitude of the Highlanders to Drummond. Everyone knew that there was an attitude, that it was peculiar and intense and that there was probably something very important about it, though it did not concern them directly. Looking back from the *fait accompli* of his murder, few would deny that this attitude betokened an intention that was tantamount to being an open secret. Only Drummond and those closest to him did not know this secret – no one knows what is inconceivable to him. All in all, then, it was a much-foreseen death. If it came as a shock, it was because our trials had forced us to think only of our own fates. We had simply forgotten what was due to Drummond, just as we had forgotten to forewarn the man himself.

Accordingly, Mr Paterson's semi-delirious project, of persuading New Edinburgh that what was universally known to be true was not in fact true, did not meet with success. It was one of those solemn absurdities that mark the space between the point at which failure becomes inevitable and the point at which men accept that it is inevitable. There was an indignant muster before the Meeting House. Jardine ordered about the few remains of the original redcoats and two dozen of the louts who had been training for piracy. The call for volunteers, however, was not met by anyone outside this group. The prospect of slaughtering the inhabitants of the nearest Indian village without the complicity of the whole colony gave even Jardine pause for thought. A vicious downpour was claimed as reason for a postponement till the next day and nothing more was heard of it.

Equally predictable (or so it seemed after the event) was that Drummond's demise was quickly followed by that of Caledonia itself. No sooner had we dispensed with his services than we were confronted with that situation for which he had been uniquely qualified. It fell to Jardine to do his best and, though I am no judge of military matters, I believe it would not be unfair to say that the dog proved no match for his master.

Three days after the murder I became aware of alarms and disturbances a couple of hours before dawn. I came out of my cabin to find Jardine on the quarterdeck – he had inherited the *Rising Sun* without a word of objection from anyone. Someone from Point Lookout had glimpsed lights off-shore. A single gun had been heard and was suspected of being a signal. All eyes were straining seaward, the slimmest of moons and starlight through thin cloud our only help. I moved forward, out of the awkwardness of Jardine's company, and found a vantage-point on a coil of rope at the very apex of the bow. My half-fevered senses made shapes out of the even nothingness, insisting that patches here and there had a more absolute blackness than the rest. From behind me I could hear Jardine angrily repeating his order for silence. I twitched at everything my desperate imagination suggested. Was that blacker blackness a hull? Was that vertical line in my mind a real mast of a real Spanish warship? Was that flicker of paleness a sail? Even at the time I knew that I could not possibly see any of these things. Fever and emotion were conjuring them for me. I had only to think of what might be there for some dim trace of it to appear. And that emotion? I must make myself clear here, as those without such experiences (which is all humanity) or of an excessively goodwill towards the current writer will no doubt mistake my meaning. There was none of the apprehension natural when expecting sight of one's enemy, and still less of that ardent desire to come to grips with him that the lesser poets like to speak of. I yearned for ships to be there and my only emotion was hope – an unalloyed and unrepentant hope of deliverance.

I jumped as someone upset a lantern and let it clatter over the deck.

'Silence there!'

Frozen like pointers we heard the sound – two ticks of a grandfather clock, or a signal musket and its reply three miles out? Some saw a flash, others said no. Jardine gave the order to prepare, and I gave thanks.

The guns at Fort St Andrew and those of the battery on the opposing side of the bay were prepared for action. Crews were made up, by necessity, of two or three men of experience and two dozen others who had until first light to learn the arts of gunnery. Captain Jolly was consulted on the position of the *Rising Sun* and the *St Andrew*, both anchored outside the bay. It was declared impossible to bring them in past the sunken rock in darkness. If Green had done it with the *Worcester* it was because he had a smaller ship and because he was a fool. Our two greatest ships, therefore, were prepared for a standing fight. As one who had been distrusted by Drummond, I received no orders from Jardine and was able to stand by and look on impassively, according to my temper. Mr Shipp, also left idle on account of his association with me, came and stood by my side when I returned to the quarterdeck. 'Well, sir,' he asked, 'what do you think?'

I did not dare to tell him and he said no more to me.

From that point until we realized the true nature of our position, I witnessed a most extraordinary transformation. The prospect of meeting with an enemy and engaging in the simple business of killing him or being killed by him flooded Caledonia with an insane energy. Lights sprang up everywhere the frantic and elated preparations were being carried out. The *Rising Sun* and the *St Andrew* shone on the water. 'Let them see us, lads,' shouted Jardine, in a tone that was enough of itself to make the crews impatient for victory. Lanterns and signal fires appeared at Point Look-out and the battery. A dawn-like glow rose over the peninsula, indicating that activity in New Edinburgh was equally intense. Everyone suddenly seemed to share the belief, unexplained, unspoken and magnificently unreasonable, that a single triumph now would undo and make good all our folly.

A boat heavily bumped our timbers. Already half full of men, it took on several more from ourselves and half a dozen kegs of powder before making off in the direction of the battery. Its oarsmen had only made a few strokes when I heard a wild shouting from it and went over to the rail to see what the problem was. A man was standing and waving his arms about and being alternately cheered and abused by his fellows. 'Here we are!' he shouted. 'Come and get it! Over here! Come on, then!'

The boat began to rock perilously. Hands seized him by the belt and collar and dragged him down. Oaths, threats, boasts and laughter diminished as the rowers pulled away. Remote sounds continued from the battery after they arrived and began their lessons. Orders and occasional general shouting came over the water as the *Sun* and the *St Andrew* busied themselves with their own preparations and manoeuvred beam on to the lightless sea, ready to deliver broadsides to whatever might be hiding there. After two hours, when some were debating whether it was first light or not, the teachers of artillery put their new pupils to the test. A single gun flashed and boomed out over the sea, brilliantly illuminating the battery and all its men in an infinitesimal moment of stillness. A cheer went up, at the end of which an angry soldier's voice could be heard, revelling in an undreamed of authority: 'Faster! What are you waiting for? You're all dead!'

After a full five minutes of silent fumbling another single shot boomed out.

'Old women!' bellowed the new-made officer. 'You're nothing but old women! You're all dead!'

His recruits laughed and cheered.

I managed to find space for myself in a boat heading into New Edinburgh. The rowers had hardly taken twenty strokes when the battery was rewarded with permission to unleash a full cannonade. Eight guns ripped into the night, their fire-flashes flickering against the clouds like bolts of lightning. Great whoops and hurrahs followed but were immediately drowned out as the gun-decks of the *St Andrew* and then of the *Rising Sun* herself added their terrifying power. In our little pinnace, curses and insults were exchanged as shoulders barged and heads banged against each other in the panic to hide below the gunwales. The planks of the hull hummed and the surface of the water was a momentary chaos as if it were being shaken violently in a glass. Through the whine in my half-deafened ears I could hear distant musket and pistol shots coming from New Edinburgh. As the explosions died away there was a crescendo of cheering and hooting and bellowing in celebration of this great victory against the night. Behind it, I could just detect the hiss of plumed water falling back into the sea where the shot had harmlessly splashed and sunk. From the quarterdeck of the *Sun* Jardine was shouting orders down to us. I paid no attention until the young lad squeezed in beside me, jumped up so quickly he almost threw himself in the sea.

'Adams!' Jardine was shouting. 'Adams, can you hear me?'

'Here, sir! Yes, sir!' the boy shouted back.

'Addition to orders of the day.'

'Yes, sir! I hear you, sir!'

'Whoever wastes another ball or another charge of powder will be shot with his own musket! Have you got that, Adams?'

'Shot with his own musket, yes, sir!'

He sat down again and started to mumble the order to himself over and over – 'Shot with own musket. Yes. If wastes powder or shot with own musket, that's right. Yes, sir. *Yes*, sir! Yes, *sir*! Yessir!'

This last phrase he agonized over with all the care of a tragedian perfecting his character's greatest line. He arrived at last at a satisfactory delivery, repeating it several times before concluding with a curt and decidedly military nod of self-approval. I tried to give the impression of looking straight ahead while examining askance the red coat he was wearing. The cuffs came down to his knuckles and I could have slipped three fingers between the collar and his neck. Threads unpicked themselves at the shoulders. Made for a man, they now sagged down on to the boy's half-starved haunches. I was considering the comedy of his appearance when our boat turned a few degrees and torchlight shone on his face. A quite different emotion surprised me and I was forced to turn away until I could repossess myself.

'It's Rob, isn't it?'

His features creased with irritation.

'You were helping Dr Munro?'

'Robert Adams, sir,' he told me, in an affronted tone. 'I'm adjutant to Colonel Jardine.'

'Doesn't he need your help any more? Has he got someone else?'

Mr Robert Adams made a contemptuous noise. 'I'm adjutant to Colonel Jardine now, sir,' he explained, unable to hear that word too often.

In New Edinburgh I found the same delirium. Every one of the surviving redcoats (about a dozen) was now enjoying the rank of an officer of some sort. They ordered about in lines and columns groups of men who seemed to take an equal pleasure in obeying their every word. The prospect of a fight had seemingly done more good for the colony's health than all of Munro's efforts. That part of New Edinburgh which had previously been reserved for the sickening in an attempt to limit the contagion was now almost empty. The hale now marched side by side with those whose appearance of vitality was nothing but the penultimate, burning stage of the fever. I even saw two or three stumble out of the infirmary and totter over to the nearest parade. Munro stood by the side of the tent flap, making no effort to stop them. He saw me across the excited mêlée and raised a hand in exhausted, despairing, comical salutation.

At the centre of this activity was Sergeant Black – or was it then Lieutenant Black, or Captain already? – standing on one of the upturned boiling pans we had used to search for the Nicaragua wood. Adjutant Adams stood on the ground beside him, looking up as Black read the orders he had just received from Jardine. I saw Adams speaking and could hear in my mind his proud delivery of the nonsense Jardine had shouted at him from the *Sun*. The scene was obscured by twenty men marching by with picks and shovels shouldered like muskets. I learned from another onlooker that they were on their way to complete Drummond's ditch. Only another three yards of excavation were required to finish it and let the waters meet. The men looked grim and stamped angrily on the soft ground as they went by. Their menial tools were as glorious in their minds as a musket is to a lad of sixteen allowed to touch it for the first time. They filed away into the trees, the light of their two torches being quickly extinguished by the forest.

I had decided to find some dark and unnoticed spot by the shore where I might wait for the dawn and was on my way there when an excited stray collided with me. I apologized for obstructing him and made to walk on.

'Mackenzie! Is that you?'

A lantern was raised and cast an uncomplimentary light on Mr Paterson's face. His skin, a deathly white by day, was jaundiced by the yellow of the lamplight. Forehead, cheekbones, nose, lips and chin caught the light, but the rest, from which the prosperous flesh had drained away, remained in shadow. He jerked his head up to demand an answer to his question. The eyes were bloody-rimmed and distant.

'Mackenzie! You're not armed!' He had a new voice for the occasion – military brusque.

A bold contempt rose in me and an even bolder need to express it. 'I see you have a pistol there, Mr Paterson,' I said.

'I do indeed, Mackenzie!'

He drew it from his belt and looked threatening. I stepped back, fearing an accident.

'And no doubt you have the will to use it?'

The reminiscence was lost on him, as might have been expected.

'I certainly do!' He looked about, holding his lantern high, in case the enemy had already arrived. 'This will cost them dear! We'll send them away with their tails between their legs. Get yourself a pistol,

Mackenzie, and a sabre. A young man like you won't want to miss this.' I assured him I would. He advanced on me and pulled me closer by the arm, making me conscious of my own emaciation. 'One good blow now, Roderick, and we're home and dry!'

I listened distractedly to his explanations while trying to take in the details of what was happening around us. It occurred to me at that moment that our language, extensive as it is, contains nothing more perfectly inappropriate than the phrase he had just used. This, more than anything, revealed his state of mind. His voice became strident and I returned my attention to him with some general expression of agreement.

'Of course it is! Of course!' he insisted. 'One good day's work tomorrow and we can still win. Even after everything we've been through – that doesn't matter now. We can still win out!'

'Win?'

'They say I've been lying in bed taking my ease . . .'

'I've never heard any—'

'Thank you, but I know it's true. People have always thought the worst of me. There are some men in the world who have to carry that burden whatever they do. But I've been busy, I assure you. Do you know what we'll be taking in ten years? Eight hundred thousand in sterling every year! Sterling, mind you! And I have only assumed an increase in traffic of two per cent and that prices will—'

I declared that I had to hurry away to get my pistol and sabre.

'But I can't waste any more time talking to you,' he almost shouted.

He went off into the night. His voice still came to me in scraps – 'Eight hundred thousand! That'll put some steel into them! *Nemo me impune lacessit!*' Wherever he went, men started important conversations amongst themselves, found it necessary to examine their equipment or recalled errands that quickly removed them from the scene.

I found my unnoticed spot, and even some moments of sleep. A dream woke me with a convulsion of fear and the needle senses of something hunted. All was still quiet under a greying sky. I walked to the nearest fire in search of some food. Three still forms lay sleeping about it. Elsewhere, the sickest still groaned and mumbled to themselves, but with these exceptions New Edinburgh was deserted. The men were either concentrated in Fort St Andrew or in defensive positions in the forest. I saw it as it must be now – voided of its humanity and of all its madness too, absurd, incomprehensible, the not very interesting remains of an ancient people whose purpose no sane man could guess at. I found a pot and started to boil some water. I marvelled at what I had seen over the last few hours. How tenacious is this strange, disastrous character of ours that even at the last extremity we can get no rest from it – like a dying dog that fancies it hears a stranger's voice and drags itself from the straw to growl and bare its gums one last time, only to be laughed at before it drops down dead. It was then that I conceived my ambition – the only one it was still reasonable to have. I knew that what I wanted most was to die at sea, out of sight of any shore. When the muskets started to fire in the forest, singly at first, then in rapid volleys, I knew also that what I feared most was victory.

In the next half-hour a position was arrived at which would remain largely unchanged for the following three days. In the middle of the third day the issue was decided (though in truth it was never in doubt) by external forces entirely unrelated to the efforts of the contending parties. The firing I have mentioned, along with cries of belligerence, fear, pain and command continued to come from the forest for some ten minutes. From the seaward side, to which three-quarters of our strength was directed, there was silence. Soon I began to hear the battle more sharply, unmuffled by the trees, and then to see the muzzle-flashes of muskets and pistols. I stood now in the company of the three sleepers who had been woken by the noise – I never did discover who they were or how they had not been joined to one of our new-made regiments. We looked on as four spectators, without exchanging a word or, seemingly, considering that we could or should take any part in the action that was slowly approaching us. A shadowy Mr Paterson emerged from the Meeting House and splashed across the open ground in the direction of Fort St Andrew as fast as he could. Dr Munro emerged momentarily from his tent to see what was disturbing his patients. A boat ran aground behind us and I turned to see Ensign Adams running up from the shore.

'What's happening?' he demanded breathlessly. 'I'm to tell Captain Jardine what's happening.'

I and my three companions said nothing, but merely turned our attention back to the forest from which we expected to see men emerging at any moment. Adams gave a soldierly oath and ran back to the boat.

A skirmish line of our men began to back out of the forest just to the left of the Meeting House. They stopped and fired into the trees for several minutes. From my standpoint there was no evidence of any enemy until a man cried out and dropped to the ground. While they retreated another ten yards, another larger group of colonists appeared from the forest to the right of the Meeting House. Drums rolled and answered in the forest and I heard Spanish voices shouting orders. There was a moment's silence before an intense fusillade was started. I saw one man drop from the left-hand line, and then another. The group on the right was retreating again, still steadily walking backwards and at first sight suffering no ill effects from the Spanish fire. Then some of the men turned and began to quicken their pace. I could see the dull forms of bodies fallen from the front and middle ranks and men picking up their feet as they stepped backwards over them. The thin line to the left was no longer a line at all, and as I looked at it I saw another man fall and then another two almost at once. I recall a strange, dreamlike absence of anxiety as I watched patches of mud near to me kick up as bullets sped into them. A kettle rang and flew a couple of yards as it was struck, gushing muddy water. Splinters flew off a post by the infirmary, the canvas of the tents was plucked by bullets as they flew through it. Through dense billows of white smoke I began to see the brightly coloured uniforms of tightly organized bodies of men. One of the fireside sleepers hopped, opened his mouth in surprise and fell forward on his face. Just as I realized that Caledonia was within minutes of an admirably efficient extermination (as one of the soon-to-be-dead I regretted that the event would go unrecorded), I found myself in the middle of our men fleeing chaotically towards Fort St Andrew. I tried to stay as close to the centre of this rout as I could, reasoning that in this way a pursuing musket ball would be more likely to find someone else's flesh first. Like the others, I clutched at those around me as I lost my footing, I elbowed and kicked obstructors out of the way and struck out and swore at those whose flailing bayonets were the most immediate threat to my life. In the last yards before safety the greatest hazard was the answering fire from the fort, cannon as well as musket. Bent double to avoid such an absurd death I cracked my collar-bone on one of the fort's gateposts and blundered into its safety.

A cautious squint over the ramparts revealed that the Spanish had not in fact moved from their positions by the edge of the forest. I tried to count the bodies on the 'field of battle', if that is the correct term. The engagement had cost some twenty lives. Firing from the Spanish line ceased completely and I slowly raised my head a little more over the rampart. By the time there was full daylight another party of Spaniards had come in from the direction of Drummond's ditch, escorting those who had been sent to complete it. A third group straggled in from the far side of the bay with a rigid Reverend Borland in their care. At noon he was allowed to walk into the fort, but the sappers and a handful of others were retained as prisoners-of-war. We had sight of some six hundred Spanish soldiers in all, a slightly greater number than ourselves. We never did find out where they had come from – perhaps landed on the coast nearby and marched from there, or perhaps brought over the isthmus from Panama by some road that had escaped our attention. Although Don Juan de Pimenta never satisfied us on that point, I tend to the latter explanation, which seems by far the most suitable.

Several hours of inactivity passed until a drummer approached us in the afternoon. He shouted his message over the palisade and Mr Spense told us its meaning. His Excellency Don Juan de Pimenta,

Governor of Cartagena, respecting our honour and pitying our condition graciously offered to stay his hand in return for accepting our immediate surrender. He was asked to wait while we considered our terms. He replied that there would be no terms and was sent away.

From that point until the end there was little change. There was the occasional exercise in organized firing, the odd heartening cannonade. The Spanish would withdraw into the forest while we spent ourselves against the trees, their picket line reappearing within a few minutes of our guns falling silent. Orders came less frequently and then were heard no more. The hours passed, day and night, with a few irregular shots a minute on both sides. Men fired whenever the Spanish line seemed to drift forward, or in darkness at the light of a lantern or a pipe being lit, or out of boredom or because they had fallen asleep and leaned on the trigger. Somehow, I became equipped with a pistol and thought it prudent to be seen making the occasional shot myself. I remembered Private Miller and his good advice on such matters – it helped me to ensure that I did no harm. We took some twelve or fifteen lives in this way and in the same period lost twice as many of our own to fever and flux. The bodies had to be put out at the back of the fort and let fall over the cliffs to pile on the shore. The odour from these miserable burials became hard to bear.

Those who stayed on the ships played little part in the drama except at the end when they were required to give them up to the victors and follow their instructions on the matter of disarming the *Rising Sun*. The smaller ships in the bay, the *Dolphin*, the *Caledonia* and the *Endeavour*, attempted a few broadsides at the Spanish lines but the shot from their lighter guns fell short for the most part, and on one occasion wide enough to poke a hole in the roof of the kirk. Outside the bay, the eight vessels of the Spanish flotilla (first reported as thirty), were content to await the outcome without ever trying the strength of the *St Andrew* and the *Rising Sun*.

During those three days in the fort we were more aware of the other non-combatant. Dr Munro had not joined the rout of the first morning and he and his infirmary remained at the exact mid-point between the Spanish lines and the palisade of Fort St Andrew throughout the proceedings. Almost immediately he was seen talking to Spanish officers. Two captains, whose appearance at least we were to get to know well, visited the infirmary tents several times. When the Reverend Borland was returned to us an effort was made to regain Munro as well. A messenger was sent out under flag of truce to ask that our physician be returned to us. A Spanish officer shrugged and indicated that it was no concern of his and that if we wanted him back we should talk to the man himself. The messenger followed this suggestion but returned with Munro's refusal on the grounds that there were still too many sick in the infirmary. That morning he had been observed walking about the ground to either side of the Meeting House where the dead still lay. He stopped by one of the corpses, the blue and yellow of a Spanish uniform just visible in the mud. I saw it myself – the pause, looking elsewhere as if he hadn't noticed it, and then the glance towards the fort before stooping to lay a hand on the neck and brush some hair from a forehead before moving on. For a moment all movement and speech stopped. The hair on the back of my neck rose as I felt something ugly shift through the fort.

The next morning, when it was assumed that there would be several fewer patients needing his attention in the infirmary, another embassy was sent to bring him back into the fort. Munro replied that he would come between noon and three to do what he could, but that he would then return to the infirmary. Jardine replied that he must enter Fort St Andrew immediately and unconditionally or face trial for his actions. The messenger returned with a note that made him flush with anger and turn away. Dr Munro remained just where he was until the end, unconcerned by the occasional shot flying over his head. Sometimes he stayed out of sight in the tents, sometimes he splashed about the ruins of New Edinburgh under the rain's renewed assault. He walked slowly, stumbled on things that weren't there, seemed always on the point of falling forward like a man in the extremes of drunkenness or exhaustion.

Late on the second day he was seen with one of the Spanish captains again. There was a brief conversation before he went with him into the forest. He disappeared from view for about half an hour before returning on his own. A shot from our side ploughed into the mud at his feet. He calmly looked down at the trench it had gouged and wiped the black spray from his face. A few seconds passed in which another such 'accident' was all that was needed to unleash twenty muskets into him. I looked back at Jardine and despised him when I saw that he was not prepared to say a word. Munro straightened himself, put his hands on his hips and stood stock-still for an hour to make it easy for them before going back into his tent unharmed. I told Jardine to his face that his men commanded him more than he commanded them. He did nothing and I knew, with some relief, that he never would.

Those three days in the fort were a final, concentrated spasm of all the misery and absurdity of our time here. The hopelessness of our position was clear to everyone, but the conspiracy to deny it was more extreme than ever. Every time the truth threatened to become undeniable, it was met with a renewed surge of enthusiastic delusion. This was the only real effect of the cannonades we occasionally unleashed and when the purpose of these displays also became doubtful Jardine resorted to conversing with Black in a loud voice, saying how impatient he was for the Spanish to attack. Optimism was quickly restored on the basis that our opponents would slaughter themselves in pointless attacks on our impregnable defences. Half the men were engaged in making up charges of grape-shot, and as they were stacked beside the cannon, victory once again became certain. As the hours passed, and then the whole of the first night without the slightest movement, I could see from the faces, exhausted and blanched by the dawn light, that the truth was gaining on them, dogging them ever more closely. I understood the mad syllogism that was keeping us there. We had become incapable of action, surrender was action and therefore we could not surrender. All we were waiting for was for things to be taken out of our hands.

In the middle of the second night, after the incident with Munro, I found myself thinking of Drummond and thanking God he was no longer with us. My fever was high and I began to believe that he was watching us in some way, looking on in contempt as the crucial hours were allowed to slip by. That was when he would have acted, at the most improbable, most difficult moment. He would have done something unexpected, uncompromising and pure in its brutality and, quite possibly, effective. With Jardine I had no fear of such a victory. I heard his voice behind me – a few quiet words with each defender as he moved along the parapet. Perhaps because the general viciousness had infected me too, but more probably because of his silence when Munro was in danger, I felt the need to torment him. I waited until he had returned to the centre of the fort. I got up and went to a brazier nearby, which smouldered weakly under the shelter of a scrap of tarpaulin.

'It's a bad business,' I said.

I waded towards him, pulling my boots from a foot of mud with every step. I looked at his profile for several seconds, the edges and gaunt bones of it just visible in the light of a half-shuttered lantern. He made no sign of having noticed me. I made sure I was visible from the corner of his eye and assumed the same position, staring out towards the invisible Spanish lines, savouring the ignoble pleasure of having the upper hand.

'I can't help thinking what he would have done,' I said. 'I had the idea that this would have been his time – but to do what? Attack the ships with the *St Andrew* and the *Rising Sun*, perhaps? Or bring one of them into the bay and use it to bombard the Spanish? No, I suppose not. Maybe leave a dozen men in the fort and spend the night going round the Spanish with the rest. Attack from behind at dawn!'

There was a noise from Jardine, which I ignored in my enthusiasm, moving on to still more extravagant ploys.

'But no – if I can think of that it can't be the right thing to do. It would have been something no one else could have thought of. Something only he could have . . .'

I stopped as I caught sight of Jardine's grotesquely twisting features. He was trembling, exerting every grain of will to hold back . . . what? Anger, humiliation, or grief? I began to understand that Drummond had been more than just himself. He had been half of all the men who followed him as well – a dangerous, exciting, unequal half, which had made them more than they could ever have been on their own, but which left nothing behind. I had caught my prey too easily. I waded back to the parapet, all the more ashamed for having left Jardine without a word of apology. I turned my thoughts to the next day – would it be the last, or the last but one? Would I survive it? I forgot all about Jardine.

In the end it was the rain that saved us. Saved . . . I have just written 'saved'! Forgive me. You cannot understand how difficult this is. The effort to make sense – every word is a great rock lifted on to the page. Who am I talking to? I don't have long. The rain, then. The rain saved no one, but it did stop things, put an end to them, took matters out of our hands. Of the three days of waiting the rain was entirely absent for an hour in twenty at most. Nothing exceptional in that, but it was more fitful than before, oddly so. We remarked on it. It was light for most of the time, but then exceptionally heavy, perhaps more so than ever before. A final paroxysm to end the season? We'll never know. Maybe the sun shines all day now – that seems suitable too. Done for by the last ditch – there's something right about that, as if it always had to be. The rain then – it drenched and doused us more than ever. By the end the only things we had still alight were two storm-lanterns. They were in demand as those who still had dry tobacco queued to light their pipes from them. Signalling to the ships by light or even by smoke had become impossible. Men no longer made any effort to cover themselves. Shelter was impossible, even to attempt it was ridiculous and, in spite of everything we had been through, that was the first time I had seen such complete resignation.

Our powder caked, some even slaked into a black sludge. Before the end men had to dig down to the bottom of each barrel to find a few handfuls that were still dry. The effort was often futile: the pans of our muskets and pistols were tiny pools of rainwater, the barrels had become drainpipes. Our weapons began to flash half-heartedly without discharging. Later, the cold click of flint on steel was a more common sound than any detonation.

But this is all beside the point. The point, if that is what I really mean, is that Fort St Andrew, an earthwork surrounded by a palisade, collected the rain like an enormous water butt. The problem had not been foreseen and no drainage had been provided. The rate of natural seepage and run-off was just enough to cope with moderate rain, but the mythical downpours that afflicted us in those last days were enough to turn it into a pool that was sometimes waist-deep. When the rain lessened again the waters would recede, slowly at first but then, for reasons that escaped us or were not thought worth considering, more quickly as the siege went on. Towards the end of the third day the lake of mud created by these rainstorms sluiced away like the water from an open lock. Most of it rushed through the gaps in the palisade, which were being worked ever wider by the force of the floods. The rest sank straight down into the soft earth with a strange rapidity. We had no engineer to tell us what this meant.

It happened very suddenly on the afternoon of the third day. Another downpour had filled the fort to our knees. Only a single small patch at the rear remained solid and this was crowded with powder barrels and the dying. We were all so feverish we probably missed the very beginning of it. It did not seem strange that things should appear to move of their own or that men, though standing quite still, should drift slightly like debris on a quiet sea. For many of us, it was a long time since we had trusted our senses. The next stage was the creaking of the palisade. At first it was like the timbers of a ship, joints flexing and easing the way they ought to. A sharp, splintering crack seized everyone's attention. We looked at each other, listened to the sound of ropes straining, of nails and dowels being eased from their holes. The drifting became more distinct. A man in mud to his knees was floundering as it suddenly lapped around his waist and then his chest. Elsewhere a great bubble belched to the surface as if the mud were starting to boil. Some instinct drove me to the higher ground on the seaward side. I started to wade and then, as the filth reached my thighs, to paddle with my hands as if I were half swimming. I became aware of objects flowing past me in the opposite direction and had the extraordinary sensation of walking half through, half on a river. A powder barrel eased past me. A storm-lantern followed it, strangely upright and steady as if still on dry land. I was more on all fours now, praying to find something solid under my feet and hands, fighting a stinking, foul-breathed Scamander for every inch of the way. It lapped at my face, threatened to fill my mouth. From behind there was a terrible commotion of shattering timbers and failing ropes and cries of terror and pain. I was suddenly tugged backwards as the flow increased and scrabbled desperately to save myself. Something sharp and immobile cut into my knee. I thrashed about and found it with my foot, pushing myself up out of the flow and flopping forwards. At last I found a surface that would support me. I was able to crawl and could just drag myself on to a shore of solid ground.

I found myself clinging to a tiny and crowded island. Some one hundred other souls crouched there, whose own attempts at survival I had not noticed until that moment. All were as fouled and three-quarter drowned as myself. I turned round and sat down, wiping the mud from my eyes. Fort St Andrew no longer existed. In its place was a steep decline, which began just in front of my feet and spread into a still creeping delta of mud. All over its surface the contents of the fort lay scattered. Barrels and muskets sank, other items emerged, being rejected by some force from below. Around the edge of the delta I was relieved to see a dense jetsam of humanity struggling to pull itself free from the mud. I watched as lines of Spanish infantry rapidly advanced on the survivors. The front rank held their muskets at the ready, the second rank drew their swords. The detachment halted ten yards from the edge of the landslide and gaped at the merciful wonder that had destroyed their enemies for them. As one they rushed forward and started to drag every human thing clear of the mud, living and dead. If there was an order, I did not hear it.

I lay back and stared at the clouds, letting the rain start to wash my face. A mad elation surged through me. It was over, I would die at sea.

*

I THOUGHT I HAD more time. I have just woken to find this book fallen on the deck and the last measure of ink seeping from the quill into the blankets. For several minutes I sat like a dotard trying to remember who I am, where I am, what these words mean. One of these faints must be the last, the one from which I do not wake. It is too late to say all I wished to say. The fever has – but no, that doesn't matter. There is no time for that now.

Don Juan de Pimenta was a better enemy than we could have hoped for. Indeed, he was hardly our enemy at all but 'merely', as he liked to say, 'a servant of His Most Catholic Majesty'. In the brief period between our surrender and our departure I never saw any indignity in him. He expressed no satisfaction at his success and required less of us than a victor had a right to. One of his captains handed a letter to the last boat to push off for the *Rising Sun*. It was delivered to Captain Jolly, who now commands us, and its rumoured contents were conveyed to me by Mr Shipp (for whose survival God be thanked). Don Juan prayed for our safe voyage and assured us that his master had a short memory for all the many sins the world committed against him. I could not help but wonder if he knew what had happened at Toubacanti.

He liked to display his English to us and talked that first night of the 'dictation of terms', which would begin the next morning. It was a busy night, spent restoring the living and burying the dead. A single cross was placed on the landslide for the fifteen who could not be found. We received assistance from the Spanish soldiers to a degree that surprised the best of us and was met with ungrateful incomprehension from the rest. By dawn we had ascertained that one fifth of our original number remained alive – a single shipload.

Don Juan's dictation hardly merited the term. He spent an hour in the Meeting House with Mr Paterson. He emerged baffled and a little embarrassed to explain that he had not been able to make himself understood. It had proved impossible to progress beyond Mr Paterson's offer of ten per cent of the Company's stock and the position of vice-governor of Caledonia, which would declare itself to be sovereign and perhaps even change its name to New Andalusia. Was there anyone else who could speak for the colony? As Don Juan de Pimenta put this question to us, I watched Mr Paterson emerge from the Meeting House behind him. He addressed an order to a Spanish guard standing by the door. He repeated it roughly and began to look about himself, unaware that he was being ignored. He made a sudden lurch forward as if to save himself from falling, held on to the shaky banister and stared at the steps in the knowledge, or so it seemed to me, that he would be most unlikely to get to the bottom of them without falling. Two of our men understood and helped him down. As a new delegation was proposed to Pimenta, Paterson was led away to the shore, talking loudly about tolls and percentages and capital and something about canals.

Major Jardine and Captains Malloch and Jolly signed the document Pimenta put before them. At first we were to be denied the *Rising Sun*, but when Jolly asked for it in return for the surrender of all the other vessels Pimenta agreed, on the sole condition that all her guns be thrown overboard under the supervision of his own men. This passed as a great act of diplomacy on Jolly's part and gained him the command of all that remained of Caledonia. We provisioned the *Sun* as best we could from the stores of the other ships, submitting every parcel of goods to inspection before being allowed to take it below. During this work the great splashes of the ordnance kept time for us as they were dropped into the sea one by one. They worked through her gun decks a side at a time making her list to starboard when all the port guns had been drowned and then slowly right herself as the other side was cleared. Officers from the Spanish ships inspected our other vessels. The *St Andrew* was taken as a prize and the *Dolphin*, the *Endeavour* and the *Caledonia* declared unseaworthy and burned. The conflagration was at its height just after dark and lit up the whole of the bay. Only the destruction of the *Caledonia* elicited any strong emotion in me. I watched with an eerie fascination as the remaining timbers of the quarterdeck crashed down into the hull in a great cloud of flame.

New Edinburgh was treated likewise. Even before the last colonists had boarded the *Rising Sun* the huts that would burn were burned and those that would not were knocked to the ground. The Meeting House, doused with turpentine and pitch, was reduced to a rectangle of ash in less than an hour. The infirmary went the same way, the only body to be removed beforehand being that of Munro himself. I found him still sitting at his desk, head down as if asleep, covering a half-written sheet of paper – 'Account of a New Fever of Particular . . .' The fingers of the right hand obscured the rest. Virulence? Fatality? I moved a finger and smiled at what I saw there as if recognizing a friend in a crowd. Outside I gave orders for everything in Munro's tent to be removed to the *Sun*. I don't suppose they were carried out. He was the last of our number to be buried in the graveyard.

By the time the Spanish burned the infirmary it had become so corrupted that no one was willing to do anything more. Every bed and pallet was occupied with a rotting body and the whole was a humming hive of blow-flies that drifted from every gap in the canvas like smoke. Its cremation completed the destruction of New Edinburgh. Only the kirk remained untouched and it had never really been part of our little town.

I sat on the great rock by the shore, hugging my knees, violently shivering with fever. The last two or three boatloads of colonists stood silently and waited. I was there just long enough to notice amidst all the smoke and burning the smell of earth and trees. It came to me that the Spanish were irrelevant to our destruction. Darien had never tolerated us. It was throwing us off, cleansing itself. The empire of Spain had made a fortnight's difference, a month at most. She will make no more of it than we did.

I had to accept some help in boarding the pinnace and squatted in the stern as New Edinburgh shrank – a smoky gap in the trees. We rowed through a charred scum of debris from the ships. The water was black, the air bitter with burning. The three keels floated still, a few timbers protruding a foot or so above the surface. We passed the swirl of water about the sunken rock. I was hauled aboard on a rope but somehow found the strength to climb to the quarterdeck and stand by the rail. Captain Jolly stood in command. I found his position there painful and could only offer the briefest acknowledgement.

We made sail, slowly moving past the Spanish squadron. I tried to focus on the faces of the men on deck, mildly curious at best as to the cause of this minor episode. The *Rising Sun* turned for the open sea. We passed the angle that made the opening of the bay invisible – one of its great virtues as we once thought! The tock of axes attracted my eye to the cliffs and I saw the look-out tower tumble over and crash on to the rocks below.

The coast thinned. I stared at it with all that remained of my strength, determined not to be deceived. When the land was gone a hint of smoke remained. Two ships were sighted and came close. The captains inspected us through their telescopes. All was in order. They unfurled their flags and turned to the north-west – English frigates out of Kingston, bearers of good news.

I checked the horizon again. Water only. No land and nothing that came from land. I turned round and round, seeing nothing but sea. I thanked God, over and over again, aloud as I turned, thanking God for that perfect, watery horizon. I went below.

In six hours or ten or twelve I shall return to the deck and be let slip into that empireless sea. No pain now. I feel soft. A strange heat in the belly. Something is melting, breaking down. I think it will be easy.

God forgive me.

RODERICK JOHN MACKENZIE
At sea
17 April 1699

Part Three

19

HOW STRANGE IS FORTUNE!

The impossible becomes the everyday, the inevitable never happens. Best of all, the dead live! I am one such. A tall tale. A violation. A quiet life now, little to look at, but from within the constant leavening surprise of being here at all.

My life, then, is the first thing to be explained. It was Shipp who died, taking the fever from me. This is what I chose to believe, although it was two years before I saw his name on the official list, blown in here by chance from the big world outside. I enquired. No one knew his name. I wrote to Milne Square and received a reply from a clerk who did not know my name either – that at least was something. No surviving relative was all I could conclude. No one to praise him to, no one to tell what should be told. Not surprising, really – he was a true seaman. I took a bottle of whisky one night and locked my door and wept for him from dusk till dawn. The men looked hard at me that morning but said nothing, as ever. His stone is here now, far from the sea. Far above it too.

Stranger still that I should open this book again. Since returning to my senses I have seen it only once. I was repacking a trunk in preparation for coming here and came upon it unexpectedly. I threw out a waistcoat stiff with old sweat and tropical mud and there it was. Hidden at the bottom, half wrapped in a shirt, unrecognizable at first in its sailcloth jacket – Shipp's thick-fingered work, I suppose. I bent to pick it up and then stopped, fingertips not quite on its rough cover. I received a queer, repulsive charge and thought better of it. Maybe later, I thought, or maybe never. When was that? Six years ago, seven now? Not long enough. I entombed it in as many layers of workaday things as I could find and watched it strapped precariously on to the back of a cart, pretending to myself that I couldn't care less if I never saw it again.

And so here it is – the cure for this disease is not so easy. If there was a clock here it would be striking two now. I am too stirred up to sleep, too stirred up altogether since the letter. Departure in four hours, fool that I am to leave this dreary but most necessary asylum. How many times have I told myself I don't have to go? Every time there is an answer: 'You do have to go. You have to see it through!'

That's it then, seeing it through, though I'll be damned if I know what I mean by it. Wouldn't say if I did, just in case – it might not happen. So it's not the letter, really, or not that alone. It's the news from Edinburgh. It often doesn't make much sense by the time it gets here, half remembered by people who don't know or care much what it means. Of course, I'm no different now. For the first few years I used to go down to the inn at Sanquhar every month to get the mail from the Dumfries coaches. Mr Wardlaw would gather any papers that had been left and I would spend half a day reading them and drinking his beer. The habit dwindled as they became less and less comprehensible to me and was finally given up altogether, there being no mail to collect either. Gradually my view of the world became like that of the miners themselves – obdurately incurious, resentful of intrusion. It serves them well and has done the same for me although, I would say, for different reasons. The letter shattered all that. It flattered me, but I cursed it too. I wanted to let it alone, but couldn't. I started to ask more questions, borrowed a paper from the doctor we summoned two weeks back from Crawfordjohn (Rae's leg crushed below the knee by a kibble – his last ten shillings for the fee and still dead – unpleasant memories for me). Then I went down to Sanquhar to see what I could learn.

'What do you make of it all?' asked Mr Wardlaw, as I leafed through the leavings of more worldly travellers. I made a noise to which he replied, 'Aye, I reckon so.'

I settled down with a jug of ale to see what I could work out. There were several I had never seen before, single sheets for the most part – the *Caledonian*, the *North Briton*, the *Free Unionist*. I knew from my early days in Edinburgh how quickly such things came and went. They didn't answer any questions. I found the facts dull, unconnected. Nevertheless, there was something in them that unsettled me, a tone I would have preferred not to hear, like an old argument being helplessly returned to. As I rode back up here that evening I turned it all over in my mind and tried to make sense of it. Surely, it was nothing to do with me? Why should I care? By the time I left the banks of the Mennock Water and crested the last hill to look down on the village, I had abandoned all such ideas and accepted that I would see it through, or have done with it, or whatever. I would go.

I have just noticed how out of practice I am and what a mess I have made of these first pages. If I have retained anything of value from my experiences it is surely the small, square nature of a chief clerk and quartermaster. I shall use it now, arranging my poor stock and making up my accounts in full and proper order. What is this place, then? What am I now?

*

ONE DAY I AWOKE in a small room. Brilliant sunlight struck across it. It puzzled me for a while until I realized that it was strange because its angle and hue could not possibly be tropical. I stretched my head back and could just see one pane of the window, brilliant gold and flowered with frost. From that moment I remember everything, but one of the first things I was told was that I had been in that room for months. I had slept, dreamed and raved the whole summer through.

At first I had no memory at all of what happened between boarding the *Rising Sun* and waking on that extraordinary morning. Over the next two years parts of it came back to me until, it seemed, I had remembered all that I ever would. Of the voyage I still know nothing. I do not believe I ever will, and can only deduce that my energies were so entirely occupied in the battle for life that nothing was left to form even the lightest impression on my conscious mind. I did know that it was Captain Jolly who brought us into the Clyde. Much later I learned that the passage had been eight days shorter than the voyage out, even taking account of us not stopping at Madeira. My informant, a fellow survivor encountered by chance, was of the opinion that he owed his life to Captain Jolly. We drank to his memory and praised him extravagantly. He had entered our conversation only because of the news that he had captained the *Beauregard*, one of the seventeen vessels sent to the bottom of the North Sea in the great winter storm of that year.

When we dropped anchor off Greenock the worst must have been over for me – I could hardly have been alive otherwise. I have no recollection of the moment itself but must somehow have absorbed the information that we were home. What I do remember, and this is typical of what has remained to me from those months – a series of motionless images like lightning flashes through a long night journey – is standing by the rail and seeing that we had entered a wide firth bound by low hills. I suffered a brief moment of confusion. Perhaps we had not moved at all, it was just another turn of the fever. Other inlets ran off to the north and beyond the coastal land mountains could be seen. A boat was approaching us, a man standing in the prow. Our appearance. He hailed us. Our tongue. There was no mistake.

The lightning flashed again and there was my hand on the rail – cadaverous, crocus-yellow, gruesomely exhumed from some other world. I remember also the plague flags fluttering from the rigging. I remember delays, arguments, anger. There was something about Port Glasgow and something else about Port Glasgow requesting us to stay where we were off Greenock. A licence was needed to go further up the Clyde under the plague flag. The city fathers deliberated, heard the shouting in the streets and deliberated again. Beyond that coast, which we already regarded with resentment, Scotland was waking to the truth, learning the whole story in all its many versions of how its money and hopes had been conjured inexplicably into air. From conversations, and oftentimes the remonstrations I had to listen to later, I was reminded of the blithely baseless certainty I had once shared. On encountering it again I found it strange and even ridiculous. Though it had once been my faith too, I now found myself having to pretend a sympathy that was very far from my true feelings. When I heard too much of it, which was often, I felt nothing but contempt. I don't say it was not harder for them – what we had seen over many months they had to accept all at once. More than the colonists, much more, they had already reaped and spent the profits. They had paid off their debts and nightly delighted in the satisfaction of their just desires. None of it was to be. The news came with our own arrival: there had been no warning. Again and again after my recovery I heard how all the news had been good, how our little victory at Toubacanti had been celebrated. It was all so incomprehensible.

Many had every right to give us a cold welcome, but I soon learned that those who had been bereaved only of their money were the ones I really had to fear. They formed a vengeful tribe, admission to which was gained by subscribing to a single, identifying conviction: namely, that they were entirely innocent and that we, the survivors, were entirely guilty of their ruination. It was men of this sort who deliberated in Greenock and Glasgow while two more of our number died.

I have some vague memory of leaving the *Rising Sun*, though even to this day I have no clear understanding of it, or who I had to thank for arranging my escape. There is another spark of lightning in my mind, which illuminates a small boat, rowlocks muffled with rags. There were ropes cutting into me, there was swinging and lurching in darkness, curses and loud demands for silence before I landed heavily in the bottom of the boat. I remember feeling my feet dragging through sand as I was pulled up a smuggler's beach. I remember a crude cart, its leather cover and the lantern swinging from one of the hoops. I remember someone lying beside me (I think), and being woken by the rattle of cobbles and wondering where I was and who I was and being sure that I would die after all. A seeming instant later there was sunlight and frost.

*

THE ROOM WAS PACKED tightly under the eaves, the ceiling sloping acutely so that I could stand, when that became possible, only in the middle part of it. A single small window poked through the roof and was, at that moment, the source of the most beautiful light and exquisite coldness I had ever experienced. With difficulty I raised myself until I was kneeling on the bed. Suddenly things twisted and went dark and I was falling. I threw out my arm and found the frame of the window, which burst open. I pitched forward until my chest jarred painfully on the casement. Brilliant light and freezing air instantly restored me to my senses. I was leaning half out of the window, pulling at my nightshirt to let my skin drink in as much of the dazzling, crystalline air as possible. My breath plumed thickly over the slates as I looked down in wonder at the slow, majestic, populous river of Edinburgh's High Street.

I was startled by a shrill cry of horror from behind me. Before I knew what was happening I was seized from behind by someone of terrifying strength and thrown back on the bed. A young woman stood over me, face red with anger and exertion, fists resting on hips. I made to demand who she was and what she thought she was doing. I adopted a tone of insulted authority in my mind but could only produce a few hoarse syllables.

'Never you mind and only what I ought to. What do you think you're doing is what I'd like to know? Trying to ruin all our good work?'

I became aware of the lie of my nightshirt and immediately pulled it down.

'Hm!' exclaimed the girl, in matronly contempt for my modesty, though she could not yet have been twenty. She bent over me and with a few deft movements had me encased in my bed as tightly as a child in swaddling.

'Who are you?' I whispered.

'Your nurse,' she replied, with distaste. 'And it's not what I bargained for, I can tell you.'

I asked whose house I was in, how I had come there, what her name was, but she would tell me only that if she found me leaning out of the window in my nightshirt again she would take me by the ankles and send the rest of me after. She paused in the doorway before leaving, slender and by no means tall. She smiled very slightly. It was a thrifty gesture but enough to let me know that there was more to her nature than I had just seen.

Over the next fortnight I resigned myself to the infantile pleasures of patienthood and slowly learned the truth of my situation. Angela, for so Providence had named her, brought me broth and stern admonitions four times a day. I progressed to boiled beef and potatoes and a little red wine, but when I asked for a piece of fruit I was rebuked and told that I should have brought some back with me. Nevertheless, a dish of sour apples stewed with honey appeared the next day. Lest this should be mistaken for kindness I was brusquely informed that the mistress had said I might have whatever I could pay for. As to who that mistress was, and to all my other questions, I was told that she had her instructions and that she would lose her place if she said another word.

After several more days of this mystery the mistress herself appeared. My recovery was still in its early stages or I would have recognized her at once – ample, authoritative, dressed with a discreet precision and of an age and demeanour that suggested a woman with nothing more to learn of the world. Here, indeed, was the mistress of whom my spitfire attendant lived in fear.

'Ah, well,' she said archly, 'I suppose you wouldn't be the first of my customers not to recognize me – Mr Mackenzie.'

I stared hard, certain that I knew her but still unable to find a memory that would make any sense.

'You've changed more than I have, I can tell you. When I first saw you I could hardly believe what they were telling me.'

'You're . . .' I paused, looked about the room and wondered if I could possibly be right. 'You're the . . .'

'The what?'

'Mrs Gilbert?'

'Widow Gilbert I am and this is my house.'

'And this room – this is Sus—'

'The smallest room in the house, Mr Mackenzie, or the smallest and least inconvenient we could put you and that God-knows-what into.'

She indicated the stack of trunks, portfolios and tarpaulin sacks that filled a third of the room.

'It's not mine.'

'It's your baggage. You came with it, whether you own it or not.'

'What am I . . .'

'As I said, the smallest room of the house but a proportion of my assets, nevertheless. You are sleeping on my assets, Mr Mackenzie. You are . . .' She stopped, suddenly struck by what she was about to say. 'You are consuming my capital, Mr Mackenzie. This is no poor-house. I haven't changed my profession since you were last here.'

She stood by the window, looking down at the street, flicking her keys from one side of the ring to the other.

'What am I doing here?'

'I'll ask you that when you can give me a proper answer.'

'Where's Susanna?'

'Angela said you were talking sense at last. I just wanted to see for myself.' She left, gesturing at the sacks and trunks as she went. 'I'll find a man who'll give you something for that.'

Slowly I grew stronger. When the days were good I was moved to a back room, which took the sun for several hours. I watched the comings and goings in the back courts, the endless procession of sheets and linen being hung out and collected and hung out again. I watched the light on Blackford Hill and on the Pentlands beyond, and urged on my recovery by thinking what a pleasure it would be to walk there. I was even brought books, the parts of an odd collection left by the patrons of the house. I read Colvil's *Scotch Hudibras*, which, by its marginalia, had greatly displeased a previous owner and found no more favour with me. I browsed a few theological works and drifted aimlessly through *Leviathan*, inhaling only a few of its sonorous, antique phrases before letting it drop to the floor. Only a little Rabelais, done into our particular English with scandalous zeal, did my spirits any good. It was the only part of that library of orphans not to be out of place. In crimson leather and neat fresh gilt, it presented something of a mystery as to why its owner had not come back for it. I have it still and can breathe the air of those days merely by touching it.

A suit of clothes was found for me and I began to walk, gradually reversing through the ages of man from infirmity to my proper state. I was permitted only the back stairs, Widow Gilbert being firmly of the view that she could not afford to associate her house with 'squanderers'. 'Those gentlemen who can still afford to enjoy my hospitality, Mr Mackenzie, and it is not so many as before, do not come here to be reminded of their misfortunes. The disappointments of cooled marriages, the importuning of creditors, the unspeakable price of grain, the failure, for whatever reason, of their investments must all cease to exist as soon as they come within these walls.'

I suggested that her patrons might as well aim to be parted from themselves. She told me it had not been her intention to converse with me, and if she found my liverish features upsetting one of her gentlemen she would have me on the streets before dawn.

I came to know Mrs Gilbert's employees very well. At first I often had to stand still on the stairs to regain my breath and calm the trembling of my legs. Conversations would start with whoever was passing and I was soon in receipt of all the gossip. As someone with whom there was no possibility of commercial relations I had a peculiar position. I was not really a man at all for them and became something like a sister, but one so odd and removed that she could be told anything without there being the slightest possibility of consequences. I learned their alliances and enmities. I learned the complaints of the trade and the character of the customers – who was good news and who was bad. I learned their ambitions, on which my opinion was always asked and which I always praised as laudable and most likely to succeed. Strangest and most remarkable of all, I learned how women talk to each other. For countless hours I listened to the innermost intimacies. I was amazed at what I heard – it amazes me still – and was still more amazed at hearing it in voices that could be just as well used to predict rain or hire a horse. At certain moments I would become aware of myself and blush. The girls would laugh and stroke my cheek, but the conversation never continued.

This innocence, coupled with my physical weakness, made me the child of the house and everyone down to Ruth, the half-simple kitchen maid, acquired a maternal authority over me. I would receive dictates on my health from all sides and was severely scolded for sitting out in the back court on a morning that was too cold for me. I accepted such treatment without the least indignation. In truth, I was made much of and could not have found a better berth.

By early November I was beginning to feel quite well, though weak and in appearance still sallow and thin. The house had become accustomed to me and I to it. An agreement on the matter of money had smoothed my relations with Widow Gilbert. On gloomy afternoons I sat in the warmth of the kitchen talking with Ruth or with the girls who sometimes came in from the front where they did a little work as seamstresses and dressmakers for the benefit of that small part of Edinburgh's population who preferred not to know the real business of the house. It was on one such afternoon that Widow Gilbert herself came in and gave Ruth a coin, telling her to go and buy some eggs.

'Well, then, Roderick Mackenzie,' she said, 'is there anything more you can tell me now?'

I told her that I knew nothing more than on the first day I awoke under her roof.

'A pity. You were brought here by two men late one night. They insisted that this was where you belonged, and by the time poor Ruth could gather what little wits God gave her they dropped you on the floor right there and went. I caught them the next day when they returned to deliver your baggage. They said they didn't know who you were and that they had asked all round the town. They could only find one person who thought they knew you and he believed this might be your home! What about that?'

'Who were the two men?'

'Porters, they said. What porters? I said. Just porters, madam. Whose "Just porters"? I asked. Who pays you? That got rid of them – you'd have thought they'd seen the watch coming!'

I suggested they might have been from the Company.

'I tried them.' She took the dough Ruth had left in a bowl and started to knead it. '"I expect he's passed away, my dear," some idiot told me. I told them to try harder and they sent me a letter saying they had no responsibility for former employees.'

'Former!'

'I can show you the letter, Mr Mackenzie.'

I said there was no need. She took a knife and slashed the dough into four. Each piece was slapped and kneaded in turn, rolled over and into itself again and again. When she took up the third piece I asked her, 'Where's Susanna?'

'Dead.'

The answer was very quick and sharp as if she had been taking a run at the word ever since she had come into the kitchen. It was what I had expected to hear.

'What happened?'

She took up the fourth piece of dough and worked it angrily.

'Nothing unusual.'

The silence was long and I was about to ask again when she went on.

'Childbirth.'

She raised her head to look at me, but I remained fixed on her hands.

'Yes, she died in childbirth, right here in this house.'

'You were with her?'

'Of course.'

'The child?'

She shook her head. 'Too soon. Like a little doll he was. You could have made three of him out of that.'

She put the fourth unbaked loaf in a row with the others. They seemed horrible to me, like shrouded infants.

'Five hours he lived in this world. A crying shame. Bonny black hair. Never saw the light of day.'

Her hands disappeared for a moment and then were in front of me again, being rubbed harshly on a cloth. When I looked up I saw that one cheek was marked with flour.

'I'll tell you something fine,' she said. 'You can go and see her if you like. Right in the middle of Canongate churchyard. A little High Street whore and her baby amongst all those baillies and ministers and merchants and lawyers. "Susanna," I said to myself that day, "you lay with them in life, you're good enough to lie with them in death."'

'How?'

'I know the people, Mr Mackenzie, and I have the money. It wasn't hard. Of course you'll see some things on the headstone that aren't exactly true, but I don't suppose that matters to her.'

Since hearing the word 'childbirth' only a single possibility had been in my mind. 'When did this happen?'

Widow Gilbert screwed her eyes up and looked at me with a little smile. 'A few months back.'

'A few months after I left, then?'

'That would be right.'

'Mrs Gilbert, whose child was it?'

She forced a laugh, but had her answer ready. 'Edinburgh's.'

She took up the knife again and went along the loaves putting two deep gashes in each. Suddenly she dropped the knife and turned her back to me. She put her hands to her face. For several seconds there was no sound. Then she shook herself and growled and turned to look me in the eye, daring me to insult her with a word of consolation. She finished with the loaves, sliding them into the oven and muttering to herself: 'You're just a stupid old woman. Spilt milk, that's all it is. Spilt milk.'

'Where?'

We both turned to see Ruth standing in the doorway, a basket of eggs over her arm.

*

A WEEK AFTER this interview Angela lingered in my room in the morning. She said I was looking much better. The girls all thought so. She sat beside me on the bed and made a play of stroking my forehead to check for fever. To my surprise, I felt myself capable of accepting this offer and did so right away. When spent, I lay on her trembling and then sobbing on her shoulder like an abandoned child. When she twisted her fingers in my hair and repeated the words 'There now, you're home. You're home now,' I felt that only grief had been consummated.

This transaction broke all the charms under which I had been living up to that moment. The privileges of convalescence ended at once, and although I was still readily greeted by everyone, the intimacy that had existed before was no longer possible. I had reverted, inevitably no doubt, to being a man in a brothel. Both Angela and I had to endure a storm of anger from Widow Gilbert. The commission of such an act free of charge greatly offended the morals of the trade and we were both very nearly cast off. The day was saved by my agreeing that it was all my fault and that I should pay the usual fee for 'entertainment'. For my part, I contracted with Widow Gilbert as an ordinary tenant on condition that I continued to abjure the front door – a discretion that suited me very well.

I began to go about the streets, merely crossing the road at first or walking a few doors in either direction before returning, already quite exhausted. By the time I started to regain my strength it was November. I favoured the afternoons when the light was already fading and went so thickly muffled against the cold (still an exquisite pleasure to me), that it was all but impossible that I should be recognized. I peered out from between my hat and my scarf, nervously examining every face, quickly glancing away for fear of that jolt of recognition. From thinking, as I looked down at it from the top of Widow Gilbert's house, that the city had not much changed, I quickly came to see the marks of failure. Some were obvious – the darkened windows where shops and coffee-houses had been, the women on their knees in the haymarket brushing grains of barley into their aprons and others begging, their cries continuous, one hand extended in appeal, the other dragging some pale, pitiful scrap of a child. I never saw one of them given bread or money, and often watched them being pushed out of the way or roughly spoken to. Amongst them was an entirely new species of the streets: boys from ten years or so upwards who would trot along at your elbow and demand to be sent on errands or to sell you a stick of sealing wax or a packet of tobacco dust or to tell you for fourpence where you could borrow money. When the watch appeared they fled at once down the wynds and closes as if someone had opened the door on a barnful of rats. One day I saw a woman with a board – 'Husband Dead in Darien'. The next day there were ten and the day after that fifty. They seemed to do little good and disappeared just as quickly.

I walked three times past my old tailor's address before realizing he was no longer there. I saw a cobbler huddled on the pavement with his tools, moving his head from left to right as he followed the holes in every third pair of shoes that passed before him without ever doing a penny's worth of business. I watched two men shout at each other and raise their hands merely for brushing shoulders. I watched another stand on a corner for a full ten minutes before choosing his way. He spoke to himself, gesticulated, fell quiet again, seemed not even to notice the young woman who approached him. Everywhere there were harsh words and contempt and the certainty that no one had lost more than one's self.

One Sunday I found myself approaching Dr Sinclair's close. I paused by a brazier for a few minutes and kept an eye on the entrance. I crossed the High Street and went past, trying to see down it. The light was already half gone and I decided that this was my best opportunity to take a look without any embarrassing encounters. The lightless grimy windows and the sign, limping a bit to the left but with my own crude handiwork still visible, were exactly as before. I bent down to one of the window-panes to check for light within and noticed then the broken chain hanging from the door. I pushed it open slowly and went inside, cautiously feeling for the two steps that had caught me out on my first day there. My entrance stirred up a miserable aroma of dust, mould, vinegar, urine and rats. The dull glimmer from the skylight that had once shone on Mr Watson's ledger like an annunciation was just enough to let me see the emptiness of the room. The oversized mantelpiece was still there, a rubbish of twigs and birdlime on the hearth. From the ceiling a cable hung down a few feet to where it had been cut in two by whoever took away the candelabrum. I thought at first that the door to the inner office was open, but when I got closer I saw that it had been removed entirely. The oak panels had also gone and the room felt damp and colder even than outside. I stood where Colquhoun had sat on his absurd, second-hand throne, curious to see how the room appeared from that spot which I had secretly coveted but had never once dared to occupy. Under my feet I could feel the dimples in the stone where the chair legs had ground. Only the strong-box remained, stubbornly riveted to the floor. The lid was open and I went over to look inside – a piece of rag, the neck of a broken bottle.

My physical recovery progressed well, but my mind lagged behind, becoming even more troubled. Everything my senses received was woven with my memories and changed into new and alarming forms. Any sudden noise was a musket-shot from which I flinched. When I heard a horse coughing, it was not a horse but one of Munro's patients coughing out his last. An onion on my plate, picked up with a knife, became a man and a bayonet so lurid and real that for a moment I could not see what I was doing. When I passed some filth uncleared from the gutter it became, in my nostrils, a seething corpse. My mind seized on the likeness in every face I saw, however slight, and turned it into a perfect portrait of one of the colonists. On some days I would see more dead men than live. The existence of Edinburgh became partial to me, a half-way reality towards which I struggled against Darien's mad pull. I would walk all the daylight hours of December's short days, going out past the palace, turning up to the coast, dawdling on the shore, coming into Leith, pausing by the few poor ships to see what might be new, passing the idle, empty warehouses – not least my own fallen empire – spend an hour in a tavern there, safely concealed in a haar of pipe-smoke, breath and bitter talk. I would turn in again towards the city, skirt the loch, climb up past the castle in the last of the light, made thick with the exhalations of chimneys, gutters, middens, men and women and walk down the High Street again, finishing my circuit on the back stairs of Widow Gilbert's house, suddenly not at all sure that I had not walked round the shores of Caledonia Bay and through New Edinburgh rather than the old. Darien was within me.

Almost to the end of the year I passed my time in this way – mechanically sustaining my existence, walking and looking at the real and the unreal in equal measure. I had no thoughts of my own, made no decisions, had no intentions beyond those required by the most immediate necessity. More than once I contemplated the choice between one tavern and another, sensibly getting hungrier and colder, only to find myself in the very same spot half an hour later, like a natural idiot waiting for instructions. I heard of Paterson's recovery and how some rejoiced and others cursed. I saw the Reverend Borland's pamphlet and spent a few minutes by the bookseller's stall ensuring my own name was not there. And on the title page? What else but 'I alone am returned to tell all'? It is what we all say. I read the directors' proclamation of Captain Galt and Mr Cunningham's treason and watched an old shirt and trousers stuffed with straw go up in flames, little boys laughing and pushing to be the first to stamp out the embers. I read how Captain Green had been a spy, Capitano Verde in fact; the *Worcester* was really the *Santa Maria*. 'Ah, yes,' a man in Maclurg's told me. 'How like the English to pay a Spanish whore to commit their crimes for them!' This is how the truth is made. On one of my walks I saw the little Palmer warehouse burn. The crowd threw stones to break the windows to make the fire burn faster. The watch stood by just in case things got out of hand. Old Palmer was there himself, running up and down, appealing, weeping at the end. How they laughed! How they cried, 'Go home!' He did, and all the others like him. Scotland wanted to be alone. At last I followed Widow Gilbert's suggestion and went to see Susanna. It stood near the middle in space preserved by a tree, granite amid sandstone, costly, angry: 'Susanna Walker beloved wife of Adam, 21 years, and son, 1 day'. My son, I said.

The little money I had was soon exhausted. Poverty shook me out of my indulgent mood and began the long, slow cure that was completed here by solitude and stillness. My first thought was to search the mysterious chests and cases that had come with me in the hope that I might have inherited something of value. I found only specimens of plants, papers of all sorts with many drawings, the remains of a leathery, brandy-smelling thing amidst shards of glass, and in one case all on its own, packed about with leaves and cloth, an unborn manatee floating in a jar. All this I had transported to the university and left at their door with no name. I kept two sets of surgical instruments, and with these became a street-hawker for a day, loitering about the entrance to the Anatomy Theatre selling one for three pounds, the other for fifty shillings.

When this fund came to an end I was at a loss for what to do. For a while, my mind evidently not yet fully recovered, I thought I should try to find Colquhoun. One man told me not to waste my time, another said that if I should find him he would like to know where. At last I was provided with an address, but found that it was Mr Watson's house. A physician came out and began to walk up the hill. I ran across and pretended to mistake him for Colquhoun. He drew himself up very sternly and told me I knew fine well he was not. Was he, by any chance, attending on Mr Colquhoun in that house? He shouted at me furiously, 'Would I tell the likes of you, sir? Would I? Do you think I don't know you?'

I stepped back in amazement.

'You're a pack of wolves! You've driven that poor man to within an inch of his grave and still you're not satisfied. Have you no shame?'

He pushed past me, leaving me the subject of hostile stares from all directions. The wickedness of creditors, the saintliness of debtors – I saw it all in a moment. It might have been, indeed it was, in effect, Colquhoun himself who had spoken. I returned to town laughing at myself.

I had resolved never to visit Milne Square again, especially after I had learned of my status as a former employee. Nevertheless, when Munro's legacy had run out and I was still too ashamed to approach any of my former acquaintances I accepted that I had no better alternative. I found the ground floor occupied by some clerks belonging to the new bank and the first floor given over to several advocates. Only on the second floor did I find the shrunken remains of the Company of Scotland.

I entered and addressed myself to a man seated behind a large desk. He did not raise his head, but pointed to a printed notice that stood by his elbow. It advised subscribers to refer all questions and demands to a lawyer and gave directions to the lawyer's office. I said I had come on other business and after several minutes of pointless manoeuvring wrote a note and insisted that it be passed in to someone in authority. An older man came out very promptly and made a show of welcoming me and congratulating me on my recovery. We went into the private office – a rough patch on the polish of the door where my name had been. This man showed a very different character when installed behind my old desk. Compliments and regrets alternated with each other in a well-practised flow, the theme of which was 'Whatever you have to say to me, the answer is no.' I told him how I had learned that I was a former employee. He said he was sorry. I asked when I had been dismissed. He told me he could no more give me information than he could give me money and wished me well for the future. I recognized a clerk on my way out and made sure that I encountered him in the street later that day. As he had a great appetite for hearing of the voyage and the colony, it was an easy matter to cultivate his acquaintance. Within a week I obtained through him, by means of a venial deception, a document showing the date of my dismissal and the address of Sir Robert Blackwood in London. A correspondence ensued, the happy result of which was a payment of eighty pounds in settlement of unpaid salary.

As the bank in those days would hardly have lent to the King himself, this was a considerable capital. The newspapers, noticeboards and coffee-houses were full of men in search of funds. I found the simplest and most vital proposal I could and bought a half partnership in it. Mr McCrindle did all that was required in the business of carting in potatoes and turnips from the fields of Fife and ransoming them in the markets of the city. I received my share of the profits at the end of every month over a brandy in Maclurg's. My only role in the business was to listen to this unpleasant creature of necessity and agree six times in the space of a half-hour that one could not feed another man by going hungry oneself.

In this way I spent the rest of the winter and the first weeks of spring. The future remained a cancelled appointment, an opaque and threatening nothingness, my only connection to which lay in the effort I spent not thinking about it. I would rise late, sleep in the afternoon, discard books half read. In coffee-house or tavern I would find the dimmest corner and put on an expression to discourage any thought of conversation. With my back leaning against the wall I examined my countrymen through the object glass of my experiences, at once magnifying and diminishing. I regarded them with a contempt that brought me no satisfaction and for which I could find no reason.

Whim and boredom led me to church one Sunday morning. After the service I turned at the sound of my name and found myself facing Baillie Ritchie in a state of what seemed to be very genuine surprise and delight. He shook me vigorously by the hand, said how glad he was to see me and called over Mrs Ritchie and their two younger daughters. 'Look, my dear!' he exclaimed. 'Isn't this wonderful? It seems we were misled.'

Mrs Ritchie appeared with Caroline and Anne by her side. 'Mr . . . Mr . . .'

'Mackenzie, dear.'

'You're alive!'

The conversation continued with much inconsequential excitement with me explaining my presence in the flesh and Baillie Ritchie explaining that they had heard a rumour to the contrary some months before. I was even informed by Mrs Ritchie that the eldest daughter was not present because she worshipped elsewhere with her husband and that a child was expected in the summer. Caroline and Anne nudged each other and inspected me through their eyelashes. The curiousness of such a reception from a former landlord did not escape me. I considered that it might be the pleasing effect of, as it seemed to them, my suddenly coming back to life on a fine Sunday morning outside St Giles. I also knew that Ritchie had not lost a penny in the Company. In any case, I spent little time on such questions, so engrossed was I with the idea that here at last might be a change of fortune.

I made myself visible every Sunday morning from then on and was soon encouraged by an invitation. Once again tales of my experiences proved a useful currency – the pleasant and the curious for the whole family around the lunch table, and the pitiful truth for Baillie Ritchie himself after the ladies had withdrawn. He could not hear enough of the worst I had been through, and would listen intently with the occasional 'Ah, yes' or 'Of course' to let me know that he had foreseen all. When Mrs Ritchie began to sing the praises of Caroline and to favour me with invitations in the afternoon, I knew that tests were being applied and, it seemed, passed. Afterwards, I was not untroubled by this but would say in my defence that I was in every part of the business nothing more than the respondent to their approaches. Furthermore, if marriage had resulted I would have accepted it with, I think, sufficient sincerity. The actual outcome was undoubtedly the best for both parties.

It was during one of these talks with Ritchie – it was rather late and we had got the better of a bottle of Canary – that he surprised me by raising Borland's pamphlet. It had displeased him greatly. He became quite exercised by it and denounced particular points with vehemence, especially the conclusion, to which I had paid no attention in my brief examination of it. This was, in short, that the revealed purpose of the scheme was to rid our country of the most worthless and hateful part of its population. A 'madman's eschatology', he called it – a borrowed phrase, I think. He wanted my opinion on the Reverend Borland's state of mind – surely it was deranged? I said that this was undoubtedly true, that some had noticed it even from an early stage.

'Of course,' he said.

Drifting somewhat, I spoke a little of Mackay, that he had been much preferred to Borland, that he had been his superior, that he had died of a fever.

'There you are,' concluded Ritchie, 'the man was consumed by ambition.'

It was only a moment before taking my leave that the purpose of this conversation became clear to me.

'Surely,' he said on his doorstep, 'if even half of what you have told me is true, and I'm sure it all is, they must have been the best of men, not the worst.'

I whistled all the way back to Widow Gilbert's and, sure enough, an offer was made within the week. I accepted by return and after my second and very brief meeting with Ritchie that day I stood in the High Street, in the midst of its powerful current, and had a sudden and sweet memory of my first sight of it. I had the sense again of receiving something heaven-sent. This time it was something simple, solitary, certain and dull. Something quite perfect. Baillie Ritchie and certain other gentlemen had obtained a mineral lease for part of the estates of the Earl of Queensberry and I had agreed to supervise their interests. I would mine lead from the Galloway hills.

And so here I am, not twenty yards from where I dismounted six years ago. In my own house too – a great pleasure that – built on my orders and still the only stone house in the village. When I first got here there was only a handful of timber and turf dwellings – they stirred difficult memories and I got out of mine as quickly as I could. Now there are three times as many. In ten years we will be a town!

I came in late spring, leaving the Carlisle road at Elvanfoot and plodding steadily for hours along the banks of the Elvan Water, just as I had been instructed. The way was always upwards, the hillsides steep and the few sheep on them disconcertingly starved. I began to think that I should have asked more questions, to wonder if Ritchie had known exactly what he was offering – he admitted that he had never been here himself. I followed the first clear path that diverged from the river, continually thinking at every turn and brow that I must be about to arrive at my new home and continually being met by new vistas of desolation. I noticed buzzards in the sky and, when the gradient lessened and became an undulating plateau, found the hollows still white with snow. I saw a ptarmigan not yet out of its winter colours and scared up flights of larks every hundred yards. I encountered a man with dog and gun and took directions from him. After descending for a while I found myself looking down at the course of another small river and beside it all that then existed of Wanlockhead. As I approached it a huddle of three men walked slowly backward out of the largest structure there, a shed with two chimneys both putting out a good deal of smoke. They dropped their burden on the ground. A boy ran with a bucket from the river and doused the object with water causing much hissing and steaming. I dismounted beside them and we all admired the long bar of fresh, silver-bright lead.

'You'll be Mr Mackenzie,' said one of the men to me, in a northern English accent.

'I am.'

'Ah, well,' he said, 'all good things come to an end.' But he put out his blackened hand all the same and shook mine very honestly.

I soon learned the sense of his remark. My role was to charge the miners too much for their supplies and to pay them too little for their lead, remitting the difference to the leaseholders. My arrival ended for them a brief and profitable interregnum. However, the miners being close and the leaseholders far, the effects of time and human sympathy soon brought about some changes to this system. I introduced into the accounts what I privately refer to as compassionate inaccuracy, the moderate and balanced application of which has allowed me to remain friends with all parties.

The work is not onerous and, with respect to my time at least, I soon established for myself the life of a gentleman. I learned to shoot and acquired a dog to accompany me on my expeditions and to listen and nod to my prescriptions for the world's ills. I built this house. I patronized Mr Wardlaw at Sanquhar, read his papers and collected the books I ordered from Glasgow. I learned to cook for myself and passed what remained of my evenings by the lamp. At first, thinking that my time here would be short, I read what I believed would equip me for a triumphant return to the city: *The Villany of Stock-Jobbers Debated*, *Considerations for the East India Trade*, *The History of the Rebellion*, Adair's *Description*. My room would fill with merchants and bankers and even the occasional professor. They were amazed by my knowledge. I was offered directorships of the most promising concerns. Sometimes I would read a letter from Caroline. They became less frequent and my replies less prompt. At the end of my second year here my conscience was relieved by the news that she had become very satisfactorily engaged to an official at the bank.

I learned the attractions of this place, acquired a taste for solitude, thought less about return. I closed my coffee-house and opened a theatre wherein, *sans* stage, *sans* actors, *sans* everything, I saw whatever had most recently been printed: *The Lying Lover, The Rivals, The Way of the World, The Relapse.* This too palled. I am out of fashion now, by four years or more. Four years in which I have walked, hunted, slept by the fire in winter and under the stars in summer, with only the occasional shock of finding it was not the month I thought it was, or even the year, to jog my arm and tell me that time still passed.

Such is my whole history here until a week ago when I received a letter.

Dear Roderick Mackenzie,

It has taken no little labour to turn up this address and I hope you will not take it amiss if I say that it seems a most improbable location for a man of your sort. I am seriously alarmed this will never get to you. In any case, time is short and I must write at a venture and hope that on this occasion, at least, we have some luck.

I know nothing of your present situation and am aware therefore that the substance of this letter may be inopportune or even unwelcome to you. If that is so, I can only hope you will accept my apologies and take a generous view of the motives that have led me to risk stirring unpleasant memories. In case we should not meet, let me confess now that it is not solely your own interests I have in mind. I am sensible of the injury I have done you, more so perhaps than you are yourself. Ever since I incurred it, I have carried this debt over in my accounts without knowing how or whether it were even possible for me to clear it. I now see a way, and am obliged by the selfish demands of my own conscience to make the offer.

The precarious state of our country makes this both possible and urgent. I have, and expect still to play, some small part in these affairs. These exceptional days will present some opportunities, over which I may be able to exert some influence. Nothing is certain, but in these circumstances when it is so unclear what will be left behind, it is perhaps once again time to risk all.

If you could make yourself known to me in Edinburgh as soon as possible, I can assure you of my every effort on your behalf.

Your sincere friend,
Samuel Vetch

Today I return to Edinburgh.

I ARRIVED IN EDINBURGH three days ago. To look at the streets and the buildings (to which there have been a very few changes), I might think that I had been away a year or two at most. And yet this calming delusion lasted a mere hour or so after I turned from the Selkirk road, tired and sore from my second day in the saddle, to amble down the Cowgate. I rode slowly, enjoying familiar sights and an unreasoning optimism about the mysterious purpose of my visit. I soon realised that I might as well be a Chinaman, fresh-landed from his ship, and I still understand a bare half of what is happening.

I was just about to turn up St Mary's Wynd when I witnessed an exchange between a grey-haired man, of some substance by the look of his clothes, and another younger man. This latter was talking very earnestly, but there was nothing remarkable about the scene until he handed over a sheet of paper. The older man flung it in the air, started to abuse his interlocutor and to make frantic appeals to those around him.

'I'll have none of it, sir! You saw that, it was his, it hardly even touched my fingers! I didn't touch it at all!'

The other man's arms were spread wide with amazement. He seemed to be apologizing and was beginning to retreat when he was seized by two roughs who clearly frightened him very much. There was a violent struggle, some wrestling on the cobbles from which the poor unfortunate was hauled up with blood streaming from his forehead. Amidst the general uproar some objections began to be heard to which his captors shouted, 'Watch, Watch!' though I never saw any insignia. The grey-haired gentleman was now nowhere to be seen and when the watchmen, if that is what they were, dragged their prey into a close the disturbance was over. The sheet of paper lay forgotten on the ground and I was eager to know what could cause such violence. I manoeuvred my horse until I was directly above it and was about to dismount when a heavy boot landed on the sheet. A belligerent, unshaven face stared up at me. 'Did you know either of those two gentlemen, sir?'

I told him I did not.

'Perhaps you were interested in them?'

I told him sharply it was no business of his and demanded to know who he was.

'A man of reason, sir, and a patriot,' was all he would tell me.

He crumpled the paper and put it in his pocket before walking away. I began to get that itchy feeling of being intensely observed. There was something about my reaction to that incident which marked me out. There was a quietness around me, an excessive attentiveness, which told me that I had committed some terrible offence without giving any hint as to what it might have been, or to how I might avoid repeating it. It was with some relief that I turned the corner and started to climb up towards the High Street. It soon became clear, however, that I had been followed.

'Good afternoon, sir.'

I looked down to find a young man walking at my stirrup.

'Just come into town, sir?'

I walked on in silence, in no mood to buy.

'Come in for the business perhaps, sir?'

'What business?' I asked.

He was encouraged by this question and adopted a more confidential tone. 'I'm well connected, sir. I know all the gentlemen.'

I asked which gentlemen these might be.

'All the gentlemen, sir. I know them all, or where you can find them – for or against. Are you for or against, sir?'

'For or against what?' I asked, with such genuine bafflement that he hesitated, unsure of himself for the first time.

'The proposals, sir!'

I declared impatiently that I knew nothing of any proposals. He shrugged his shoulders and walked away.

'Wait! Do you know Mr Vetch?'

'Is he for or against, sir?'

'Don't you know?'

He pondered for a moment but had to admit he did not know the name.

I came into Nether Bow and paused to consider whether I should go left or right to find some lodgings. The High Street was crowded. I watched a printer's boy struggle to make his way through to the boards and saw how the eagerness of the people made it almost impossible for him to tear down the old sheets and paste up the new. I turned into the relative calm of the Canongate and soon found what I was looking for – an inn that had not existed the last time I was here. The place is adequate enough, though not cheap. A man carried my bag to my room and assured me that 'The house is most discreet, sir,' before sidling out.

As it turns out, my choice was not of the best. Yesterday afternoon I returned to find a bottle of hock and two glasses on my table. Mr McCrindle appeared almost at once and spent an awkward half-hour telling me of his pleasure on seeing me again and asking questions he had no business to ask. He is, it seems, the half owner of the place. He is also, I am sure, the reason why my presence here is so widely known and has been made much of on account of my former connections.

That first day I rested a while in my room and went out in the evening, determined to put an end to the mystery without, if it were possible, revealing too much of my own ignorance. I looked at the papers on the news-boards and read of Commissioners and Articles and the Equivalent and Petitions and Lord Seafield and Lord Belhaven and the Dukes of Hamilton and Argyll. But nowhere could I find a simple explanation, which could have been of any use to my imaginary Chinaman. I went to Maclurg's and Mrs Purdie's and to two or three others new to me and took a glass in each and sat in the darkest corners I could find.

'He's a scoundrel!' one man shouted. 'He's thinking of his estates in England.'

'That's right,' said another, 'that's the very truth. They would all rather be pages in London than dukes in Scotland.'

'You would not say that if you were a linen merchant, sir. These last three years the linen trade has—'

'The linen trade! They complain too much to make a living. Work harder!'

'And if I did who should I sell it to?'

'Zell it to mee, Monsieur, I am a Frenchman,' came in a comic accent from the other side of the room.

'We're supposed to be at war with you.'

'English war.'

'Scots dead!'

The linen merchant was leaving. 'Be poor, then!' he shouted at everyone. 'Let hunger mend your wits! If you'll not take it now, you'll take it in ten years.'

As he reached the door there was a chorus from the happily drunk of ' 'Bye, 'bye. 'Bye, 'bye!' I noticed, however, that several of the better sort were going with him. They formed a group in the street and I left too.

'You're absolutely right, sir,' one of them was saying. 'There's no other way.'

'They're all fools in there,' said another, 'but they don't matter. It'll pass.'

'It had better.'

'It will, it will.'

'It must.'

This last turned abruptly to me.

'And who are you listening for?'

I denied the suggestion and said, naïvely no doubt, that I was merely trying to understand.

'I'm sure,' my questioner said dismissively.

I thought, nevertheless, that these gentlemen might be a better source of information and I asked them if they knew Mr Vetch.

'Something of his reputation,' said one.

'Do you know where he lodges?'

'London!'

The linen merchant stepped forward and examined me more closely. Did I recognize him? Not exactly, but by a fraction of a second I knew exactly what he was going to say.

'Have I not seen you before?'

'I doubt it, sir.'

'Wait now . . . Yes, that's it. Weren't you involved in the Company? You were the—'

I pulled my hat down and dashed across the street, almost under the hoofs of a coach and pair coming from the direction of Parliament Close.

'Idiot!' yelled the coachman.

I just glimpsed a coat-of-arms and a worried face peering out.

Mrs Purdie's was of an even hotter temper. I had to push my way in sideways and to duck a wild punch (not aimed at me) before I could lay my hands on a glass of hot rum and work myself into a space by the wall. The force of the debate had turned the place into a cockpit with tables, chairs and crushed and angry people arranged in a rough circle. Contenders shouted and gestured at each other across a few feet of open space, the flagstones slick with various fluids and spiked with the shards of a dropped jug.

A man was standing on the edge of this space, struggling to make himself heard. 'No, no, no! You're not thinking at all. Sovereignty never put meat on your table. And even if you'll not give that word up – though I never heard it much spoken of before – that's not what you're being asked to do. It's as if . . . as if a private man were to put his stock into co-partnership with other persons. Should he be looked on as giving it away? Is not a man's property in common as real as what he has in a separate estate?'

A dozen replied at once.

'What's yours is what you can do as you please with.'

'Your country's not your shop, sir!'

'I still say it's changing master for servant.'

'What of your wife? Shall I put my stock into her six nights a week and leave the rest for you? It's not as if you'd be giving her away.'

The original speaker made a gesture of despair and turned back to his own small group of supporters. A young man stepped forward from the other side. He had the manners of a gentleman and the dress of one who would pass himself off as a merchant.

'Wait! Please! Perhaps there is something in what this gentleman says. We should at least examine it more closely. Anything less would not be fair.'

The first speaker gave a hostile glare. The sweating crowd pushed in more tightly around the tiny circle of space.

'Every grain and hair of this proposal must be scrutinized if we are to be sure of making a wise choice. As some of you may know, marriage is a hazardous venture. Strange things can happen on the way from the altar. In less time than we thought possible we can find ourselves with quite another bargain from what we intended. We must put a microscope to this marriage – for it is easier done than undone. Consider the happy couple on the very first day. Here they are . . .'

The audience laughed as he put himself astride an imaginary animal, hands in front to hold the reins.

'. . . the placid English dog going out into the world with his incorporated spouse the Scots flea. I play the flea, if you please.'

'You do it well, sir!'

'My thanks! At first all seems well. Then I open my mouth. "Go left, if you please, dear husband." Perhaps he's a little deaf, or perhaps he dislikes the left. "Go right, if you please, dear husband." Still nothing. I realize that my little voice cannot easily be heard so far away and in such big ears. I shout, "Go left! Go right! Stop! Sit!"

Nothing at all. I panic and appeal to passers by, "Help! Save me! I am being borne off by this brute. Is there no one who will help me?" They ignore me, indeed, they do not even notice me. It is as if I did not exist. But then I realize how stupid I have been. I had my protector in my pocket all along.'

He took a white handkerchief from his pocket and waved it frantically.

'But, sir, sir, I have a treaty, an Act no less. Will you not do what you promised? It says you must listen to me, just a little bit at least. Oh, won't you please? The dog stops and speaks, as if to himself; "Madam, one day when I am turning left you may say, 'Turn left,' another day when I am turning right you may say, 'Turn right.' So much will I listen to you. For the rest, I advise you to be quiet lest you cause an itch and force me to scratch."'

The 'flea' stood up to his proper height and rearranged his handkerchief in his coat pocket. His antagonist stepped forward once again, shrugging a hand off his shoulder.

'You're a very witty fellow, sir. Worth your pay, no doubt.'

'I say what I believe, sir. Your own services are, I believe, a guinea a day to talk to all who'll listen.'

'A lie! A lie and you know it!'

The younger man held two guineas high above his head. We all helplessly looked up at this morsel before quickly returning our eyes to the debate.

'Here's something that will change your mind. Will you see reason for these?'

One of the older man's seconds came forward.

'You've no manners, sir, and you've no sense. You're nothing but a clown. Our country needs better than the likes of you.'

The object of these remarks had already turned his back.

'I think we should go,' he said loudly. 'The town is so full of common whores these days.'

This was too much and the other party, four or five in all, hustled after them.

'Out in the street with you! That's where we deal with your sort!'

I listened for the commotion, but heard nothing and stayed where I was. The rest of the company hardly seemed to notice they had gone.

'It's all the Darien business that's behind it,' cried another voice. 'Those that lost the most will gain the most, and where are they if not in Parliament?'

'You've a short memory,' came the reply. 'There's many ordinary folk who put their money there, and honestly so. Some are still suffering. Are they to refuse?'

'We know where you stand.'

'You've not learned that lesson, sir. What happened to Caledonia was their doing. Everyone knows that. They cheated us then and they'll cheat us again – burnt bairn fire dreads!'

'Aye, that's the way it is. If there's any gain to be had from this it'll be for the English merchants. Sign on Monday and you'll wake on Tuesday to find a pack of them licking the butter off your bread!'

'Take that for your losses and go back where you belong!'

It was difficult to see what happened next. It was a coin, I think, that hit the union man in the eye. While he held his face and shouted in pain, a glass shattered somewhere. A stool landed on someone's shoulders and then the air was thick with missiles and fists. As the debaters surged forward from my side, a channel opened beside me and I dashed out to the street. I looked for the merchant and the 'flea', but they were nowhere to be seen. There didn't appear to be any blood on the cobbles.

I spent the rest of the evening descending through similar scenes in similar taverns before finally coming to rest in Crawford's at two in the morning. At that hour it was a sparsely populated bedlam for those who were simply too mad or dull to be tolerated anywhere else. I was approached by a particularly hopeless fellow who helped himself to a place at my table. Unkempt, unwashed, threadbare, I reflected with amazement that someone had seen fit to employ this man to distribute their ideas. He began with irrelevancies, like a beggar trying to detain you in the street, and quickly moved on to surmise that I had heard a great deal of nonsense about the 'current business'. Perhaps it would interest me to learn that the most informed and able men agreed with me that it was all nonsense, and that the only salvation for our country lay in immediate incorporation with the Dutch. This, as he put it, would ensure at a single brilliant stroke no poverty and no popery.

I could see his face turned towards mine as I ignored him and observed the other drinkers. I remarked quietly that it would also ensure an English invasion.

'Not for the first time,' he replied casually, as if this could not be a serious objection. He slipped a leaflet into my pocket. I continued to pretend he wasn't there but could see, nevertheless, his exhausted shrug as if to say, 'Contemptible, I know, but what should a man do? All the other places were taken and a man must eat.'

He shrank from something, and at the same instant my view was blocked by an expanse of tightly stretched cloth. I looked up to see the mountainous tapster standing over us. 'Is this fool troubling you, sir?'

For the briefest moment I hesitated, but it was enough to seal the poor fellow's fate. The tapster leaned over the table and expertly seized his victim. With one hand on his collar and the other on his belt he hoisted him up in the air and bore him off towards the door, his limbs flailing at the air like a helpless sheep. From outside came a grunt and a soft impact with which my own body winced in sympathy. The tapster returned and walked past me with majestic impassiveness, grumbling that a warning was a warning.

The only conversation with any life continued in the opposite corner. Three men were at the table – one with his head on his arms as if asleep, another pushing his jaw into his chest so that he should not yawn openly in the face of the third, who was explaining something to him.

'Well, there's no point in bothering about it because it just isn't going to happen. How could it? It's just so much nonsense, and haven't we heard it all before? It didn't happen then and it won't happen now. And why? Because it's impossible! It's impossible for a thousand reasons and I'll give you just one – weights and measures!'

He paused, waiting for the brilliant spark of recognition to show in his companion's eyes.

'Look,' he went on, 'I'll explain. What's the basic weight in Scotland?'

His companions seemed not to hear him.

'That's right, the French troy ounce. That means, as everyone knows, that their ounce is one and four-fifths per cent lighter than ours. Now the Scottish pint, on which all our measures are founded, should weigh fifty-five of those ounces, that's our ounces, of the running Water of Leith or, put another way, some ninety-nine square inches. Consequently, their pints are to ours as two hundred and ninety-seven is to two hundred and eighty-two. That being the case, their beer gallon is some five per cent better with near a hundred and three of such pints going to our beer barrel. And that's only the start of it! Our ordinary peck consists of twenty-one and a quarter such pints, but the peck used for oats, barley and malt near thirty-one and our boll is made up of four such pecks. All of which makes our ordinary peck about a fifteenth part less than their bushel, but the extraordinary about a fourth part more!'

'I hadn't thought of it like that before,' said the second man.

The sleeper raised his head and gave a despairing groan. 'Betrayed! And for what? Nothing but peace and prosperity!' His head fell back on his arms immediately, putting me in mind of a figure on a fancy clock whose hour had just struck.

I returned to my lodgings where I had to wake the bag-carrier to be let in. He further disendeared himself to me by once more trailing me to my door, keeping up every step of the way an appalling speech explaining that it was never too much trouble to get up for a gentleman, and that I should not even have considered apologizing. I gave him a penny as I took one of his candles. He abased himself and said it was much too kind.

The door would not open properly, and when I lit the lamp I saw that all sorts of rubbish had been pushed under it. I kicked it out of the way and sent a little book slithering across the floor. I told myself I would ignore it and got half undressed and sat on the bed and drank the water from the jug. Of course, I weakened in the end and got down on my knees to fish it out. It was exactly as I might have expected: *An Enquiry into the Reasonableness and Consequences of a Union with Scotland – Proceedings of the Wednesdays Club as Recollected by its Secretary Lewis Medway*. A card fell into my lap:

> What a great prize we will shortly salve from this wreckage. Who could value it more highly than ourselves? Hoping to see you with us soon.
>
> W.P.

An address was written on the back.

I lay on the bed and read over Vetch's letter in my mind. Only then did it occur to me that I have no clear idea what it means, and no idea at all about why I am here. Am I a born fool, perhaps? The question presented itself very forcefully to my drunken mind (and still does).

Exhausted from such a night and from my journey, I awoke late the next day. The city seemed less feverish by daylight but was still far from normal. I took my breakfast in a nearby coffee-house where the talk, though sober and calm, never strayed far from the same issues. I walked up the High Street and found a large crowd of people in and around Parliament Close. I walked through them, listening to snatches of talk, catching the tension. Members of the watch stood about. Twenty or so gathered in a group near the entrance to Parliament Hall by an odd construction of fresh timber, the purpose of which soon became clear. A sudden agitation swept the crowd and a carriage drove in at reckless speed. There was a moment of hesitation as the new arrival was identified, and then a threatening push towards him, shouts of abuse, fists and sticks waved above heads. The twenty watchmen were quickly around the carriage, the occupant of which I glimpsed only by part of a leg and his head as he entered the hall between the protection of the high wooden shutters. The coachman stood up by way of a warning and let his two huge greys feel the whip. The carriage started forward, scattering people in all directions. One was thrown to the ground and was instantly the centre of a dozen excited admirers. Elsewhere, the crowd returned to its former state, as quickly as an actor stepping off a stage.

I carried on until I stood outside Widow Gilbert's house. I had reasoned, as I lay in bed that morning, that this might be the best place from which to obtain some more reliable information. Colquhoun, I assume, is long dead while Baillie Ritchie believes I am still looking after his mines in Wanlockhead. Although I have learned that the residue of the Company maintains a small office somewhere, I cannot contemplate showing my face there. It must be admitted then that I had little choice. Besides, I felt drawn to the place.

I was a little amused and also pleased to see how much bolder it has become. From the anonymity of my days there is now a large sign –

SEAMSTRESSES AND DRESSMAKERS
Small and Fine Work Undertaken

– the purpose of which, I fancy, is more to advertise than to conceal. Certainly, I received a look of severe reproof from a passing matron as I went in. Inside, I found an even greater transformation. Carpets covered the flagstones of the hallway. The first flight of the stairs (perhaps the whole of the stairs) had a new banister with elaborately turned balusters. The old cracked doors have been replaced by new ones half as thick as ships' timbers with smart brass around the handles. Varnish and paint glinted. I was regarding this scene, not without a certain nostalgia for what it has replaced, when a young woman appeared and ushered me, without a word being spoken, into the front room. Several wholesome girls concentrated on various half-made garments. Two older gentlemen, waiting amongst them, took fright at the appearance of my unfamiliar face and at once started innocent conversations with the nearest seamstresses. When I commented later that a great deal more trouble was being taken over this show than in the old days, I was told that it is now a genuine part of the business. As Mrs Gilbert liked to put it, the house often had the honour of serving both the husband and the wife of the same family.

I gave my name and asked if I might see Mrs Gilbert herself. I found her sitting in the kitchen, at the same floury table at which I always seem to find her. A small strong-box and a few piles of coins were before her. She held thick spectacles on her nose with her left hand. Her hair was quite grey. She looked up. 'Well, then. Don't think you haven't changed yourself!'

I made my apologies while she scowled at me just long enough to make me really believe I had offended her.

'Sit down, then. Sit down. You don't need to be asked in this house. You're well?'

I said I was.

'I should think so!' She turned to the kitchen-maid. 'We saved this man's life once. I would have been sorry to hear it was all for nothing.'

She took her spectacles off and rubbed a hand over her face. The changes shocked me. She screwed up her eyes, craned forward and laughed at herself. 'Oh dear, you might be anybody.'

'You're exaggerating,' I said, 'surely.'

'Just a little.'

I spent more than an hour there. For the most part we talked about things that even now I can't remember. I was struck by how little the Union business had penetrated her world. She had heard one of her gentlemen say it had something to do with the Whigs being in power in London, but quickly disclaimed any understanding of what that meant. She thought it must all be part of 'that misfortune' a few years back, and of things never being much good after that, for most people at least, and of everyone feeling tired and having had enough.

'Enough of what?'

She shrugged. 'I don't know. Themselves. I don't take much of an interest in it, Mr Mackenzie, but I would say that it's a sort of boredom. You know, some of the girls have been asked to do things not even I've heard of, and that's saying something. And then there's the money.'

'What money?'

'I couldn't say where it's coming from. I mean, not exactly. But there've been more English sovereigns spent in this place in the last six months than in . . . well, since I don't know when. Now that must make a difference, wouldn't you say?'

'I suppose so. It hasn't done you any harm, then?'

She laughed. 'What does? Contentment, I suppose, but I don't worry about that.'

She asked me where I had been all this time, why I had been neglecting them. I repeated the name of my home for the last six years, but still she shook her head. We spoke of old friends and of my convalescence under her eaves. She asked what had brought me back to Edinburgh. Was I going to stay?

A bell rang and I looked up to see another novelty. Five little bells were attached to a board on the wall by means of coiled springs. Cords ran from each spring up to tubes that disappeared into the ceiling. Below each bell a name was painted: Alice, Mary, Caroline, Joanna. Beneath the fifth the painted name had been scratched out. Chalked below it I read 'Ruth'. The bell above 'Alice' was still quivering. 'A sweet girl,' said Widow Gilbert, 'just joined us from the country.'

I made my apologies and returned to the High Street. Though on one level fruitless, I am glad I went. As I stood under that sign and put on my hat I had an odd, abstracted sense of completion.

I started back the way I had come, but found the crowd so swollen that it had flooded out of Parliament Close and was now blocking the whole High Street. It was clear that some news had just been spread and that something particular was being anticipated. The mood was easier than before, jocular even. A fine carriage made its way slowly through the crowd, which parted respectfully. I asked a man whose it was.

'Lord Belhaven's! Don't you know anything?'

The carriage stopped and I stared at it expectantly for several seconds before realizing that the rest of the crowd's attention was elsewhere. A cart appeared from the direction of the Canongate, its sides draped in brown cloth like an enormous closet bed. All eyes were on it when it stopped. The cloth dropped away, revealing the scene to an enthusiastic cheer. A huge scarlet apple, a yard high, stood to one side. Beside it there was an embarrassed boy of about twelve years, long bleached straw wig, saltire bodice and skirt with paper leaves stitched on about the middle. Despite the modesty of his dress, this little Scots Eve was immediately the subject of lewd whistles and many indecent proposals. The boy reddened and shifted. A serpent approached him from the left, or at least a man in green with something protruding from behind that suggested a tail. More cheers as he pressed his unwelcome attentions on the bashful little Eve and gestured invitingly towards the apple. He turned to the crowd to deliver his speech in the common conception of an English accent.

'Behold how lovely and comely a thing it is, how pleasant to the eye. Think, madam, how sweet it will be if only you will taste it.'

The boy shook his head emphatically. The crowd abused the serpent and shouted advice to Eve.

'Consider, madam, what good nourishment such a fine-looking fruit must be. Think on the advantage that must come from it. I tell you, it shall make you wise, you shall be as gods.'

Eve leaned towards the serpent and whispered in his ear.

'What's that?' shouted the serpent. 'Someone told you you would be thrown out, that you would have no home of your own? But, my dear, is that so very bad? To be ejected from this little place, this worthless hovel of a garden? Oh, no, my dear. You have been misled. Someone has lied to you. They only want to keep you low. This little cabbage patch may be yours, but it is no paradise. Paradise is elsewhere.'

Still Eve was unconvinced. She shook her head, shrank away. Then, by some device I could not see, the apple began to turn. The other side became visible – rotten, half eaten away and with a rolled-up copy of 'Articles of Union' sticking out of it in a suggestively worm-like fashion.

'Told you so, told you so, told you so!' chanted the crowd, like children at a fair.

The serpent plucked the Articles from the rotting flesh of the apple and applied himself once again to his audience. 'Gentlemen, ladies, be not affrighted with their ugly shape, they are better than they are bonny. Come, taste. Come, make a narrow search and enquiry. They are good for Scotland – the wholesomest food a decaying nation can take. You shall find the advantages, you shall find a change of condition, you shall become rich immediately. You shall be as the English, knowing gold and silver.'

A third figure appeared, bewigged, black-coated and blustering. He brushed the serpent aside. 'Enough of this, sir, you have no skill. The world will not wait for you.' He produced an apple from his pocket and began to force it down the throat of the unfortunate Eve. 'Eat, I say! Swallow down this incorporating union. Though it please neither eye nor taste it must go over. You cannot know your own good, madam. You must trust your physicians. Swallow, and you shall have reasons afterwards.'

The physician abruptly disappeared, and a violent disturbance began in front of the cart. I saw his wig fly off, two men seizing him and others from the crowd coming to his rescue. Another man, very like those I had seen bearing off that young gentleman in the Cowgate, clambered up on to the cart from the far side. The straw-haired Eve jumped down in alarm and ran off as a general conflict began. Everywhere I saw members of the watch I had not noticed before. I saw a hand around the serpent's ankle, pulling him down from the cart and then one of the watchmen taking his hands from his face and looking in surprise at his own blood. The yard-high apple was knocked off its stage. My last sight of it was as the bone of contention between two very red-faced and passionate antagonists.

I pushed my way to the edge and emerged with nothing worse than a bruised jaw and a dented hat. At the same moment Lord Belhaven's carriage made its way clear and began to pick up speed. It had only gone a few yards when a bottle arced out of the blue and smashed on the roof. A man leaned out of one of the topmost windows. He shouted after the disappearing carriage, 'Sorry!'

For the rest of that day and all of this I have kept to my room, disturbed only by the sound of broadsides being pushed under the door and by two gentlemen who thought I could help them on account of my once having been 'something in the Company'. As everyone's business seems so well known to everyone else I am assuming that Mr Vetch, if he is in Edinburgh and wishes to find me, will have no difficulty in doing so. I tell myself there could be a thousand good reasons for his absence, but am filled with doubts and fears all the same. I learned from Widow Gilbert that the business in Parliament will not go beyond next Thursday at the very latest. I shall wait till then, but no longer.

*

ALL IS SAID AND DONE. The decision is made, though not by me. I should be asleep. It's a miracle that I am not, and a torture too. If only for an hour or two – sweetly to know nothing of this crime. Two in the morning and still I have to listen to their triumphs. What could be more bitter? But I'll not complain of that. Let it come, let me hear it all. I'll steel myself, and if later I should backslide or cavil with my own conscience I'll see their faces again and hear their voices. Their cruelty will keep me true.

In a few hours I will be in the saddle again, going south with James. I must think of that. I must hold to it if I am to stay sane between now and dawn. All I can feel is the need to go, a painful hunger for distance between myself and everything I have known. A cleansing, an effacement. Shall I change my name? Comical too, is it not? I will be the one fleeing from the scene like a criminal while the betrayers drink and swagger, red-handed. Will the roads south be busy tomorrow? That is the question. We'll see what we're made of then.

How else could I spend these few hours but with this book? So long idle, unnecessary, finished even – did I think that? I need it again now more than ever. It has become a shelter, a home of sorts – the story of myself my only home? Well, maybe, but no time to play with that now. There is another motive, too – the lure of completion and, with that, never having to write another word. The consummation is horrible, no doubt, and I would shrink from it were it not for the thought of making a perfect end, of laying down the burden, paid to the last penny. Now is the time to cover the last few pages bound in by the good and foresightful Mr Shipp. I shall end with an oath never to take up the pen again if not for the honest simplicities of the ledger and the bill.

What Vetch told me, I believe now – that he made no difference, that I made no difference, that none of us did. Even the beasts bellowing outside my window, stamping with joy for their loyal murders, are not to blame. There's not one who couldn't say he made no difference, that the dead would still have been dead and in the same place and at the same time and in the same fashion all down to the very last if he had stayed at home that day. I want to condemn them, I want to hang them all and would do it too if their advocate were not so clever. For each one he trails before me so many witnesses to his good character, he shows me his children, the evident products of his decency, the unanswerable proof of his necessity. I hear his customers or his employer attest to his fair-dealing. The minister of his parish appears and says he knows him well, that what he has heard is not true, it cannot be, it is impossible, an outrage. And yet . . .

Who is the culprit, then? For whom shall we get the rope ready now? How shall we know him? One line in the mirror, a tic, a blemish in the eye, the brand of possession, the daylight signature of that black power that seizes us by the ankles and pulls us down to beasthood. It grunts and we hear singing – 'Now is the moment. Now, of all your life, you are free. You were made for this. Do your worst!' It is a darkness lurking behind my head, turning as I turn. I can smell it. The stench strengthens every minute, oozing through the window-frames.

Who woke it? Who set its course? Paterson? In my mind I have hanged him too. I saw him an hour ago, conjured in this very room, laced and smiling, as sane and solid as in his best days. I was dizzy with hatred. I felt the hemp in my hand and pulled every bit as hard as the rest. Then I remembered the truth – face ashen with shock, trembling behind his door with pistol in hand, at the edge of his wife's grave and then later, feverish and raving. In the end all that can be said is that he should have known better. We should all have known better.

So Vetch is right. He didn't make any difference and is not to blame. I didn't make any difference and am not to blame. There was nothing I could have done and all my efforts to the contrary were . . . what? Mere youthfulness? Outrageously, I make myself the centre of all this and think how much better it might have been for me if I had been back in Wanlockhead. It's a sort of daydream I will always have, harping on the narrowness of the chance by which I witnessed these events and received their bitter impress. I was so close to escaping them, to deciding that I had been deceived, that I would return to those untroubled hills, go on as before, hearing of it only as a piece of old news, the sting long since drawn. I was going to order a horse, to pack and be gone when I came back and found the note amongst all the rubbish pushed under the door. Now there will be another life.

*

I SAT IN THE CHAIR by the window for a good while, contemplating the letter on the floor, half suspecting that it might turn me from my purpose. I scrutinized the writing on the outside and tried unsuccessfully to force a recognition. I snapped it open and found, with undeniable relief, that it was indeed from Vetch – brief, apologetic, persuasively earnest. I tried to pick an argument with it: it was too brief, surely; it explained nothing. I was owed more than that and should leave anyway. I read it again and decided, as I put it to myself, to grant him another day.

I spent that day filling my time as best I could. In the afternoon and early evening I walked through the town seeing more of what I had seen before only more heated, more desperate. The final vote was then a mere three days away. Faces were angry or drawn, or secretively expressionless.

I returned to my room in twilight and fumbled for a taper. I turned and froze, at once putting all my resources into staying still and silent. A ripple of cold crept up my neck as I became certain that the shape I could see against the windows was the head and shoulders of a man sitting in my chair. We were as still and silent as each other and my mind formed a picture of the little pistol I kept in my saddlebags. Believing that I must be invisible to him and that he must somehow have missed the sound of my entry, I spent the next three minutes creeping towards this pistol and pushing my hand into the bag until I could lay firm hold of it. It was only then that I realized I had neglected to form any intention as to what to do with it. During another three minutes in that awkward and increasingly painful position the sound of heavy and regular breathing from the direction of the chair disturbed me a little. At last, when I had despaired of him moving and when the pain in my left leg had become intolerable, some external force mercifully intervened and made a decision for me. I took two great strides towards the door, threw it open to let in some light from the corridor then charged down the hapless sleeper with a wordless roar, the only significance of which was my own fear. The poor fellow exploded with fright and on seeing himself confronted by a madman with a flintlock, let out a similar yell. This resolved itself into semi-articulate gabblings the gist of which was 'No!' Other people had already begun to rush into the room, the bag-carrier to the fore with a lamp in his hand. There was a general uproar as men demanded to know what had happened, who had been hurt, where the criminals were, who were these two statues staring at each other and trembling? I took the lamp into my own hand and held it over the man in the chair. What I saw flickered on the edge of recognition, but made no immediate connection.

The man leaned towards the light and peered at me. 'It is . . .' A few inches closer. He cocked his head to one side and checked my features with a squint eye. 'It is Roderick Mackenzie, is it not?'

He became sure, and as the lines of fear eased away there appeared before me Mr Samuel Vetch, changed only by the nine years that had passed since my last sight of him. An embarrassing error was declared, the room cleared, food and wine ordered.

For the first half-hour and the first half-bottle we spent our time apologizing to each other. I briefly recounted my life, dismissing everything about the colony with a curt 'You know all about that.' I explained Ritchie's favour to me and a little of how I had subsequently earned my living. He received the information with the expression of one comforting the bereaved. I asked in turn how Fortune had treated him. I heard of a partnership in ventures to the Gold Coast, the margins obtainable on the importation of port after the Methuen treaty, which I knew about, of course (I nodded). I listened to his enthusiasms on the subject of insurances – I had heard of the Sun Fire Office? A most promising start. He was lucky enough to have three per cent. I heard of his house in London, of the desk with drawers stuffed full of Bank of England stock. He stopped suddenly, gave a little smile of remorse. 'Well, that's not for today.'

'Our lives have been very different,' I observed.

'Perhaps we can change that.'

'Oh, yes?'

There was an instant of concern in his face as I let him catch my tone.

'If you want to,' he said.

Bag-carrier entered with our meal. He took his time, speaking incessantly as he arranged the table, praising the pheasant, describing its sauce. 'It's the Seville oranges, gentlemen, they have the bitterness.'

He had taken the liberty of bringing another bottle, thought we would not object. Vetch dismissed him with silver, told him he would be called when needed.

'You made good your losses, then?'

'Losses?'

'From the Company.'

'Ah.'

'You were more fortunate?'

'Mm?'

'Perhaps you didn't make any losses?'

'It's true, I didn't. I disposed of my share three weeks after the fleet sailed.'

'Good.'

There was a long silence. A knife shrieked against a plate.

'You didn't think it a sound investment?'

'You knew that?'

'What?'

'You knew that I had sold out?'

'No.'

'You seemed to know.'

I shrugged. I returned my attention to my meal, crushing a coil of orange peel between my teeth. I distributed the last of the first bottle between our two glasses.

'You got my letter, obviously. You understood it?'

'I'm beginning to. You're here to see justice done, or something like that. Tell me, what did you know?'

'I knew that the English colonies would be instructed not to sell you so much as a cup of water. In the event of an attack from Spain, the English navy would observe and report. Nothing more. It was the advice of a man called Vernon. It was almost certain that the government would take it.'

'Of course,' I said, 'I knew that too. It's just that I had been in Darien three months before I knew.'

Vetch threw down his knife and stood up abruptly. For a while he stood silently by the windows, looking out into the street. He turned to me angrily. 'Don't you remember what it was like? If I'd had it printed and pasted up on every wall in the city do you think it would have made any difference? No! What would they have said? The English are against us. Together with the Spanish, half the seagoing world is against us. So much the better. All the greater triumph for us! They weren't listening, Roderick. There was nothing I could have done.'

He returned to his chair, drank. I could count his heartbeats as the wine shimmered in his glass.

'Do you remember the note Fletcher handed you that day when you came to see me?'

It took me a few seconds to think what this referred to.

'I remember a note,' I said, 'and I remember another later with the letter to Sir Robert Blackwood. Yes.'

'Do you remember what they said?'

'I remember what they did for me.'

'Yes,' said Vetch quickly, 'but do you remember what they said?'

I sent my mind back and suddenly, as it were, broke through into a scene of myself opening those letters and the reply from Blackwood, confirming my joy. The emotion returned to me, the smell of my office, the feel of the paper between my fingers. I had everything I wanted. I was going to Darien! I experienced the pleasure of a sudden, perfect, unbidden memory of childhood. The motionless happiness of running in a field under the sun, going nowhere, untainted by all that would come after. I looked over my own shoulder and read the strangely incongruous words. Could that be right? Was that really what he had said? There was a tremor of anxiety and all at once the black history of the last nine years poured in and destroyed it all. Vetch had been speaking to me.

'I said I'm sorry. I should have said more. I should have made it clear.'

The exact words of that brief correspondence ran through my mind.

'Is that your "wrong"?' I asked with a smile.

'For a long time I thought you were dead.'

'Many are.'

I regretted this when I saw its effect.

'Mr Vetch,' I declared, 'I must forbid you ever to apologize to me again. I want to tell you something that I am sure will shock you. When I came to find you when you were ill – believing you were ill, I think I can say – I prayed with all the passion my little soul was capable of that you would remain ill until the fleet left with me in your place. Indeed, if you had died – don't think I didn't consider it! – I would have accepted it as something done for my sake, as a blessing straight from God. I do remember those days. There was nothing you could have done.'

We stared at each other in deep and slightly drunken seriousness. I mumbled something about it not being the first time I had profited from death. Glasses were raised.

'Forgiven?'

'Nothing to forgive!'

We talked of other things. I learned the more precise truth behind what I had already heard as gossip and brawling and pantomime. The Union men were in the ascendant again and had found the key to unlock all the obstacles to their project. The Company's accounts had finally been closed and made up. Certain important gentlemen had determined that it had lost its subscribers £232,884 and a quantity of shillings, pence and farthings that I forget. This sum is in addition to the several tens of thousands still awaited by countless chandlers, drapers, tanners, sailmakers, printers, ironmongers, gunsmiths and widows. The problem is to be solved at a stroke by a payment from England, which will more than cover the loss they were so pleased to help make in the first place. All that is required of us in turn is to dissolve our small estate into the body of a much larger, the nature and fitness of which we may only guess at, trusting to the good nature of our new masters. The outcome of the vote was not in doubt. According to Mr Vetch, that had been 'settled' many weeks before. Other sums or, as he put it, 'persuasions', had been expended far from the prying eyes of the public accounts. Men of influence, in and out of Parliament, had been made agreeable. Even Belhaven, the darling of the crowds, was spending more on his London house. Paterson had not been forgotten in this process. Though it was nowhere written down I was assured that after a certain period he would be generously compensated. I showed Vetch the book I had received and the card that had come with it.

'He is Medway, of course.'

'So I assumed.'

He read the card.

'You haven't met with him?'

I shook my head.

'Don't. He's out of credit.'

I reassured him on that point and expressed my surprise that Paterson had added his voice so loudly to the unionist side.

'Why not?' said Vetch. 'The man's a merchant, not a patriot. Besides, he always wanted the Union.'

I felt as if I had missed a step and my recovery was too slow by half.

Vetch smiled. 'At last I've said something that surprises you.'

I struggled to find some convincing dismissal of this, but in the end said nothing.

'If Darien succeeded, England would have been all the more eager for union to get her hands on such a prize. If it failed and the country was pauperized she would have a bargain on her own terms. Only the price would change.'

'Is that true?'

'I had it from the man himself. In any case, how could it not be true? There's a law to these things, whatever men think. You see, Roderick? There really was nothing anyone could have done.'

I remained silent.

'I'm sorry,' said Vetch.

'I shouldn't be surprised. I suppose I shouldn't be surprised at anything now. I don't know – it's just that for . . . what?, near ten years now again and again I've thought, "Then I was deceived, but now I understand." And every time I said it I became more sure that I had passed through all the deception there was and that I really did understand and could not possibly be deceived any more. And then a year later I would be saying it again and swearing to myself that I was stripping away the very last veil and seeing everything as it really is. And now . . . Well, does it never end?'

Mr Vetch looked perplexed and suggested, rather easily, that this must be a sort of progress.

'Mr Vetch, may I ask you what you're doing here? You didn't come up here to see me.'

'True.' He paused. 'Shall I tell you?'

'Please.'

'If you promise to understand.'

'I promise to try.'

'I'm spending the Government's money.'

'You're a part of all this?'

'Wait, please. I'm neither for nor against, I swear, and I haven't turned anyone. I was approached in London several months ago because of my old association with the Company. The Government had got into a panic for some reason, I don't know why, and wanted to send confidential agents north to make the business more sure. They sent Defoe . . .'

'Who?'

'It doesn't matter – others also who were to be well supplied with money for persuading influential people and compromising potential trouble-makers. I had the choice of telling them that they were wasting their money, whereupon they would simply have commissioned someone else with the same task, or taking it and seeing that it got into some more deserving pockets.'

I told him frankly that I would have preferred some other explanation.

'I've helped many people who were hurt by what happened in Darien – people who won't get a penny from the official settlement.'

'Did they not ask where the money came from?'

'Some did and held their noses. Others asked and were all the happier to take it. They appreciated the irony. Most didn't ask at all – I told them I was from the Company, which they know full well isn't worth a farthing. A widow isn't a traitor for putting a little more bread on her table.'

'That depends.'

'Listen . . .'

There was a sudden burst of shouting from outside. As I wanted air I went to the window and looked out, but could not at first see anything. The sound seemed to be coming from directly opposite and I realized that it was the reflection of a crowd approaching down Leith Wynd. I opened the window further and leaned out. They soon appeared in the crossroads, milling tightly about a collection of lanterns and torches. They turned away from us, going up through Netherbow to the High Street.

'Death throes,' said Vetch.

I sat down again, unaware that I had witnessed the beginnings of a tragedy.

We stared gloomily at the carcass of our pheasant, the odour of which was beginning to offend our sated appetites. Mr Vetch brought his hand down sharply on the table.

'Let us change the tune!'

Bag-carrier was summoned and the table reset with coffee and a decanter of Malmsey.

'I have an offer to make you, Roderick Mackenzie.'

'English gold?'

'No. But if you need money . . .'

I shook my head.

'A position.'

'I want to be able to say I had nothing to do with this.'

'It hasn't anything to do with this. It's between you and me.'

'In return?'

'Nothing.'

'I've never been made an offer like that before.'

'It's just what it seems, Roderick. The business I mentioned on the Gold Coast? I still have a small share of it and am occasionally in touch with the other investors. They've done well and I know they want to open a London office. I told them I knew the ideal man.'

'What sort of business?'

'Trade.'

'No complications?'

'Such as?'

'National companies, empires, flags, patriots?'

He shook his head firmly. 'They don't know the meaning of the word. Just merchants. There's no one else there – not yet, anyway. You should at least try it. If it's not to your taste you can always find something else.'

'As easy as that?'

'For you, in London, yes. It's another world, Roderick. You should be there.'

I said I would think about it and we passed on, dawdling through trivia for another half-hour before he pulled on his gloves and picked up his hat.

'I have to go south tomorrow,' he told me. 'Do you remember James Minto?'

'Certainly.'

'You could give your answer to him. He's going down too, but will be here for another few days. May I tell him where you lodge?'

He held out a card on which he had already written an address. 'Write to me there if you don't see him.'

He trusted that I would do the right thing and I assured him that I would. In the corridor he stopped and feigned a sudden memory.

'D'Azevedo!' he exclaimed. 'Cohen d'Azevedo, you remember him, surely? I see him now and again. Once a year or so in London. He still speaks of you.'

With that we parted.

*

IF I FELT BEFORE that I had missed a step, what happened next took the whole earth from beneath my feet.

In the morning I found the streets unusually busy. Through all the city's ports there was a steady inward stream of people, drawn by a desire to be present for the final vote. The High Street by Parliament was almost impassable, but the most excited and vicious part of the crowd was clustered about the Tolbooth. I went there myself, thinking some spectacle must have attracted them. A nervous face looked out of one of the prison's uppermost windows. The crowd growled like a dog. I questioned a man and learned that they were there to see justice done. The night before an English ship had come into Leith Road. Its captain and several other crew-members had been seized by the mob and thrown into the care of a terrified magistracy. Some were shouting about pirates, others about spies. I heard the name Green. I heard *Worcester*. I began to fall.

I ran down the street towards Nether Bow, cut through Hart's Close and took a horse from the New Port inn. I rode recklessly against the thickening influx, making a catechism in my mind of the commonness of the name Green and of the certainty that there must be more than a single ship in the world called the *Worcester*. This idiocy brought me no comfort and I felt no surprise when I clattered along the quays and saw her there brilliantly painted and prinked out, unique and unmistakable amidst all the dowdy decay around her. All her hatches were open and a jubilant rabble was already busy with her cargo, stacking bales and chests of all sorts on the quayside. I heard what would be repeated many times over the next day and a half – that her cargo was worth three hundred thousand sterling and that our taking of it was a great blow to England. I heard it even in the mouths of those who had their hands on that very same precious cargo and who could see for themselves that there was nothing but calico and coir and a ton or two of coffee, which could not be worth a twentieth of what they claimed.

When I arrived a young man stood officiously above these thefts and made a show of directing them. He informed me with evident embarrassment that he was the harbourmaster's assistant clerk (the harbourmaster himself being indisposed), and that the cargo was merely being sorted through for the purposes of making an inventory for the Court of Admiralty. He had hardly completed this explanation when a violent brawl broke out on the matter of a brassbound chest with a promisingly stout lock. A knife appeared and was waved at the other contenders. The chest was dragged away and, with the help of some confederates, was thrown on a waiting cart, which at once set off and disappeared behind the warehouses. All eyes were on the hapless youth who had been sent out to do his master's duty. He walked towards the nearest warehouse, quickened his pace along its side and then, almost at a run, darted through a stout door. We could hear the sound of bolts being thrown. A cheer was raised and I looked on in disgust as an unrestrained despoliation began.

A delighted audience gathered and chorused a multitude of justifications. Of all the absurdities I heard, three soon came to dominate. There was the old story, harking back to their first disappointment, that Green was a spy and an agent, sometimes for the Spanish and sometimes for the English, and his only part in the colony at Darien was to destroy it. Others forgot that he and his crew had ever been there and said that the *Worcester* was taken as a reprisal for one of the Company's ships seized off Gravesend for offending against the privileges of the East India Company. For the third party this was too dull – they insisted they were pirates, notorious for countless thefts, rapes and murders along the Malabar coast. The most extraordinary thing was that whenever the adherents of these three opinions met they found themselves in full agreement. A pirate man would listen to a reprisal man, or a reprisal man to a spy man and would at once shout, 'That's right!' or 'The very truth, sir!' Contradiction had become confirmation. I hoped until the last minute, or at least I pretended to hope. But when I heard this insanity, an appalled, constricting fear rose up from some simpler part of me, which knew how it had to end. I remounted my horse and began to ride back to the city. I looked back from the corner of the last warehouse and saw them cutting down her rigging and sails with axes, taking down her spars and preparing to dismast her. Though nothing but a mob, there was a strange order to everything they did. There was something repulsive about it, the way a spider moves its limbs.

As soon as I was back in town I busied myself with uncovering the whereabouts of the more substantial privy councillors and then in embarking on a day of fruitless embassies. In spite of the importance of the next day's business I could get the scent of only a few of them, and in every one of these cases I failed even to catch sight of my quarry. I was informed at the Marquis of Tweeddale's house that he was taken with a violent cold and hoarseness, which made an interview impossible. At the lodgings of the Earl of Roxburgh a servant insisted he had never been near the place, even as he wore the Earl's livery. The Earl of Crawford had not yet entered town, having been delayed by a lack of horses. Cockburn, the Lord Justice Clerk, was home but suffering from such a sprain that he could not even descend the stairs. A window slammed as I looked up.

I pushed my way through the crowd around the Tolbooth and, through a two-inch slit in the door, lied about important papers for the keeper. I found him in a small room on the second floor, pale and greatly preoccupied with his own misfortunes.

'Well?'

I apologized for my deception and quickly stated my true name and business. His only reaction was disappointment. He looked ill, feverish. I said something about my attempts to find some privy councillors.

He suddenly came alive. 'And will they not speak to you? I'm sorry to hear that. I don't know who you are, sir, but I'm the keeper of the Tolbooth and since last night they've not had a word to say to me! This is too rank a business. They're all . . . They're—' He stopped abruptly, shook his head, put up his hand. 'I didn't say that!'

I asked if I could see the prisoners.

'On no account!'

'Why not?'

'You might kill them.'

I protested.

'You are a friend to these men?'

I hesitated. He lunged over his desk. 'A friend, eh? Twenty letters I have sent out, more. Not a word in reply, not a single word!'

Had he spoken to Captain Green?

He told me he had and briefly related their story. They had been trading in the Caribbean for six months and were returning to London with their cargo. Bad weather forced them north around Cape Wrath. As a consequence they were short of a few days' water and had put into Edinburgh to make good. They denied all knowledge of what had been put to them.

'Do you believe them?'

'Not my business. Now that's not right – I did receive one reply, from my deputy. He's ill, if you please. Ill!'

He started to pace the room, occasionally glancing down through the narrow window, which was already missing several panes of glass.

'I may not leave the building except in the charge of my deputy. It is one of the terms of my office. The terms of my office are many and not very pretty. The terms of my office are cunningly constructed, sir, to ensure that in certain rare and unpleasant circumstances it is I who have to sit on this ton of powder.'

I asked him what he would do.

'Nothing at all. I shall execute the terms of my commission as I understand them, and I understand them to mean that I should do nothing. I shall sit on my office, sir, and do nothing until I can sit on it no longer.'

He began to descend the spiral steps behind his desk, muttering as he went, 'Pilates! Cowards and Pilates!'

I shouted after him that his prisoners were good and innocent men. The words 'I didn't say that' were all I had for reply.

Night fell. A hooting, howling vigil began around the foot of the Tolbooth. Bonfires were lit, fiddlers played for dancers, beer and brandy flowed. From time to time men disagreed with their fists before reconciling themselves with more furious abuse hurled against the walls of the prison.

At dawn the crowd was swollen with fresh levies and it soon engulfed both the Tolbooth and Parliament Hall. By nine I saw the first weapons and sensed the horrible excitement caused by the glint of clean steel pike-heads in unlicensed hands. Detachments of the watch came out of the guard house and paraded themselves almost up to the edge of the crowd before retiring under a shower of stones and bottles. An hour later the castle governor tried his strength. A squadron of horse came jingling down from Castle Hill and exercised itself in the Land Market. The crowd remained unabashed and the dragoons withdrew a little, though not out of sight. The despairing features of the Tolbooth keeper were seen at his window and there was a renewed frenzy of shouting and jeering. After a minute, this resolved itself into the chant of 'Justice! Justice!'

By noon all parties were tired of these overtures. A jolt ran through the crowd, affecting everyone like the limbs of a single startled body. I could see nothing but soon heard the information, flowing back from the western edge of the crowd, that the dragoons were advancing. I had drifted to the north side of the street and was able to clamber on to a mounting block to see for myself. They approached at a slow walk in a double line across the Land Market. At the word of command they drew their swords. The crowd flowed threateningly towards them, confident of its indestructibility. The chests of the horses were now pushing against the hands and faces of the crowd. The dragoons held their swords high and, for a few paces more, waded on into the deeps. I saw the swords start to fall, heard the jeers turn to panic and anger. I was prepared for flight, but was amazed to experience a sudden more violent lurch forward. In an instant the single intelligence of the crowd understood that victory was theirs. The dragoons had been ordered to use the flats of their swords at first and that half-heartedness against such an opponent was enough to ensure their failure. I saw horses rearing, one with bloody flanks. Hands grabbed for reins, pulling them sideways. Dragoons toppled and were instantly surrounded. Terrified animals began to back away and collide with those behind them. In less than a minute the line broke and retreated. Half a dozen dragoons were allowed to follow on foot.

A new cry was taken up: 'Treason! Treason!' The object of this abuse could just be seen by the weigh-house and at the corner of West Bow – several carriages waiting in a line, each with a coat-of-arms on its doors. The crowd was momentarily drawn back to its original purpose. If the final vote could be prevented its great country would be preserved, for a day or two at least. More carriages appeared, separated from the crowd by a hundred yards and a disorganized screen of soldiery. A figure stepped down from one of them and played the gentleman's part, walking calmly up and down behind the dragoons, causing the air to cloud with insults and missiles.

Whether there was a signal, or whether the keeper of the Tolbooth had at last received some instructions I cannot say, but the crowd turned like a vast, single, lumbering idiocy, just sensitive enough to feel the twitch of a halter about its neck. The greater noise was once again about the Tolbooth and the current flooded rapidly back towards it, leaving the dragoons and the lords in their carriages without another thought. More people flooded in from the sides and I was borne along in a press of humanity so dense that I could neither lift my arms nor take more than half a step at a time without treading on ankles and toes. An undertow caught me and swung me round so that I could see the door of the Tolbooth. Two or three men were ineffectually stabbing at the doors with pikes. At the next blow the doors swung open without the least resistance. Twenty or thirty of the crowd rushed forward, causing a vacuum that reverberated through us all as a sudden forward tug. There was an explosive roar of triumph and another change of direction. The crowd started to flood northward by every possible outlet. I was carried downstream towards Nether Bow before being violently plucked to the left and propelled down Halkerton's Close. The crowd struggled to force its way through New Port and then began to flow around it by the shores of the loch. There was a sudden release of pressure as it battered its way into the Physic Garden and rushed over it, trampling everything into a worthless mire. Having achieved the openness of Leith Road it was joined by further flows coming up from Nether Bow and westward along Canongate Backs. In full spate, it bore down on Leith Sands. The beast knew its mind.

It spilled eagerly on to the sands and arranged itself round the scaffold, constructed in certain knowledge of what was to come. It was a simple frame, consisting at top and bottom of spars from the *Worcester.* Three nooses were already hanging from the upper spar. A shudder of excitement ran through the crowd and I turned to see pikes moving towards the scaffold. When they got there the prisoners were pushed up a few steps at the back. Only then did I see them. The other white man and the black man I had never seen before, but there was no mistaking Green. I was pressed forward to within twenty yards. Only the crowd held me up as I stared at Green's face. I don't believe he saw me.

The hangman appeared, or a clown playing the role of hangman, black-hooded. The crowd quietened, moaned and whimpered to itself, shifted from foot to foot. Green and the crewmen were forced to balance on the lower spar and had the nooses placed around their necks. The hangman hesitated and looked out to the Firth. There was the hull of the *Worcester*, still in her festival colours. Small boats were rowing away and thick smoke already oozed from her hatches. The hangman held up hoods to the crowd and placed them first on the black man, then on the white man. He came to Green who jerked his head away and started to speak. 'People . . .' he said.

The hangman kicked his feet off the spar and set him swinging over the heads of the crowd.

I refused to take my eyes off the *Worcester*. I watched the smoke thicken and the first flames appear. Dull red at first, soon brilliant and furious. They burned up the ship as if it was nothing but paper.

On the scaffold the men died and were still. The crowd glared at the bodies in sulky, disappointed silence. The hangman cut the ropes with a hatchet. The bodies fell and were thrown on a cart.

Only when the great sullen mass formed a procession behind the cart did it begin to find its voice again. Even so, the attempts at jubilation were never whole-hearted. Songs disintegrated and trailed away. Chants were weak-voiced and embarrassed. The crowd was jaded and resentful. As it approached the city and was pressed together by the narrowing road it began to tear at itself. Insults and accusations were thrown from group to group. It kicked and punched and bit. A blow landed on my face. I tasted blood and saw it streaked on the back of my hand. I caught a fellow with his hand in my pocket – two frightened faces asking questions of each other, the feel of fresh paper which I grasped and pushed further down. Beatings began wherever victims could be found – questioners, objectors, bearers of the wrong accent, the wrong expression. I saw one dragged by the collar, indignant at first, then the terror as he realized the hopelessness of it. Cudgels and fists rose and fell over him, boots staved in teeth and ribs. His coat had been too costly and I felt my own begin to burn on my back. I had stopped in the middle of the flow and saw that others had stopped too and had begun to stare at me. I tried – the mere thought of it scalds me with humiliation – I tried to make my face look like theirs, I took up a line of one of their idiotic songs, I shouted something against the Union. I might as well have tried to change my smell with a pack of dogs at my heels.

A circle had almost closed around me when someone grabbed my arm. I pulled away. He shouted at me. 'Come on, you fool!'

Then I was running behind him. We darted to the left along the North Backs until the crowd thinned. Then up a close – the wrong one as it turned out – and into a closed court. We ran on through a back door, through a kitchen – screams, apron flying – through a hallway – a poker waved, shouts of 'Thief!' – through the front door and into the Canongate itself.

'Don't you lodge here?' asked the man.

I took the lead. We half battered down the door to McCrindle's inn and stumbled into my room.

That was some fourteen hours ago, when I was someone else. Dawn greys the windows and my bags lie packed by the door.

The man took off his hat, laboured to regain his breath.

'You do recognize an old whoremonger, don't you?'

I thanked him, and then again and again until he laughed and begged me to stop.

He asked if I had spoken to Mr Vetch. The crying of the mob grew louder as it regained the High Street with its horrible trophy. We could hear glass breaking. The smell of smoke became stronger.

He asked if I had made my decision.

THE LAST OF THE LAST. I thought so once before, but now it cannot be otherwise.

Mr James Minto and I left the city at dawn, paying twice what was fair for horses. Even at that hour we did not have the road to ourselves. From the first we saw four or five other riders to the mile and the occasional coach. Only after several miles were we passed by a man going north and he wore a worried expression as if already aware of the disturbing uniqueness of his direction.

We began to talk and found that on the events of the last few days we were at one, but that on their origins and true character we were sharply divided. His views were as harsh as he knew how to make them and I can see now that there is little more in them than the practice of his profession. Even so, at times we both became vehement and twice we rode apart. Some companionable force always made me slow or him quicken so that it was never long before we were back together again. We talked more of the future and were reconciled.

At noon we stopped for an hour and watched pass the ever-thickening traffic that had been building behind us all morning. We rode on and made Lauder by nightfall. My sleep was very disturbed.

Today we took an easier pace and stopped here in Coldstream late in the afternoon. We were presented with a choice between this place and the New Inn. James tossed a coin. We disagreed about the meaning of the result and came here because it was closer. James was discussing money with our host when I saw him. I experienced an instant of startled recognition before telling myself that it could not possibly be so. I crept a little closer to see a monumental figure, his back and huge shoulders almost horizontally slumped on a chair, which rocked back on two legs, his thick-stockinged feet propped on the hearth rail. His chest was bound in a leather jerkin, the buttons of which pulled tight at their holes and creaked when he breathed in. At the high tide of these great inhalations the leather would buckle just enough to reveal a glint of heavy gold chain lying against the chest beneath. About him lay boots, saddlebags and a travelling coat, all of which seemed to have been thrown off in careless haste. I tiptoed closer still and was about to lift the edge of the enormous hat that covered his face when the inn-keeper appeared at my elbow. He gestured for silence and firmly escorted me upstairs, explaining that Mr Cohen, as he called him, was one of his best customers.

The singularity of his appearance and the curious feeling I remember from my first sight of him – I do not know how to express it except to say that he is simply more present than other men – should have put the matter beyond doubt. James, however, was sceptical and the more I thought of the improbability of the coincidence, the more I dismissed the idea. I slept a little and then went downstairs with James to find something to eat, whereupon the question was most emphatically resolved. Joseph Cohen d'Azevedo was standing by the fire, mightily pleased with himself. Our appearance was greeted with a great cry of 'Brothers!' We were embraced and honoured in the most extravagant terms, myself particularly. He asked if we, too, knew the secret of the place. James admitted we had tossed a coin.

'That is what you think,' said d'Azevedo. 'You have been blessed. God himself has guided your steps. Come!'

We followed the inn-keeper to the back of the house and were ushered into a small room directly opposite the kitchen. We took our places at a table neatly set for three with silver, large sea-green goblets and a stiff white cloth.

'I shall indulge you,' declared d'Azevedo. 'I insist! You will never eat better, not even in Paris herself. You'll not believe me, of course. Why should you? You are young men with all before you, but I swear all the same that each of you on your dying day will say, "I never ate better than on that night!"'

The door opened to admit the inn-keeper with a bottle of wine. I glimpsed the kitchen beyond, caught a draught of its smells and heat as an arm stirred something in a pot and was gone. D'Azevedo put his glass down, head tilted back, eyes closed in ecstatic transport. 'Mr Coleman, I believe you are in league with the devil himself!'

The air filled with violets and blackcurrants. Mr Coleman respectfully inclined himself towards the table and left. We talked of coincidences, exchanging examples from our experience and agreeing that none was as remarkable as the present. Over a dish of larks, rolled in on themselves each with a single leg bone protruding like a cherry stalk and dripping in a deep red sauce that confused and delighted my senses equally, we recounted our histories since we had last met.

'Buying, selling, making losses, making profits, accumulating, the voyage out, the voyage home to see how my children have grown. Next year the eldest will be a merchant himself. Last year we lost the youngest.'

James said even less, and after mumbling something about being a paid complainer declared that he had no past and that from this day on he would have nothing but a future.

'I managed a lead mine,' I said. 'Before that you know.'

The legs of six larks were cleared away and a haunch of venison placed in the middle of the table. Mr Coleman sang its praises as he carved it, explaining proudly the use of cow's udder in the making of the stock, alerting us to the varieties of pepper, the sliced ginger and horseradish root, the addition of a little vinegar (only that made from sweet wine was 'deep enough'), the sweet herbs and juniper and pine kernels. He discarded the remains of the first bottle and replaced it with another.

'Something's happened, I think,' said d'Azevedo.

Together James and I told him the events of the last few days. He listened in silence and concluded that he was sorry. James started on his theories again, more strident than before. I tried to keep silent as long as I could, listening to how everyone involved in the Company had been a fool, how its failure had been predictable to the very last detail, how the country had played the Prodigal Son and now, having thrown its money in the sea, was whining all the more for being welcomed back, for having all its losses restored by its kindly southern uncle. This was too much and I told him angrily that the only place Scotland was being welcomed into was the house of a thief, permanently indentured to earning back what had been taken from her. He laughed at this, called it poetry and asked me if I really believed it. Because I didn't, I shouted at him, 'I've lost my country!'

D'Azevedo, cleaning his plate with a piece of bread, looked at us both benignly. 'Ah, youth!' He nudged me in the ribs. 'Listen, son, to what an old Jew has learned about countries. I know it wasn't God who made countries. What are they for? I ask. No one could ever tell me. What sort of a thing is it that no one knows what it's for, I ask you? Countries? Forget about them! God grant we never have one of our own to break our hearts. No one needs a country.' He waved his hand imperiously towards the south. 'There's always plenty of space in someone else's, if you make yourself amenable.'

I sat dumbfounded while James exploited his advantage.

'We have no quarrel over the last few days, but the rest, the whole thing together, there's something good about it. The world is growing up, Rory, our days are getting lighter. Can't you see it? It doesn't matter who you are any more. Soon it won't even matter what you believe. All that matters is what you do, what your power is. The future is simple, Rory. It's not honour or pride or loyalties stuffed down your throat before you can say your own name, it's power, it's getting what you want, it's doing what works, and it can't come soon enough.'

'You're a good lawyer, James.'

'I am.'

'You'll get what you want.'

'And so will you.'

'Perhaps I'll employ you one day.'

'At your service, Mr Mackenzie.'

'Much obliged, Mr Minto.'

D'Azevedo assumed an expression of dismay. 'Gentlemen, gentlemen, you are doing the cook an injustice.' He diagnosed too little food and too much wine, but refilled our glasses all the same. We ate and he talked.

'It puts me in mind of an encounter last summer, in the coach from Bristol to London. One of my fellow travellers was much taken with the subject of light and explained to me at great length that it is not instantaneous as ordinary folk suppose, but has a speed and travels and takes time to get places as do other things. "In the manner of the London coach?" I asked. "Exactly so," he says, complimenting me on my intelligence. "It is the case then," I say, "that when I light a candle in my room I do not, as I have always supposed, see it at once but must wait until this light whips up its horses, rides round the walls, up and down to the ceiling and the floor, pays particular attention to the mirror, the gilt of its frame, the polished toes of my boots in the corner and when it has satisfied itself as to its illuminations canters up to my eye and only then provides me with a picture of everything it has touched?"

'"Ah," he said, "if only I could put it as well as you, sir, the whole world would believe it!"

'He explained that my not having noticed this daily occurrence was due solely to the great speed with which it happened, as a measure of which he told me that it took eleven minutes only for the light of the sun to reach us from where it is created.'

'"Does that account," I asked, "for my long-held suspicion that the sun rises eleven minutes before we see it?"

'"Not in so many words," says he. "It shines as it rises, but has not its present appearance. Rather it is the image of itself eleven minutes before."

'"Then," I say, "I do not see my wife as she is."

'"Ah," he says, "what a pleasure it is to speak to a man of sense."

'"If my wife dined at one end of the table and myself at the other and it were long enough, I would see her as she was the day before."

'"Just so. And if you made your table twice as long the next day you would see her just the same, not aged by so much as a second."

'"Longer still and I would see her as a girl, when she was the most beautiful thing in the world."

'"Yet longer, sir, and you would see her grandmother."

'At Marlborough I took him for a fool, by Newbury I was not so sure and by the time the coach reached Reading he was the wisest man I had ever met. He told me of the new microscopes, ten times better than before, and showed me a book he had, full of pictures and already forty years old! He described the invisible force that holds the heavens together and told me that Sir Isaac Newton himself had said that soon everything would be understood. As we approached London I told him of my world, poor by comparison but not without its surprises. I asked him to guess how much money there was in the world and proved there was a million times more than he supposed. I told him about stock markets and the new insurances and how a man with a hundred guilders in the morning can do business for a thousand in the afternoon. We took our leave of each other with the very same phrase on our lips – "You amaze me, sir!"

'Since then I have seen steam pumps shown in London – fed with coal and water they go up and down on their own and, when they are made larger, will do the work of a water-mill or of a dozen horses. In Amsterdam I have watched gypsies charge a penny to let people see a dog float up in the sky under a huge bag of hot air and in the papers I have read of a lake in America which is all salt and no water, a thing I would certainly not have believed when I was a boy.

'I think of my poor father. He died of many things, no doubt, but one, I am sure, was boredom. How could that happen now? From now on we will leave a world more full of wonders than when we entered it.'

All this he said and more besides, talking ceaselessly for half an hour. James and I pushed our plates forward and looked at him in confusion. He clapped his hands sharply to summon the inn-keeper. 'There!' he said. 'Have I kept you apart long enough?'

Candied oranges were served, filled with their own marmalade and then a carp poached in white wine, flavoured with lemon and mace, stuffed with oysters. A syllabub followed, of sack and orange and lemon and nutmeg and rosemary. At the last a covered dish was placed on the table and the bell raised with a flourish. A palace quivered. Dark chocolate steps led up to coffee walls, which paled as they rose to pure milk and then to saffron and raspberry red.

'The Temple of Solomon!' announced Mr Coleman. 'See, gentlemen? The sun touches the towers. It is dawn in Judaea.'

'God bless you, Mr Coleman,' said d'Azevedo.

He swallowed hard, sniffed, wiped a tear from his eye. We took up our spoons and within minutes had left not one stone upon another.

When Mr Coleman returned we were all wiping tears from our eyes. Cognac was served, dark as caramel. Side dishes were brought – slices of quince in brandy, bright yellow rings of crystallized pineapples. Pipes were filled, coffee poured. I had been telling the story of the Reverend Mackay. How we laughed! How we roared with indecency!

I stared down at my coffee, watched the vapours twitch and the almond oil sparkle on its surface. We looked at each other and smiled – speechless and only a little ashamed. How easily the sting of tragedy is drawn.

We press on at sunrise, d'Azevedo coming with us as far as Newcastle where he takes ship for Amsterdam. James and I pulled ourselves up the stairs and stumbled into our rooms. I stood in the middle of the floor half senseless, wholly stranded, unable to do anything but watch the candle burn. The sound of snoring came through the walls. A mouse foraged. From outside I heard midnight chime, and then again more faintly. With each stroke the wonderful spell melted away.

Sleep threatened, and even as I thought of it the shadows advanced on me, thick with voices. And so what else but to sit down with this? To write a little and then to read the night through, to read it all, to see it faster and faster as phrases and faces pour in whole pages at a time down to this point, the very scratch of this pen.

I opened the window, listened to the river, saw more clearly the bridge and the toll-house. I have changed my shirt and repacked my bags. I have tightened the straps.

Here it is now, all that was seen, all that was felt, all the cruelty, all the vanity rolled up all at once into a single infinite jewel.

The sky lightens. The stable-boy clatters in the yard. He talks to the horses as he feeds them. He tells them he must saddle them as he saddles them. Birds sing. The house stirs. The sun clears the hills and turns the river to gold. I hear d'Azevedo's voice and now James's. They are shouting in the yard, laughing. They say I am asleep. They say I am still dreaming of the London girls. A pebble strikes the window. I pull on my boots.

All is present now, held up between forefinger and thumb. Encompassed at last, and in a mind still my own, somewhere untouched.

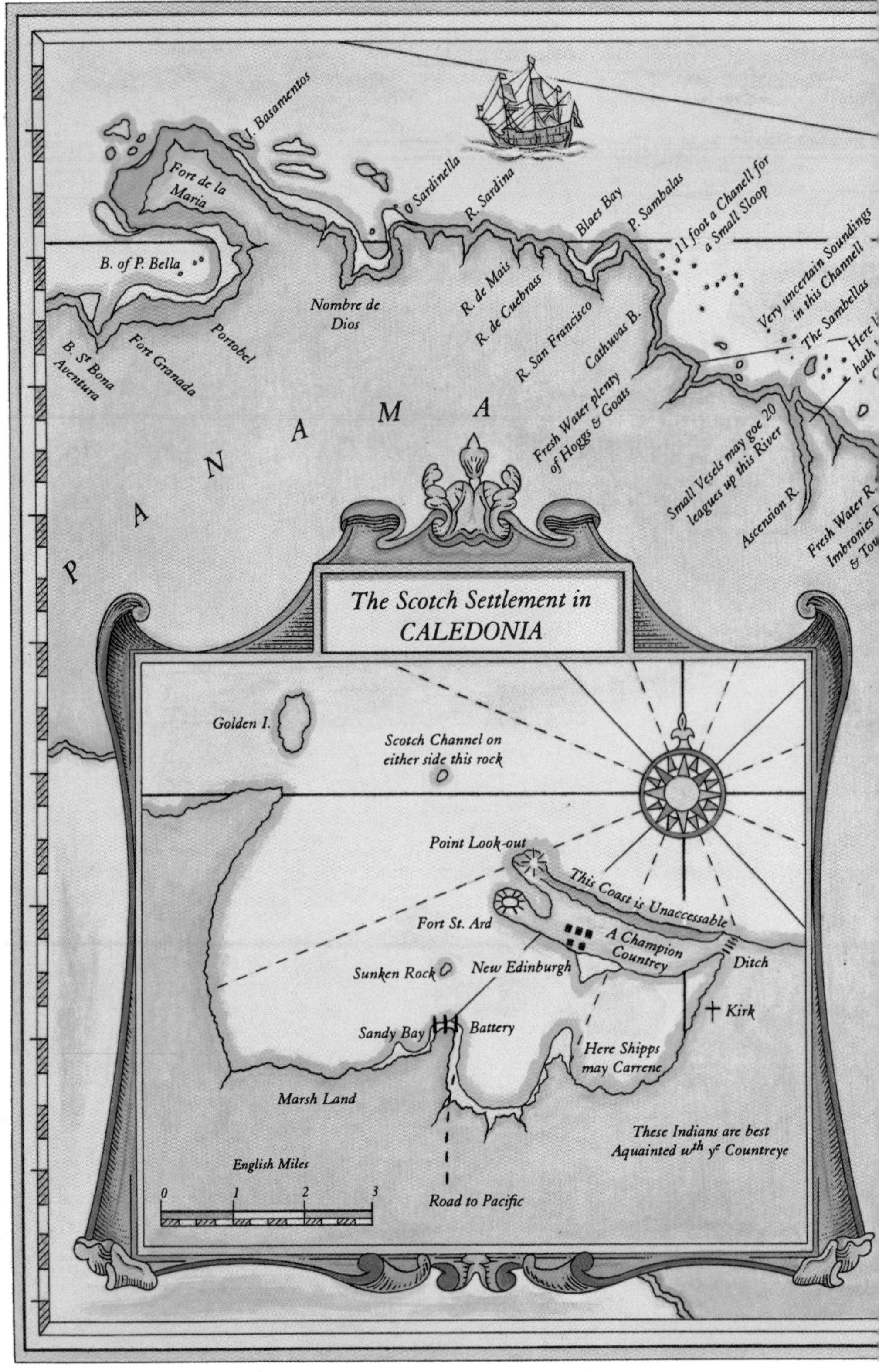
I. Basamentos
Fort de la Maria
Sardinella
R. Sardina
Blaes Bay
P. Sambalas
11 foot a Chanell for a Small Sloop
Very uncertain Soundings in this Channell
The Sambellas
B. of P. Bella
Nombre de Dios
R. de Mais
R. de Cuebrass
R. San Francisco
Cathuvas B.
Portobel
Fort Granada
B. St Bona Aventura
Fresh Water plenty of Hoggs & Goats
Small Vesels may goe 20 leagues up this River
Ascension R.
Fresh Water R.
P A N A M A
The Scotch Settlement in CALEDONIA
Golden I.
Scotch Channel on either side this rock
Point Look-out
This Coast is Unaccessable
Fort St. Ard
A Champion Countrey
Ditch
Sunken Rock
New Edinburgh
Kirk
Sandy Bay
Battery
Here Shipps may Carrene
Marsh Land
These Indians are best Aquainted wth ye Countreye
English Miles
0 1 2 3
Road to Pacific